MIND BOMB

BOOK ONE
OF THE LANDMINE CHRONICLES

LUKE
MITCHELL

Published by

MELROSE BOOKS

An Imprint of Melrose Press Limited
St Thomas Place, Ely
Cambridgeshire
CB7 4GG, UK
www.melrosebooks.com

FIRST EDITION

Cover designed by Nikki Bovis-Coulter

ISBN 978 1906050 38 2

Printed and bound in Great Britain by:
Biddles, King's Lynn, Norfolk

To Zorba the Buddha.

CONTENTS

Landmine Chronicles

Good my lord, will you see the players well bestowed?
Do you hear, let them be well used; for they are the abstracts
and brief chronicles of the time.
William Shakespeare, Hamlet act 2, sc.2.

1

A BLESSING OR A CURSE

Southeast Cambodia, 14 February 2005.

The metallic click heralded the arrival of a ten-second eternity. Red light flashed in his brain. Eardrums buzzing, a torrent of adrenaline screamed through his bloodstream. Swirling mists of vertigo sucked him into a whirl of violent emotion. Paralysed by fear, heart racing, his mind pulsed with a superimposed confusion of final moments.

He experienced the sensations of a freefall paratrooper tearing through the clouds as he rushed down to meet his destiny. Below him and gouged into a vast open plain pockmarked by craters was the panorama of a battlefield littered with wrecked military vehicles, smoking ruins and dead men. Mortally wounded, he joined them. As an unknown soldier lying in a sludge-filled trench he watched his lifeblood ebb into the mire. The angel of death stood by him. He cried out for his mother upon seeing his name chiseled out on a black granite gravestone in some forgotten corner of a cemetery.

His ears twitched when the still night air was rent by howls from those most diabolical of God's creations – the dogs of war – unleashed by power-mad generals driven by primitive compulsion to conquer and destroy. Overhead, bombs whistled, their metal casings printed with the numbers of those they sought. A young pilot had dropped the payload. His angst-ridden face glowed neon green in the muted light of an instrument panel. It was flashing a warning. A heat-seeking missile had locked on to his doomed jet's afterburners. He reached down to the red handle at his side, which when pulled would hurl his automatic ejector seat through the cockpit's shattered canopy and out into the ice cold stratosphere. The mechanism that could save his life wasn't there. In its place he found the switch for an electric chair ready to be thrown by an executioner's hand. The same anonymous hand that pulls a lever to release a trapdoor beneath feet tottering on creaking gallows, or frees Madame Guillotine's blade to rumble down with a farewell kiss upon her razor sharp lip.

Eyes looked up from a head in a gore-spattered basket. They stared lifeless at the sky. The same sky he now gazed at in an endless moment crammed with shock, nausea and the extremities of horror. One question burned in his mind. Why me? No answer came to him and in those ten flesh-creeping seconds he recognized who he was – Hamish Macleod, the man who had just sat on an unexploded landmine.

In a grim spontaneous parody of a Zen master, he simply sat without moving. Not a muscle in his body stirred. His jaw started to judder up and down. Words began to form, swear words; a string of profanities poured out of his mouth that would have embarrassed the bejesus out of an Irish navvy suffering from Tourette's syndrome. The demon of foul oaths having exorcized itself in a verbal catharsis, Hamish fell silent and struggled to come to terms with his predicament. While sweating dumdum bullets, his mind spun into fast rewind.

It was Saint Valentine's Day on a remote stretch of Cambodia's coastline close to Vietnam. Earlier that evening Hamish and his wife Jean had celebrated the occasion by dining on succulent swordfish steaks and rice. They'd eaten their self-made meal sitting on the sand outside of a beach hut. To quench their thirst they'd consumed a couple of bottles of lukewarm Tiger Beer. Unaccustomed to alcohol, Jean had drunk enough to send her into a deep sleep, which left him free to slip off into the dusk.

Over the years Hamish had built up a strong self-image. He saw himself as solid as a granite boulder sitting midstream and never fazed by the ever-changing waters of life that rushed around him. The sad reality was that during the course of his life, he'd become nothing more than a mass of acquired habits. All of his personal traits could have been judged to be socially acceptable, except for one; he was a cigarette smoker.

The moon was beginning to rise when he decided to go for a stroll along the beach. While stretching his legs he inhaled deep draughts of balmy sea air. He walked a kilometre or so, came upon a solitary coconut palm and decided to sit underneath it. Click!

Raw fear's pungent odour stung his nose with a bitter stench. Questions ricocheted off the canyon walls of his mind. 'Why hasn't the mine exploded? Will it go off if I move? Why does the only palm tree in sight have a mine planted at its foot?' He looked up and thought, 'Coconuts are waiting to be harvested. Somebody has cut notches in the ribbed tree trunk to make it easier to climb. Who was so wicked as to plant a bomb in the hope of blowing up some hapless victim?' He studied the palms of his shaking hands and wondered, 'Is the mine a leftover from the Khmer Rouge? The genocidal regime of Cambodia's Pol Pot and his murdering minions brought this country to its bleeding knees over twenty years ago. Was the thing planted here as a result of a more personal matter? Like a stupid tribal feud over ownership of a bloody water buffalo? Jesus Christ, what the bloody hell am I going to do?'

Of one thing he was certain. Some nameless person was responsible for this heinous creation. He pictured a shadowy figure in a dark grey business suit with a debauched face and a triple chin. The fat bastard was sipping cognac from a snifter and smoking a Havana as he sat counting piles of money in an air-conditioned office above a munitions factory. The sale of this mine stuffed an extra dollar into his already overfull wallet. Hamish decided there and then that anyone who had anything to do with the manufacture and distribution of landmines should be given a mandatory lifetime prison sentence with only mouldy bread and vinegar for sustenance and no tobacco to smoke.

'Cigarettes!' Hamish remembered why he had sat down in the first place. He was dying for a smoke. Careful not to make any sudden movement he became acutely aware of the detonator's hard roundness pressing into the soft flesh of his right buttock. He dug his fingers into the sand underneath him. When they touched the top of the mine he felt something about two and a half inches in diameter. 'Fuuuuck!' he cursed and jerked his fingers away as if they'd received a powerful electric shock, realizing as he did so that the thing he was sitting on must be big. Words like claymore and anti-tank mine sprang into his consciousness as he nervously fumbled in his breast pocket for his packet of Marlboros and lighter. His hands shook as he lit up. The cigarette burnt down to its filter in four long drags. Feeling dizzy from the nicotine rush he tossed the dog-end away and steadied himself by focusing on his surroundings.

Five kilometres away, made visible by pinpricks of light, was the nearest outpost of civilization. Some days before, Hamish and Jean had visited this somnolent village, which was little more than a straggle of shacks. Surrounded by strung-up strips of drying fish, the stench had been overpowering. There they had met the toothless fisherman Mister Po, mending blue nylon nets in front of his lean-to home. A knotted lungi covered his emaciated loins at the top of a pair of stork-like, knobbly-kneed legs. He was a jovial old cove with a permanent smile fixed upon his taut lips. An intricate web of fine wrinkles fanned out from the corners of his translucent eyes to cover his entire face, a consequence of casting nets for decades in waters reflecting bright sunlight. Mister Po owned a beach hut along the coast that he occasionally lent to tourists. Bereft of creature comforts, this rudimentary shack of thin bamboo-mat walls supporting a thatched roof was home to a legion of insects that would have kept an entomologist busy cataloguing for a month. Exhausted from the heat, being constantly on the move and waking up every morning in a different bed, Hamish and Jean planned to stay for a week and rented the hut for a pittance.

The view was priceless. Unblemished powder-white sands hugged the coastline in both directions. There was little in the way of vegetation, coconut palms being a rarity. Clumps of tall, spindly Ephedra pines dotted the landscape. During the heat of the day these hardy evergreens provided welcome shade from a sun that roasted the sand to such an extent it became impossible to walk barefoot.

Give him his due, the landlord had warned them, as had the *Lonely Planet Guidebook to Cambodia*, that it was dangerous in places to stray from the beaten path because of the risk posed by buried landmines. On the other hand, Mister Po had assured them that the beach was safe. Yet here was Hamish sitting on top of one of these devices barely five metres from the sea's gently lapping waters.

Hamish had a clear recollection of the many disfigured people he'd seen on the streets of Cambodia's capital Phnom Penh, one of the strangest places he'd ever visited. Thronged by bicyclists, the city had a tangible air of tragedy hanging over it, an unpleasant reminder of the atrocities committed there in the past by the Khmer Rouge. In many areas it was dangerous to walk at night along the badly lit streets. In daylight hours numerous beggars employed outrageous innovations to capture foreign tourists' financial sympathies.

He remembered, not in words but in images, one hot afternoon when he saw a man pushing a steel-framed hospital bed on rollers along the pavement. He was transporting a person missing both arms and legs. The bed pusher had accosted him and begged for money. The memory made his blood run cold. Normally Hamish was able to shut out the colossal suffering that so many people in the world endure. Now that he was on the hot seat himself it had become more difficult.

'A blessing or a curse.' He recalled a conversation, more like an argument, he'd had three months earlier with his brother. In many ways a complete enigma to him, he found it impossible to sum Angus up in so many words. He enjoyed being in his company but at the same time there was something about him that made Hamish feel unsure and ambivalent about himself. Through the judgmental lens of his logical mind, his brother appeared to be a gentle madman. Ironically Angus was the sanest person he knew. One morning over breakfast, he had asked a question that made Hamish bristle.

'Why is it that a warm-hearted man like you is married to a cold calculating creature like Jean?'

Hamish had almost choked on his coffee when his brother fired this one off at him. 'Who ... who ... who the bloody hell do you think you're talking to? How dare you speak about my wife like that.'

When it came to his spouse, Hamish was as blind as a myopic bat hanging from the roof of a subterranean cavern. A devotee in the cult of personality, Jean's bible was Hello, the society magazine. Within the glossy publication lay her sole aspiration in life, to one day have her glamorous features printed upon its hallowed pages. Jean was a well-proportioned channel for the spirit of pure selfishness. Her substantial lips gave her away. Held in a petulant pout, they occasionally parted to form a practised smile. They were home to a set of perfect pearl-white teeth, which framed a tongue sharper than a surgeon's scalpel when it came to the callous dissection of others' lives. Her devious psyche contained more snippets of gossip than the minds of a busload of hairdressers.

As her three daughters were now grown up with children of their own to take care of, Grandmother Jean had become a keep-fit fanatic. Aerobics, yoga, Pilates, if it enhanced her looks, she was practising it. Although middle-aged, Jean appeared to be in her early thirties. When she cruised down the street young men stopped to ogle at her gliding by. Keeping her lustrous black hair in a loose pile on top of her head added to her overall appearance of looking like a tall Amazonian goddess full of youth and vitality.

Hamish was crazy about Jean. He was a voluntary victim of a thirty-year infatuation who treated his high-maintenance wife like some rich men treat their expensive sports cars. Whatever was needed to keep her running smoothly, he footed the bill. Unknown to him, she made frequent trips to the garage, on her own, to have her hi-octane, fuel-injected engine lubricated by skilled mechanics who kept her fine-tuned and humming. Back home in Oban, on the West Coast of Scotland, every Peter, Dick and Roger knew about Jean's tireless enthusiasm for riding on hot rods, the more horsepower and thrust the better. Hamish was a cuckold, living in a contented cloud of blissful ignorance, totally unaware of his wife's unbridled promiscuous activities. Nothing breaks like a heart and had he discovered the truth, his unsuspecting one would have been shattered into bleeding pieces.

Apart from making her husband a laughing stock among Oban's well endowed studs, she also nagged him incessantly about his nicotine addiction. Hamish had lit a cigarette and blown an aggressive cloud of smoke at his brother, who used his hands to waft the offending cloud away.

Angus, upon meeting Jean for the first time, had immediately sensed what kind of woman she was, and his brother's reaction came as no surprise to him. In his eyes Hamish was no different from most people when it came to hearing an unwanted truth about their lives. They either don't believe it or resent being informed. Angus had raised his palms in mock innocence. 'You have some anger management issues that need working on. If you don't learn how to deal with your anger it's going to bring you into serious trouble one day, if it hasn't done already.'

'What are you talking about? It's you who's making me angry with your provocative question.'

'Hamish, you might be a success as far as the world goes, but as for your inner life, you are a robot, an automaton. Look at you, one question and you're furious. I couldn't make you feel angry so easily if there wasn't already a stockpile of it inside you waiting for an excuse to vent itself.'

Hamish felt there was truth in what his brother said but his mind was aflame. 'If you're so bloody well smart, how is it that you've ended up in so many bad situations in your own life?'

Angus clasped his hands together, rested his chin on them and remained silent for a few moments before he spoke. 'It's the mind that interprets life's events in terms of good and bad. In this world there is no way of knowing what is, in fact, a blessing or a curse. All we can do is live through the process – here and now.'

As Hamish sat remembering his brother's words, the present was pressing in on him. His thick shoulders heaved and a groan escaped from his throat. In an attempt to break free from his external reality, he applied himself to practising a meditation technique, which Angus had taught him. He closed his eyes, concentrated on his breathing and focused on a bright star, which was shining in the sky directly in front of where he was sitting. Ten minutes later his body jerked. The initial rush of adrenaline had worn off. Drowsiness overcame him and darkness set in. He lit a cigarette to ward off his lethargy.

The moon rising in front of Hamish was full. Its reflection was fragmented by the wavelets on the sea, creating thousands of little dancing flashes. A few kilometres out, he could identify the outlines of two small islands that he knew were uninhabited. On the distant horizon he could see the glow of artificial light from halogen spotlights mounted on the superstructures of Cambodian fishing vessels. When they were switched on at night, schools of curious squid were attracted to the dazzling luminescence, mesmerized, and lured into the fishermen's waiting nets.

A mild breeze came in from the warm waters of the sea. Overhead dry palm fronds rustled ominously. The last thing Hamish needed was for a coconut to fall on him. He examined his wristwatch's illuminated face. It was 20:16. What did that mean? He'd been sitting on a bomb for approximately half an hour. Time was not exactly flying by and he was aching all over.

'Heeeelp! Help me! Jean, help me!' Pathetic, his shouts were futile. He soon gave up.

Sleep had become a dangerous foe to be kept at bay. He had to stay awake. Jean was bound to come looking for him when she woke up. When she found him help would soon arrive. Scenes from an American war movie flashed through his mind. Spurts of soil are flying up from a hail of bullets fired by a battalion of dirty commies when G.I. Joe steps on a landmine. Click! He freezes instantly on the spot and avoids being vaporized into pink mist. He then shouts to a comrade, 'Hey Sam, help me out here, will ya?' A fellow grunt crouches down beside him and deftly slips his bayonet under the thick rubber sole of Joe's army-issue

7

boot. There just so happens to be a heavy rock handy. The sweating soldier places it on the haft of his knife as a counterbalance. Joe lifts his foot off the mine. He spits out a stream of dirty brown tobacco juice and raising his automatic weapon, lets rip with a quick burst of well-aimed fire in the direction of the bad shot brigade. A dozen gooks fall to the ground. They are either dead or writhing in agony. All in a day's work for an American hero – the jarhead smiles and reloads. As long as Hamish remained still on top of the mine all he would have to contend with was the vague possibility of a falling coconut.

His mind moved in a more practical direction. It was back to meditation. This time he tried another technique his brother had taught him called zazen. He sat with his eyes open and allowed his body to relax. Thoughts marched by in a ticker tape procession. Each time he identified with one of them he pulled himself back into the present. The intervals between each thought lengthened until there was more space than thought. Eventually there was only emptiness.

Hamish the silent watcher sat stock-still. He heard a 'pop'. He blinked in surprise and looked around to locate where the sound had come from. The beach was as empty as his mind had been a moment before and nothing seemed to be out of place. Hamish was sure he had heard something but could not figure out what it was. He took a deep breath in an effort to bring himself more into his senses and raised his left arm in order to examine the liquid crystal display on the face of his waterproof diver's watch. It was 20:26.

Way in the distance, flying high above the earth, an aircraft's flashing red and white lights appeared. Hamish envisaged a jet full of passengers crammed into economy class seats. They were eating soggy pre-packed dinners, drinking bitter coffee and laughing at a comedy film starring Mr Bean. This was being shown on an array of mini TV sets running along the length of the cabin above their heads. Loneliness and isolation were his companions as he followed the plane's progress until its blinking lights disappeared out of sight. All that was left behind was an expanding silver-grey streak of vapour trailing across the sky.

He caught a movement to his left. Something was making its way towards him. The hair on the back of his neck began to tingle. He took another nervous glance at his watch. 20:29. Puzzled, he shook his wrist, pondering over how a digital timepiece could run slow and if, in fact, that was even possible. He stared at the watch. The minute number changed to 30. Something was odd. He realized this had happened in slow motion.

His attention was drawn away from the time by the movement on the sand. Whatever it was, it was getting closer. He lowered his hands to his knees and focused single-pointedly on a thin shadow zigzagging across the beach. He rolled his dry tongue over the roof of his mouth. It tasted like rusty nails. Like an octopod's slimy tentacles, a horrible anxiety began to creep over Hamish as it dawned on him what he was looking at. It was a snake, a long snake. Hamish's ophidiophobia was so profound he couldn't even stand to watch snakes on television.

It was a cool evening. His denim shirt was soaked through with sweat. While sitting on the mine, he'd been unremittingly terrified, except when he'd been able to escape into the refuge of his mind. The miasma of fear clung to him like a malevolent spirit. He found himself experiencing an adrenaline-fuelled level of mortal dread beyond his wildest imaginings. As the serpent drew closer every hair on his body began to bristle, including his pubic hair, which stood to attention while his genitals shriveled up and retracted. Hamish felt like a human pincushion. He nearly rose up and ended it there and then but fear had paralysed him. His heart was ready to burst. He was starting to have aural hallucinations. From the coconut tree's trunk came the sound of Morse code tapping out an SOS.

'Pop.' This time he knew where the sound had originated: from his head, in the centre of his brain. The snake continued to slither over the sand towards him. Hamish had completely forgotten about the landmine. His mind had shut down.

The serpent reached a spot in the sand directly in front of him, coiled itself into a compact spiral and rested its head at its centre. Hamish stared at it. Shaped like a timeless sculpture made from hi-tech alloy, the shiny scales of its dark skin glinted in the moonlight.

There was a constriction in his chest as paranoia beat against his ribcage. The build-up of pressure was booming in his ears. He had stopped breathing. A pellet of panic exploded in his throat. Gasping, he sucked in air. This sudden noise startled the snake and part of its body reared upright in front of Hamish. It was a hooded cobra. It began to sway to and fro in a hypnotic motion. A delicate tongue darted in and out between its gleaming fangs. Its head was level with Hamish's face. A condensed and refined reptilian scent flooded his nostrils. A recess in his brain registered that this lethal and graceful creature was a female.

Hamish's eyes were still and unblinking. He was unable to focus on the patterns upon the cobra's glossy hood. All he could see were the shiny black balls of its eyes. Within them burned two sparks of ruby red light. The tiny crimson fires grew brighter as the serpent's head moved closer to his face. The two lights merged into one. Through this magenta crystal glow Hamish looked into the cobra's soul and saw a vibrant intelligence that was awful. A forked tongue flickered over Hamish's lips, flipping a switch at the base of his spine. With tremendous power, a bolt of primordial energy shot up through his body and discharged itself out of the top of his skull. Hamish heard and experienced the popping sound again, like an over-inflated balloon full of warm liquid bursting inside his cranium. The cobra hissed. Hamish stared directly into its mesmerizing eyes. He felt strangely dislocated from the encounter, as if watching a three-dimensional holographic drama. There was no sense of fear or repulsion; only the feeling of being held spellbound by the power of fascination. Death felt suddenly familiar to him, like an old friend he'd taken for granted and forgotten.

The snake quietly hissed again. She wanted to keep his attention in order to share a secret. An Adam with no Eve in sight, Hamish was intrigued by the possibility of becoming intimate with a venomous serpent. Transfixed, he listened intently to what the cobra had to say. She communicated with a latent part of his brain, formed in the jungles from prehistoric times. Flicking her tongue she spoke not words but faint hissing sounds. Her voice was soothing and sapient. It filtered through his conscious mind and was translated into coherent thought forms. The reptile was indeed a female and lived nearby under a large flat rock. In essence curious and non-aggressive by nature, she'd sensed Hamish's presence and slithered over to investigate. He had nothing to fear unless he made a sudden move that could be interpreted by her highly developed sensory system as threatening. If this happened, she had no choice in the matter; she would strike automatically and deliver a shot of toxic venom via her fangs that could kill him. There was no malice in her being. She was a secretive creature who shed her skin from time to time and in sleep dreamt her ophidian dreams.

The cobra made one last sound, not so much a hiss, more a forceful fah. Hamish blinked and came out of the trance induced by her hypnotic gaze. He refocused his eyes. The dark skinned female was coiling herself once more at his feet, a little closer this time, giving the impression she felt safe in his physical proximity. Hamish felt a tremendous rush of energy stimulate every cell in his body, which almost succeeded in making him cry out in liberated exaltation.

His rational mind began to rise to the fore. He started to question what had occurred only a few moments ago – communicative cobras did not fit into his world. He looked down at the serpent and knew she was real. He stared at his watch, somehow believing that what a plastic chronometer had to say would make everything all right. It didn't. The watch read 20:35. This was impossible. The serpentine session had lasted at least half an hour but according to the time only six minutes had passed. He tapped the watch's face with a finger in the hope of reconnecting a broken circuit. His thoughts returned to the earlier puzzling slow motion movements of his watch and how it had seemed to take forever for the jet's flashing lights to cross the sky.

He remembered why he was under a coconut tree. He should have been petrified. What was happening to him? Was he going mad? He knew he was sitting on an unexploded bomb. Suddenly it dawned on him. His fear had evaporated. The thin line between life and death had dissolved. He saw that the two apparent opposites were interlinked – one could not exist without the other. Hamish smiled. At this stage in his life proverbial clichés formed the basis of his philosophical understanding. He was now starting to delve into the mysterious marrow of existence. He began whistling 'Amazing Grace' but broke off mid-blow due to the presence of his sleepy companion, 'Miss Serpentina'.

Angus reappeared in Hamish's mind, accompanied by an empty feeling in his stomach. Something was gnawing at his guts. Three months of lengthy breakfasts where Angus had recounted his life story had drawn to a close six weeks earlier. Hamish's personal history had only required an afternoon to relate. He had more or less written Angus off as a Bohemian crackpot with too much time and money on his hands. Hamish was now awakening to the realization that his brother had been endeavouring to enlighten him.

An expression Angus had used came to him: 'Near death experience.' Was that the explanation for the strange things that he was going through now? How much closer to a near death experience can one come than sitting on a bomb and being kissed by a cobra? He couldn't help reflecting on it. He only had one skin and he wasn't ready to shed it.

Angus had lived a very full and intense life and had come very close to death on several occasions. He would have been familiar with what Hamish was now experiencing. An echo from the past came to his ears and he heard his brother's voice rise in his head. 'When death draws near, the veil of illusion lifts and your whole life unfolds in front of you. You can recall your life's impressions in minute detail and relive their emotional impact.'

In a shuddering moment of penetrating insight, the truth about his relationship with his brother came to him. A twinge of guilt snapped in his chest. He had been jealous of Angus. Ordinarily he would never have admitted this. However, faced with his possible annihilation, he came clean with himself. He'd been envious of his brother because it was Angus who'd really lived life to the full and was thus in a position to know how to die when the moment arrived. Angus had risked his life and travelled roads fraught with danger. He on the other hand had opted for security and chosen to walk a straight and narrow path, marked out by a materialistic society. He'd reaped the comforts and rewards that came with such a life. Now faced by the great unknown and the prospect of dying he felt he had no inner life to fall back on. It was Angus who had risen out of the mud of human existence to open like a lotus flower in the rays of a new rising sun. He felt lost in the dark. It was Angus who'd found real meaning in his life and not the shallow deceptions he felt he'd adopted. It was Angus who had entered into a freedom loving relationship with another human being, a liaison that Hamish had coveted. Yes it was true; unlike himself the odds had been stacked against Angus, yet he'd gambled everything to win it all and be surrounded by friends who truly loved him.

Hot tears of remorse streamed down Hamish's cheeks and fell onto his lap. The cobra blinked a beady eye at him, and then looked away. Relieved and feeling purified Hamish acknowledged that he had underestimated Angus. He said a silent prayer of gratitude to his brother for telling him fundamental truths about life's mysterious nature.

Angus had told him that witnessing life as a drama enables one to recognize his or her true spiritual identity. At that time it had made no sense to him, but now, faced with the very real possibility of dying on the spot, his brother's statement was beginning to ring true. Hamish realized that if he let go of everything and entered totally into the world of his brother's experiences he might be able to find the key to overcome his present existential crisis. After all, he'd already lived his own life and now recognized its dull routine of conformity.

He glanced at the time again. 20:45. 'So what?' Unfastening the strap, he threw the watch into the sea and in so doing almost blew himself up. The cobra reared up and hissed. Staring into the snake's black eyes, he spoke to her. 'Ssh, now, sssh, take it easy, I will not harm you, sssshh.'

The cobra wavered for a moment, lowered herself and curled up. Hamish stretched his arms in the air and said one more word: 'Yes!'

His cumbersome thoughts were no longer controlling how he felt. He was now able to witness them as something apart from himself and watch them lumber by like a herd of tired elephants.

He looked up, chuckled and blew a kiss at the sky. All things considered, it felt like a crazy thing to do. Hamish knew that his brother, had he been present to witness the gesture, would have appreciated it and loved him all the more for it, because it was just the sort of thing he would have done.

Propelled by fate, Hamish felt like he'd performed a metaphysical giant leap across time and space to land in Angus's well-worn soul boots. The truth was far more down to earth. Hamish had come directly in contact with the most powerful and basic of human needs, the need to survive no matter how. He now wanted to live more than anything else. Faced with the prospect of losing his life, it struck him how incredibly precious it was. Like a barnacle stuck to the hull of an ocean-going liner, he would cling onto life by whatever means possible. Evolution had programmed him to do so. In the process he'd been given a wonderful survival tool – his mind. He had to use that tool to stay still, overcome his body's sensations of extreme physical discomfort and employ it as a weapon to combat sleep.

He closed his eyes and went back to the beginning. What had started out as a terrifying encounter with a landmine and a dangerous snake was about to be transformed into a revelatory inner journey: or so it felt to him in that moment. The night was only in its infancy and therefore barely able to crawl by.

2

WOMBMATES

Allahabad, Uttar Pradesh, India, 1992.

'Who is this Angus?' Hari Sahaj Vichara was reading a letter. Seated on the white marble floor in front of him was a gathering of two hundred or so spiritual seekers who had travelled from every corner of the world to sit at his feet. Born in Islamabad in 1909, the master was now eighty-two years old. He was built like a retired heavyweight boxer gone to fat. When he was a young man he'd been strong enough to heft a full-grown water buffalo upon his broad shoulders. In his dotage, he still retained a little of that physical power, but alas, not his health. Head shaved smooth, he wore a grey flannel knee-length shirt and matching baggy pants, clothes more typical of a Muslim than a Hindu. Hariji, as he was affectionately known, put down the letter, took off his reading glasses and let his rheumy eyes roam over the congregation before him. There was a hint of mild irritation on his pugilistic face.

Angus, who had written the aforementioned letter, raised his right arm and called out, 'That's me, Hariji.' Motioning with his hand, the master beckoned Angus to come forward from the back of the assembly and said, 'You, come here.'

Angus stood up and made his way through the audience. When he reached the empty space on the floor at Hariji's feet, he sat down on its cool polished surface and looked up at the master. In company,

15

Mr Vichara was a disarmingly charming man with a jovial and playful personality. Close up, one on one, the master was all business. His job was to awaken people from the sleep of ignorance. At that moment he appeared to Angus like a cross between a wild-eyed Brahminy bull and a laughing Buddha, although he wasn't actually laughing. Now that he had the master's undivided attention, Angus was unsure what to do with it. He felt like a man who, having convinced himself that he has wings, was ready to launch himself over an abyss in order to prove that he can fly.

Hariji nodded at Angus to acknowledge his presence. He then motioned for Angus to come closer and whispered in his ear: 'You have no desire to be in the womb again, isn't that it?'

To an outside observer the situation would have appeared unremarkable. A big old man seated in a white armchair bends forward and says something to an alert and wide-eyed fellow half his age sitting cross-legged on the floor in front of him. This is what happened inside Angus's mind when he heard the master's question. He closed his eyes. He then saw a panel open up on the right side of his head. Focusing his mind's eye upon this space he was drawn into it. The next thing he knew, he was back in his mother's uterus.

Living conditions inside the womb were cramped. Curled up beside Angus was his twin brother. A picture of perfection and harmony, Hamish was floating in his liquid dreams. A restless spirit had taken possession of Angus's tiny body. Unlike his wombmate, he was full of nervous energy and squiggling around like a tadpole trapped in mud. It was hot, claustrophobic and noisy inside life's pulsating orange and red walls. The beat of his mother's heart thunderous, Angus could no longer wait to get out of there. He pushed and shoved his way round to what he instinctively knew to be the escape hatch leading to the outside world.

Working his way down the birth channel, the soft walls around him were expanding and contracting, making him feel like a sausage being squeezed out of its skin. One final push and he managed to pop his head out into the harsh bright light of the world. Aunt Rose, the midwife, was waiting to ambush him. She grabbed hold of Angus and yanked him out into the cold room. He was dangling upside down when he received his welcome to Planet Pain; a slap on his bottom that felt like a shotgun blast on his sensitive skin. His sensory system hit overload and a primal scream ripped through his organism.

16

Angus took a deep breath, opened his eyes and found himself once more gazing up at the master's inscrutable, yet compassionate, countenance. Hariji remained silent. He looked at Angus in a way that implied he knew everything there was to know about him. Angus felt like he'd been stripped to the core, leaving his essence bare. In that spiritual nakedness he felt humbled.

Remembering being in the womb and his birth had only taken a few moments, although the emotional intensity of the experience had made it seem much longer. Hariji raised his chin, prompting Angus to reply to his question. It had required forty years of living for Angus to recall the trauma that accompanies birth into the human realm. It was clear in that moment that he had no desire to be born again.

'Yes, Hariji, that is correct. I never want to be in a womb again.'

The master gave a sagacious nod. 'Good,' he said. 'And remember, as long as there are sheep there will be herders. How many lions do you see being herded?'

Angus did not have to think about his answer. 'None, Hariji.'

The sage chuckled. 'Yes, that's the right answer. Now wake up and roar. Declare your right to awaken. If the need arises, feel free to come and talk to me.'

'Thank you,' said Angus. He bowed with reverence at the old man's feet, stood up and returned to his place at the back of the hall.

The Isle of Iona, Inner Hebrides, Scotland, 12 December 1951.

Margaret Macleod was sitting up in bed panting. Body slick with sweat, her once lustrous dark hair hung damp and lifeless. Before becoming pregnant at the age of twenty-three, she had been slim and athletic. Meg's pregnancy had been an arduous one, mainly due to water retention, which had swollen her body to such an extent that she now resembled a barrage balloon. During the past few months her positive outlook on life had been eroded by extreme physical discomfort, leaving her in a state of perpetual melancholia. The only desire that remained within her bloated frame was to give birth. She'd been in labour for eighteen hours and was tremendously relieved that her searing pain-filled ordeal was finally over. Meg thought she was having a nightmare when she heard her sister-in-law's voice pierce through the red haze in her brain.

'Come on, Meg. You've got another one in there. Breathe out and push, woman. Breathe out and push!'

Another contraction came. Meg wailed and tears streamed down her face. Her body went on automatic pilot and began to push as instructed. It required half an hour of pushing and pulling to dislodge Hamish from his cosy refuge. Arriving feet first he managed to rupture one of his mother's blood vessels on the way out. After being inverted and receiving an excruciating slap on his buttocks, he was laid on a towel that felt like a bed of nails. He immediately began to express his discomfort by screeching as loud as Angus. Rose was glad to hear it because she knew that those lusty screams were expanding his lungs, causing blood to be sucked into his body from the placenta. She cut Hamish's umbilical cord, tied it and lifted him up to place him beside his brother inside the large prepared wooden drawer from the bottom of a wardrobe.

In her early thirties, Rose was medium height and fair skinned with a smattering of golden freckles below her prominent cheekbones. Her ancestors had been Scandinavian, and as a consequence she had thick shoulder length blonde hair that was the envy of every female on the island. She usually kept it tied up in a tight matronly bun on top of her head. Rose had learned the profession of midwifery through hands-on experience. She'd taken up this part-time occupation because she was unable to bear children of her own. Over the years, assisting many women in childbirth, she had become a valued member of the small island's community.

When Rose saw the amount of purple-brown blood seeping out of her sister-in-law, she knew that something had gone seriously wrong. There were no medical services or trained physicians on Iona at the time. Even had there been, Rose knew in her heart that there was little that could be done to save the life of the woman who now lay dying in front of her. Removing a fresh handkerchief from the bib of her apron, the midwife wiped beads of perspiration from Meg's hot feverish brow and upper lip. She tried to comfort her. 'There, there now, my dear, don't fret. I'll soon have you as right as rain.'

A faint moan escaped from Meg's anaemic lips, while a look of consternation grew on Rose's face, betraying the fact that she held little or no belief in her own soothing words. Rose had been performing her duties alone because Meg had succeeded in making herself very unpopular during the last few months of her pregnancy. Due to her physical condition, she'd become an obnoxious grouch and as a result all of her friends had deserted her.

The babies had momentarily fallen silent. The midwife heard a shoe scuff on the stone floor behind her. She turned, half expecting to see a concerned neighbour entering the room to find out if she needed assistance. Rose was dismayed to see that it was Nancy Stewart, the local madwoman, dressed in a bizarre combination of hand-me-downs. Long strips of mud-stained fabric hung over her torn ankle-length dress, a fitting match for her matted brown hair.

Like most village idiots, she played the important social role of the psychological yardstick. As long as a person could not relate to Nancy's frame of mind, they could rest assured they were sane. She was as nutty as a sack of almonds and had she been living in the Middle Ages, she'd have jumped the queue to be burnt at the stake. The crazy witch lived in a dilapidated hovel on the outskirts of Baile Mor, Iona's only village. She'd been a reclusive spinster for all of her adult life. Starved of human company she'd taken to having conversations with trees, sheep, crows and country pancakes. A regular feature of island life was to see the old bat engaging in a one-way heated argument with Iona's signal-red letterbox. Apart from being completely bonkers, Nancy smelled like a thing long dead that had been dug up from the ground. She hadn't had a decent scrub in years.

When the midwife saw the disgusting hag was about to pick Angus up in her filthy claws, she shouted at her. 'Nancy, get the bloody hell out of here this very minute, you scunner that you are.'

Nancy's fanatical eyes, burning with madness, shone as if she'd just had a brilliant idea. She smiled to display her buck-toothed testimony to never having visited a dentist in her entire life. The midwife was unimpressed.

'Out, out, out.' Rose tried to shoo the loony away with her hands. She wouldn't budge. 'Out with you Nancy, or so help me God, I might do something that I will live to regret.'

Exasperated, it seemed to Rose that it took a long time for Nancy's damaged brain to register that she was unwelcome. The poor nutcase eventually shuffled out of the room muttering incoherently.

Rose returned her attention to the babies. Disturbed by the commotion, they'd embarked on a wailing competition, sounding off like a pair of burst bagpipes.

Ten minutes of wooing and cooing persuaded them to fall asleep. Rose stood over them watching their tiny faces peeping out from the swaddling clothes she'd wrapped them in. Hamish looked grotesque, a human frog with red mud drying and cracking on his face. She whispered under her breath, 'Heavens, look at the state of you, ya poor wee soul.'

Wanting to wipe the offending substance from Hamish's forehead, Rose searched for her hanky in her apron pocket. She'd left it at Meg's bedside. The midwife turned and walked across the room. Meg looked as pale as a bucket of milk. Her face had collapsed inwards upon its bones. Most of her blood had drained away to leave her lips the mauve colour of a drowning victim. Rose bent over her and realized Meg had gone into shock and was now dead. She'd passed away while Rose had been trying to get rid of Nancy Stewart.

The midwife remained calm. She knew from her past experience that it was inevitable her sister-in-law would die. It came as a shock because it happened so quickly. Margaret's body lay with a large, dark pool of congealing blood sinking into the sheets beneath her swollen legs. Rose's first task was to tidy the situation up. She was just thinking that the job would be a lot easier if someone had been around to help her when Lizzie Allan entered the room. She'd been one of Meg's closest friends before they'd fallen out a couple of months previously. In her late twenties, Lizzie was as skinny as a worn broom handle and tended to wear clothes a few sizes too big. She was best known around the island for her singing in the church choir, for her voice was the soprano of an angel. Rose was glad to see her.

'Thank God somebody's come. Meg's passed away. She's had twin boys.'

Lizzie was stung by remorse. Her delicate jaw dropped when she looked at her ex-friend lying there dead. She also noticed Meg's face had taken on an unsettling beauty.

'Twins?'

Rose looked over to where the babies lay on top of a wooden table in their makeshift cot. Lizzie followed her gaze and walked over to examine the newborn infants.

'They're so beautiful,' sighed Lizzie. 'Crivens,' she gasped, 'what happened to this one? He's a' covered in blood. Is he alright?'

'Don't worry, both of them are going to be just fine.'

'Have you been on your own all the time?' asked Lizzie, turning to examine Rose's tired face. 'You look knackered.'

'Aye, you're right, I'm finished. I'm thinking to myself that after this I might give up the role of being Iona's midwife. I did have one visitor though, Nancy Stewart.'

'What in God's name was she doing here?'

Rose shook her head, hardly believing it herself. 'That's a good question. She just wandered in here away in a dwam. I had to stop her touching the bairns with her dirty hands.'

'Strewth! I'm sorry I wasn't here to help you Rosie. It's just that me and Meg—'

'There's no need to explain, Lizzie. I know what happened. What's done is done. C'mon now, give me a hand here.'

The two women worked together in silence. They cleaned up Margaret's corpse as best they could and changed the bloodied bedding. Rose raised Margaret's head and put a pillow with a fresh cover under it. She busied herself with tidying the dead woman's hair, while Lizzie went outside into the garden. When she returned, she carried a small red rose in her hand. She placed it by Margaret's head on the white pillowcase. Like Meg's face the flower's beauty was stark.

Lizzie spoke to Margaret as if she were still alive. 'I'm sorry Meg. I'm really sorry. I wanted us to be friends. It was so hard for me.' She broke down and cried.

'Now, now,' cautioned Rose, 'Meg's spirit might still be hovering above us in the room watching over the wee ones. If it is, letting go of your emotions will disturb her. The past is a graveyard. It's life we're concerned with right now. Do the right thing and show her how much you care about her bairns.'

'Aye, you're right, I'm sorry. It's just—'

'It's just nothing,' said Rose. 'Awa and fetch some milk. Those two will be waking up very soon and when they do there will be hell to pay if there's nothing to put in their empty wee stomachs. Off you go now. Tam Davidson always has fresh goat's milk. Hurry back.'

Lizzie rushed out through the doorway, happy for the moment to be doing something useful. Left alone once more, Rose opened the window to let fresh air into the stuffy room. She looked at the view over the Sound of Iona to the plumb coloured, snow-capped hills of the much larger neighbouring island of Mull. The wind was strengthening and whipping up the sea in its path. The agitated ink-black water was lined by white. Rose leaned forward and turned to her right in order to see the open waters of the Atlantic Ocean. The sky was darkening in the distance, heralding the arrival of a storm. A troubling thought surfaced in her mind.

'Jesus!' she exclaimed, her hands moving to her cheeks as she stepped back. 'What's Norrie going to say when he gets home?'

Rose closed the window, as if by doing so she could shut out the thought and prevent its recurrence. Three hundred nautical miles northwest from where Rose stood, Meg's husband was standing facing the wrath of his mistress – the sea.

Norman Macleod was the captain of a twenty-ton trawler called the *Northern Lights*. Norrie was the youngest skipper, by far, in the West Coast of Scotland's deep sea fishing fleet. At twenty-six he'd taken command of the *Lights* and within the short period of four years earned himself a reputation of being a master mariner. He was a hard-working captain who brought his boat safely back to port after every trip, loaded to the gunnels with fresh fish, much to the delight of the trawler's owners who sold the catch on the open market for big profits.

Extremely stubborn, Captain Norrie's one major character flaw was instrumental in bringing him to meet his fast-approaching nemesis. On the morning of the eighth of December, he had pigheadedly ignored a mid-Atlantic storm warning issued by the meteorological office. He should also have been at home with his wife in her hour of need. Instead he set out to sea from the coastal fishing village of Mallaig. He'd pushed his vessel's six-hundred horsepower diesel engine to its limits as it crawled up mountains of water at two knots and, cresting their summits, shot down the other side into deep troughs at sixteen. Now, four days later, he realized he'd made the biggest mistake in his seafaring career. The seas had attained proportions beyond anything he'd ever encountered. Waves as high as four-storey buildings were crashing over the trawler's battened-down hatches to cover them in boiling white spume.

The boat was sitting low in the water. The previous evening a cloud of gulls wheeling in the sky had alerted the captain to the presence of a large school of herring. During the night, the crew had struck on the shoal and the nets had hauled in a record-breaking catch. Everyone on board had been in a jubilant mood when they opened the bursting nets above the hold and dropped over fifteen tons of silvery fish into the darkness below. Apart from the crack they'd had hauling the fish on board, the seven-man crew was excited at the prospect of being paid a healthy bonus when they returned to Scotland's mainland.

Now, the extra weight was turning into a catch-22 that was working against the crew's interests. Apart from being too low in the water, the trawler's rudder cable had snapped and she was now drifting in dangerous waters. Below the heaving decks, Nils Skogland, the Swedish engineer, was desperately trying to repair the broken steering cable. If anyone could fix it, Nils could. Unfortunately, destiny was working against his normally incredible improvisational skills in the realm of marine engineering. Using a length of copper pipe and a mixed assortment of nuts and bolts, he'd almost succeeded in joining the frayed ends of the thick wire hawser together. A violent movement jerked the rudder in the opposite direction. One end of the cable ripped across Nils's oily right hand and severed three of his fingers. Flailing like a bullwhip, the hawser disappeared down a steel tube in the ship's stern. 'Javla,' Nils cursed as he stared in horrified fascination at his damaged hand, thinking to himself that Mrs Skogland was going to give him hell when he arrived home minus three of his digits. Many were the nights when she'd whispered in his ear, 'Oh, Bo, I love your strong hands.'

Out on the ocean the *Lights* was drifting backwards about to crest a forty-foot wave. The trawler tilted at an impossible angle, throwing the engineer hard against the metal bulkhead. His head took a terrible knock and he collapsed unconscious into the bilge water swilling around on the floor.

Up above in the wheelhouse Captain Norrie's fists were white as he gripped the trawler's wooden wheel to steady himself. A week's stubble on his chin, he appeared a lot older than he was. Three long days without sleep had left him gaunt, with eyes bloodshot from exhaustion. His steel-blue pupils shone like living drops of the ocean that surrounded him. Standing with his feet set firmly apart to counter the rolling motions of the ship, he turned to Jimmy Johnson, his first mate, whose ruddy face was contorted by worry.

'Away down to the engine room and see how Nils is getting along. If he doesn't fix that cable, we're done for.'

Dressed in green oilskins, Jimmy said nothing as he staggered out the door to go below deck. Norrie stared, hypnotized by the sea's turbulent grey mass. It occurred to him that it was time to send out an SOS. He was just about to switch on the radio when the first mate returned. He could see at once that Jimmy was even more dejected than when he'd left.

'Skipper, Nils is out for the count. By the look of it he's taken a nasty smack on the head and something's happened to his hand, there's blood all over the place.'

Norrie let out a groan and went back to the wheel. 'Don't tell me! Is he going to be all right?'

Jimmy shrugged. 'A wee bit the worse for wear and tear. He'll have a right headache when he wakes up. I had to pull him out of the bilge or he would have drowned in six inches of stinking water.'

Smiling grimly at his friend, the captain nodded. Jimmy reached into the inside of his oilskin jacket and produced a hip flask. Screwing off its round cap he offered it to his skipper. 'Would you be up for a wee dram, Captain Macleod?'

Norrie gratefully accepted the metal bottle and raised it to his lips. 'Cheers Jimmy.' The captain took a swig. 'It's an honour to call you a friend. There's no other man on earth I'd rather have by my side in a moment like this. I was just thinking to myself, it's a pity it wasn't the auld days when ships had wooden rudders. Then we could have shot a hole in the damn thing and strung a pulley through to steer with.'

The first mate watched his captain take another healthy shot of Scotland's finest. He was delighted to have received such a grand compliment from a man whom he respected and admired. The grin that was spreading across his face vanished in a second when the whole ship shuddered from the impact of a huge wave that engulfed her. He pointed to the trawler's half-submerged foredeck.

'Norrie, we're heading sideways into thon waves and they're no' getting any smaller. If a big one catches us we'll keel over.'

Handing the flask back to his first mate, the captain agreed. 'Aye, those are my thoughts exactly. I'm sorry. This is my fault. I shouldn't have brought you and the lads out into this grey hell. How are the boys doing down below?'

'Holding on to their bunks, throwing their guts up and cursing your name, no doubt.'

'I couldn't blame them for that,' said Norrie, half to himself. 'I'm cursing my damned name as well.'

Jimmy studied him curiously. 'Oh, aye, listen to you. "Captain Remorse", is it? I didn't hear any of the hands saying they were unwilling to go to sea because there's a wee bit of a swell on. So I'll hear none of this "I'm sorry" nonsense, Captain, Sir.'

Norman MacLeod had to chuckle. It seemed at times that the pair of them lived inside each other's heads.

'Ach maybe you're right, any firewater left in thon flask of yours?' Jimmy shook the metal bottle. 'Aye, there just might be a wee drop left if you—' Jimmy broke off in mid-sentence as an enormous wall of water bore down on the trawler. 'Jesus, Norrie, will you look at the

24

size o' that.'

There was no way the skipper could have failed to see the freak wave. As its gargantuan bulk drew closer, the mid-Atlantic roller began to block out the sky, which created an ominous half-light inside the wheelhouse. The captain let go of the powerless wheel. He extended his right hand towards the first mate. Everything appeared to be moving in slow motion.

'I reckon this is it, auld pal. Are you up to it, Jimmy?'

Gripping his skipper's hand, Jimmy turned to face the ocean's wrath. 'With you by my side skipper, I'm bloody well ready to face anything.'

The trawler started to roll over. The two men clung to each other. Jimmy yelled, 'Yee haaww!'

The end, moments later, was swift and furious. Dumping thousands of tons of water on top of the upturned trawler, the massive wave broke her back in an instant. Captain Norman Macleod was knocked off his feet and thrown against the wheelhouse ceiling like a matchstick in a flooded drain. His neck broken, he was dead before the Atlantic Ocean's cold waters engulfed him.

By the time the giant wave had rolled over them the *Northern Lights*, her entire crew and their foolhardy captain were tumbling down into a dark abyss.

For the first month of their lives, Angus and Hamish slept, fed and cried together under the slated roof of 'Braeside'. This was the name of Aunt Rose's rented, three-roomed cottage. A small wooden outhouse with a bucket full of ashes served as a toilet. It stood adjacent to a tall rowan tree that had been planted to ward off evil spirits. However, this tree proved to be ineffective as far as abominable smells were concerned. Her 'wee but and ben', as she liked to refer to her home, was situated on a cobbled road three doors along from the house where the twins were born.

Rose lived with her husband, Daniel Macleod. Dan was thirty-five, but looked ten years older. His weathered face resembled a tan-coloured mask made from a piece of leather, dried and wrinkled from being exposed too long to the sun's damaging rays. Apart from a few months during World War II when he'd been conscripted into the army, he'd spent his entire life under the ever-changing skies of

Scotland's Western Isles. He eked out a living by doing odd jobs and using hook, line and sinker to fish from his small wooden boat. Most days, except the Sabbath, he rowed to the island's western coastline to reach deeper waters where cod roamed in abundance.

Dan was a talented fiddle player, making him popular at social gatherings. Be it a jig or a lament, he could always provide a tune for the occasion by deftly drawing his bow over his instrument's finely tuned strings. His company was also much sought after by the island's children, for nobody could tell a story quite like 'Uncle Dan'. He was a mimic who possessed the ability to imitate any voice: man, woman or child. Confident by nature, he could cast the storyteller's spell and draw his young listeners into an imaginary world. There they experienced the thoughts and emotions of the vivid characters who lived in his tales.

Dan's creative spirit expressed itself in many forms. The small garden in front of 'Braeside' was full of sculptures he'd made. These consisted of driftwood, unusually formed rocks, seabirds' feathers and crustaceans' shells that clattered in the wind. Most of his neighbours found his *objets d'art* peculiar. However, if words were spoken behind his back they were said only to praise him. Wherever he went Dan always emanated an air of infectious contentment. With the exception of his narratives, he was a man of few words. His thoughts, when he had any, were as simple as a child's. Illiterate, his intelligence came from the heart. His greatest love in life was the company of other people. There was nothing, within reason, that he would not do for his fellow man. If an extra hand was needed, Dan would be there to provide it.

Since Rose and Dan were a childless couple, he was over the glen about playing host to the twins. Every evening after work he'd hurry home to spend time with the two baby boys. Angus was his favourite of the pair. There was something in the infant's spirit that Dan felt inexplicably drawn to. Angus was by far the noisier of the twins but even when he was bawling for his bottle of warm goat's milk his penetrating cries came as music to Dan's ears. He picked up Angus with his gnarled hands. He held him close until the nursling was lulled into sleep by the warm resonance of his voice.

'My, my, dearie me, what a fuss you're making. You're a wee noisy bundle so you are. Hush now, aye, that's right, you're with yer Uncle Dan now. Ssssh, no harm will come to you when you're in my arms.' Dan's soothing voice entranced most people he talked to. One only needed to hear it once to know and experience its hypnotic magic. Angus was no exception.

Entering the small bedroom, Rose walked up behind her husband. 'You're home are you? Since we've had those bairns in the hoose you've had very little time for me. C'mon now, your supper's on the table.'

'Aye, aye, woman, can you no' see I'm having a blether with my wee pal here?'

Rose returned to the kitchen while Dan lowered Angus into the cot beside his sleeping brother. Before going through to join his wife, he stood for a moment looking down at the sleeping babes in admiration. Identical, they were perfect. He pushed his thick cloth cap back from his furrowed brow while wiping tears away from his eyes. Such was the depth of the love he felt in his kind heart for Angus in particular, that had life chosen to grant him one wish, he'd have asked to have the quietly sleeping infant as his very own son.

Most indoor life took place within the fair-sized kitchen that also served as a living room. Its coarsely laid stone walls were lined from floor to ceiling with pine planks, black and reeking of tar from decades of peat smoke. Protruding from the walls were big nails and hooks for hanging various things: lobster pots, farm implements and Rose's prize possession, a large iron frying pan with a long handle. There were no ceilings, only beams, slats and the sloping underside of the slate roof. Below a cracked window, a solitary brass tap was the only source of running water in the house. In need of a washer, the inefficient tap dripped into a grey marble sink and marked out the seconds like a water clock. The fireplace was the size of a small cave. Three feet above the grate, a thick horizontal iron bar was set into the bricks for smoking mutton and herring. Flat stones were home to soot-blackened pots. At times Rose used these for cooking when her ornate cast iron stove wasn't on the go. A functioning relic from the previous century it not only burned peat, wood and coal, it baked beautifully also.

In those dark times there was no electricity on Iona and at night the islanders lived by the light of oil lamps, candles or the glow cast by an open fire. Over a simple candlelit supper of boiled cabbage and potatoes the couple discussed the imminent arrival of Dan's father on the island. They reached an agreement to ask him if they could legally adopt Angus.

Dan was Norrie's only brother. They'd liked each other but had never really been that close. Dan's love of the land had lain in stark contrast to his younger brother's tempestuous love of the sea. When news finally filtered back to Iona about the disappearance of the *Northern*

Lights, Dan had intuitively sensed his brother was gone forever. He had always felt that Norrie's passionate obsession with the ocean would lead to his demise.

The topic of passion was a touchy subject in Daniel and Rose's home. In fact, it was a matter that was never discussed. Rose was infertile and gradually their sex-life had dwindled away to almost nothing. The last time they'd come close to performing the act together had been a disaster. A few months previously, Dan was invited to play his fiddle at a local wedding reception, where he'd brought the house down with his renditions of various reels. He'd managed to coax everybody into their dancing shoes and soon had them yelling for more. As a reward for his accomplished musical skills he'd been supplied with an excessive quantity of whisky and gotten blazing drunk. Later that evening he'd staggered home, climbed into bed with his clothes on and tried to make love with his wife. Dan failed to rise to the occasion and soon passed out on top of a disappointed Rose. Having sex together had never been their forte but this did not stop them loving each other wholeheartedly.

Over time, they'd learnt to sublimate the sexual urge. Dan had his manual labours and creative projects while Rose, having said goodbye to her part time job as a midwife, said hello to the world of baking. She delivered bread, scones and pies fresh from the womb of her own oven. The joy Daniel and Rose shared in each other's company would become one of the constants during Angus's childhood years.

Robert Macleod, Angus and Hamish's paternal grandfather, arrived the following afternoon on the ferry. Rab Macleod had, like his deceased son, been a trawler skipper in his time. Due to an accident on the high seas he'd taken early retirement. He now lived out his days in a white-painted cottage on the outskirts of the town of Portree on the Isle of Skye's east coast, the place of his birth. The unfortunate accident had occurred a decade ago, changing his life forever and leaving him a somewhat sardonic and frustrated man. Whilst fishing off the coast of Norway his trawler's nets had become entangled with those of a Norwegian boat competing for the same catch. In the chaos that ensued, both of Rab's legs were crushed beneath the knees when the two vessels collided. Rab almost died as a result of his injuries, but thanks to his iron will managed to retain his grip on life until he was eventually ferried to a hospital in Oslo. The multiple fractures and breaks in his shin bones were set in place by a group of dedicated surgeons, who'd used metal screws to join them together. He'd had a massive blood transfusion and later the orthopaedist in charge of Rab's case informed him that it was a wonder he was still alive. The bone doctors did their best, which was nothing short of being miraculous, but even with their skilled help, Rab, once he was on his feet again, was to walk with a peculiar limp for the rest of his life.

Nine months into a two-year period of convalescence, Rab's feisty wife, the mother of his two sons, eloped with a Danish trawler man. Six months later, Rab received a picture postcard from Copenhagen. All it said on the back was, 'I should have left you years ago. I never want to see your grumpy face again. Elaine.'

It was true that since his accident Rab had begun to complain about what life had put him through in the school of very hard knocks. There was however a lot more to him than being a cantankerous old git. He was a man who wore the mantle of responsibility with dignity. Never one to act on impulse, he was hence a good man to have around when a clear-cut decision was needed. Rab took life seriously and was candid about his personal shortcomings. This quality of honesty extended into his social life. If someone among his many friends or family needed to have something pointed out to them for their own good, he'd let them have it. To balance this forthright tendency in his personality, Rab had developed a robust and bittersweet sense of humour.

With regard to his sons, Norman had always been perceived by his father as being the one who carried the lion's share of his genes. Norrie had been Rab's favourite since the day he watched his second son be born into the world. If Rab Macleod were asked to sum up Daniel in two words, he would have said, 'A failure.' He saw his eldest son as a man at odds with the world, barely able to support himself and with very little in the way of personal ambition. Rab was aware of Dan's finer qualities but tended to disregard them, for they reminded him too much of his runaway wife.

A black tam-o'-shanter upon his head, Rab hobbled up the road that led to the village of Baile Mor, straightening his tie as he gathered his thoughts in order to deal with the problem of what should be done about taking care of his own blood – his orphaned grandsons. Had they wished it so, Rab would have allowed his son and Rose to adopt both of the twins, except for one important detail: they were poor and barely able to feed another mouth, let alone two. As he pushed open

Braeside's garden gate, his course of action became clear.

He rapped on the blistered paint of the front door's wood panelling with his ebony walking stick's brass handle. When Rose opened the door she had plastic curlers in her hair and flour-smudged cheeks from her baking chores in the kitchen. Coming face to face with Rab, she stepped forward and gave her father-in-law a hearty hug. She stood back from him and said, 'My, Robert, you're looking grand.'

The old seaman removed his black bonnet, ran a liver-spotted hand over his grizzled grey head and gave Rose a sideways look 'Aye, lassie, you know what they say about creaky doors.'

In unison they said, 'They last the longest', and shared a brief laugh together.

'Come away in with you,' invited Rose. 'I'll put the kettle on. You can have a cup of tea with a big slice of freshly baked rhubarb tart. I'll bet you're famished; the sea air aye makes a man hungry. Dan will be home in a wee bit.'

He limped into the kitchen, paused and sniffed the air, much the same as an old stag on the side of a mountain does when picking up on the scent of a hind in heat in the valley below. 'I can smell something good and my belly is rumbling like a wagon rolling over a bridge at the thought of tasting your pie.' Upon hearing this, Rose gave Rab a curious glance.

It occurred to her that no matter how painful the situation was she had to broach the subject of the death of his youngest son. She braced herself and said, 'Rab, what about Norrie?'

His eyes became focused on things only he could see. 'Aye, Rose, I appreciate your asking. 'Tis indeed a sair fate that is mine. Let the dead bury the dead, is how I choose to see it. Now lass, if you permit me to, I'll say no more about the loss of my darlin' son, for it was he who was the comfort of my soul.'

Over tea and pie they chatted about what had been happening in their lives since last seeing each other.

'And the midwifeing?' asked Rab.

'Aye well, to tell the truth, after Meg's death the wind went out of my sails. Now that I'm a baker there's no more blood and a lot more fat.' Rose patted her midriff bulge to emphasis her point.

'Ach, away with you, I like a woman with a bit of meat on her bones.'

'Robert Macleod, you're no' flirting with me are you?'

'Aye, that will be right; I'm out to pasture now. The days of sowing my wild oats are a long forgotten dream.'

'Well, listen to you. You've still got thon twinkle in yer eyes. I do believe there's a good bit o' life left in you yet.'

'Aye lass, maybe yer right, but the life's in a' the wrong places, if you catch my drift.'

Rose smiled. 'And those legs of yours? Are they giving you any bother?'

Robert grimaced. 'To be honest with you, I feel like a bloody weather station.' Pointing to his right leg, he commented, 'If this one aches it's going to rain. If it's the other it means snow. When my ankles are sore there'll be frost on the ground in the morning.' Rab paused to produce a conspiratorial smile. 'I've got a joke for you.'

Rose raised her eyebrows and said, 'I'm all ears.'

'There's a naked Scotsman walking down Prince's Street in Edinburgh. He's got his willy stuck inside a welly boot. A bobby comes up to him and says, "Here! What do you think you're doing, laddie?" The naked man looks at the bobby and says, "Nothing, officer, I'm just fuckin' aboot."'

'Rab Macleod, as you very well know, I don't tolerate the "eff" word in my house,' said Rose, feigning outrage. 'Anyway, you told me that one the last time I saw you!'

'Damn it, I do believe you're right.' Rab slapped his forehead. 'My memory's no' what it used to be.'

The kitchen door swung open and Dan walked in looking like he'd just spent the last few days down a coalmine. He was working at present as a chimney sweep cleaning soot out of blocked lums.

'Och jings,' said Dan, 'I didn't notice the red carpet was rolled out. Hello father.'

Robert looked his son up and down. 'Jesus, Danny, what a fright you gave me. I thought it was one of thon darkies from Africa come to murder us. Away and get thon muck washed off you, before you sit down with us.'

Dan took a moment to take in his father's appearance. The fastidious old seaman was dressed in a dark Harris tweed suit with the chain from his pocket watch hanging over one side of his matching waistcoat. Dan smiled knowingly. 'Taking control of the situation already, are we, Da? Don't tell me you're scared of a wee bit o' dirt. Some of us have to work for a living, you know.'

Robert glared back at his son, annoyance tugging at the corners

31

of his mouth. 'I will have you know that I've worked more in my life than—'

'Save it, Da. I can see you haven't changed a bit since the last time I saw you. Drink your tea. I'll away and get cleaned up.' Dan caught his wife's eye and winked before leaving the room.

When Robert was first introduced to his grandsons, they were sleeping in their cot. As he approached them, Angus's eyes popped open. He began screaming like a tomcat with his tail on fire. The old codger put his hands to his ears.

'Good God Almighty, what a bloody racket, can you no' shut the wee bugger up? He'll crack the glass in the windows with that noise he's making.'

Daniel lifted Angus up and held him close. He calmed the baby down for a moment until Rab peered into Angus's wide-open eyes. He took one look at his granddad's deeply lined face and, once again, hit the decibel switch in his lungs.

Rab shook his walking stick at the squealing infant. 'That one will be trouble. You can mark my words on that.'

After supper, father and son put their differences aside and sat down with Rose by the warmth of the hearth. There was not much of a discussion to be had over the fate of the twins, Rab having made up his mind beforehand. Once the old sea salt had made a decision, come hell or high water there was nothing that could be done or said by anyone to change it. Stubbornness was a family trait that all the men folk of that particular offshoot of Clan Macleod carried within their personalities. Rab laid his cards on the table with little in the way of an introduction.

'Now, let's get down to it. Rose here has informed me that the pair of you would like to adopt the wee screamer. That's fine with me.'

Daniel could not conceal his joy. A stern look took possession of his father's features. 'And you can wipe that puppy dog expression off your face for a start. There's more to rearing bairns than playing with them. They require patience, feeding, clothing and a whole lot of other things.'

'I know that, father.'

'Aye well, if you don't you soon enough will. There's one other matter I've given a lot of consideration to.' Rab paused to add gravity to what he was about to say. 'I'm aware that some might judge that life has twisted and bent me out of shape. Physically, at least, I'm forced to agree with them. Whatever the case might be, there's one thing left that I'm going to ask the pair of you to do for me. I'll have you know I don't care a tinker's toss for folk's promises and oaths; easily given and too easily broken is how I see it. That said, I want you to swear to me that, until the laddie turns eighteen, neither of you will reveal to him that he has a twin brother and that they were orphaned as newborns. Now then, what do you have to say to that?'

Dan and Rose exchanged a puzzled look. Rose gave a slight inclination of the head, signalling that if a question were to be asked, it was he who should ask it.

He turned to his father. 'That's fine with us, but what I want to know is, what has brought you to make such a strange demand?'

Rab tapped a wad of Black Twist tobacco into his briar pipe, lit it with a match, took a few draws and spat into the fire. Hot coals hissed back at him. With a face as long as a tombstone he said, 'As you very well know, I'm no' a man who is accustomed to having his authority questioned, but in this case I can see a wee bit of an explanation is in order.' He tweaked his veined nose before continuing. 'These eyes of mine have seen a lot in their time. I once watched a married couple who I was acquainted with, in a situation that you will one day encounter, trying to explain to an adopted youngster that they are no' his or her real parents. If it's done at too early an age, it's my opinion that it could work out badly. It's like pulling the rug out from under them. They lose their footing and become unstable.' Rab tapped his pipe on the grate. 'A bairn is ill equipped to deal with such an eventuality. In fact, such a revelation can affect the course of a young person's life for many a year to come. Now, have I made myself clear on the matter at hand?'

Not for the first time Daniel felt respect for what his father had to say. He might be a quarrelsome and self-righteous old dog but short-sightedness was not a label that Dan or anyone else would ever be able to stick on Robert's bottle of personal characteristics. Whether he was right or wrong was another question.

'Father, I speak for both of us when I give you our solemn-most word that we will abide by your decision. But what about—'

'That's already taken care of,' said Rab in answer to the question that Dan was about to ask.

'What do you—'

Rab cut his son off again by raising his voice and saying, 'I said it's already taken care of. That should suffice. What happens to the other bairn is no concern of yours. I dare say you'll have more than enough on your plate to be going on with.'

Rose listened in silence to this exchange and hoped Rab's self-righteous demeanour didn't succeed in getting her husband's dander up. She let out an audible sigh of relief when she saw Dan swallow his pride and lighten the situation by saying, 'Oh well, I suppose that's that then. Which means there's only one thing left to discuss and that is, what are we going to call the twins?'

Rose stood up. 'Hold on a minute here, laddies. Before we get down to the name game a wee drink is called for. What do you say Rab?'

Pointing to the kitchen cupboard with his walking stick, Rab said, 'Well now Rosie, if my memory serves me well, it's telling me that you always have a bottle of malt stored away for special occasions. Am I right about that?'

'You most certainly are, but you're no' exactly answering my question, so I'll ask you again. Would you be up for a wee dram?'

'C'mon now, woman, you're winding me up here. Of course I'd like a dram, or maybe two. It'll do my aching bones the world of good, so it will.' Rose deposited a full bottle of whisky on the table, cleaned three glasses with the end of her apron, and poured the malt half way up in the tumblers before them. The glow from a paraffin lamp found the glass surfaces, transformed itself and reflected back into the warm kitchen as splinters of glittering amber light. Before tasting the single malt Rab held his drink under his nostrils and inhaled the spirit's bouquet. 'Ach,' he sighed. 'Ye cannae whack it.' Raising his glass, he proposed a toast. 'Here's to the twins, may they live long and prosperous lives in interesting times. *Slainte.*' They clinked their glasses together and in true Celtic style got down to a spot of serious drinking. It was almost midnight when Dan squeezed the last drops of whisky out of the bottle into his father's glass. During the course of the evening it was Dan who had won the debate over what name should be given to his new son. Then Rab and Rose finally settled on the name Hamish for his brother. 'Angus and Hamish, braw Scottish names,' was the last thing Rab said before falling asleep in front of the hearth, where little crimson flames danced and disappeared upon a glowing bank of peat.

The following morning, Daniel rowed his father and Hamish across the mile-wide stretch of choppy water that separated Iona from the island of Mull. From there Rab would make his way over to the mainland and then south down the coast to Oban, where Hamish's new parents awaited him. The previous week, Rab had met Duncan Johnson, the brother of the now deceased first mate of the *Northern Lights*. After a memorial service for the lost crew of the ill-fated trawler, Duncan and Rab had gone down to the local pub in Mallaig for a drink. In the course of their conversation, Duncan informed Rab that he and his wife Mary had lost their only child, a wee laddie of only six months, to pneumonia during the autumn.

One thing led to another and over a pint of McEwen's, that became several, the two men exchanged a firm handshake after having decided the fate of one of the yet-to-be-named baby boys. The alcohol had done its job of dissolving their psychological barriers, allowing them to expose to each other the true complexion of their characters. Duncan had been on good terms with Norrie when he'd been alive. His wife had been a close friend of Meg, as they'd grown up together on Iona. Therefore Duncan could gauge to a certain extent what would be coming in the adoption package, and he knew his wife would be delighted at the prospect of having a family again.

Half way over the Sound of Iona the wind picked up, making Dan's job of rowing more arduous. Rab sat in the small boat's stern, holding the baby as they were cradled by the rocking waves. For a change, that morning it was Hamish Macleod Johnson who was kicking up a fuss. The moment they'd pushed off from Iona he'd started crying his tiny heart out, and he would not stop until they came ashore on Mull. Perhaps some part of him realized that, for the first time in his life, he was being separated from his twin brother. Hamish would get used to this because fifty years passed before they were reunited again.

Fifty-four years later Hamish opened his eyes and found himself back on the beach in Cambodia. He'd completely forgotten where he was. It had worked; he'd managed to break away from his own reality.

'I'm remembering to forget,' mused Hamish. The paradox sounded so absurd to him that, for the second time that evening, he wondered if he was losing his mind. Then he recollected how he'd scoffed at his brother telling his story of how he relived life in the womb, sitting at the feet of some Indian guru. Angus had admitted that it sounded incredible but swore on his life that what he'd described had really happened to him. Hamish looked down at the cobra curled up on the sand and asked himself, 'How many people would believe me if I tried to tell them what I've experienced so far this very night?' He hoped that he'd live long enough to answer that question.

Very carefully he stretched his legs, crossed them, took a deep breath, let it out slowly, closed his eyes, and shot through the escape hatch back to Iona.

3

THE CHAPPATI CONNECTION

Baile Mor, Iona. August, 1957.

Angus began to crawl and, much to his parents' delight, proceeded to take his first unsteady steps six months later. Once he was walking and talking, trouble began.

It was midnight and Angus had just been woken up from a deep sleep by an unusual sound. He lay still, staring up into the darkness. There it was again; it was emanating from the kitchen. He'd never heard this before. It was the sound of his parents arguing. Sitting up on the side of his bed he rubbed his eyes and then crept off to investigate. The kitchen door was ajar, allowing a pale beam of light to escape into the hall. Angus stood in the shadows and listened.

His mother's voice was distraught. 'I'm telling you the boy's no' right in the head.'

'How can you say that about our son?' asked his father.

'Well, how else to explain these strange goings on? There's something no' right with him. It's no' natural for anybody, let alone a six year old laddie, to be like that.'

Silence.

'Maybe he's got the sight.'

'The sight, the sight,' echoed Rose. 'Just listen to yourself. Maybe we should take you to see the head doctor as well.'

'It'll be over my dead body that you'll be taking Angus over to the mainland to go and see a psychiatrist.' Dan's voice grew louder. 'Over my dead body, do you understand?'

When Angus heard this, he wondered if his father was going to die.

'All right, then,' Rose relented. 'If you put it like that, I'll let it go like I've done so many times before. But if it happens again that I see Angus talking to invisible people, or telling me about places and things that there's no way on earth he could possibly know about, I'm putting my foot down and taking him to see a doctor. Do you hear me?'

'As I say, there's no way I'll let you take the boy to see a quack. It's just a case of an overactive imagination. He'll grow out of it.'

'Overactive imagination! Who are you trying to kid? How could he have imagined the things I've told you about?'

'Listen woman, you know I don't have the answer to that, but I ask you, what harm does it do?'

'Well, for a start, if anybody finds out about this—' Rose remembered something and then continued. 'Maybe some people know already. I was just talking to Mrs Hepburn the other day, and do you know what she said to me?'

'No, I wasn't there, so how could I know what she said to you?'

'Don't you be smart with me now,' chided Rose. 'Remember these were her words, no' mine. She said, "Young Angus is a strange wee laddie. Sometimes I could swear he can read my mind." What do you have to say to that then?'

'It sounds to me like idle gossip. What does an auld wifie running a shop know about anything, anyway?'

'That's your big problem, Daniel Macleod. You just don't care enough about what other people think.'

'Aye right,' retorted Dan. 'That's because maist people are thinking a load of nonsense maist of the time, you included. Taking our son to a mental hospital. How could you entertain such a thought?'

'Right then, have it your own way. But I warn you, if he doesn't grow out of it, as you're so very fond of saying, I'm going to do something about it.'

'Are you threatening me?' Daniel asked, his words chilled by cold anger, 'because if you are—'

Rose cut in, her voice sharp with irritation. 'No, I'm telling you. Don't you dare talk to me in that tone of voice again or I'll take the frying pan to your head.' Both parents fell silent. The charged atmosphere seeped out of the kitchen and sent a shiver up the boy's spine. He decided to sneak back to his bedroom before they called it a day.

Back in bed, his body moulded itself into a warm cocoon beneath the thin woollen blankets. Angus lay mulling things over in his mind. He knew exactly what the source of his parent's argument had been – 'Amah'. She was a figure who had existed in his life for as long as he could remember. Non-existent to everyone else, she was as real to him as the wooden rafters that were now creaking above him in the darkness. Her skin was the colour of chocolate and the whites of her eyes were enormous. A vibrant streak of scarlet powder ran down the centre parting of her long, thick, jet-black hair. Dressed always in the same red cotton sari draped elaborately around her body, she would appear out of nowhere and speak to him in a singsong voice. The rolls of fat that hung around her waist jiggled when she laughed, while the coloured glass bangles on her thick wrists jangled like sleigh bells. She smelled of curry, although back then Angus had no idea what the pungent scent was. When he was younger, she'd rocked him in her strong chubby arms as she sang him lullabies in a language he liked but did not understand. Now that he was older, she told him about her life in India.

These encounters with her had caused a lot of problems in his young existence. On several occasions he'd spoken to his parents about the contents of some of his talks with Amah. He soon discovered this was a mistake.

One morning, while luxuriating in the warmth of his bed, Amah instructed him how to make chapattis – a simple baking task. After the lesson was over he dressed and then rushed off to see his mother with a very special request in mind. Rose was in the kitchen, hard at work and up to her elbows in dough. She had become the main supplier of bannocks, biscuits and mutton pies for the whole island.

'Mammy, could you help me make something?' Angus asked as he approached her.

Rose glanced up from the kitchen table where she was busy cutting out circles from a flattened slab of shortbread mix. She smiled when she saw Angus's cheery face. He resembled Dennis the Menace, his favourite comic strip character. He was wearing his black and red banded tee shirt and had intentionally made his mousey brown hair stick out like a dirty haystack that had been blown about by a gale.

'You're needin' a haircut, laddie! What is it?'

'Could you help me make chapattis?'

'Cha…cha…what?'

'Chapattis.'

'Chapattis! What in God's name are chapattis?'

'Well, you mix flour with water and add a wee bit of salt.' Angus paused for a moment trying to get his instructions right. 'Then you make wee balls and roll them out with your rollin' pin to make thin pancakes, then you heat up your chapatti plate and—'

Rose looked up sharply from her biscuit making, an expression of mild alarm upon her face. 'You've no' been talkin' to this Amah of yours again, have you?'

Angus knew better than to reply to that question. He realized he should have kept his mouth shut. Amah was a no-go area with his mother. Feeling silly to have gotten so carried away with the idea of making chapattis, he remained silent.

'Cat got your tongue, has it? Out of my kitchen now! And no more of this chapatti malarkey, do you hear me?'

'Aye Ma, I'm sorry.' Dispirited, Angus had turned on his heel and left his mother to her baking.

Unknown to Angus, a week after the chapatti incident, his mother had taken time out from her work to take a stroll down to the pier. Every now and then she liked to do this as she enjoyed talking to people waiting for the ferry. On this particular sunny afternoon Rose met a friendly woman with a gold ring in one nostril who'd emigrated from India and now lived in Edinburgh. Her husband worked as a bus driver in the busy city. Like many other tourists during the summer, she and her family had come over to Iona for a day trip. After exchanging names, Rose remembered something and asked, 'Mrs Singh, do you know what chapattis are?'

Mrs Singh started to laugh energetically, causing her thick, black-framed spectacles to tumble from her face onto the wooden pier. Rose bent down and picked them up, noting that the thick lenses were still intact. Handing them to the amused woman, she asked, 'What's so funny?'

'Oh dear, please don't to be thinking me rude, but you see, to us Indians, chapattis are the equivalent to what bread is to you Scots. Now if you are to be reversing this situation and I am to be asking you, 'Do you know what bread is? You would be laughing instead of me.' Mrs Singh chortled.

Rose wondered if the dark-skinned woman, dressed in what looked to her like a bed sheet, had been drinking. She persisted with her enquiry. 'How do you make these chapattis?'

Mrs Singh pulled herself together, smoothed out the creases in her pink sari and then launched into a detailed description of the fine art of flat bread making. As the Indian housewife was describing how it was most important that the griddle be made very hot, Rose began to feel the hair on the back of her neck rising.

'Goodness gracious me,' said Mrs Singh, 'so sorry to be saying but you are suddenly looking as pale as chapatti flour. Are you feeling unwell?'

Rose put her hand to her forehead and discovered she'd broken out in a cold sweat. She was asking herself how it was that a small boy, living on a remote island off the west coast of Scotland, could know how to make chapattis.

'Oh, well yes, Mrs Singh, now that you mention it, I do feel a wee bit queasy. We're no' used to the sun in these parts, you know. Well, it's been interesting, but if you'll excuse me now, I must be on my way.'

Puzzled, Mrs Singh stared at Rose. 'Strange people, these islanders,' she thought, saying, 'Goodbye now Mrs Macleod, it's been so very nice to be meeting you.'

Rose hurried home. Feeling a headache coming on, she took an aspirin and then went to lie down for the rest of the afternoon.

Angus was wide-awake when he heard his parent's bedroom door close. Soon the cottage was still and silent, except for the sounds it made as it too settled down for the night. A ship's horn blew in the distance. It was a lonely sound.

He lay in bed dressed in pyjamas, tossing and turning as a powerful force gripped him. Sorrow welled up inside his sensitive heart because his parents felt the need to argue about him, especially over the subject of his dearly loved Amah. Unexpressed, this feeling of sadness soon began to transform into anger. Clenching his jaw, his face muscles hardened at the thought of what his mother had said about taking him to see a doctor on the mainland. He sat up, took off his pyjamas and put on his striped tee shirt, black shorts and a pair of gym shoes. A plan formed in his mind; he would creep out into the night and give the grown-ups something that they could really talk about.

4

THE GENIE IS OUT

Iona is well known for two reasons. The lesser of these being the great fascination the island holds for geologists. Many of the rocks that can be found there are over 1,600 million years old and belong to some of the oldest geological formations on the planet. Over the course of hundreds of millions of years, the sea level had risen and fallen, ice ages came and went, and taken their glaciers with them. Volcanoes had blown their tops while violent Atlantic storms cooled them and battered the island into what can be seen today: Iona the beautiful isle surrounded by white sand and pebble strewn beaches fringed with seaweed the colour of mustard. Within its curving boundaries lie grassy hillocks and steep granite cliffs worn into their sloping sides. At the foot of these knolls, fields of wild flowers and pasture are home to herds of bleating sheep, walled in by drystone dykes shaped and formed by the labours of countless generations of islanders.

Apart from the small isle's unique natural beauty and geological interest, another more significant reason has been drawing people to Iona's windswept shores for over two thousand years. Before the time of Christ, the Druids, the Celtic priestly caste, were aware of the blanket of peace covering the island and viewed Iona as a sacred place to bury their dead. However, it was the efforts of one man that caused the Isle of Iona to become well known.

In the sixth century, Saint Columba sailed over to Iona from Ireland with twelve of his followers. The saint was impressed by the island's remote location and pristine environment. He'd found what he was in search of – the perfect place to inspire and train missionaries. He established a settlement on Iona.

Columba was in many respects a visionary and is considered to have been a most remarkable man for that particular period in time. A Christian priest, poet, prominent preacher and aristocrat, he was also a passionate humanitarian. He believed life was a unity that encompassed all people as God's children. This was a conviction he must have laboured hard with because every once in a while a dragon-prowed longship would beach itself on Iona's shoreline. Whereupon hostile marauding Vikings, driven by their God Odin, would disembark, set fire to anything they couldn't steal, murder a few people and then sail off into the pale rays of a dying sun.

Columba and his cassocked brigade set to work building a church, a refectory and a dormitory. The acolytes' lives were full of hard and rigorous labour. The saint kept the shop stewards of the monk's union at bay by convincing them that work was worship and worship was salvation.

Once the commune was set up, it became a powerhouse from where positively charged missionaries set out to bring Christianity to the mainland. There too, the monks had their work cut out for them. In those days Scotland was inhabited by wild tribes of pagan Picts who worshipped standing stones, tattooed spirals on their bodies and ingested the psychoactive skin of fly agaric toadstools. The poisonous mushrooms left the Picts fighting mad and energized them with heroic impulses bereft of any sense of self-preservation. Roman legionnaires were sent packing when Caesar's mafia tried to muscle in on the Picts' tribal lands. As a consequence, the Emperor Hadrian decided to build a fortified wall right across the border between Caledonia and Britannia in case the blood-crazed maniacs tried to head south.

Colomba persevered and set up a franchise of churches in Scotland, which provided outlets for the now much sought-after Word of God. At the age of seventy-seven, Saint Columba went off to meet his maker, leaving behind his legacy.

The fortunes of the Iona settlement ebbed and flowed with the tides of time. For centuries it was the place to be buried if you were a dead monarch. There was a slow train coming round the bend by the time a parish minister in Glasgow heard a voice in his head and believed that God himself had taken time out from the destruction, creation and maintenance of whole galaxies to have a wee word with him. The

Lord instructed him to get busy restoring some ruins on an island in some backwater of the universe. The Reverend George F. Macleod (no relation to Angus) became a man with a mission and brought his organizational skills into play. Iona Abbey, as it stands today, bears testimony to the good works of the inspired minister.

Like pieces taken from half-a-dozen different jigsaw puzzles, Angus managed to join various incongruous snippets of information together to form his own personal take on Iona Abbey and who had been responsible for its construction. He believed that Saint Columba was an entrepreneur who'd come over to Iona from Ireland a long time ago with a workforce to build a hotel. He realized that over the years things had changed and now the hotel's ruined buildings had been reformed and converted into a church.

Angus knew what Columba had looked like because he was depicted in a large stained-glass window set in a perpendicular cut-stone arch at the back of the abbey. Mister Columba was a tall, bald man who had a penchant for dressing in women's clothes. Over his shoulder he carried a big wooden cross, presented to him by Mr Jesus Christ. A hundred years ago he'd come over to stay at the Columba Hotel, during his summer holidays, with his girlfriend Mary MacDellen. Jesus needed a break from fighting the Romans and working in the circus as a conjurer where he performed tricks that he called miracles. Angus reckoned that the magician must have been making a few bob because every adult on the island had a book of his, called The Bible, in which he'd described his miracle show. He'd heard all this at Sunday school and it beat him how Jesus walked over the sea. He'd tried this himself a few times and got soaked for his efforts. His conclusion was that it must have been an illusion created by walking over ice.

Changing water to whisky was an easy deception to work out. The illusionist had a quick-handed assistant called John MacBaptist, who swapped the bottles over while his boss kept the audience distracted with one of his unbelievable stories.

Angus knew how to perform Jesus's burning bush miracle. It was easy. All that was needed was a bottle full of stolen diesel oil and a box of matches. He'd shown his pals how to do this trick on several occasions. The last time he'd done it he'd poured too much fuel over

45

a hedge and when he'd put a match to it there was a loud 'whoomp', which blew him off his feet. The flames singed off his eyebrows and fringe. When he returned home that evening, his mother had given him a right telling-off, which brought his career as a magician to a sudden end.

Angus had heard people say that the great performer was going to return one day. Even though he must be a ripe old age by now, this came as good news to him because maybe then he could ask the magician to teach him some new tricks.

Right now the second coming of Mr Jesus Christ and his miracle show was of little concern to Angus. He had more important things on his mind.

Like a naughty little genie released from the confines of a bottle, Angus climbed out through the rectangular space provided by his bedroom's open window. Sticking out of his back pocket was a catapult he'd obtained in barter for a woollen sock full of dazzies. The glass marbles had been a valued possession left to him by Santa Claws. One cold night, the jolly man with the long fingernails had deposited them in a long stocking at the foot of his bed after having first descended into the house via the chimney. It was a mystery to Angus why Mr Claws couldn't enter the house through the front door like everyone else. It was never locked and a lot easier to use than the soot-covered lum. Perhaps Santa was a crazy alkie? Drunkard or not, it was thanks to his present that Angus had his catty, a primitive and effective weapon that contained within its simple mechanism a lot more destructive potential than a bag full of little glass balls. Over the past weeks he'd been practising in secret. Now with a well-aimed shot he was capable of knocking a tin can off a dyke from fifty feet away.

Outdoors a sea breeze was blowing. Stars had come out to play and made a luminous black velvet vault out of the sky. There was no moon. Darkness was the perfect cloak for Angus's clandestine mission. In the distance a barn owl screeched, inducing fear and dread into his heart. The nocturnal predator then fell silent and the young boy's nerves settled. He strode up the cobbled road until it passed the last house in the sleeping village and turned into a dirt track. He reached an iron gate leading into the abbey's grounds. He inched it open while rusty hinges squealed in protest. Thinking it would be quieter to climb over the wall, he then pulled the gate closed. Its metal latch clicked into position. His soft-soled canvas shoes hardly made a sound as he walked along a gravel pathway towards the abbey's main building. He stooped to gather rounded pebbles and stuffed them into his pockets to use as ammunition.

Angus skirted the building until he faced a large stone frame set into the back of the abbey. Contained within this framework were a number of stained-glass windows and at the centre was Saint Columba's image.

Angus's first shot whizzed straight through the Saint's forehead. Such was the force contained within the catapult's strip of black rubber cut from a bicycle tyre's inner tube that the pebbles passed through the thick glass making little sound.

Inside the building high velocity projectiles ricocheted off the stone walls and any other surfaces they came in contact with. When his fusillade was over, he'd worked up a sweat and put holes in all of the windows. Returning the catty to his back pocket, he turned and set off in the direction leading back to Baile Mor.

He hadn't gone far when he heard the crunch of footsteps on gravel behind him. Angus darted for the nearest cover, a collapsed drystone dyke. Behind the mossed-over rocks the only noise he could hear was his heartbeat pounding on the insides of his eardrums. The pulsations slowed down and sounds began to filter in through his twitching ears. He listened to waves breaking down on the shoreline. Up by the village a cat yowled. To his left, a gentle wind rustled the leaves of a solitary holly oak.

Angus heard laughter. Somebody was laughing hysterically. His caution gave way to intense curiosity, which compelled him to take a peek over the broken wall to see if he could locate where the sound was coming from. Over by the abbey he could make out the vague outline of someone standing on the very spot he'd vacated after having fired his catapult. He focused his eyes enough to be able to see that whoever it was had their hands on their hips, looking up towards his handiwork. The figure started walking directly towards him. Angus hunkered down behind the wall, wishing the earth would swallow him.

A high-pitched woman's voice rang out. 'Come oot o' there, you wee bizzum! I know you're hiding behind thon dyke.'

Angus knew who it was immediately. It was Nancy, the local madwoman. He scrambled to his feet and made a run for it. In his haste he tripped in a rabbit hole and fell over a sleeping sheep. The startled ewe sprang to her feet, shook herself off and bleated in anger at having been so rudely awakened from her woolly dreams. Angus picked himself up and continued running in the direction of home. Climbing over the garden gate, he crept round to the side of Braeside and slipped through the open window. He pulled it closed without making a sound, threw off his clothes and lay down on his bed. His heart was thumping again, so loud that he worried the banging would wake his parents. By the time his pulse returned to normal, he was fast asleep.

Cambodia

A subtle movement caught Hamish's eye. The cobra was beginning to uncoil herself. She slithered off along the beach seeking the warmth of her reptilian burrow under a slow cooling rock. Before she had gone far, she stopped and raised her head to look back towards him. Satisfied that all was well she continued on along the beach, a moving black S against the chalk-white sand until she merged with the shadows.

Hamish sat looking at the seashore. An empty bottle was being washed up on to the beach in front of him. The motion of small waves was gently rolling it back and forth. He lit a cigarette and continued to observe the bottle. He could hear the sound created by the sand's abrasive surface on the glass's rounded contours. A larger wave pushed it further onto the shore, leaving it stranded where it gave off a dull blue-green reflection in the moonlight.

Three months earlier, over breakfast by the sea in Sri Lanka, it was Angus who had used the genie in a bottle metaphor to describe himself as a young boy setting off on a mission to commit an act of vandalism. When he finished narrating this particular anecdote from his childhood, he added his own personal reflection on the window-smashing incident. The genie, for him, represented his competing emotions as a child. Not content with such a simple explanation, he took it much further and turned young Angus into a microcosm of what was going on in the world at large.

'When I did that as an angry wee boy, I wanted to go out and leave a strong impression on the world because I felt frustrated and also misunderstood by my parents who, I might add, I loved with all my heart. In much the same way, mankind gives emotion freedom to do what it wants today, but instead of smashing a few windows, it destroys whole environments. Forget about global warming, it's global roasting the world's political leaders should be trying to do something about. The earth's running a temperature that has been brought on by a massive infestation of Homo sapiens parasites. It's time to invest in plastic rain barrels and prepare for water wars because water is going to become a big international issue in this century.' As if to emphasize his point, Angus paused for a moment to wipe sweat from his brow and take a sip from a glass of aerated water. He then went on. 'You see, emotion is the genie that is bottled up in our senses. The genie is by nature an excitable and callow energy, seeking to experience itself in the world through our eyes. Extremely vain and narcissistic, it looks for its reflection in the mirror of emotional reaction. From almost innocuous, unconscious actions such as talking badly behind a friend's back or becoming unnecessarily angry in a traffic situation, to large scale, more violent acts, like flying passenger planes into buildings full of people or invading a country and murdering its citizens. These are all examples of what happens when the genie of uncontrolled emotion escapes into the world to wreak havoc. I mean to say, back in 1997, when that drunkard, Boris Yeltsin, was supposed to be running the show in Russia, over a hundred suitcase atomic bombs went missing – a hundred atomic bombs – think about it. If that's not out of control, what is?'

Angus was watching Hamish as he said these things. It was therefore that he commented, 'I see you're nodding your head as if to say I'm talking nonsense.'

'But you can't—' Hamish tried to protest but he couldn't get a word in edgeways. His brother was on a roll.

Angus continued, saying, 'The problem with the genie is that we are always identified with it – that is, with the emotion that we are possessed by at any particular moment. Part of our destiny as human beings is to break free from the genie, rein it in, and become the master of it. If we fail to do this there's going to be big trouble on our little planet.

'For the first time in history we have a global civilization, united under the banners of consumerism and a belief system based in philosophical materialism, which limits reality to what we perceive through our senses. As a species we are obviously at a primitive stage in our evolutionary development because our greatest tribal status symbols are still our weapons. There's no need to club our enemies to death anymore because nowadays all we have to do is pull triggers and press red buttons to exterminate them.

'As far as the global environment and terrorism are concerned, it has occurred to me that, due to the genie's increasingly irrational demands and compelling influence upon us, mankind won't wake up to what's going on, unless there's a major catastrophe of some kind. Some prophets of doom say that it will require such a global cataclysm to propel man on to the next rung of the evolutionary ladder. I choose not to believe that, but I have to admit there is evidence to support such a theory. The proliferation of nuclear weapons, the population explosion, decimation of rainforests and industrial pollution concern everyone living on the planet today. These issues must be addressed and controlled now, before the balance tips and we begin a rapid descent into hell. We have to move away from a carbon fuel economy. The Four Riders of the Apocalypse have been signing on at the dole since human beings took over their jobs and began pumping billions of tons of poison into the atmosphere. God knows what our grandchildren will have to say about the diabolical mess we are in the process of leaving them as an inheritance. The way things are going, it will no longer be necessary to inform the children about the birds and the bees. Well, at least not the honeybees, because those minuscule, workhorse creatures who pollinate one-third of the human diet will soon be extinct.' Angus raved on without pausing to catch his breath. 'We have to eradicate poverty, the lack of education that leads to women having too many babies and the reasons why anyone should resort to using terror tactics in order to bring attention to the fact that there's something happening in their life that is driving them insane. If we don't act now it's only a matter of time before an Apocalypse-hungry maniac or group of kamikaze terrorists get their hands on a nuclear or biological weapon, smuggle it into Manhattan or the City of London in a container and push the—'

Hamish interrupted his brother's verbal outpouring by raising his voice. 'Hold on a minute. What on earth has all this to do with a genie in a bottle?'

Angus snapped out of it and said, 'Oops, thanks for pulling me up. I was completely carried away there. That's what happens to me when the genie of emotion gets tangled up in my thoughts. I start talking too much and, as Lao Tsu the Chinese mystic wrote in the *Tao Te Ching*, "Those who know do not talk. Those who talk do not know."'

'Sounds a bit boring to me, does that mean we're all supposed to sit around like mutes?'

'No,' answered Angus, 'but considering the confusion that too much talking can cause, it's maybe not such a bad idea.'

'So what does it mean then?'

Angus placed a forefinger over his lips and considered the question before answering. 'The first thing that comes to mind is a painted sign at the main gate of an ashram I used to frequent in my India days. It said, "Leave your shoes and mind at the door".'

'More riddles! I still don't get what you're driving at. I'm starting to feel stupid. What does leaving your mind at the door mean?'

'I'd say, start to meditate and familiarize yourself with silence. That way you won't have to ask such a question.'

Hamish sighed in exasperation. 'Don't patronize me. The only time I've seen you sit down and meditate was a few days ago when you took the time to instruct me in those meditation techniques.'

'Ah-ha, there you're making the same mistake a lot of people make. Meditation techniques are not meditation.'

'What are they then?'

'You use meditation techniques to bring you into a meditative state. Once you have the hang of it, you don't need the techniques anymore. Or, to put it another way, a person with a broken leg uses crutches to walk, when the leg heals the crutches become obsolete and can be thrown away. It's only a stupid person who uses crutches when there's no need for them.'

'All right,' said Hamish, 'so what exactly is a meditative state?'

'Meditation is a state of no mind.'

'No mind, here we go again, what's that supposed to mean?'

'It's difficult to say in so many words, but if you permit me to, I can demonstrate it to you very easily and perhaps, if I'm not mistaken, catch that aggressive genie at play.'

'I've no idea what you're talking about, but anyway you have my permission. Go ahead and show me.'

As quick as a flash Angus leaned over the breakfast table and delivered a hard slap to his brother's face. For a few seconds Hamish sat in silence, doing nothing.

'That's no mind,' said Angus.

Suddenly, Hamish was possessed by anger. He leapt out of his seat shouting, 'You fucking arsehole!', and dived over the table, sending crockery flying to the floor where it smashed to pieces.

Angus was too quick for him and dodged out of his way. 'And that's the genie of emotion out of its bottle.'

Hamish came after him. Angus escaped down to the beach with his furious twin brother in hot pursuit. They ran a long way. By the time Angus let his brother catch up with him, Hamish's anger had dissipated.

'That really hurt,' panted Hamish, putting a hand to his red cheek.

'Sorry, that's the problem with awakening. It's sometimes painful,' said Angus. 'In my opinion the pain is worth it because a person who is unable to stop thinking is someone who is suffering. Unfortunately this is the case for almost everybody and therefore being identified with your mind is considered normal. ' Angus ran his hand over his sweating brow and continued by saying, 'Looks like the genie's finished with you for the moment. Mark my words though, he's like a ghoul who feeds on whatever he can stir up in your pot and like the Terminator said, he'll be back.'

Still trying to recover his breath, Hamish shook his head and looked at him. 'You're bloody well nuts, you know that?'

Angus bestowed a prize-winning smile upon his brother, thumped him good-naturedly on the shoulder, stood up and said, 'Come on, I'll race you back along the beach.'

He'd just sat where he was and watched Angus's muscular body recede into the distance as he jogged along the shoreline.

Hamish let go of the memory and noticed his cigarette had burned down to its filter between his fingers. He flicked the dog end away, watched it spiral towards where the bottle had been and realized that it was no longer there. The sea had reclaimed it and taken it elsewhere – leaving the genie free to feed on Hamish's angst.

5

HITLER AND BARNEY'S
MAGIC POTION

A door slammed. Angus awoke from a troubled night's sleep. He'd been dreaming about Amah. She'd come to scold him for breaking the abbey's windows. 'You naughty boy,' she'd shouted, a look of extreme displeasure on her normally jovial face, 'what a terrible thing you've done. I'm never coming to see you again.' Amah had been shaking an admonitory finger at him but disappeared the instant Braeside's front door banged closed and woke him up.

Angus sat up in bed and ruffled his hair. He shook his head, trying to clear the dream from his mind. His belly was growling. Stretching his arms, he searched around and picked up whatever clothes he found discarded on the cold flagstone floor. He dressed quickly then made his way through to the kitchen. When he opened the kitchen door the first thing he saw was his mother, down on her bended knees cleaning smouldering ashes out of the oven. The second thing he set his eyes on was a bowl of steaming hot porridge. He made a beeline for it.

'Angus Macleod,' shouted his mother, brandishing a small metal shovel. 'Don't you dare sit down and eat that porridge until you go back to your room and change that filthy shirt you're wearing.'

Angus's chin touched the top of his chest as he looked down to examine the source of his mother's complaint. His tee shirt was smeared with sheep droppings. He did as he was told, hurried back to the kitchen and sat down at the table. The porridge tasted like the

53

nectar of the gods with a touch too much salt in it.

He wolfed down his breakfast while his mother continued her chores. As she worked, Rose informed her son that his father had been summoned to a gathering down at the manse with the rest of the island's menfolk. The meeting had been called by the moderator because of an act of sabotage that had been carried out during the night. Wisps of smoke spiralled up from her aluminium pail as Rose paused in her labours for a moment to ask a question.

'You don't know anything about this vandalism, do you?'

Angus scuttled around in his mind, hoping he could come up with the right response. 'Vandalism?' He spoke the word as though it were new to him. 'What's vandalism, Ma?'

'Och, never mind, eat your porridge.'

Angus could feel his mother's eyes watching him as he spooned another load of the thick gruel into his mouth.

'Heavens,' exclaimed Rose, 'your hair looks like a crow's nest! It's a haircut for you at the weekend, my lad.'

'Aw, Ma, don't say that. I like it the way it is.'

'I'll hear nothing out of you on the matter. C'mon now, hurry up with your breakfast or you'll be late for school, and don't forget your schoolbag.'

The village of Baile Mor stood on a gentle rise. At the foot of this grassy bank a stretch of single-track asphalt wound its way up from a small harbour. A short distance along the road sat Iona's schoolhouse. It was built from stone. The year of its construction was carved into a granite lintel above the front door: 1921. It was situated near to a roofless ruin that had been a nunnery in ancient times. Behind the school, a fenced-off area of flattened grey earth was used as a playground during the pupils' midday break. There was only one room inside the building large enough to serve as a classroom.

Seated on plywood chairs, shiny from the rubbing of countless fidgety backsides, a dozen or so children between the ages of five and twelve were pulling textbooks out of their bags and placing them on scarred wooden desks in preparation for the first day of the autumn term. Facing the class Mr Napier, the school's only teacher, sat behind a broad oak desk. He had on a pair of horn-rimmed spectacles and was fussing over a pile of papers. There was an air of smugness about him, as if he were a business executive preparing to sign an agreement on a billion pound trade merger he'd just executed. Angus retrieved his jotters and pencils from his olive green canvas satchel that, in a previous incarnation, had been an army gas-mask holder. There was a loud knock on the door and then two uniformed policemen strode into the classroom.

In those days a man had to be at least six feet tall to make him eligible for joining the lofty ranks of the police force. Dressed in black, the two policemen were built like chiselled boulders. Their big leather boots gleamed with the lustre of polished marble. Staring from clean-shaven pale faces, their cold steel-grey eyes looked like rivets as they scanned the room and its occupants. Angus had never seen a real live bobby before and now here he was looking up at two of them. Instinctively, he did not like them. He kept his eyes down and examined his English jotter's open pages as if upon its faint blue lines were written the universe's greatest secrets.

The taller of the two men stepped forward and loudly cleared his throat in front of the school children. The class looked up like a herd of startled gazelles by a waterhole in Africa who've just heard the roar of a hungry lion in the vicinity. The flatfoot introduced himself. 'Good morning, children. My name's Sergeant Murdoch and I've come over from Mull this morning with my colleague here, Police Constable Donaldson.' The big sergeant turned to the man standing behind him and nodded, just in case the kids in the class were so dumb that they did not know to whom he was referring. He continued. 'We've come over to Iona to investigate a serious crime committed in the abbey's grounds last night. I'd like to ask a few questions because you children might be able to help us with our enquiries. Before I do that I'll let you ask me a few questions to begin with. Now then, do you have anything to ask?'

Morag Simpson raised an eager arm.

'Yes, lass, what's your question?'

Morag was seven and had a narrow face capped by an unruly mop of ginger curls. 'Sergeant Murdoch, have you ever had tea with the Queen?' It was an innocent query that succeeded in setting the sarge on the wrong foot.

'Ehm … no, lass, I've never had the honour of having a cup of tea with Her Majesty the Queen. Next.'

Billy Smith's arm shot up, Nazi style. He was an eight year old brimming over with physical energy. He was dressed in short checked trousers suspended by a pair of bright red braces stretched over a striped shirt. Billy grinned. exposing a gap between his teeth. His impish face was crowned by an exaggerated quiff hairstyle, held in place by lard. He was proud of his hairdo and referred to it as his 'Little Richard'.

'Yes, son, what is it?' The sergeant was barely able to suppress a smile. Billy's appearance affected everyone in this way – apart from Mr Napier, who only smiled when he was punishing his pupils.

'Sergeant Murdoch, how many Jerrys did you kill in the war, sir?' A great fan of war comics, Billy gave a curt salute.

'Ehm … Son, I did not kill any German soldiers during the war. I was in the Home Guard.'

'Did you shoot down any Messerschmitts, Sir?'

'No, I did not.' The sergeant was starting to become irritable. 'Next!'

Neil Ferguson put up his hand. Neil was almost ten and the smarty-pants of the class. He had on a pair of patched denim dungarees. His jaw jutted out. He had fair hair styled in a spiky crew cut that he called a 'Tommy Steele'. Nobody except Neil knew who Mr Steele was, but judging by his name he was probably like Neil, a bit of a hard nut.

He tried, unsuccessfully, to keep a straight face when he asked, 'Sarge, do you take off those great muckle boots of yours when you get into bed at night on top o' Missus Murdoch?' The class laughed. Like a predator who had just spotted a tasty snack, Mr Napier glanced up from his important paperwork. Sgt Murdoch's air of bonhomie vanished.

'I'll have none of that kind of cheek out of you, sonny. The police have ways of dealing with the likes of you.' With this thinly veiled threat, the sergeant blew it with the school children.

Neil raised his hands together in front of him, as if preparing to be handcuffed. Feigning timidity, he said in a pipsqueak's voice, 'A'm sorry sarge, I'll no' do it again.' The schoolmaster stepped out from behind his desk and took control of the situation.

'Ferguson! Go and stand over there!' He pointed to a corner that had a big canvas map of the world hanging from one of its walls. Turning to the police sergeant, Mr Napier made a suggestion. 'Officer, perhaps it would be easier if you simply ask the children your questions directly.' The teacher returned to his desk while the copper did an about turn in his tactics.

'Did any of you children notice anything suspicious yesterday evening?'

Silence. You could have heard a spider walking across the classroom's wooden floorboards.

'I will repeat my question,' persisted the bobby, spittle accumulating at the corner of his lips. 'Did any of you see anything at all that appeared suspicious on Sunday evening?'

'Yes, I did, sarge,' said Neil from his corner.

The policeman was by now wary of Neil, but his curiosity had been tweaked. 'Well, out with it, lad, out with it.'

'I saw them on Sunday night over by the nunnery. They were lying on the ground.'

Sgt Murdoch couldn't conceal his excitement. He walked over to Neil and said, 'Aye lad, aye, go on, go on. Who did you see?'

'A pair of wifie's drawers, they were pink and they had great big skid marks on them.'

The class's uproar was cut short when Mr Napier rose from his seat and strode over towards Neil. Taking hold of his ear and twisting it, the pedagogue led him out of the room. When the teacher returned, he held a short hushed confab with the two policemen over by his desk. After much nodding of heads handshakes were exchanged, the policemen marched out of the room without so much as a glance at the children. Mr Napier was as relieved as his pupils to see the back of the bobbies. He did not like outside interference in his domain.

Now that he was in complete control again, the first thing Mr Napier did was to open a drawer in his desk and bring out 'Nessie'. This was the name given to a thick brown leather strap that Mr Napier used to administer corporal punishment. He brought Neil back into the room and made him raise the palms of his hands together in front of him. The classroom despot brought the belt's split end down upon Neil's palms with all the strength that he could muster from within the frame of his wiry body. Neil received six of the best. The thwacks rang out, making the rest of the class sit up straight in their chairs. Neil's eyes watered a little from the pain, but there was no way he would ever have allowed a tear to fall in front of his warped sadist of a teacher, a Sassenach who imagined himself to be a pillar of society.

Mr Napier's nickname was 'Hitler'. He knew that was what his pupils called him behind his back because he'd seen the name written in chalk up on the blackboard often enough when he'd returned from having left the room for one reason or another. Like the Great Dictator, his rule was autocratic, but there existed nothing of greatness within the rigid confines of his personality. The reason he'd earned his moniker had more to do with his physical appearance. A bachelor from south of the border, he always dressed in a shapeless grey tweed suit. He was a short man in his mid-forties who had gone bald at a premature age. In a pathetic attempt to cover up his baldness, he'd taken to letting his black hair grow long on one side of his head and combing the greasy strands over his pate. If there was one meteorological phenomenon that Hitler feared above all else, it was a windy day. To complete the picture, Mr Napier had a stunted grey moustache stained brown in the middle, a telltale sign of a heavy smoker.

Angus enjoyed learning, but like the rest of his classmates, he hated and detested his tutor. Although Angus was three years younger than Neil, he shared the top of the hit list with him for being the most punished child in the school, which in turn made him popular with his classmates. Within a year of having taken up the position of being the island's sole schoolmaster, Mr Napier had managed to destroy all of his pupils' chances of ever graduating to any sort of refined work that required sensitivity in their fingertips. This was because their nerve endings had been smashed into non-existence by liberal applications of Nessie the belt.

Mr Napier was in a particularly foul mood that morning, even going as far as punishing Morag, his pet pupil. She'd made the mistake of accidentally knocking over her inkwell while refilling it. Unlike the boys, Morag cried an overflowing burn of tears after feeling Nessie's bite for the first time in quite a while. Smiling benevolently, Hitler took pity on her and offered his snot-stained hanky to dry her eyes.

Angus looked on and felt a lump in his throat. His heart began to beat in an agitated way that gave birth to an emotion of outrage. He liked Morag a lot. It hurt him to see her experience pain at the hands of such a beast. He felt helpless, for there was nothing within his limited realm of power that he could do to aid her. Frustration churned in his guts and a new sensation began to form in his young heart. He had no way of identifying the feeling because it was new to him. It was to grow over the years and one day manifest itself as desire for revenge upon his wicked and cruel tormentor.

In the following weeks, rumours and gossip were rife within the island community about who was responsible for the breaking of the abbey's windows. Angus was never a suspect, being perceived by the islanders as a curly-haired innocent incapable of carrying out what was viewed by many as the Devil's handiwork.

Iona was a slow-moving place where the passage of time was measured by observing the passing seasons. Months flew by like the clouds that scudded over the island, driven by strong winds that blew in from the North Atlantic. Angus grew taller and by the time he was nine he'd graduated to his first pair of long trousers. His friends called him 'Monk', courtesy of a large pair of blunt sheep-shearing scissors, a shallow bowl and his mother's very limited skills as a hairstylist.

At school Mr Napier continued to dole out retribution. In between belting sessions, he provided his pupils with an elementary education. Angus had three things to thank him for. Mister Napier had taught him to read, to write and to disrespect authoritarian figures for the rest of his life. Any spare time Angus found himself with was used to feed his insatiable appetite for the written word. As for the other subjects he was taught at school, he achieved passable marks on his report card, except for geography, something he excelled at. Instinctively he knew that one day all those cities with funny sounding names like Istanbul, Bangkok and Kathmandu would be places he could travel to and explore.

Angus detested algebra almost as much as he hated the man who tried to hammer the meaning of its equations into his head. One evening he'd broken into a sweat trying to decipher the hieroglyphic inscriptions of his algebra homework. In the end he gave up in frustration. It all seemed like gobbledegook to his unenlightened mind. When Hitler discovered his failure, Angus had to pay the price.

'Macleod! Get over here immediately and put your hands up, boy.'

Angus was by now immune to Nessie's bite with the palms of his hands calloused due to repeated encounters with the leather strap.

Later that day he'd been sitting by some fishermen at the end of the pier and overheard a word that he'd never heard before. Next morning in school he looked the word up in one of his favourite books, the *Concise Oxford English Dictionary*. It said, 'bastard: informal; an unpleasant or despicable person.' He liked the feel of the word as his lips sprang apart to expel it.

It did not take long for Angus to violate another of Hitler's stringent laws, and like so many times before, he stood holding his hands out in front of him, waiting for the despicable tyrant to do his best to inflict pain upon him. Angus watched the pervert work himself up into a heated state of agitation. Beads of sweat were streaming down over

Hitler's flushed face. When the sadist ran out of steam, Angus dropped his throbbing hands to his sides and stared into the creep's beady eyes. The schoolmaster realized something was not under his control. Faced with his pupil's unfaltering gaze, he felt uncomfortable in his own skin, a sensation somewhat akin to that produced by wearing cast-iron underpants. To Angus, he looked like a skinny rat whose eyes darted around the room, furtively seeking a way out of the situation. Angus intensified his stare.

'We-well, boy, what is it?' blustered the teacher.

A spasm of rage erupted inside Angus's chest. He channelled the raw power into two words and literally spat them out into Hitler's face. 'Ya Bastard!'

'Wh-wh-what did you say?' puffed the tyrant, small flecks of spittle sticking to his livid face.

'I said you're a bastard and I hate your guts.'

Provoked, the tutor rose to the challenge. 'How dare you speak to me like that, you … you … you insolent scoundrel. I've a good mind to expel you, but I have a better idea.' Pointing to his oak desk he ordered, 'Bend over there.'

Angus did as he was told. The sadistic teacher started laying into his backside with the belt as if he were being paid in gold for every whack. The pain on the top of Angus's legs and buttocks was excruciating. He clenched his jaw in order to prevent any sound escaping from his tightly sealed lips. The class stared on in disbelief. Hitler was flailing away at the young boy's backside, possessed by the spirit of a slave-driver below the decks of a Roman galley coaxing his oarsmen up to ramming speed.

Neil Ferguson sprang to his feet and shouted, 'Leave him alone! Angus is right. You're a rotten old bastard!'

The rest of the schoolkids rallied to the call. Their booing soon changed to a chant of 'bastard, bastard', even though half of them had no idea what the word meant. For a moment Hitler continued hitting Angus, but the violent wind was fast leaving his furiously flapping sails.

With a sharp intake of breath, Mr Napier dropped his belt and clutched his chest. He staggered across the wooden floor and collapsed into his seat. His face had taken on the colour of curdled milk. He was perspiring like a pig in a sauna, and his camouflage hairstyle had come unstuck. Angus had almost passed out from his vicious beating. He opened his eyes when his lashing came to a sudden end. He was astonished to see that Hitler was in worse shape than he was. Mr Napier's hair was sticking out all over the place, which made Angus realize that something was seriously wrong with him.

For a moment their eyes met and the teacher wheezed, 'Get out of my sight.' He raised his voice and hissed at the rest of his pupils, 'Class dismissed.'

Nobody moved.

He repeated his command. 'Class dismissed.' A note of desperation lent emphasis to his words.

The children quickly gathered their things together and hurried out of the classroom. Colour was returning to the deflated pedagogue's face by the time Angus had put his jotters away and walked to the door. Just as he was about to make his exit, he turned and looked back at Mr Napier. The angry heat streaming out of Hitler's eyes could have blistered paint.

'Bastard.' The word flew out of Angus's mouth with the force of a verbal bullet. Mr Napier winced, but said nothing.

Angus went home to find his mother in a cheery mood, humming the melody to 'Over The Sea To Skye'. She was sweeping the floor with a broom as her baking orders for the day cooled on the table. After staring at the evil countenance of his teacher all morning, Rose appeared angelic to Angus. It was warm and her cheeks were flushed. Her long blonde hair was tied back in a pleat. A stray tress hung free over one side of her face giving her a heart-warming ragamuffin appearance.

'You're home early today. How was school?'

Angus screwed up his face. 'I hate algebra.'

'Now, now, we'll have none of your complaining in this house,' chided Rose. 'You've got to stick in at school if you want to get anywhere in this world.'

'Aye right, Ma.'

'Don't you get lippy with me, young lad. How about chopping some kindling?'

'Aw, Ma, no' the now, I'm away oot to play.'

'All right then,' conceded Rose. 'Away with you and get out of your school clothes before you go.'

In the privacy of his bedroom, he took off his grey flannel trousers and white cotton underpants. There were bloodstains on the seat of his pants. Using a cracked shaving mirror that had once belonged to his father, he examined the damage inflicted upon his backside. Raised red welts lay across his buttocks and the tops of his hamstrings. In places the skin was broken, the obvious source of the bloodstains. He whispered the word that so aptly described his antagonist. 'Bastard.'

He decided to ditch his stained underpants. He had no desire to answer the questions his mother would doubtless ask if she found blood on his drawers. If there was one thing Angus had learned from his window-smashing escapade three years before, it was to keep his mouth shut and share with no one any information that could bring him trouble. It had never occurred to him that his teacher might be the one who deserved punishment for his atrocious behaviour. Besides, Angus already saw himself as being big enough to fight his own battles, although the strategy for conducting an attack on Hitler hadn't quite come to him yet. He put on his football jersey, a grey tee shirt with a small blue and white Scottish flag stitched onto a shoulder. A good kick about would help him to forget the agonies of his run-in with Mr Napier.

Angus jogged down to the grass pitch behind the social hall and arrived in time to join a game of five-a-side football. Teams were being picked and an argument broke out over which side was to be Scotland and which England. As usual, nobody wanted to be on the Sassenach team. Neil Ferguson settled the dispute by tossing a copper penny into the air. The losers were, of course, the English because, unlike their neighbours who lived south of the border, the Scots at that time didn't have to struggle to gain a sense of national identity. From an early age the children on Iona had it drummed into their heads by their elders that they were Scottish and to be proud of it.

'Hey Monk, you're in luck, you're on the Scottish team with me,' said Neil, punching Angus lightly on the shoulder. They walked together over to one side of the pitch.

'You're the goalie, Monk,' said Neil, well aware of his friend's lack of skill in the beautiful game.

'Aye, okay Neil.' The worst footballer on the island, Angus was always the goalkeeper. Neil pulled his young friend closer.

'You took a right hiding today. Are you okay?'

'Aye, a'm all right. Bit of a sair bum, that's all.'

'That auld shite's going to get it one of these days,' said Neil. Angus said nothing, though he shared exactly the same sentiment.

'C'mon, Monk, let's have a game of fitba'.'

Neil broke into a trot and headed for the centre of the field. Angus took his position between the white-painted goalposts and watched the kick-off. He stared at Neil's back, moved by his fondness for the older boy. Some of the teenagers from the village had made up the numbers for the game, and one of them was now heading towards Angus with the ball in his possession. Like a runaway train, Ian MacFarlane was steaming down the unguarded right wing. Angus ran out to meet him. Just as Ian was about to take a crack at the goal, Angus recklessly dived at his feet. He smothered the leather football with his body and sent his opponent flying. Ian was fizzing at the rough tackle and after Angus had booted the ball upfield, the muscular youth came up behind the goalkeeper, gave him a hard slap on the back of his head and shouted, 'You lanky cunt, you nearly broke ma fuckin' legs.'

Neil was nearby and ran to Angus's assistance. He pushed Ian in the chest and spat to one side. 'Keep your hands to yoursel', or you'll have to deal with me.'

Ian was a strong youth and, if he'd felt like it, could have beaten the crap out of Angus and Neil with one hand tied behind his broad back, but there was something in Neil's fearless demeanour that made him hold back.

'Aye okay, Neil, no problem, just tell your goalie to take it easy like. It's a friendly match, right?'

'Awright, Ian,' replied Neil, his flinty-eyed expression turning into a smile in the late afternoon sunlight.

They shook hands and the game proceeded until Calum 'The Tank' Docherty tripped Billy Smith up in front of the goal and a penalty was awarded to England. Ian took it. The ball came in like it was shot from a cannon and, by a complete fluke, Angus managed to get in its way.

'Save!' cried the Scottish side.

Ian shook his head in disbelief and cursed, 'Jammy bastard.'

By sunset the friendly drew to a close. Scotland had romped home to a 7 - 3 victory over the Sassenachs, a reality the 'Tartan Army' dream about but unfortunately rarely get to see in the real world of International Football; although, it must be said, not for the lack of having enthusiastic supporters. Angus was fairly chuffed with himself. Not only was he on the winning side, he'd also made a miraculous save. With the wind in his hair he whistled 'Scotland the Brave' all the way home.

He'd forgotten all about the damage to his backside until he sat down at the kitchen table for his evening meal. Then he remembered the hard way. The pain evaporated through the seat of his pants when he saw what was for supper. Mince, tatties and the father of all culinary delights, a great big mealy Jimmy. The long grey sausage was made from a short length of sheep's intestine filled with fried oatmeal and spices. A coronary specialist's nightmare, it was Angus's favourite dish. Its contents were mixed with the minced beef and mashed potatoes, and before him lay a feast the likes of which would have satisfied a Clan Chieftain.

'Angus, you're eating like a pig,' scolded his mother as he attacked his food like a glutton who'd been on a cabbage soup diet for a month.

'Can you no' see the lad's hungry after his game of fitba',' said Dan, winking in his son's direction.

'We're no' a pack of savages. You're nearly as bad as him,' said Rose, turning to her husband, a smile showing at the corner of her lips.

Like most mothers of the time, she took great pleasure and satisfaction in watching her family enjoying her cooking. She knew the magic ingredient that won over their stomachs and hearts, time and again. It was pure unadulterated motherly love.

Mr Napier curbed his aggressive behaviour for more than a week. His motives were entirely selfish; he did not want to die from a heart attack at the tender age of 46. Within a fortnight it was punishing business as usual.

Summer gave way to autumn and what few deciduous trees there were on the island lost their leaves, leaving their naked branches to claw at the pale blue mid-October sky. Towards the end of the month, an unexpected warm front rolled in off the Gulf Stream and herded the clouds away to the east. Panic gripped the Ionians' hearts when the sky took on an unusual azure colour and a flaming orb appeared over the island. The phenomenon, known as 'The Sun' and commonly found in Mediterranean countries situated thousands of miles away to the south, unleashed a frightening heat and bright light. This prompted many of the islanders to tear off their woollen hats, scarves and jerseys. Others feared they might be burnt or blinded by radiation. Religion being strict on Iona, nobody would dare to work on the Sabbath. Down at the Kirk on Sunday morning the pews were packed. It was standing room only when Reverend Gray's reedy voice called out and urged the congregation to remain calm. He reassured them by saying he'd witnessed this kind of meteorological phenomenon before, back in 1946 when it had been put down to being an after-effect from the war. He guaranteed his flock that their shepherd, the Lord Jesus Christ, would take care of everything and that they'd soon be able to return to their normal lives wherein they complained all the time and were suspicious about everyone. When Reverend Gray fell silent everyone stood up and sang 'Onward Christian Soldiers' as if they were troops marching towards a war where their survival depended on the loudness of their voices.

That afternoon, Angus retreated to his secret hideaway, a cosy nest between some boulders on top of Dun I, the highest hill on the island. It was there he'd sit for hours reading books he'd borrowed from the school library. There were qualities about this spot that he enjoyed more than anywhere else on the six square miles of land that made up the island's territory. He loved the peace and silence wherein the beat of a gull's wings sounded loud, the distant bellow of a rutting stag in search of his harem on the hills of Mull nearby and the occasional passing thought noisy. The panoramic views and the sensation of being high above the cares of the world added up to more than the sum of their parts. Angus did not see the place as being beautiful. He experienced it directly and felt nature's wild splendour.

With a sigh of pleasure, he leaned back to feel the reassuring warmth of a granite boulder pass through the thin cotton barrier of his tee shirt. He was a Highland Lord alone on his treasure island. The complete lack of gold doubloons and pieces of eight was more than made up for by his emerald-studded kingdom, set in a sparkling sapphire sea and illuminated by a sun whose brilliance left the Koh-i-noor diamond in the shade. He looked at his bare feet, enveloped by thick moss and grass, transformed by imagination into a primordial Jurassic forest where giant black rhinoceros beetles preyed upon striped caterpillars as long as trains. Flying out of primeval mists, screeching pterodactyl moths used ivory talons to carry off baby woolly mammoths for lunch.

On this particular afternoon, he'd just finished reading Robert Louis Stevenson's *Kidnapped* for the umpteenth time. He put the well-thumbed paperback down and admired its cover, printed with a picture of the novel's hero, David Balfour, dressed in a kilt whilst hanging on to the edge of an outcrop of rock. His favourite read, this classic tale of adventure and friendship had become part of his soul and filled his heart with inspirational joy. He sat remembering one of the most exciting chapters in the famous story. David had been a castaway on the nearby island of Erraid after his escape from The Covenant, a brigantine crewed by seafaring pirates. He'd made his way from there to Mull where he'd navigated through treacherous bogs and over heather-clad mountains. Angus looked over the Sound of Iona to the southeast where, a few miles away, he could see, bathed in the afternoon sunlight, the islet of Erraid. He pictured how it must have been for David a century ago, dragging himself ashore only to find he was in a deserted and solitary place with nothing to eat or drink. His fantasy was interrupted when, down below on the road, a bright splinter of light was reflected towards him from the shiny surface of polished chrome.

A month earlier, curious stares were exchanged when the Caledonian MacBrayne ferry docked one afternoon and a brand new car rolled down its ramp to rumble onto the pier. It was the first motor car to arrive on Iona. Up until then Massey Ferguson tractors were the only form of motorized transport on the island. It soon became known that the dark blue Ford Anglia's proud owner was none other than Mr Napier, the schoolteacher.

There was only a mile of surfaced road on the island and the car's driver used it as often as possible. Each morning of the working week Mr Napier drove to the school and parked his Ford for all to see and admire. Angus had peeked through the Anglia's driver's side window to see that the oval shaped speedometer went up to eighty miles an hour, an inconceivable speed in such a slow-moving environment.

As Angus sat watching the car below him proceed along the dirt track that led to Coracle Bay, where his teacher rented a small isolated cottage, the natural algebra within the boy's mind began to reel out equations.

Billy Smith owned the largest collection of war comics on the island. Angus had borrowed a pile of these pictorial pulp magazines from his classmate a few weeks before. One of the comic book's stories followed the exploits of a platoon of American GIs stranded behind enemy lines, led by a hardened war veteran called Sergeant Samson. The non-commissioned officer was so tough he ate the wooden lids off ammo boxes for breakfast. He and his men were surrounded by the enemy; well-armed, grey-uniformed German Wehrmacht soldiers who were either called Fritz or Heinz. The Jerrys spoke German with each other using words like *Schweinehund*, *Gott im Himmel*, and *Achtung Mienenfeld*.

Hamish, sitting there on the landmine, had read the same kind of comics when he was a boy. It was therefore that he recalled the German word for minefield. Shocked out of reliving Angus's adventures, he quickly glanced around, only to realize nothing had changed in his immediate vicinity. An involuntary shiver passed through his body. In no way wishing to think about his current reality, he forced himself to dive back into the imaginary world of Sergeant Samson.

The Jerrys had parked a squadron of tanks outside the bombed-out ruin of a farmhouse that Sergeant Samson and his platoon were hiding in. The GIs had run out of bullets and grenades, but they still had to find a way to destroy the enemy panzers. Sergeant Samson hit upon an idea when he just happened to find a few bags of sugar hidden in a secret cellar below the farmhouse, where a family of terrified French peasants huddled in a corner, waiting for the war to end. Under the cover of darkness the GIs screwed off the petrol caps from the unguarded war machines and sweetened up their gas tanks. Next morning the black-clad German commander threw a fit when he discovered his heavy tracked Tiger tanks had been immobilized by a crafty act of sabotage. He called the guards Schweinhunds and shouted up to Gott in Himmel that his panzers were 'Kaput! Kaput! Mein Gott, kaput!' Sergeant Samson and the lads were soon safe behind American lines, shaking hands with each other, congratulating themselves on what a smart bunch of cowboys they were. Kaput – Angus liked the sound of that word.

Next morning, his face lopsided with pent-up rage, Mr Napier arrived at the school on foot because his car had mysteriously spluttered to a standstill half a mile from his cottage. He was a stickler for punctuality. A victim of his own rules, a storm cloud hung over him when he entered his classroom half an hour late.

Hitler had taken to smoking his Navy Cut cigarettes in front of the class. In those days, nobody had ever heard of secondary smoke. Therefore nobody thought about it, except the primary school kids who had to sit there all day long breathing in and smelling the disgusting stench of stale cigarette smoke. The nico-addict always had a fag on the go. His large glass ashtray, lying to one side of his desk, was filled to overflowing with dog ends and ashes. In his haste to get to work, he had left his smokes behind in the car and was absolutely dying for his fix by the time he sat down behind his desk.

On the edge of the ashtray was one unsmoked cigarette. Reaching into his waistcoat he retrieved a packet of Swan Vestas. His hand was shaking as he lit the end of his fag with a sulphury smelling burning match. With a short sigh of satisfaction, he blew a noxious cloud in the direction of his pupils. He gazed at his fag with a look of relief spreading across his face. Just when he was about to take another drag, the cigarette exploded. There was a flash, a dull whoomp and then Hitler disappeared in a pall of smoke. Some of the younger girls in the class squeaked in fright, but for the most part the pupils looked on agog.

When the smoke cleared, Hitler did not look like the Great Dictator anymore. He resembled a shell-shocked black and white minstrel and if he'd started to give a rendition of 'My Dear Old Mammy' nobody in the room would have blinked. Mister Napier's watering eyes stared out of his head. Had he looked in a mirror they would probably have popped out because his eyebrows had gone to the same place as his moustache and hairstyle. He was as bald as a blackened ostrich egg. The teacher began to tremble, screeching out the kind of scream a porn star would make if his oversized penis was dipped into molten iron. His fist banged down so hard on his desk that his pens, pencils and inkwells began doing the Highland fling. The kids loved it. Their cheering was loud enough for Rose to hear it up in her kitchen.

'My,' she muttered, 'the children sound like they're having a great time of it today. I always knew Mister Napier was a good teacher.'

School was cancelled for the rest of the week while Hitler had his right hand and lips treated for second degree burns.

The following Monday morning, Sgt Murdoch was standing talking to Mr Napier when the schoolchildren filed into the classroom. This time the big bobby did not waste any time on pleasantries. As soon as the whole class was seated in front of him he cleared his throat and got straight to the point.

'Right then, I've been called over to Iona for two reasons. As you all know, someone pulled a very dangerous prank on this very spot last week that, I might add, almost succeeded in putting Mister Napier in hospital. Do any one of you know who put the gunpowder from a shotgun cartridge in your teacher's cigarette?'

For a moment it was quiet in the room until someone cut a loud fart. Some of the younger kids tittered. Angus looked over to Neil because that was where the rude noise had originated. Neil sat staring straight ahead. The picture of innocence, he looked like a Christian saint who'd just picked up his halo from the dry cleaners.

The sergeant continued. 'The other criminal incident that I'm here to investigate is the sabotage of Mister Napier's Ford Anglia motor car. Somebody put sugar in its petrol tank. Do any of you know anything about this?'

Billy Smith's hand shot up like he was trying to catch an annoying midge.

'Yes, lad, what do you have to say for yourself?' barked the copper.

'Sergeant Murdoch, Sir.' Billy snapped off a quick salute. 'Sergeant Samson did it, Sir.'

The bobby's eyes narrowed and Angus felt a sickening drop in his belly.

'And who, may I ask, is Sergeant Samson?'

'He's the leader of Dog Platoon, Sir.'

The policeman scowled. 'Listen laddie, I'm here on a serious police matter. If this is your idea of a joke, it's not very funny.'

Billy's jug ears turned strawberry red. He remained silent, realizing his intelligence was of no value to this stupid bobby who was now towering over him.

The sergeant looked at each of the children's faces in turn, leaving Neil until last.

'I seem to remember you. What's your name, boy?'

'Neil.'

'Neil what?'

'No, Neil Ferguson.'

The sergeant took a step closer to Neil. 'Mind your lip, son. What do you know about these crimes?'

'What crimes?'

Sgt Murdoch glowered at Neil. 'I'll get to the bottom of this. I have my suspicions, but as yet there is no hard evidence to back them up.' Bending forward, he looked directly into Neil's eyes. 'When I do find my evidence, there will be hell to pay.'

The teenager sat unblinking and stared right through his antagonist.

Sergeant Murdoch left the island by late afternoon. The only thing he got to the bottom of was the small motorboat that ferried him back to Mull in choppy seas. Mr Napier resigned a week later. He'd taken to wearing a woollen bonnet to cover his baldness. There were still bandages on his hand when he walked up the ramp of the Friday afternoon ferry, followed by his ruined car, which had to be shunted onto the boat by a tractor. A few of his ex-pupils showed up to give him a send off. They waved and cheered as the ferry pulled away from the end of the pier, a cauldron of bubbling grey water at its stern. Billy gave him the Nazi salute and clicked the heels of his tackety boots

69

together. Mr Napier kept his back to the island as the ferry plowed out through the waves into the open sea. He was never to be seen again on the island. Gone forever, and guess what – nobody missed him.

Angus kept his sugar-in-the-petrol-tank mission to himself, as did the gunpowder-in-the-cigarette culprit. It was Neil who had made the world explode in the iniquitous tin god's face. Like his young friend Angus, he knew when to keep his lips hermetically sealed.

In mid-November a temporary replacement teacher came over from the mainland to take the schoolchildren through to the Christmas holidays. Miss Crawford was every schoolboy's wet dream come true. A tall brunette in her mid-twenties, her hair was cut in a pageboy style with a neat little fringe framing her sultry brown eyes, pert nose and red painted lips. She wore pointed high-heeled bootees, which gave her a difficult time on the potholed road outside the school, but did wonders for her tight posterior, which stuck out almost as far as her bulging breasts. Her bosom was displayed in a tantalizing fashion by wearing a skin-hugging, finely woven Fair Isle jersey. When Neil first set eyes on these magnificent mammaries he almost swooned. He later described them to Angus as looking like the nose cones of guided missiles that bounced when she laughed, something that, much to his delight, happened often.

The girls in the class also liked Miss Crawford. She was an enthusiastic tutor who took a special interest in each of the children she taught. The young teacher was a whiff of French perfume compared to the foul-smelling monster who was her predecessor.

Due to Miss Crawford's presence in the classroom, testosterone levels were shooting up in most of the young lads' hormonal systems. Neil Ferguson cashed in on the spate of spontaneous erections among the male members of his class by constructing a device he described as a shagging cushion. He'd found an old sheepskin pillow, cut a slit in it and filled it full of jelly. For sixpence you could have a go at it. Angus never tried the thing out as the sexual urge had not quite yet grabbed him strongly enough to make him feel like doing such a thing. However, one cold evening he did accompany Billy Smith over to the cemetery to see how the shagging cushion worked. Billy paid his sixpence to Neil, pulled down his pants and got to it with the pillow on top of old Mabel McPherson's gravestone. As Billy's bare ass bucked up and down in the moonlight Angus was not quite sure what to make out of his antics, but he laughed and slapped his sides trying to figure it out.

A few days later Neil threw his moneymaker into the sea because it was starting to smell a bit ripe from overuse. There were enough dead spermatozoa contained within its padded interior to impregnate the entire female population of Zombie Planet.

Angus was down on the pier the next day when old Barney, the fisherman, caught the love cushion on the hook at the end of his line. The old codger was mystified by the fact that he'd just landed a sheepskin pillow full of red gunk. He dipped his finger in the watery jelly and tasted it. Licking his lips he figured it was salmon spawn that had dissolved, or roe from the ovaries of a deep-sea female fish. Whatever it was, Barney enjoyed the taste of the stuff; it had the aromatic flavour of liquorice, sweet with a salty tang.

Barney decided to take the cushion home with him to his nearby cottage. Once there, he emptied its liquid contents into a plastic basin and noticed there were lots of short, curly black hairs in it and bits of foam rubber. He found a sieve and poured the red goo through it. The liquid now resembled half-set jelly. Barney tried a couple of soupspoons full of it. Half an hour later he felt revitalized and then realized he'd struck gold. Diluting the jelly with water from a wooden rain barrel, he then used the solution to fill fifty half-pint whisky bottles he'd been storing in cardboard boxes in his garden shed. With a bottle of the finished product in his hands, he took a mouthful and found to his delight that the liquid still retained its distinct flavour. He was now ready to go into business.

'Try this. It will do you the world of good,' said Barney to one of his mates, an old-age pensioner who went by the name of Davey Watson.

'What is it, Barney? It tastes like liquorice,' said Davey after swallowing a mouthful.

'Why, it's the elixir of life,' replied Barney with an air of self-confidence. 'It's an old recipe handed down in my family for generations. I found it written in one of my dear old Dad's diaries after it had lain forgotten in the bottom of a drawer for well nigh forty years.'

Davey looked into his old pal's watery blue eyes and wiped the back of his hand over his sticky mouth.

'It tastes good but what does it do to you?' asked Davey, smacking his cracked lips.

'Well, for a start, it will get your wee man standing to attention,' replied Barney, pushing his seaman's cap back on his head.

'Come on noo, you're pullin' my leg.'

'You won't be needin' anyone to pull your leg with this stuff in you. You'll be doing it yourself because your pudenda won't go down.'

'You've got to be bloody well joking.'

'I kid you not. This is not a humorous matter, Davey. Why, just the other day I was out for my constitutional after taking a spoonful of my tonic, when I came across Nancy Stewart over by the back of the abbey. She was bending over talking to a hoody crow at the time and when I saw her rear end I felt a tingle in my tadger for the first time in over a decade.'

'Nancy Stewart!' exclaimed Davey in disbelief, his wheezy voice whistling through badly fitted false teeth. 'I wouldn't touch her with a barge pole. Good grief man, are you out of your mind?' Davey's glasses steamed up from the heat of his embarrassment. 'C'mon now, please tell me you're havin' me on.'

'As I said, Davey, this is a serious matter. I've only told you about what happened when I saw Nancy to give you an idea of the potency of the stuff we're dealing with here. I'll no' lie to you, Davey.'

'I'll admit, you've got me interested now. How much would you be asking for a bottle of your tonic?'

Barney stoked the grey stubble on his chin, spat on the ground and turned the question over in his dawdling mind. 'Well,' he said, turning to his friend, 'I've given it some consideration and seeing as how we're auld pals, I can let you have a bottle for a couple-a-quid.'

'Two pounds,' gasped Davey, squinting through the condensation on his spectacles, 'that's a lot of money.'

'Aye, but it's still cheap and that's a friendship price, mind.'

'Okay, Barney, you're on, but no' a word of this to anybody. I don't want the misses to know how come my passions have been reignited after all these years.'

'Your secret's safe with me,' said Barney giving his first customer a sly wink.

Within a week the secret was out. Barney's wonder tonic was in great demand. Its reputation as a powerful sexual stimulant had spread through the island's community faster than an ugly rumour. In less than a month he'd sold the lot, causing him big problems because many of his pals had become reliant upon his love potion to throw petrol on the dying embers of their sex lives.

'What do you mean you've lost the recipe?' asked a very distraught Davey Watson a few weeks later.

'I'm sorry. I threw it in the fire one night by accident,' lied Barney.

'Good heavens, man. How could you have been so careless? I can't believe you've done such a stupid thing.' Davey cradled his head in his hands as if the news entering his brain was too heavy for his neck muscles to support.

For years to come, stories were recounted about Barney's magic potion and its legendary powers as an aphrodisiac. Come rain or shine, Barney continued to sit on the end of the pier every afternoon, living in hope that he'd one day hook another sheepskin cushion filled with the magic elixir.

On the last Friday before Christmas, Miss Crawford's high heels clicked up the ferry's gangplank. She stood in the stern of the boat, waving goodbye to all her pupils who had come down to the pier to see her off. The lassies waved their hankies and the laddies blew her passionate kisses. As the ferry pulled away, old Barney looked up from his fishing and admired the bonnie lass waving goodbye from the ship's deck. He felt a stirring in his loins. Barney died on that very spot a few years later with his rod held tightly in his arthritic hands and a contented smile upon his lips.

Miss Crawford waved until she could no longer distinguish the children on the jetty. She'd enjoyed the few weeks she'd spent on Iona, unaware of the chain reaction that had been set off among the island's population because of her stay there. Perhaps it was better that way.

On top of the landmine, Hamish tried to alleviate the numbness spreading up from his buttocks into his lower back by stretching his spine and limbs. He chuckled as he did so, remembering the ribald laughter that had risen from Angus's belly to erupt out of his mouth, while recounting the story of Barney's magic potion. Later that morning,

Hamish had asked him if he had ever thought of writing a book about his exploits.

'Yes,' replied Angus, 'I can see it now, my entire life condensed into a blurb on a book cover – "Reads like Billy Connolly meets The Fabulous Furry Freak Brothers."' He screwed up one side of his mouth and went on. 'Seriously though, I've often contemplated the idea, but that's as far as it will go. I have neither the special kind of discipline that a writer requires, nor the inclination to retreat from life's stage to write about it. Besides, I've spent more than enough time on my own in the past and as a result have no desire left for the pursuit of such a solitary profession. Apart from that, I believe Sir Walter Scott put it best when he wrote on the first page of *Rob Roy*, "The tale told by a friend, and listened to by another, loses half its charms when committed to paper."'

'Just think though,' said Hamish, 'about how much laughter you could bring into the world by letting people read about your adventures.'

Angus arched a dismissive eyebrow. 'I think you're getting a wee bit carried away with yourself here. From what I've already told you, it should be clear to you by now that part of the reason I developed a strong sense of humour was to counterbalance the tragedy that so often accompanied me through life.' He stopped talking and, across the space that existed between them, looked deep into Hamish's eyes. Angus broke the silence by letting a short sigh escape from his lips and saying, 'You know, I've often thought life is a great big school. A school where one only has two choices, those choices being whether or not to accept that everything that happens to you is preordained.'

With the echo of that conversation bouncing around in his head, Hamish reflected for a moment, both in the past and in the present, where his very own existence was now threatened by misfortune. Yes, he had to admit, Angus's life may at times have been comical, but as often as not his path led him through dark valleys where, ambushed by the hand of fate, he was dealt heavy blows and the only light available to navigate with came from a lamp fuelled by his indomitable spirit.

6

DANNY BOY

India. 1990.

The fierce heat thrown off by the funeral pyre felt similar to that experienced when standing in front of the open door of an iron foundry's blast furnace. Angus's robe clung to his sweating body like an extra layer of thick skin. He wanted to stand back from the ferocious flames but he was hemmed in by hundreds of people. They were crowding round to say a final farewell to their beloved master.

The sage died in the milieu he'd become accustomed to living in. During the last thirty years of his life he had been constantly surrounded by controversy, buffered by the ceaseless love of the people around him. The current debate was centred on the cause of his death. Was he, as the guru claimed, a victim of thallium poisoning, a highly toxic chemical element slipped to him by employees of the U.S. Government, a plot hatched and implemented in 1985, when he was arrested and detained within the shadowy confines of the American penal system? Or had he, as others claimed, succumbed to the combined effects of a chronic neurological disease and an alleged addiction to prescription tranquillizers coupled with massive inhalations of nitrous oxide, or laughing gas as it is more commonly known?

Standing by the funeral pyre, none of these arguments coloured Angus's perception of the death of this man he had loved so deeply.

He was certain that the world had just lost a crazy diamond from its crown of creation when this anarchistic Zen-like Master departed from the earthly plane.

The searing heat of combustion was not the only phenomenon that was intense down at the burning ghat that evening. The powerful charge of psychic energy permeating the atmosphere was so tangible it could have been bottled and sold in a New Age shop as 'Incredible Vibrations'. Angus felt like he was witnessing a scene right out of the Bible or some other religious storybook. Everyone present, including himself, was wearing a white robe that, by reflecting the light from the fire, glowed with vibrant shades of orange. The master's family of devotees and disciples could be seen going through the whole gamut of human emotion: grief, desolation, anger, joy, ecstasy and even madness. It was all there, registered on the faces of those gathered around the blaze. In the background loomed a tall banyan tree. Upon its thick boughs, people sat like a tribe of nature spirits. The pupils of their eyes were glowing like girasols, illuminated by the fire and highlighted by the jet black backdrop of a moonless night. By the banyan's long hanging roots stood a small Shiva temple. Over the past few years, Angus had gone there on numerous occasions to share the company of wandering mendicants, who would use the pilgrim's shed by the shrine as a stopover for the night on the road to nowhere.

The fire crackled, roared and flared when an updraught of cool air fed the flames rising from the pile of wood soaked in boiled butter. At the heart of the inferno the sage's body was burning and vaporizing, his once noble head now reduced to a charred and broken skull full of bubbling brain matter. It was he who had first introduced Angus to the radical idea that death could be seen as a cause for celebration rather than sorrow. He'd described death as a beautiful experience which is so intense that nothing in life can be compared with it. Nevertheless, the master had often drawn comparisons. On numerous occasions Angus had heard him portray the release that came with death as being like a cosmic orgasm or, to use a more down to earth metaphor, like removing a too tight shoe from one's foot. During the last years of his life, the sage had been plagued by ill health and suffered extreme physical discomfort that would have driven a lesser man to distraction. Now that the master had stepped out of a pair of shoes that were a few sizes too small for him and dissolved into an ocean of bliss, Angus let out a cry of exaltation. The physical form of the most remarkable man that he'd ever had the pleasure of meeting was gone. However, the master's rebellious spirit would live on unabated as a palpable presence in the lives of Angus and others like him all over the world who had been touched by the mystic's crazy sense of humour, grace, wisdom and boundless love.

How different this experience was from the first time Angus encountered death, when it came to take someone away who had become a part of him.

January 1962. Iona, Scotland.

Winter's icy breath blew in early that year. The poor man's television, the fireplace, was the main source of entertainment in the evening for most of the islanders. Angus loved it when his father used these fire-gazing sessions as a setting to tell him stories. The tales usually revolved around the heroic exploits of the fearless warrior chieftain of Clan MacGregor.

Sometimes known as the Scottish Robin Hood, Rob Roy MacGregor was engaged in a permanent running battle with the King's men. Armed with muskets and clad in bright red tunics fastened with big brass buttons, these luridly dressed English mercenaries made life hell for the clan folk, they stole their livestock, molested their women and forced the Highlanders to pay taxes with money they could ill afford. A forerunner to modern day methods of ethnic cleansing, the Highland Clearances threatened Clan MacGregor with absolute extinction.

When Rob Roy showed up to teach the wicked soldiers a lesson, the accursed Sassenachs paid a heavy toll for their iniquities. Wearing a tartan kilt and the white cockade of a Jacobite in his bonnet, the Highland liberator would dispense swift and lethal justice with his double-edged sword's razor sharp blade. The way Daniel told it, this ancient incarnation of Sergeant Samson was covered from head to toe with blood and gristle from the carnage he created with his weapon. Grand Guignols of historic proportions, these bloodthirsty reckonings would come to a grisly climax after the Redcoats' butchered corpses were formed into a macabre pile on top of a hill covered in purple heather. Ascending to the apex of this mound of death, the blood-crazed vindicator would raise his bloodied claymore above his head and swing it in an arc, creating a whooshing sound. A primordial roar would erupt from Rob Roy's throat when he gave voice to the clan's rallying call.

'Gregaraaaa!'

Below him a crowd of Highland partisans raised their broadswords in a victory salute to their vindictive chieftain. They flung their black bonnets in the air and bellowed with pride. Their voices echoed like thunder through the glens. The sound of bagpipes cut through the air, signalling that it was time to return to their hideouts. Forming up into a column, two abreast, the Highlanders would march off behind Rob Roy, the pleats of their kilts swaying in time to the beat of a drum and the piper's tune. They disappeared over the hills but if you listened hard enough, way in the distance, you could still hear the skirl of the pipes.

Angus never tired of hearing these legendary tales. When his father fell silent, it was always the same word that came to Angus's lips.

'More,' he would plead. 'I want to hear more. Please, Da, just one more story.'

Daniel would look over to Rose, for it was she who would always have the last word in such matters. If it were late, she'd shake her head. Daniel in turn would say to his son, 'That's enough for tonight, laddie. You'll be having bad dreams if I tell you any more stories before you go away to your bed.'

Angus knew better than to argue with his father. It was true that sometimes he woke up in the middle of the night from the depths of a nightmare in which he'd dreamt the Redcoats were outside, preparing to storm the house in order to capture him and throw him, his ma and da into a dank dungeon.

He'd sit for a while and gaze at his father perched on a stool by the fireplace. Shadows cast by the flickering fire would sometimes dance upon Daniel's weathered face. One moment he would appear youthful to Angus, the next old and wizened. These were the moments he felt closest to his father. When Angus had been younger he'd dreamt of growing up to be just like his hero Rob Roy. Knowledge gleaned from books had put paid to those dreams and now, in their place, came a new vision – that of one day becoming a storyteller like Daniel.

The winter in progress was to be later recalled as being the coldest and harshest in living memory. Within the thermometer's glass confines the mercury atoms that called it home became more intimate with each other and settled down at a new subzero basement apartment on Minus Thirty Degrees Centigrade Street. Arctic winds shrieked in from the ocean, dumping millions of tons of fresh snow all over the Hebrides, chilling their inhabitants to the bone. Everyone on Iona had resorted to dealing with the most basic necessities of human existence, especially the need to keep warm.

The main source of energy on the island was supplied by burning rectangular bricks of peat. There were no bogs on Iona to provide this indispensable fuel. During the summer months, the menfolk would venture over to Mull, where peat moss was in abundance on the moors. After the sodden peat blocks had been cut out from trenches called hags, they were stacked and dried. When the drying process was complete, carthorses transported the hard black bricks to the coast and from there they were ferried over the Sound of Iona to be stored in readiness for the onset of the cold winter months.

By the end of January the normally adequate supply of briquettes was starting to become severely depleted. A cruel wind screamed in the chimney pots. No longer belching clouds of thick grey reek, sad wispy white feathers of smoke rose into the freezing air to create a dismal reminder for the islanders of their forlorn fate. Wrapped in sheepskins, the Ionians huddled beside their cooling ovens to keep the bitter cold at bay. Crofters who were less prepared took to chopping up their few pieces of wooden furniture to feed their hungry stoves when their peat ran out. The ninety or so permanent residents on the island were, in many respects, one large extended family. During hard times all socio-economic differences were set aside to make it easier to help and support one another.

January passed. Lack of food, vying with almost non-existent fuel supplies, had become the problem that superseded all others. There were plenty of sheep around, and a few other livestock, but unfortunately they were frozen solid, buried beneath six feet of hard-packed snow. Nobody on the island had a mutton detector to locate the dead sheep, so lamb chops would have to wait until the thaw set in.

By mid-February it was down to boiling leather boots and handbags to make watery soup that tasted of shoe polish. For a few days the sky cleared, but it was still so cold that when some of the Ionians woke up in the morning their noses were blackened by frostbite. People had tried fishing from the shore but the only thing biting was the frost. The fish lay further out to sea. The only way to reach them was to organize a fishing expedition and set out in a boat. This was not so easy as it sounded because drift ice had built up along the coast and turned into pack ice, stretching out into the water to a distance of sixty yards.

Pushing or pulling a heavy wooden boat over the treacherous frozen surface was deemed too dangerous a task to attempt. Instead, a channel had to be cut to launch a vessel into the sea's icy waters.

Swinging a sledgehammer upon the slippery ice was a tricky task requiring the balancing skills of a tightrope walker. If a man slipped or fell while wielding a heavy iron hammer, the consequences could be dire. Under the glaring eye of a frigid sun, a dozen men were battering away at the white plane. The repercussive racket could be heard all over the island, despite the fact that the thick snow acted like an audio sponge. The sound reminded Daniel of howitzers firing.

In 1944 Daniel had been called up to serve in the Army. He'd been enlisted into the ranks of the Gordon Highlanders, where he had served as a loader in a gun crew. During the Normandy landings on D-Day, Daniel had been running up the beach after his unit had disgorged itself from the rusty interior of a landing craft. There were dead or wounded soldiers everywhere and he'd joined them when an accidental discharge from an Enfield rifle, being carried by a comrade behind him, sent a .303 round into the right side of his upper back. The bullet passed clean through Dan's body and hit the corporal in front of him square in the middle of his neck, severing the top of his spinal cord and killing him instantly. Daniel passed out from the intensity of the pain caused by the projectile that had torn a hole in his infraspinatus and pectoralis major muscles, clipping the top of one of his lungs on the way through. A nearby medic's prompt action saved Daniel's life by stemming the flow of blood and putting him in the right position to stop his lungs filling with his own sanguine fluid. He was lifted in a stretcher and returned to Britain before he'd had a chance to fire a shot in retaliation.

Another man from the island had also served in the Gordons. Unlike Daniel, Arthur Barker was already a professional soldier when war broke out, and had risen in the ranks to become a Company Sergeant Major. He'd been knocked out of the war a month before it ended when, advancing north on the outskirts of Bremen, an enemy sniper's bullet had shattered his left wrist and forced him into early retirement. It was Arthur 'Dog' Barker who was now walking over the ice sheet towards Daniel, who was smashing at the white surface with his sledgey. He was Dan's best friend.

Arthur gave Daniel a hefty slap on the back and said, 'Whoa there, Private Macleod.' Arthur liked to rub it in that Daniel had been a lowly private during the war, although there was no malice in his voice when he said it. 'You look like one of thon black slaves from the Wild West

80

hammering steel pegs into sleepers when they were laying the tracks for the Union Pacific Railroad.'

Daniel laid his hammer down, the ice below him groaning from the pressure created by the shifting tide. 'Now, Dog, take it easy with that imagination of yours. We don't want you straining your brain now, do we?'

It was well known on the island that Arthur was allergic to anything that vaguely resembled hard work, even though he was a mountain of a man who was six-foot-six in his socks and had upper arms as thick as most men's thighs. Arthur's strength was legendary. Over by an abandoned quarry lay a marble slab that weighed over two hundredweight. This flat piece of rock was used by the Ionians to measure a man's strength. Arthur was the only man alive on the island who'd ever hefted this heavy slab above his head. In his youth Daniel had tried to lift the strength tester himself and managed to raise it six inches off the ground before popping a disk in his lumbar region, leaving him flat on his back for a fortnight. Some said Arthur's strength came from eating handfuls of the bee pollen he'd collected from his hives. Daniel thought Arthur looked a bit like a gigantic bumblebee, the profile of his ruddy features came together to form a cone shape that would have fitted right into the trumpet of a giant bluebell.

Apart from his bees' honey, another of Arthur's sources of income was the production of rotgut vodka, made with the help of a mini distillery situated round the back of his cottage. It was a bottle of this firewater that Arthur now produced from the inside of his knee-length leather coat and offered to Daniel.

'Here, take a slug of this. It'll give you the strength of Hercules.'

Daniel uncorked the bottle, took a swig of the clear liquid, screwed up his face, gasped and did an impromptu jig.

'Hell's bells,' exclaimed Dan. 'It tastes like paint stripper but it warms the cockles of your heart, so it does.'

'More like pickles them, I'd say,' said a voice behind him. It was old Barney, the fisherman. He'd seen the bottle and come over to sample its contents. Soon the whole ice-breaking gang was gathered round enjoying a wee taste of Arthur's notorious bootleg liquor. The bottle was passed around and sucked empty in a few minutes, but Arthur was not a man of limited resources when it came to supplying strong drink.

'Hey, presto,' he cried as he produced another bottle from the spacious pockets sewn to the insides of his fur-lined coat. Joining in the spirit of the occasion, the men tried to outdo each other by telling the most obscene joke. Viewed from a distance this spontaneous gathering could have been easily perceived to be a group of Arctic explorers congratulating each other on having just made it to the North Pole on foot.

'I'll keep an eye out for you.' Grouped together in a loose circle, the men let out hoots of bawdy laughter when Barney delivered this punch line to a joke concerning the sexual practices of a prostitute with a glass eye.

All of a sudden, cracking sounds could be heard as fissures started appearing in the surface of the ice below the men's feet. Cracks shot out like bolts of white lightning from a frozen epicentre.

Somebody shouted, 'Run, its going to give.'

The men scattered as if they were snooker balls that had just been struck by the white in a strong break. Daniel was the only one to remain where he was. Standing with his mouth open, his warm breath was streaming out in a cloud of vapour. There was another loud crack. This time the sound originated from directly beneath Daniel's boots. The ice split apart and swallowed him.

Submerged in freezing water, the stupefying effects of the vodka left Daniel's body in an instant. Trapped under the ice sheet, he kept his wits about him, knowing full well that if he didn't he'd be a goner in no time. The water was only a few feet deep. Holding what breath he had, he stumbled over rounded granite rocks and thick seaweed. It was hard going. His clothes dragged on him like cold liquid lead. Daniel pressed his mouth into an air bubble trapped, like him, beneath the ice. Once he'd sucked it in, he drew back, leaving skin from his lips on the underside of the frozen surface.

He could hear the thuds of his comrades' boots thumping around above him as they frantically tried to locate his whereabouts. He knew he was headed in the right direction because up ahead the water was ice blue. The sun's rays were penetrating the open water, unimpeded by the opaque filter created by the ice. Another air pocket supplied him with enough oxygen to make it to the jagged edge. Gasping, he bobbed above the water's surface where eager hands pulled him out of the sea. Daniel lay on his back gazing up into Arthur's wide-open eyes.

'Jesus,' said Arthur, 'I thought we'd lost you.'

'Y-you're no' the o-only one,' spluttered Daniel. 'F-for a minute there I thought m-my number had c-come up.'

Some of the men helped Daniel struggle to his feet. He was all for going back to hammering at the ice that had nearly taken his life. His teeth were chattering like Morse code being sent by an operator with a shaky hand. Daniel started walking back to his abandoned hammer, water squelching in his boots. A strong hand gripped his arm and spun him round. It was Arthur.

'What do you think you're doing?' he barked, making no attempt to conceal his annoyance.

Daniel looked into his friend's eyes for the second time in a couple of minutes. Relief had left them, to be replaced by anger.

'I'm g-g-going b-b-back to w-work,' stuttered Daniel.

'Like hell you are. Have you taken leave of your senses? You're soaked through to the skin and chattering like a frozen monkey.'

'B-but I'll m-miss the fishing trip.'

'Fishing trip,' repeated Arthur. 'You've had your bloody fishing trip for today. I've a good mind to throw you back in the sea again if you don't get away home this very minute.'

'B-b-but—'

'But bugger all, get the hell out of here right now.'

There was a despondent look on Daniel's face as he looked down at his feet; his trouser legs were beginning to freeze solid.

'Private Macleod,' roared the ex-drill sergeant, 'this is an order. You'll go home to your wife, right now.'

The military command cut through Daniel's stubbornness. 'Aye, okay,' is all he said, as he bowed his head, turned and walked over the pack ice towards the village.

When Daniel creaked into his wife's kitchen he could hardly move. His clothes were frozen stiff and brittle as glass. When Rose saw the state of her husband she nearly had a fit.

'Mary Mother of God,' she exclaimed. 'What have you done to yourself now?'

Daniel tried to chatter an explanation but it came out sounding like the noise made by a woodpecker high on amphetamine getting busy on a tree trunk in an Alpine forest.

'Angus!' Rose shouted to her son, who had risen to his feet from a stool beside the stove. 'Break up thon chair you've been sitting on and get the oven on the go. We need boiling water.' Her voice shot up an octave. 'Come on now, don't just stand there gawking like an idiot. Do what you're told!'

Angus began chopping up the stool while Rose busied herself

83

with trying to get her spouse out of his frozen clothes. Daniel was shaking and wisps of steam were rising off the crown of his head. By the time Angus had transformed the small wooden stool into a pile of neat kindling, Rose had managed to remove her man's rigid clothing. She wrapped a woollen blanket around Daniel and hurried him off in the direction of the bedroom. The oven crackled into life when Angus blew some air into its open door through a copper pipe to conjure up a ball of flames. Soon the kettle came to the boil and Rose filled an earthenware hot water bottle. She wrapped it in a towel and returned to the bedroom. Lifting the layers of blankets off Daniel, she placed the roasting object between her husband's legs. Although still unable to speak without his teeth chattering, he tried to protest. Rose was in no mood for it as she pulled the blankets back over him.

'Shut up, you bloody great fool that you are. Can you no' see I'm trying to help you? Don't make my job any the more difficult than it already is.'

Chastised, Dan rested his head on a pillow, as meek as a newborn lamb. Back in the kitchen Rose broke out the last of her whisky stash, poured it into a mug and added two spoons of sugar and boiling water, a hot toddy being the household cure-all medicine of the time. She returned to her husband's bedside with the steaming mug in hand and poured the scalding concoction down Daniel's throat. He gagged and spluttered.

'J-Jesus, woman, are you trying to k-kill me?'

He succumbed to the effects of what must have been a quarter bottle of whisky and, closing his eyes, quieted down.

Angus was heating his cold backside by the oven. When he saw his mother had a moment he asked, 'Ma, is Da going to be all right?'

'God willing, I think so, son, but he's still shuddering like a sail in a blinking hurricane.'

Rose opened the door to her larder and searched around for anything that was still edible. She recovered an old jar of Marmite with a teaspoonful of the brown sticky substance stuck to its curved interior. She also found a cupful of macaroni and a Maggis soup cube. That was it, but it would have to do because that was the last of the food in the house.

Twenty minutes later, Rose propped Daniel up in his bed and fed him spoonfuls of her improvised soup through his damaged lips. Angus stood at the foot of the bed watching on. When Daniel had finished, a touch of colour returned to his pale cheeks. He looked over to his son. 'Hello my lad, how are you doing?'

Angus was happy to see his father's teeth had finally stopped making that strange noise. 'A'm fine, Da, how about yourself?'

'I'm grand. I don't know what all the fuss is about. There's nothin' coming over me.' A true stoic, Daniel made little of the fact that his body was still shivering.

'That's enough of that,' said Rose, relief manifest upon her face. 'You get some rest now. A good night's sleep will do you the world of good.'

'Aye, aye, woman,' said Daniel. 'Will you stop fussing over me? You'd think I was a wee bairn the way you're going on.'

Rose pulled the blankets up under his chin. 'Aye, that's because you're acting like a big bairn. Now pipe down will you, and get some rest.'

That evening Dan became feverish. Lying in the adjacent bedroom, Angus heard his father calling out in the night. In the morning Dan's bed sheets were soaked through with sweat. As Angus assisted his mother to help Daniel out of bed, he noticed a sour cloying smell of sickness in the room. Daniel sat shaking on a chair in the corner, watching his wife and son change his sodden sheets.

'W-what a carry on,' he complained. 'You'd think I was a d-dying man the way the pair of you are going about.' The effort of speech proved too great for him. He was overcome by a coughing fit. It was a rasping cough, which sounded like it was tearing at his lungs.

'You hold your wheesht,' said Rose. 'You and that damn stubbornness of yours.' She patted a pillow into shape. 'C'mon now, son, help me put your da back to bed. The quicker he's back under the covers, the better.'

Later that day Arthur came round to Braeside with a few small haddock and a glass jar full of honey. Handing his apian produce to Rose, he said, 'I was saving this for an emergency.'

'Thanks, Arthur,' said Rose. 'You're a real friend, so you are.' She was tense and tired, as was Angus who looked like a refugee leaning against the cold oven dressed in his father's oversized sheepskin jacket.

'Well,' said Arthur, sitting down on a rickety chair, his cheeks splotched red by the cold, 'that's the last jar of honey we'll be seeing for a while. This damned winter's taken care of that. My wee buzzing pals will buzz no more thanks to Jack Frost and his icy breath.' He dropped this depressing subject, raised his eyebrows and studied Rose and Angus. 'You two are no' exactly looking too chirpy. How's Danny?'

Rose peeked in a speckled wall mirror and saw that she was looking whiter than the snow drifts that lay outside her house, even her freckles had vanished.

She said, 'Thanks for asking. He's sleeping now. Daniel's still with fever and I'm more than a little concerned about him.'

Arthur shook his head, remembering something. 'Do you know the silly bugger actually wanted to go back to work after falling through the ice? I had to play Sergeant Major Barker and order him to go home.'

'Aye well, that's the Macleods all over for you,' said Rose. 'A more stubborn tribe of mountain goats never walked upon God's earth.'

'Right then, Rose, I'll take my leave of you now. I've been press-ganged into going out on the boat again for a couple of hours' fishing. If I have any luck with my hooks I'll pass by tomorrow to share my catch with you and check up on my auld pal.' The big man stood up and headed for the door.

'Och,' said Rose, 'you're a guardian angel so ye are. God bless you, Dog.'

Fastening the buttons on his lambskin collar before he went outside to face the elements, he glanced over his shoulder and called back. 'Rosie, an angel is something I am not, but I do try my best. Cheerio now.'

'See you later, Uncle Arthur,' said Angus with some enthusiasm, feeling lucky to have a good uncle like him around.

During the night Daniel lapsed into a coma. By morning he was dead.

'No, I tell you. No!' cried Rose.

'But, please, Ma, I want to see my da one last time,' pleaded Angus.

'No and that's final. Your father is gone from this world. That's just an empty shell lying next door.'

'Ma.'

Rose stepped towards her son. She raised her hand to slap him, but thought the better of it. Tears came to her eyes.

'You listen to me now. This is for your own good. I want you to remember your father when he was alive and full of life.' She gripped

Angus's shoulders, bent her knees, looked into his eyes and said, 'Your da's gone forever. He's up in heaven now. Do you understand, son? Daniel won't be coming back.'

Angus began to sob. Rose took him in her arms and pulled him to her breast. They wept together and created a choking, wordless lament, joined as one in their vale of tears.

Daniel's body was to be buried in a small graveyard to the south of the abbey, in the vicinity of an ancient burial ground called Reilig Odhrain. He'd be enjoying better-heeled company in the earth than when he'd walked upon it. Not far from his grave lay the remains of over fifty Scottish kings, most famous of whom were Macbeth and Duncan. Macbeth had been given a bad name due to William Shakespeare's 'Scottish Play'. Like many a good storyteller, Shakespeare was not a man to be hindered by fact when it came to writing an epic tale. The way he told it, Lady Macbeth was a stunning redhead possessed by deadly serious ambition. She incited her husband to creep into the night and murder King Duncan while he lay sleeping in a guest room in their castle. Their diabolical behaviour brought the power-mad couple onto the highway to hell, and from there it was only a short downhill ride before they entered the nightmare-filled arena inhabited by the criminally insane.

There exists little truth in Shakespeare's fantasy. The well-documented, historically correct version of events is that Macbeth was born with a legitimate claim to the Scottish throne. King Duncan was not assassinated in his sleep but met his end in the way many of his predecessors had: at the end of a sharp sword on the battlefield. Macbeth had raised an army to march against the king and after clashing with the monarch's forces outside of a town called Forres on the Northeast Coast of Scotland, Macbeth emerged victorious and ascended to the throne. He was to be remembered as a king who ruled with a magnanimous hand that earned him the love of his subjects.

All this had now become the rotting bones of history a few feet beneath Angus's boot soles. His eyes were downcast as he trudged through the snow on his way to experience the most traumatic part of the process surrounding his father's death, the funeral. The islanders had a strong leaning towards viewing death over-seriously, as if something unnatural and evil had happened. Angus was to experience this depressing and uninspiring social tradition first-hand by the side of a rectangular pit hacked out of the ground, his father's final resting place.

The wind whispered and moaned as it blew flurries of large snowflakes into the waiting mourners' faces. There were no women present. Tradition dictated that the fairer sex be forbidden from attending burials on Iona.

Daniel's black-painted coffin was to be lowered into its place of interment with the aid of seven tasselled hemp ropes. There were tears in Arthur Barker's eyes when he said, 'Be a brave lad and take a haud o' this.' Arthur handed Angus the thick rope at the head of the casket. The planks supporting the coffin above the burial place were removed. As the eight-sided wooden box was inched down, it bumped against the grave's earthen walls. Within its confines, Daniel's corpse shifted position in Angus's direction. The increase of weight tightened the hemp rope that Angus was already straining to a keep hold of with both hands. He held his breath as the rope's rough fibres cut into his palms. Although it was very cold, sweat was beginning to break out on his brow. The casket's underside crunched against loose gravel, making a sound both unsettling and final. Angus gasped in relief. He let go of the rope and shook his wrists to disperse the pain in his red-raw hands.

Dressed in a frock coat, the minister, Reverend Gray, embarked upon a long-winded portentous sermon. It sounded to Angus like the cleric was trying to bore his listeners to death so they could join 'dear departed Daniel Macleod'. A man who, going by what the dour minister had to say about him, was now in heaven receiving his just reward from God. Upon hearing this, Angus really hoped this was true and meant his father would get that new fiddle he'd always wanted but never been able to afford. Angus's feet were freezing. He stamped his boots on the hard ground trying to bring some circulation back into his toes. The 'Holy Joe' rattled on and on while Angus kept on stamping. He suddenly slipped and tumbled headlong into his father's grave. Angus's chin was the first part of his anatomy to slam into the coffin lid. With a resounding thump, the rest of his body crash-landed a quarter of a second later. Groaning, he sat up. The first thought that entered his head was that his mother would murder him when he got home and she saw the blood from a gash on his chin had ruined his only collared shirt.

Someone called from above, 'Angus, are you all right, lad?'

He looked up and saw about twenty people's heads outlined against the forbidding grey background of the sky. Angus stood on his father's coffin and helping hands hauled him back into the world of the living. Somebody gave him a handkerchief that smelled of fish to help stem the flow of blood oozing out of the deep cut on his chin. Tam Davidson, the kindly dairyman who had supplied the goat's milk to nourish Angus when he was an infant, ushered him over to a waiting rank of dour-faced men uniformly dressed in black coats and hats. Angus had to shake hands with each of them in turn. Some of the cheerless mourners offered their condolences.

'He was a good man,' said one.

'Daniel took a bit of us all when he left,' said another.

'You're the man of the house now, Angus.'

'Aye, lad, you're the breadwinner now.'

Rather than supporting him, these consolations and encouragements were pulling the cold ground out from right under his frozen feet. 'Breadwinner', 'Man of the house', he had not a clue as to what these poker-faced men were talking about. He only needed to run a hand over the pimples on his hairless face to know he was still a long way from being a 'breadwinning man'.

His steps began to falter as he continued down the line, shaking hands with these well-meaning, misguided men with grim expressions etched into their haggard faces. The only hand he really wished to hold in his own was that of his father, now lying dead, nailed into a wooden box at the bottom of a pit a few steps away from him. In those lonely moments he sorely missed Daniel's reassuring presence more than at any other time in the whole tragic affair. His stomach convulsed. Bile caught in his throat. He felt dizzy. It all came rushing in upon him, his father's death, the physical shock of falling into the grave, and the fact that there was an ache where his heart should have been. He felt like he was in the midst of a nightmare from which there was no escape. Angus's arms fell to his sides. He blew out a long, despondent breath and began to cry. A distressed, aggrieved sound forced his jaw and lips apart. 'Maaaa!' He bawled for his mother.

Rose sat staring at the snow falling outside her kitchen's cracked window. Like everything else in the house there was a memory of Daniel attached to it. He'd promised, on numerous occasions over the years, to buy a pane of glass to replace that window but never gotten around to it. Rose could hear his voice as if he were standing next to her. 'Och, come on now woman, don't nag me over a thing like that.

I'll fix it one of these days. Besides, you can still see out of it can't you?' But he never did repair it. And he was right. She could still see out of it. 'Aww Danny,' she cried out, making a sound in her throat that was a bitter-sweet fusion of sorrow and amusement. 'How could you go away and leave me like this?' And then an unexpected echo from times long gone came to her. 'The past is a graveyard. It's life we're concerned with right now.' Those were the words of advice she'd given to Lizzie Allan when the twins' mother had died giving birth to them.

'Angus!' Rose had just remembered where he was and felt his desperate call in her heart. 'To hell with it!' She wasn't going to let local custom stand in her way when it came to protecting her son. The mother in her could feel Angus's pain and it was that pain which hurried her out into the cold morning light without a coat on and guided her. She stumbled through deep snow towards the cemetery. When she arrived at her husband's graveside, Rose pushed her own feelings of grief aside. The disapproving stares being directed her way by the all-male gathering made their owners look as if they were under a spell. She ignored the mumbled complaints and headed straight for Angus. When Rose reached his side she put a comforting arm around his shoulders and guided him away from the stony-faced men.

'What happened to you?' she asked. 'There's blood on your shirt.'

'I fell into my da's grave.'

Rose shook her head. 'I can't leave you alone for five minutes, can I?'

She leaned into him and spoke in a soothing whisper. 'Come on now, son. I can see you've had enough of this morbid pantomime. Let's away home and see if we can find something to burn in the oven to heat up a wee bit o' water for a cup of tea.'

When they reached the cemetery gate, Angus turned to take one final look at the scene in the graveyard. The snow was so deep that most of the headstones were submerged. Over by his father's grave two men were shovelling chunks of frozen black earth back into the excavation. The soil looked like lumps of coal, contrasting sharply with the snow's neon brightness. The hollow thump of rock-hard earth landing on the coffin lid was carried over to him by a raw, icy wind that stung his ears and made an eerie wailing sound. He turned and slipped an arm around his mother's waist.

They walked home in silence. When Rose opened the front door, Angus enquired, 'Ma, is death always this bad?'

Rose replied, her voice husked, 'Aye, son, I'm afraid it is. It's never a cause for celebration. It's dreich for sure, although things will be a bit more cheery at the wake. It's no' only us who'll miss your da. A lot of people loved your father almost as much as we did.'

The wake, as it turned out, came as a welcome change after the bleak scene at the cemetery. Everyone on Iona pulled together and brought every morsel of food and alcohol they could muster to try and ward off the depressing spirit that was hanging over their lives. When Arthur showed up with a dozen bottles of what smelled like napalm, the drinking began in earnest. What with Daniel's passing, the terrible cold, and little in the way of sustenance, everybody was feeling the strain. Everybody, that is, except Nancy Stewart, who showed up cackling like a wacky witch. How she was managing to survive the winter was a mystery. Nobody had seen her in a month. She had, in her own way, tidied herself up for the occasion. Wearing a fresh assortment of rags, she'd topped off her get-up with a green woollen tea cosy. It was tilted at a precarious angle upon her head, making her appear even madder than ever. This was difficult because she always had the look about her of a psychotic inmate who had just escaped from a mental hospital.

By early evening everybody was getting seriously plastered on Arthur's booze. 'Danny Boy' was the anthem for the occasion. At first it brought all the singers to tears. Daniel had loved the song and been fond of playing the melancholic tune to 'The Londonderry Air', which this particular love song is sung to, on his fiddle at the end of social gatherings. When Arthur's rocket fuel started to kick in, the mourners began to forget their sorrows. By the end of the night the song was being delivered with such gusto one could have been led to believe that their very own Danny Boy had just won the football pools, instead of having been buried under the ground in a pinewood box.

Angus got drunk for the first time in his life after Neil persuaded him to swallow a full glass of hooch. The alcohol lifted his spirits. He tried to join in with the singing by yelling at the top of his voice. It wasn't long before Angus threw up over his empty sporran and red Macleod tartan kilt, and then quietly passed out in a cold corner of the kitchen.

7

THE GRIM REAPER AND THE SEASON
OF FAREWELL

Before Daniel's giving-up of the mortal coil, Angus had never experienced a hangover or paid any attention to the fact that death was an ever-present thread woven into the fabric of life. He started to become more aware of animals being slaughtered, the occasional dead seabird washed up on the shore, worms wriggling in their death throes on fish hooks' barbed ends and a hundred and one other mortal events taking place on the stage of life around him. He began to make enquiries among Iona's adult population and soon discovered that death was a taboo subject that nobody, including his mother, wanted to talk about in too much depth. He tried doing some research in the school library, even going so far as to study the bible for a week. 'Ashes to ashes, dust to dust', sounded poetic but it did not really answer the question of what happened to someone when they died.

There remained one person who might be able to help answer Angus's question and that was Uncle Alfie. Alfred Docherty was an uninhibited alcoholic cabinet-maker who lived in a ramshackle cottage situated near low dunes on the island's north coast. It was Alfred who'd made Daniel's coffin. It was nothing short of a miracle that he'd managed to construct it on time for the funeral, because most days he was paralytically drunk, being Arthur Barker's number one customer for rotgut alcohol. Alfred spent nothing on food, living instead on a liquid diet; the higher percent proof the better. The last time Angus talked to him was just after his father's death, the day he

93

and his mother waded through the snow to order the casket from the inebriated carpenter.

It was a beautiful, clear, blustery afternoon in late March when Angus strolled over to Uncle Alfie's house. Colour was creeping back into the world and nobody was happier to see it than him. The roadside was scattered with pink lupins and purple thistles. In the fields red tractors chugged up and down, spewing out clouds of diesel smoke, as farmers ploughed away the detritus of the old year's crops in preparation for the new. Taking pleasure in the season's fragrances, he inhaled the smell of freshly tilled earth blended with the oily scents of yellow gorse and wild lavender.

Visibility was good. Fifteen miles away to the east he could see the great grey-green bronze mass of Ben More, neighbouring Mull's highest mountain. Streamers of cloud trailed along its flanks, driven in from the Atlantic by a strong wind that carried a refreshing nip upon its cold air. Sheep were slowly beginning to reappear in grassy fields after the terrible winter. When the snow had melted, hundreds of dead animals had been gathered together and incinerated over by the disused marble quarry. The smell from these burning carcasses was noxious. This stench, composed of singed wool and burnt mutton, had hung over the island for a fortnight until the wind picked up and carried it away.

When Angus arrived at Alfred's workshop the double wooden doors were wide open. He found him sitting on top of a half-finished coffin with his back turned. The old drunkard was engrossed in an intense conversation in Gaelic – with himself, as was often the case with him. Alfred's breathing was audile and came in rasping sucks – his lungs riddled by tuberculosis years before. The carpenter did not realize he had a visitor for some time. Angus stood behind him thinking that Uncle Alfie and Nancy Stewart would make a right good pair.

Alfred coughed and spluttered when he noticed Angus's shadow on the wall in front of him. He spun around. 'Well hoots, if it isn't my favourite laddie, Andrew.'

'Angus,' corrected the laddie. 'Uncle Alfie, my name's Angus.'

'Aye, so it is.' Alfred frowned, as if in search of something but not knowing what. 'Well then, how are you keepin', son?'

'Fine,' replied Angus, looking around the workshop. It looked like it had taken a direct hit from a big bomb. Alfred was a decorated war hero, and Angus reasoned that maybe his motive for keeping the place in such a mess was to remind himself of Dunkirk, where in 1940 he'd lost an eye, a thumb and a leg during the British retreat. His injuries had resulted from taking out a German heavy machine gun emplacement single-handed. Stuka dive-bombers were screaming overhead when he'd lobbed a hand grenade and blown the enemy gunners to bits. Unfortunately, the ammunition also went up, taking various parts of Alfred's anatomy with it.

'So, laddie, what can I do you for?' The carpenter chuckled at his own tired joke.

'I'd like to ask you a question.'

'Fire away son, fire away.' Grimly jolly, Alfred raised his hands and pretended to fire a tommy gun, imitating the weapon's sound with a 'Rat-a-tat-tat.' When his lips parted in a smile, Angus noticed that Uncle Alfie's big false teeth were amber from smoking too much tobacco in his pipe. The old soldier had a dark red birthmark running over one side of his forehead and his unshaven face played host to a dozen large warts that looked like blobs of pink wax. A sunbeam shone through a crack in the roof, illuminating his unmoving glass eye in an odd light. His good eye was bloodshot. His overall appearance was that of a weathered garden gnome who'd seen better days.

'Uncle Alfie, can you tell me what happens to people when they die?'

Blowing his nose into a dirty rag, Alfred pulled himself together and in a brief moment of clarity focused his single rheumy eye, sizing up the stripling standing before him. He asked, 'And what's a young loon like you asking a question like that for?'

'Well, since my dad died I—'

'What! Don't tell me your father's passed away, has he?'

'Uncle Alfie, you made my da's coffin and I remember shaking your hand at his funeral.'

'Oh … aye, that's right. Go on laddie, what were you saying?'

'Well, it's just that nobody seems to want to give me a decent answer to my question.'

'What question is that, son?' Alfred was making it clear that he had the attention span of a midge suffering from short-term amnesia. Angus began to wonder if it had been a good idea to visit Alfred in the first place.

He asked his question more forcefully. 'Uncle Alfie, will you tell me what you know about death?'

'Ah, well then, you've come to the right person to ask your question, Andrew, my boy.' Angus let the name slip pass, wishing this crazy old-timer would get on with it.

'Why,' said Alfie, 'many are the times I've stared into the maw of death. The Grim Reaper's come for me on a number of occasions, but so far I've always managed to escape from the grip of his bony fingers. I'm no' as stupid as I look. It's all up here.' He tapped the side of his head with a grubby finger.

'Who is this Grim Reaper?'

'Well, lad, that's the spectre of death himsel', so it is. He comes into the world of the living to harvest souls for the Day of Judgment. If they were good in their earthly existence they fly off to Heaven.' Alfred blinked up at the crack in the ceiling. 'And if they were sinners, they're escorted down the broad stairway that leads to Hell.' He spat on the floor.

The old buffer recovered a hip flask from the bib of his sawdust-covered dungarees that were tucked into a pair of green rubber boots. It was obvious to Alfred that he'd captured the boy's imagination, but he needed a little spiritual booster before continuing further with his elucidation. He whetted his whistle with a shot of whisky, hiccupped and then went on. 'Personally, I'm Hell-bound myself. I've had about enough of this world, but Heaven's no place for a man of my calibre. Why, the place is full of bloody do-gooders and I've seen enough of their kind in my lifetime to last me for all eternity. A ship of fools on a fool's sea, if you—'

'Tell me more about the Grim Reaper,' persisted Angus.

'Ach him, he's never far away. As sure as death you can find him hidin' in the shadows and lurkin' in the graveyard at night. He'll be doin' a wee jig on top of the graves, that's him all right. He's always ready to pounce on another unsuspecting victim, aye that's the Reaper for you. Came for me in Dunkirk, he did indeed, but I was too strong for him. I was young then. Let me tell you, I can remember the sound of the officer's whistle and going over the top when the Boche gunners were … bullets buzzzzing … barbed wirrrre … gassss…' Alfred's speech slurred as he launched into a rambling tale about being in the trenches during the First World War's Battle of the Somme and how British military doctors were recommending that the front line troops grow moustaches and smoke lots of cigarettes to fight germs. The memory of those terrible times made the old carpenter feel dizzy. He flumped on to a burst leather armchair and the pressure pushed brown stuffing out of big rips in the chair's padding. His mumblings became incoherent as he staggered down the twisted labyrinth of his past. Alfred was in search of better days when he didn't feel the need to prop himself up with bottles of strong alcohol to deaden the harsh impact of daily living.

Filled with lively curiousity, Angus walked over to examine a dusty plaque, which was nailed to a wall. Fixed to it were a neat line of a dozen or so bronze and silver medals with strips of brightly coloured ribbon attached to them. They looked impressive and valuable. Turning to Alfred he asked, 'Did you win all these medals in the war?'

Alfred looked up startled, having just returned from a sojourn on the dark side of the moon. 'What? What's that? Andrew, where did you come from? What are you doing here?'

It was plain to Angus by now that the old boozer's fondness for the liquid contents of his flask had taken him over the hills to the glen of forgotten dreams, and nightmares. He took in a deep breath and inhaled the smell of newly cut timber melded with the vapours of shellac and whisky that were so much part and parcel of Alfred's workplace. Persistence was the only way to penetrate the alcoholic haze surrounding the dipsomaniac.

'Uncle Alfie, what does the Grim Reaper look like?'

Alfie's eyes opened wide in alarm, the white of the real one a roadmap of veins. He sucked in some air and gasped, 'The Reaper! Who told you to speak of the Reaper? It's inviting misfortune to give breath to the dark one's name.'

'You did. What does he look like?'

'The Reaper? Och, I'm no' afraid of him. He carries a sharp scythe over his shoulder to cut people down in their tracks whenever he feels so inclined. Young or old, makes no difference to him.' He drained his flask and tossed it on the floor, a look of displeasure on his warty countenance. His annoyance helped focus his deranged thoughts for a moment. 'The dark one is dressed in black shrouds that billow out behind him like thick clouds of smoke,' he said, waving his thumbless hand in the air. 'Instead of a face, there is a hollow skull with worms slithering out of its empty eye sockets. Maggots crawl over his rotten teeth when they clack together in a hideous impersonation of laughter. He laughs at people's futile attempts to hide from him because he knows that in the end he'll get his bony hands on every last one of them, so he will. You see son, life's cast a spell over people. Aye, that's right, a magic spell that makes a person think death's something that happens to everybody else, but never to them.'

Alfred cast his single rheumy eye upon the young lad standing before him, worry creasing his brow. 'You young scallywag that you are,' he raised his voice and shook a fist, 'getting me to talk about the Reaper. I'll be damned for sure.' He cocked his head. 'I can hear hellhounds calling my name. It's tempting fate to speak of the skinless one. Mercy is a word that has little meaning in the Reaper's lexicon, except when it's applied to killing.' Cursing to himself, he bent down to recover his shiny flask from the tangle of wood shavings on the floor. He lurched to his feet and glanced over at Angus. 'Can you no' see I'm a very busy man with important business to attend to?'

He pulled an oil-stained red beret onto his head and limped quickly out the door, surprisingly agile for a man with a wooden leg who'd fought in two World Wars. Alfred picked up speed and zigzagged over the sand dunes, off to attend to the urgent business of finding a refill for his hip flask.

For a week after his bizarre encounter with Alfred, Angus suffered a string of horrible nightmares, starring none other than the Grim Reaper himself. After that Angus decided to keep more focused upon the world of the living. Life could be difficult and cruel at times, but at least there was not a homicidal skeleton running around in it dressed in black shrouds, murdering people with a razor sharp farm implement.

During the summer, Rose abandoned her sombre widow's outfit and threw away the black shawl she'd been using to eclipse her blonde hair. Mourning for her deceased husband was over and she took to wearing a brightly coloured floral patterned dress. In June she'd met a Glaswegian man named Steven who'd come over to visit Iona on a day trip. She had liked the look of Steve the moment she'd set eyes upon him. She knew for sure that he felt the same way about her because he was always staring at her as if she were naked, something she had experienced as being not altogether unpleasant. In truth, it excited her. Rose had lost a few pounds during the winter, doing wonders for her figure, a fact that most of the male members of the community could not help but notice. Since May there had been a spate of sunny days. Her skin was taking on a tan and as a result her freckles had reappeared.

A month after his first visit Steve returned to the island. This pleased Rose because she'd thought of the sandy haired Glaswegian at some point during every day since she'd last seen him. During his third visit they'd held hands and he'd asked her to come over to Glasgow to see him in his home town. 'No strings attached,' he'd added, although only a fool could have failed to notice that his proposal immediately lit up her face and plucked a rhapsody on her heartstrings. Not one to rush into such an action, Rose had thought about Steve's offer for a fortnight. In the first months after Daniel's death she had missed him terribly. When the pain in her heart had faded to a dull ache, she was able to focus on other dimensions of her life and realized she was lonely. She had her curly-headed son of course, who was a source of much amusement and joy. Friends too, but that was not enough to fulfil all of her needs. The surge of returning life was making its presence felt in her daily existence. Channels in her body were opening after years of neglect, flooding it with long-forgotten juices, pumped into her bloodstream by a beating heart that had rediscovered it had wings.

Rose was not the only one aware of changes going on in her life; she'd been spotted on several occasions by some of the local women, holding hands with a stranger, of all things. The gossipmongers had all the information they required. Nothing travels quicker than a rumour in a small community and soon sharp tongues began to wag faster than a litter of happy puppies' tails. Behind her back, Rose was being described as a merry widow, a loose woman and person of low moral standing. Had Rose been able to eavesdrop on these backstabbing sessions, she would have laughed. Whatever it was that was circulating in her system made her immune to the social ailments of malicious gossip and narrow-mindedness.

Rose kept looking around to see if she could catch Cupid playing his mischief upon her. The naked winged boy was nowhere to be seen and neither were his honey-dipped arrows. She was not in love but she was in something and it felt good. Rose decided to go for it. She packed a small bag with a change of clothes and caught the Friday afternoon ferry.

Angus was too preoccupied with his own reality to be concerned with the strange goings-on in the oftentimes puzzling world inhabited by the grown-ups. His mother left him under the care of Agnes Cameron, a rosy-cheeked spinster who lived next door. Angus found Mrs Cameron's face interesting to look at because, although in her sixties, she had the eyes, nose and mouth of a pretty young girl. Agnes was a hearty old soul, fat from overeating in spite of the fact that she was a dreadful cook who did not know how to fry an egg properly. The lumpy porridge she was feeding Angus three times a day was making him fart louder than a backfiring tractor. The intestinal gases being expelled into his social environment had earned him the alias of 'Windy'. Like Iona's weather conditions, nicknames could change rapidly.

It was Friday. Rose had been gone for two weeks. Angus missed her a lot, especially at mealtimes. It was late afternoon when he decided to take a wander over by the abbey in search of some company. He gave a wide berth to two massive Celtic crosses that stood like holy sentinels in front of the main building. Carved with scenes from the Old Testament, they were deemed by Angus to be untrustworthy. In school he'd been taught in history class that the two ancient monuments had stood on the same spot for centuries. By now he'd learned to think for himself and question what grown-ups told him, so he made a detour round the imposing crosses, even if they were replete with carved roses and serpents as the history book said. He saw no reason to chance a visit from that homicidal maniac, the Grim Reaper, who was bound to appear if the wind picked up and blew over a five-ton cross, squashing his young body under its lichen-covered surface.

At the back of the abbey Angus stopped for a moment to admire the new stained glass window containing the revamped image of Saint Columba. By the looks of him, his break had done him the world of good. He looked younger, with a new hairstyle and bright orange halo. The cross that Jesus had presented to the saint was smaller and therefore, Angus reasoned, lighter to carry. Angus scanned the countryside but there was not a soul in sight. He was about to head back to Baile Mor, when a flash of red caught his eye. Down towards the seashore he saw Morag Simpson waving to him.

The sandy cove at the foot of the hill was an occasional meeting place for some of his friends. When Angus arrived on the beach a discussion about American tourists was drawing to a close. Morag, who was now almost twelve, was in the process of asking a question.

'Why do the Americans always say they're Scottish?'

Neil, who was just about old enough to start shaving, answered, 'Because the Yanks are daft, that's why. Wearing the tartan as if they were Highlanders and all the while talking like they've got marbles in their mouths. My dad says they could have saved a lot o' Scottish soldiers' lives if they'd come over and joined the fight a bit earlier during the war.'

'Aye, but the Americans won the war,' commented Billy, who was a bit too big to be wearing the short trousers held up by elastic braces that he had on. 'They dropped an atom bomb on Hitler's house and killed him.'

'Och, you and your bloody war comics,' said Neil. 'Like those stupid breeks you've got on, you should have grown out of them years ago.'

Angus farted loudly and blew a small crater in the sand. He couldn't control it because Mrs Cameron's porridge was working its magic on his bowels again.

'Is that you announcing your presence, Windy?' asked Neil. 'Don't worry, we can a' smell you're here.'

'Ugh, gads,' exclaimed Billy, 'it smells like the Germans are sending over mustard gas.'

Angus felt embarrassed when he noticed Morag edging away from him. He'd been thinking about the second last time he'd worn a kilt. It was when he'd attended a ceilidh where his father became so drunk that he'd crashed through a window when he was playing a reel on his fiddle.

Morag injected verve into the conversation by saying, 'I'm going to open up a hairdressing salon in Baile Mor when I leave school.'

Neil was not going to let that go by him so easily. 'A hairdresser? You've got to be joking. Look what you did to Billy.'

Turning to focus their attention on Billy's hair, everyone began to laugh, except him. His thick crop was just beginning to grow back after Morag's abortive attempts to give him an 'Elvis'.

'That's no' funny,' said Billy, running a hand over his stubbly hair. 'My mother nearly battered me for that. She said I looked like I'd had a run-in with a combine harvester.'

'It wasn't my fault,' said Morag. 'My ma's scissors were blunt.'

Neil countered her excuse. 'It's a bad haircutter that blames her tools.'

As it was to turn out, Morag never did open that hair salon. Seven years later she married one of those American tourists they'd been discussing. He was a New York Jew who went on to become a cosmetic surgeon. Today she lives in a Manhattan apartment near to Central Park, where she takes her Afghan hound called Iona for a walk every day. Her two children have grown up now. Her face looks twenty years younger than it should, thanks to her husband's skill with a scalpel and buckets of Botox.

Morag and Neil were always arguing with each other. Angus diverted their hostile attentions by saying to Billy, 'Don't tell me, let me guess, you're going to be a commando when you leave school, right?'

Billy looked surprised. 'Aye, I am, but how did you know?'

'Because everybody knows that about you, ya stupid twally,' said Neil. 'Ever since you learned to read you've had your daft nose stuck between the pages of war comics.'

'So what?' retorted Billy. 'You can learn things from readin' them.' Springing to his feet he fired off a quick salute and raising his voice he snapped out, 'Tenshun!'

'Oh my gawd!' Morag put her hands to her face in mock surprise, a girlish ploy to show off her long fingernails that she'd painted with red nail varnish a few hours before. Slowly she lowered her hands to rest on the knees of her crossed legs.

'I can't believe it. Do you really want to be a soldier?' she asked.

'Of course I do,' replied Billy. 'How else will I be able to shoot Germans?'

Neil shook his head in disbelief. 'Did you fall out of your cot when you were a bairn and land on your head? If you shoot a German you'll be hung for it. The war ended ages ago. You stupid bam pot that you are.'

Billy Smith did eventually join the Armed Forces. He became a Royal Marine and held the rank of Corporal by the time he was shipped off to the Falklands, six hundred kilometres east of the coast of Patagonia, when a war broke out with Argentina over sovereignty of the islands. He was lying on his bunk below a warship's decks when an enemy surface-skimmer Exocet missile slammed into the ship's grey armoured steel hull, very close to where Billy was engrossed in reading a war comic. When the missile's payload of high explosives detonated, Billy was vaporized. A fitting, albeit unheroic, ending for someone who had loved the idea of warfare from the first day he'd heard about it.

'It's a free world. You can join the army if you want. Me, I'm going to become a bank robber.' Everyone turned to face Neil when he came out with this. 'My dad says there's no real money in a soldier's pay packet and we Scots have been fighting England's battles for hundreds of years. It's a mug's game.'

The sun broke through the clouds and illuminated the sandy cove. Neil's eyes squinted in the bright sunshine. He raised a hand to shade his face. 'The real money's in crime. I'm going to move to London where they've got the biggest banks to rob. I'll steal lots of money, buy a big penthouse overlooking the River Thames and bring lots of lassies home with me and shag them stupid.'

★

Neil, like Billy, would one day fulfil his ambition. He became an armed robber, made a small fortune and went to live in the States when the U.K. became uncomfortable for him after he knocked over a jeweller's shop in London's Covent Garden. It was the kind of shop that didn't bother to show prices but did go to the trouble of installing a high-definition CCTV camera, which captured a perfect image of Neil's grinning face. The following morning he boarded a British Airways flight, bound for San Francisco. He eventually moved into a beachfront property on Malibu Beach, a short drive north along Pacific Highway Number One from Los Angeles and its suffocating canopy of candy-coloured smog. Neil became a playboy and began a life of Californication. After a decade of wild parties and beautiful women, who were replaced with gay men when he became bored with them, he awoke one morning, after sleeping off the effects of a three-day coke and alcohol binge, to find his coffers were almost empty. It was time to go back to work. He teamed up with a gang of like-minded unemployed desperados and after a couple of fairly lucrative hold-ups decided it was time to go for the jackpot.

Neil and his accomplices cased out a bullion transport company in Las Vegas, Nevada. They spent two weeks checking out the movements of an armoured truck. When they had it sussed, they hit the transporter just outside the city limits. It was a successful operation. There were six men involved in the heist, including Neil. Two of them drove a Dodge van out into the Mojave Desert. To the sounds of rattlesnakes rattling and the high-pitched whine of cicadas, they buried a ton of gold bullion under the hot sands at a prearranged spot by a tall trident-shaped cactus.

Meanwhile, Neil and his three other accomplices were passing round a fat joint of Jamaican weed laced with cocaine as the car they were in shot past the turn-off for Death Valley on the main highway back to LA. Neil was in the driver's seat of his year-old Lexus, thinking he'd better cool it on the gas pedal, when he caught a flash of red and blue light in his rear view mirror. It was the Highway Patrol. Neil pushed the buttons to lower the car's mirrored windows to let some fresh air blow through the automobile to get rid of the reek of marijuana. He hit the brakes, pulled into a deserted lay-by and parked beside a burnt-out car wreck. The patrol car came to a halt about ten yards behind them. Its sole occupant hailed them with a bullhorn mounted beside the flashing lights on the roof. 'Stay in the vehicle and keep your hands in sight.' The patrolman wasn't wearing a hat when he stepped out of his car and walked slowly over to the driver's side of the Lexus. He unbuttoned the strap on the black leather holster he was wearing and clicked the safety off on his sidearm. Neil was as high as a weather balloon in a tornado when the tall cop ambled up to his lowered window and stooped to look into his Chinese eyes.

'What's the problem officer?' asked Neil, a stoned smile on his face.

'Sir, do you have any idea how fast you were driving back there?' asked the cop.

'Sixty, maybe seventy,' replied Neil.

'Sir, you were driving your vehicle at one hundred and fourteen miles per hour. That's a felony in this state,' said the officer, a deadpan expression on his face. 'Sir, I have to ask to see your license and registration.'

Neil pulled down the visor, grabbed the documents in the pocket behind it and handed them to the waiting cop.

'Sir, I have to ask you and your passengers to remain in the vehicle. I'll be right back.' The patrolman returned to his car and radioed in Mr Neil Ferguson's details. It took him one minute to find out that the Lexus registered in Neil's name had a list of traffic violations tagged to it as long as its streamlined engine hood. The patrolman ambled back over to the car.

'Sir, I have probable cause to search your vehicle. Can you pop the trunk, sir? I'd like to take a look inside.'

Neil felt like he was going to start shitting bricks when he heard the cop's request. He was a very worried man. Not because of the bricks that were on the point of messing up his Calvin Klein underpants, but because of the half-dozen five-kilogram bricks of gold he and his friends had chucked into the boot as souvenirs. The gold bars were lying on top of a pile of automatic weapons that would have been enough to start a revolution in a West African state.

'I'm sorry Officer, the boot mechanism seems to be jammed,' said Neil, performing an uninspired ruse of jerking on a plastic lever by the side of his seat. This particular patrolman was no fool. He'd been doing his job for over twenty years and in that time he'd seen and heard it all on countless occasions. Stepping back from the black car, he drew his pistol in a smooth practised movement and, adopting a two-handed combat stance, levelled its barrel with Neil's slack-jawed face.

'Sir, I have to ask you for the keys of your vehicle.'

Neil hesitated.

'I want them now, sir.'

Neil did as he was ordered and handed them over to the waiting cop whose eyes were glued to his movements. Just as the police officer was about to take possession of them, Neil accidentally dropped the keys on the ground. The patrolman's knees made a ratcheting sound as he crouched. He groped for the keys with his left hand. He kept his eyes and weapon trained on Neil. When his fingertips came in contact with the keys, his eyes moved downward for a split second. This was the exact amount of time needed for the stainless-steel business end of a Sig Sauer P220R to appear in the bottom right-hand corner of Neil's open window and discharge a brass-tipped bullet. 'One of the most accurate 45s right out of the box', is what the Swiss manufacturers claim, but at that range it didn't count. The small high-velocity projectile was traveling at 1200 kilometres per hour when it hit the cop on the bridge of his nose, shot through his brain's grey matter and exited out the back of his skull in a haze of blood, leaving behind a hole the size of a tennis ball. The uniformed man hit the ground, as dead as the dust he fell on to.

Mickey 'Speedball' Dawson was the name of the Afro-American citizen sitting behind Neil who'd applied a few pounds of pressure to the pistol's trigger and as a result left the Highway Patrolman's three young children fatherless. Mickey was shouting. 'C'mon Homes, what tha fuck are you waiting on? Let's get tha fuck outta here.'

Neil's mouth hung open as he watched a wet stain appear on the crotch of the dead cop's light tan trousers. His ears were ringing from the gun's deafening blast. Mickey's yelling sounded far away. He didn't have to be told twice what to do. Opening the car door he leaned out, retrieved the fallen keys from beside the dead man's still twitching fingers, turned the ignition and hit the accelerator quicker than you could say 'Muthafucka'.

Outside of Barstow, on the freeway heading west into Los Angeles, the Lexus was stopped at a heavily armed police roadblock. Neil and his three gangster buddies were arrested, locked up and eventually tried in a court of law. For his part in the combined crimes of shooting a police officer on duty and robbing an armoured truck, Neil received sixty years in prison with no possibility of parole until he'd served at least two thirds of his sentence.

Today he wears an orange jump suit in San Quentin Federal Penitentiary where he shares a cell with his boyfriend Toto. In a violent world where fear can be quickly transformed into respect, Neil battered out a 'Rep' for himself during his first two years of incarceration. He has also earned himself a Masters Degree in Philosophy and is currently working on a book, tentatively titled, *Doing Hard Time in the United States of Babylon*.

'My mother says you've got a dirty mouth, Neil Ferguson,' said Morag, 'and listening to you right now I think she's right. You're a foul-mouthed pig, so you are.'

'Oh, dearie me, listen to Miss Hoity-fuckin'-Toity,' sneered Neil. 'Your mother's got her head stuck way up her arse and everybody in Baile Mor knows it.'

There was a lot of truth in what Neil said. Eleanor Simpson was a snob who believed she was a cut above everyone else who lived in the village.

'Don't you dare talk about my mother like that,' said Morag. 'The only thing you'll ever be shagging is woolly ewes, just like your father.'

'My ... my da does not shag sheep, you stupid wee bitch,' said Neil, more than a little surprised to hear Morag talking like this.

'Aye that'll be right,' said Morag. 'Knowin' your father, he probably wanks off to the *Farmer's Digest*.'

Neil's face turned scarlet to the roots of his fair hair. His neck was so hot it was singeing the collar of his denim shirt. Billy and Angus exchanged curious glances, not quite knowing what Morag was driving at, although there was no mistaking the venom that was flying off the tip of her tongue.

Morag gave Neil another verbal broadside, 'You, you're all talk. Look at you, you've got a reddie on. Away home and get your wellies on an' see if you can find a few wee lambs to play with.'

'What do you expect?' protested Neil. 'Of course I've got a red face. Listen to the way you're talking, an' it's you that's saying that I've got a dirty mouth. It's no' right for a lassie to be speaking like that.'

'Aye right, big man, just forget it, will you?' Morag gave Neil a contemptuous look then turned away from him.

For some time they sat on the beach, absorbed in their own thoughts, looking east over to Mull's not too distant shore. The sun was beginning to set behind them, its last rays streaking over their heads to bathe the neighbouring island's hills in molten gold. It was

Morag who broke their contemplative silence when she turned to Angus.

'What about you, Angus? You've never ever said what you'd like to be when you grow up.'

Angus looked at Morag's face. Framed by her ample ginger curls of glistening hair, her pale skin was without a blemish except for a farthing-sized tan birthmark by the left hand corner of her thin lips. She was wearing a tight red blouse and he could not help noticing that her body was beginning to develop small breasts.

'What are you staring at?' snapped Morag.

'Oh, ehm, nothing, I don't know. Maybe I'll just stay here on Iona.'

'You're dreaming,' said Neil. 'There's no banks to rob. No' even a post office.'

'He's right,' added Billy. 'There's no' any wars to fight in either. It's too peaceful and quiet here. That's the problem with this place.' Billy sighted down the barrel of an imaginary rifle and fired off a shot at a passing seagull that had dropped down out of the sky to glide above the shoreline. He missed. 'Fucking gulls, the tourists think they're romantic but the dirty bastards would peck your eyes out sooner than shit on you.'

'Well, if you do stay, you can have free haircuts in my hair salon,' said Morag, moving a little closer to Angus.

'Naw, Morag, you'll not need to do that for me. I'll probably leave the island as well. I think what I'd really like to be is an adventurer.'

'Oh, aye,' said Neil. 'I can just see you up in the front of a whaler with a harpoon in your hand.' He pointed to a breaking wave and pretended to have just spotted Moby Dick, the great white whale. Like Herman Melville's obsessive character, Captain Ahab, he called out, 'There she blows!'

Angus grinned at Neil. 'Well, at least it's better than holding up banks and shooting people.'

'Maybe you're right, but I'll tell you one thing, robbing banks pays better,' said Neil, giving Angus a friendly dunt on the shoulder.

'Och, you guys are talking a load o' nonsense,' complained Morag, striking out at an approaching cloud of midges. 'A'm startin' to get bitten.' She smiled at Angus and asked, 'Want to get me home?'

Angus's heart skipped a beat when he replied, 'Aye sure, no problem. Let's go.'

Standing up he bashfully offered the young girl his hand and pulled her to her feet. The two other lads were digging their heels into the sand and watching them. Angus nodded farewell to his mates and Neil slapped Billy on the back saying, 'Did you hear that, Billy Boy? I think somebody's in love.'

Angus heard Neil's jibe but he was already walking away behind Morag and her backside, which fitted so snuggly into her tight black shorts, seemed much more interesting.

When they were out of earshot Morag hissed, 'Sometimes I can't stand Neil. He's such a smart Alec.'

'Maybe that's true,' said Angus hurrying along behind her, 'but c'mon Morag, my ma's always saying that blood's thicker than water. I think I know what she means because Neil's like a brother to me. Anyway, he's always good for a laugh.'

'Maybe you're right, I just didn't like what he said about my ma.'

'Listen to who's talking. You're like the pot callin' the kettle black. Look what you said about his da.'

'He bloody well started it,' was her angry retort.

Darkness was beginning to cast its shadow over the island. Morag took hold of Angus's hand. When they reached the back of the abbey, she turned to face him and, under Saint Columba's watchful gaze, asked, 'Would you like to give me a kiss?

He was suddenly lost for words and glad it was getting dark because he was sure there must be smoke rising from his burning ears. This didn't stop him from moving a step closer to Morag. Their lips parted as they connected. Teeth bumped clumsily together. Morag's breath smelled of bubble gum. It was the first real kiss Angus had ever experienced. When Morag's tongue darted into his mouth, he felt his hormones race and the excitement dancing in his stomach drop down to his groin.

That morning he'd heard Elvis Presley's voice on the big wooden Marconi wireless down at the shop. The radio was tuned to a channel playing modern music. Elvis had been singing 'I'm All Shook Up'. Now, just when he was beginning to understand what 'The King' meant about his heart beating so hard it scared him to death, Morag pushed him away from her.

'What's the matter?' enquired Angus, running a finger over his lips, half expecting them to have swollen to double their size.

'You can't have too much of a good thing.'

'Why not?'

'Because, Angus Macleod, that's just the way it is. See you tomorrow.'

Morag hurried off in the direction of the village. Angus did not know what to think. He stood for a moment. His hands were shaking and his knees felt weak. When he saw Morag's shadowy figure reach the dirt track leading down to Baile Mor he ran after her. He drew close as she approached the small pebble garden in front of her home.

'Morag,' he called, almost running into her from behind. She turned and stared into his eyes. The hint of a smile worked at the corners of her lips, which were the colour of rowan berries due to a hurried liberal application of her mother's favourite lipstick.

'Aye, what is it?' she asked, her eyes dark and glittering.

'Can I have another kiss tomorrow?'

She backed away and looked him up and down. Taking her time, she finally said, 'Aye, maybe.' She turned quickly, entered the house and was gone.

Mystified, Angus stood with his eyes fixed on the door she'd disappeared behind. The smell of cut grass, Morag's scent lingered upon the still air. Feeling light on his feet, he continued on down the cobbled road thinking that girls were strange creatures indeed, but kissing them was great fun. He wondered why she had told him you can't have too much of a good thing.

When he arrived in Agnes Cameron's kitchen she was standing at the stove. Her arthritic hands grasped a big wooden spoon to stir something in a copper pot, which she was gazing into as if she were awaiting a vision of Saint Columba. She turned and her youthful face beamed at him in the wan yellow light of a hurricane oil lamp.

'Sit down, son. I'm just making you a lovely bowlful of hot porridge.'

'Aw, that's just grand, Mrs Cameron. I'm starving.'

He groaned inwardly and thought, 'Why is it that the only things I ever get too much of in life are the bad things?' The porridge tasted like salty sawdust soaked in sour milk.

'Help ma Boab,' exclaimed Barney as he turned to face Angus, who was sitting beside him with his back against a wooden bollard at the end of the pier. 'What in God's name have you been eating, laddie, to make a guff like that? It smells like rotten eggs.' The old fisherman put his rod down by his side and started flapping his hands around in an effort to clear the air.

'I'm sorry, Uncle Barney, I've been eating Mrs Cameron's porridge for a fortnight and it's upsetting my insides.'

'Upsetting your insides is it?' said Barney, putting a match to his foul smelling tobacco pipe. 'Judging by the hum, dissolving your insides is more like it. If you feel the need to let another of those stinkers off away and sit at the other end of the pier. My auld ticker's no' up to that kind of punishment.'

'I'm sorry, Uncle Barney.'

'Aye lad, that's okay. Just try to no' let it happen again.'

Pipe wedged between his false teeth, the old codger picked up his rod and gave its line a sharp tug, just in case he'd snagged a sheepskin cushion that had floated up from the ocean's depths.

Barney was right enough. Angus was giving off a pong normally only found in the vicinity of a gasworks. He was longing for his mother to return from the mainland and serve him up some decent food.

A thick bank of cloud rolled in off the sea. He heard the thrum of the ferry's chugging engine before the boat appeared out of the mist. He could make out Captain Jamieson standing on the bridge, his long grey beard split down the middle by the breeze. There was someone by his side. Angus was overjoyed when he realized it was his mother. She was wearing a burgundy coloured coat he'd never seen before. Rose waved when she saw him.

The MacBrayne ferry tied up and the gangplank was lowered. Angus stood waiting for his mother to disembark. She finally appeared. As she approached him, Angus's heart filled with happiness. He'd never seen his mother looking so good. To match her coat she'd put on a pair of red high heeled shoes. Her beautiful hair was no longer tied up in a bun, it hung down to her waist like that of a Nordic goddess.

'My, son, you're growing fast. It's only two weeks since I saw you last, but I'd swear that you've grown six inches taller.' Holding him at arm's length, she looked lovingly into his blue eyes. 'Did you miss me?'

'Aye Ma, I did that. Mrs Cameron makes the worst porridge in the whole of Scotland.'

Rose laughed at her son's complaint, embraced him and kissed the top of his head. Taking his hand, she pulled him in the direction of Baile Mor.

'Listen,' she said, 'we haven't got much time. Captain Jamieson is going to wait for us. We have to hurry.' Rose tugged at her son's hand to emphasize her point.

'Hurry Ma? Hurry where?'

'Back to the ferry. I'm Mrs Boyd now. Look at this.' Raising her left hand Rose twisted her wrist so that prismatic light reflected off a chip of diamond mounted on a gold band around her index finger.

'What's that?'

'It's a wedding ring. I can hardly believe it myself. Steve and me got married last Thursday down at the Registrar's Office. We're goin' to live in Glasgow. I'll tell you all about it on the ferry.'

'Glasgow,' Angus half shouted, his face collapsing. 'What about my pals?'

'You'll make plenty of new friends in the city. Come on now, the captain doesn't have all afternoon to wait on us.'

Rose tugged once more at her son's hand, which now clung a little tighter to her own.

Forty-five minutes later, dressed in his Sunday best, Angus stood by his mother and two tattered suitcases on the shuddering deck of the ferry as it pulled away from the pier. Looking up from the churning waters at the back of the boat, he saw Neil and Billy walking down the road to the harbour. Angus whistled and waved to them. When they sighted him, they broke into a run. The ship was beginning to gather speed by the time they reached the end of the wooden jetty. Neil cupped his hands around his mouth and shouted. 'Where are you going?'

'Glasgow.'

Neil and Billy glanced at each other. Turning at the waist, Billy raised his invisible rifle, took aim and fired. His shoulder jerked back from the recoil. Angus ducked as an imaginary bullet buzzed over his head. He stood upright and gave the marksman a thumbs up.

Billy shouted, 'See you when you get back.' His voice was carried off in the wind but Angus heard it anyway. Overhead, seagulls glided in the slipstream laughing and crying at the same time.

He stood in the stern looking back at Iona until the island was enveloped in mist and disappeared without a trace. Out on the open sea the ferry rolled with the waves. Rose held on to the guardrail for support as she gazed ahead into the white fog. Angus stood observing her. He could not get over how beautiful she looked. Sensing her son's watchful eyes, she turned to face him and smiled. He'd never seen his mother so happy before. A single ray of sunlight broke through the clouds above and shone on Rose, burnishing her hair gold. She looked like the enchanting flower she was named after.

'Ma, I didn't even get a chance to say a proper cheerio to my pals.'

'There's no need to fret over that,' said Rose. 'You'll love Glasgow. It's a great place, full of wonderful people.'

Rose's eyes looked to the right as she cast around in her mind for something that would appeal to her son's imagination. 'There's a big river, with ships on it, near to where we'll be living. You'll love the tramcars and Steve has a television set.'

'A telly,' said Angus, his face lighting up at the very thought of such a marvellous thing. 'Will I be allowed to watch it?'

'Of course you will. That's what it's for.'

Angus came forward and put his arm around his mother's waist. It was much slimmer than it used to be.

Just then the ferry broke through the sea fog. Lying before them, across the dark grey waters of the Firth of Lorne, was the coast of Argyll. Angus had never been off Iona, except when he'd accompanied his father on fishing trips round the island's coastal waters. Gazing in awe over to the mainland, he could see high mountains that were larger than the island he'd just left behind. They looked to him like gigantic lumps of dark-green velvet coal, fringed by pine forests. Everything was happening so quickly his thoughts rushed by like the waves below him. One thing that was beginning to register in his young mind was that the world was a lot bigger than he'd imagined it to be. Something else that occurred to him was that he no longer had to worry about the Grim Reaper, that supernatural creature whose presence, Angus believed, was exclusive to Iona. What a relief.

'What are you smiling at?' asked Rose.

'Nothing Ma, just smiling, that's all.'

He held her close and took a deep breath, relishing the scent of his mother's new perfume.

When the ferry docked in Oban, Angus could not believe his eyes. There were more boats moored in the harbour than he'd seen in his entire life. He hardly noticed his mother shaking hands with the captain as he wished her good luck and bid her farewell. Above the small town he saw a building on a hill that looked like a scaled down version of the Coliseum in Rome. He asked his mother about it. She informed him that it was called McCaig's folly and that it had been named after the banker who had paid for its construction in a futile effort to ward off the rampant unemployment in the region at the turn of the century.

Suitcase in hand, Rose had to drag her son along the street as he craned his neck to take in the sights. Well-dressed people stood chatting with each other in front of brightly lit shop fronts, shiny cars flashed by, fish lorries groaned under their heavy loads – and the noise; he'd never heard such a racket.

Carrying the smaller of the two cases, Angus passed a three-storey granite house and let go of his mother's hand to stop and gaze into one of its windows. Inside, a balding man and a plump woman were seated at a long wooden table, illuminated by a crystal chandelier above their heads. They were eating their supper. Sitting between them, with his back turned, was a young lad about the same age as Angus who had the same colour of dark brown hair as he had, although, unlike his unruly mop, this boy had a neat haircut. Observing this scene from the pavement, he thought how lovely it would be to sit down for supper in such a luxurious room. He was startled from his short reverie when his mother took a tight hold of his arm.

'For goodness sake,' she complained. 'Stop staring into people's windows. Don't you know that's rude? C'mon now, hurry up or we'll miss the train.'

The thought of seeing a steam train made Angus forget about the family eating their supper. He hurried along behind his mother as they made their way towards the railway station, blissfully unaware that he'd only a moment before been staring at the back of his twin brother Hamish's head.

8

TRAUMATIC TIMES

On the beach, Cambodia.

Raw anger was clawing at Hamish's insides. His hands were shaking with fury. Not because of the landmine, but at the memory of what had taken place within the grey granite walls of the house he'd grown up in.

Duncan and Mary Johnson had endeavoured to do their best as adoptive parents, providing Hamish with love, security and guidance. His childhood and adolescence had been normal enough, containing within them all the hurdles, leaps and bounds one associates with those formative years in an individual's life. A difficult month had followed his eighteenth birthday when, by the coal fire crackling in the living room's green marble fireplace, his parents sat down with him and revealed that he was an adopted child with a twin brother who had last been heard of in Edinburgh when the police arrested him. Hamish was a sensible young man and after considering the matter for some time he went to his parents and told them how much he loved them. The fact that he had a twin brother, whose whereabouts were a complete mystery, did not concern him very much at the time because he had more pressing matters on his mind, like his girlfriend Jean and how he was going to set about convincing her to marry him.

Hamish could recollect every nook and cranny of that three-storey dwelling, located just round the corner from the High Street.

It was easy for him to recall the dining room where every evening, facing away from the window, he'd taken his place and sat down to enjoy his mother's cooking. He could remember the perfumed scent of furniture wax, the weight of silver cutlery in his scrubbed hands, the rainbow sparkle thrown by the cut crystal chandelier and its flickering electric candles, yet it was over twenty years since he'd last been in that room.

The trouble arose long after he'd left home, married Jean and become involved in the demanding process of bringing up his own children. He'd always held his parents in high esteem and thought the world of them until the fateful day when his dream was replaced by a nightmare. Hamish's mind recoiled at the thought.

One cold January evening, Jean and Hamish had been sitting on the sofa in their living room watching the latest episode of *Coronation Street* on television. He thought this particular soap opera was an insult to human intelligence and couldn't stand its theme tune, but sat through it because Jean loved it. She related to the characters in the drama series as if they were neighbours and identified with the contents of their gossip like it had something to do with her own life. Moira, who was seven at the time and the oldest of their three daughters, wandered through from the kids' bedroom dressed in her pink silk pyjamas. She put her little hands on her father's arm and looked up into his eyes.

'Daddy, why does grandpa always want to show me his willy?'

This question set in motion a chain of events that would change Hamish's life forever. He almost regurgitated the mouthful of tea and digestive biscuit he was swallowing. Hamish asked his daughter to repeat her question. His heartbeat quickened when she reiterated, word for word, exactly the same thing. Jean was so engrossed in the soap and what was going on in the life of some old crone called Mrs Sharples, she did not hear any of this. Hamish rose from the settee and switched off the blaring TV set. Jean started to complain, but when her husband said, 'Please be quiet,' something in the tone of his voice made her do a very unusual thing, she obeyed him. During a ten-minute session of carefully couched questions, it became clear that Hamish's father had been masturbating in front of his seven-year-old granddaughter.

'Jesus fucking Christ,' Hamish swore under his breath.

'Mummy, mummy, daddy said a bad word.' Little Moira looked up at her mother and could see that she was in a state of shock. 'Has something bad happened?' she asked.

Hamish tried to put his daughter at ease. 'No darling, your mummy and I are tired, that's all. Now away back to your bed and mummy will tuck you in, won't you Jean?'

Jean was gnawing on the ends of her perfectly manicured nails, her eyes blinking nervously. He kissed his daughter's rosy plump cheeks, said goodnight and nodded to his spouse, who stood up woodenly as if under the influence of a hypnotist. Jean took Moira's hand and led her off in the direction of the bedroom, where her two little sisters were tucked up safe and sound. When they'd disappeared into the room's shadows Hamish rose to his feet and headed out the front door.

White hoar frost glistened on the ground outside. Weather conditions were the last thing on his mind. Hamish was inappropriately dressed. Wearing sheepskin slippers, a pair of jogging pants and a thin cotton tee shirt with 'I Love Scotland' printed on the back, he opened the door of his Volvo estate. He sat down on the creaking black leather of the driver's seat. The smell of the treated cowhide struck a cord with the animal instinct rising from his guts. Leaning over, he recovered a packet of Marlboros from the glove compartment. He turned the ignition key and the radio came on. Donna Summer was singing 'I Feel Love'. He switched it off immediately. It was only a short drive to his parents' house yet he managed to chain-smoke three cigarettes by the time he parked his car and stepped out onto the slippery pavement in front of their home.

There was a cold wind blowing up from the harbour but Hamish didn't notice. His blood had been transformed into molten metal. He stood in the street staring at the dark-green painted door of the house he had grown up in. When little Moira recounted what had transpired, had Duncan Johnson entered his living room in that moment, Hamish would have leapt out of his seat and strangled the man in front of his wife and daughter. He had too much to lose to chance being convicted of murder. He took a few deep breaths in an effort to cool down. It wasn't easy.

In those days everybody believed crime was non-existent in Oban. Nobody bothered to lock their doors and Hamish knew all he had to do was turn the brass doorknob to enter. Instead, he pressed the doorbell set into the grey granite frame, afraid of what he might do if he went in. He gazed up at the lead glass transom until the door swung in. Duncan Johnson looked mildly surprised when he opened his front door and saw Hamish standing on the pavement. 'Oh, hello, son,' he said, thin strands of grey hair combed over his skull lifting in the breeze.

'I didn't expect to see you this evening. Come away in, you'll catch your death out there.'

Hamish remained rooted to the spot, feelings of disgust and outrage detonating in his stomach. Sensing there was something amiss, Jack took a step forward, pushing his bifocals up on his nose in order to better scrutinize Hamish's face.

'What's wrong, son? You're looking a bit peculiar. Is everything all right?'

Hamish stood stock still, staring at this man who had been the recipient of his love and respect for so many years. A veil lifted from in front of his eyes. He looked at his father's puffy facial features and could see kiddie-fiddler written all over them. Like liquid iron his rage poured into the mould of his right hand. Balling it into a fist, his knuckles turned white with the pressure. He'd heard it said that you should never hit a man who is wearing glasses but that unwritten rule did not stop the lecherous sexual deviant getting what was coming to him. Hamish punched him with a right hook that Mohammed Ali would have been proud to deliver. It connected with such violent force that Duncan's jaw was dislocated and broken in the same instant. His spectacles flew to the ground. Duncan collapsed like a dynamited building. Unconscious, his body lay over the doorstep. When Hamish noticed the specs lying at his feet he ground them into the pavement with his slipper's rubber heel. He thought that perhaps he'd killed his foster-father until Duncan groaned a moment later.

Hamish jumped into his car. The radio came on again. The Stones were playing 'Sympathy For The Devil'. The song was halfway through. Hamish heard Keith Richard's blistering guitar solo, turned up the volume, stepped on the gas and sped off into the darkness.

After Duncan had his jaw wired back together again, he made a statement to the police claiming a violent drunk had assaulted him when he answered the ring of his front doorbell. The hunt was on for the unknown assailant who had put one of the town's most respected citizens in hospital for a fortnight. When Hamish heard this he took it as the final nail in the coffin of his father's guilt. Hamish did not bring his adopted father's deplorable behaviour to the attention of the police authorities, in order to protect his wife and daughter from the hellish scandal and proceedings that would ensue if it were to become a legal matter. Inadvertently, he'd probably saved Duncan's life; in those days a child molester would have been sent to a non-segregated prison, where the inmates would have dispensed their own rough justice upon a nonce, feeding him, perhaps, a nice bowl of porridge spiced with powder made from a crushed light bulb.

Although breaking his father's jaw had given vent to his feelings of moral outrage, it was an inconclusive way of ending the sordid episode. Hamish wanted to take it a step further. When his mother informed him that Duncan was to be signed out from hospital, Hamish sat down in his office and composed a letter to the man he could no longer call his father. He threatened to let his dirty little secret out if he did not leave town within a month. It had the desired effect. Three weeks later Duncan Johnson and his wife sold the house that they'd lived in for over forty years, for almost half of what it was worth. They told their friends and neighbours that Oban was no longer a safe place to live. At first Hamish felt sorry for his mother but eventually formed suspicions that she had been aware all along of what had happened and why. Whatever the truth was, it did not really matter because he never heard from either of them again and neither did anyone else.

Hamish changed the name of the construction company, in which he was a fifty-percent partner, from Johnson and Mann to Macleod and Mann. His shrewd business partner, Dave Mann, wasn't particularly concerned about this. As long as they were making plenty of money, Dave did not care about name changes.

The trickiest part of the whole story was explaining to their three daughters why one set of grandparents had suddenly vanished out of their lives. The girls were puzzled at first but by springtime they seemed satisfied with their parent's fabricated explanation about gran and grandpa being away on a long holiday. They started to spend more time with Jean's mother and father, who doted on their granddaughters.

Jean and Hamish began sleeping in separate beds and hardly spoke to each other for a year. Shifting responsibility is a game peculiarly human and Jean managed to blame her husband for what had happened. Hamish knew she was being ridiculously unreasonable; nonetheless, it came as salt in the wounds that were already causing him enough pain. Three of Hamish's knuckles had been crushed when he broke his father's jaw. The bones had healed themselves, but as Hamish sat recalling the incident, he kneaded the back of his right hand, trying to squeeze out the psychosomatic pain that remained locked in the tissue and tendons of his tightly clenched fist. Duncan Johnson was the only person he'd ever struck in anger. He had never felt comfortable with physical violence, but when he thought about the landmine he was sitting on, it was easy to imagine killing the person who had planted it there. 'Perhaps,' he thought, 'I will have to undergo therapy to heal the psychological impact of what I'm going through now. If I manage to get out of here alive.' He pushed the thought away and returned to the past.

After months of futilely trying to deal with the shock of discovering his foster-father was a pervert who had been messing around with his daughter, Hamish decided to seek out professional help. He found a psychotherapist in Fort William who said she could help him with his trauma.

Come rain or snow, he never missed his Saturday afternoon appointment with his therapist. The fact that he found her to be an attractive and sensitive woman had more than a little to do with his weekly punctuality. Apart from that, he appreciated the time to himself that the long drive provided. The therapeutic process lasted for over a year, and as a result he realized that a lot of what had been going on in his mind was caused by imagination. Moira had told him that grandpa never actually touched her in a sexual manner, although those were, of course, not her exact words. Hamish began to be able to enjoy a good night's sleep again. During his last session his therapist told him that she'd done all that was in her power to do for him; time, or rather its passing, would have to heal the rest. She was right. Hamish rarely thought about what had happened during that unfortunate period of his life. Apart from Jean and his psychotherapist, the only other person he'd ever talked it over with was Angus. Hamish had recounted the story to him after breakfast one morning in Sri Lanka.

Angus listened impassively as his brother narrated his harrowing account. Every once in a while he'd taken a sip of coffee, but apart from that Hamish had his full attention. When he'd finished talking Angus came over, sat down beside him and held Hamish's shaking hands in his own. They'd sat there together for some time in the early morning sunlight. A wave of emotion swept over Hamish and he allowed himself to do something in front of another man that he had never done in his adult life. He cried. Hot tears ran down over his cheeks. Hamish wept about the events that had transpired long ago and yet still retained the capacity to torment him. Self-pity wracked his frame as he mourned the loss of the love, trust and security that his parents had given him whilst in their care, all wiped out by the despicable acts of a confused old man. When his tears ran dry, he felt tremendously relieved from having once more brought this dark secret into the light of shared awareness.

Angus returned to his seat and, completely out of character, lit up one of his brother's cigarettes. He took a drag, inhaled and closed his eyes. Hamish studied him. Angus was wearing his customary white cotton shorts and high-necked shirt that highlighted his suntanned face. His head was shaved and as smooth as a snooker ball, his broad brow untroubled, with not a line upon it. Unaccustomed feelings of brotherly love stirred Hamish's heart. He felt glad to be in the company of his brother, who had shared his mother's womb with him. It was hot. He ran his hand over his damp forehead, feeling how furrowed it was compared to his twin brother's. He wondered if it might be a good idea to pay more attention to this meditation business Angus was so involved with.

'Utterly disgusting,' exclaimed Angus, interrupting Hamish's reflections. He stubbed out the half-smoked cigarette in an ashtray, took a large mouthful of coffee and swilled it around in his mouth. Hamish realized it was the cigarette his brother was referring to and not what had happened in the past.

'You know,' said Angus, 'that story you've just told me deals with a subject that is so alien to me I really don't know what to say.'

'That's unusual for you.' Hamish glanced over at his brother. 'You've usually got an answer for everything.'

'It saddens me to hear you say that.'

'Why so?'

'I feel uncomfortable with the idea that I might be coming across as being conceited. Therefore, in all honesty, I must say that I don't have an answer for everything.'

'Point taken. I appreciate you having said that. I'm sorry. It's just that what happened with my foster-father is still, after all these years, a very sensitive matter for me.'

'Your parents never tried to get in touch with you again?'

'No.' Hamish, shook his head and shrugged.

'Those poor people, what a mess,' said Angus, half to himself.

'To a certain extent, I did feel sympathy for my foster-mother. As for that degenerate of a husband of hers, none at all, in fact I hope he rots in hell.'

'Well, that's not so difficult to understand.' Angus paused for a moment to observe a flock of dark green parakeets squawking in a nearby tree. With a communal screech, they took to the air. 'Jean's a funny bird,' he continued, 'doesn't surprise me a bit how she reacted. It was a good idea to seek out professional help.'

'I don't know how I would have coped without it,' added Hamish.

'Sounds like old Mister Duncan Johnson could have done with a few therapy sessions himself, but from what you've told me about him, I doubt he would have had the gumption to make such a move. Let's hope he's woken up to the fact that he was way out of order. Want some more coffee?'

Hamish declined the offer.

'So much of what we are as adults has its roots in our early childhood,' continued Angus. 'Perhaps Duncan was sexually abused as a child and that's what led him to behave in such a perverted way in front of wee Moira.'

'I never really looked at it that way, and anyway I don't care about why he did what he did in front of my daughter. To be honest, I'd be happy to never have to think about that rotten bastard again for the rest of my life.'

'You know, I went through a bit of therapy myself.'

'What kind of therapy?'

Angus chuckled before answering. 'I knew that would tweak your curiosity.'

'What's so amusing?'

'You'll have to excuse me,' said Angus. 'It's just that my therapy experiences have … how should I put it … a certain humorous aspect to them. It's not that they were funny; in fact at times they were frightening. It's difficult to explain. How about saying, I went through a rock 'n' rollercoaster of a psychological ride?'

'Okay, Angus, I can see you're getting around to telling me more about your crazy life, so will you please get on with it. That's enough of a fanfare.'

Angus laughed, jumped to his feet and started singing the old Beatles anthem, 'All You Need is Love'. 'Love, love, love', Hamish had to sing along; his brother had the knack of defusing and lightening up even the weightiest of situations. Angus was fond of saying that seriousness was a contagious disease of the soul, best kept at bay with a healthy dose of daily laughter.

'Listen', said Angus, 'my reasons for becoming involved in the therapy process were entirely different from yours. Well, at least in the beginning anyway, when it all seemed like a bit of a lark. In the end, it boiled down to the same thing in the sense that I was endeavouring to heal myself from damage done in my past because…'

'All right, all right, I've got the picture.' Hamish nodded towards the chair beside him. 'Will you please sit down and tell me what happened to you.'

Angus stretched his arms out until his elbow joints cracked and then did as his brother requested.

India 1978.

Angus had already participated in a number of psychotherapeutic groups by the time he enrolled in a weeklong intensive called 'Encounter'. He'd found that these groups provided him with a creative environment wherein it was possible to express himself in a freer, less inhibited manner, bringing him in touch with his social conditioning and psychological defence mechanisms. Angus wanted to feel more open and came to realize, through the therapeutic process he'd embarked on, that he was a tough nut who'd forgotten how to cry. He'd been told that he was in need of professional assistance to help break down the protective hard outer shell he'd surrounded himself with, a shield that was formed during his violent adolescent years in Glasgow. He'd reached a point in his inner development where it was necessary to clean out the dark basement of his unconscious mind in order to build a healthier and more stable foundation for the new person he was evolving into.

The Encounter group was the psychological equivalent of a can opener. It took place in a converted air-conditioned cellar beneath a two-storey building. Angus pushed the thick soundproofed door that led into a large square room with padded walls. Upon entering the therapy chamber, he was surprised that the door opened easily because the room's atmosphere was so dense and heavy it would have required a bulldozer to shift it. He sat down on the mattress-covered floor and joined a loose circle formed by the seven women and six men who were to be his companions for the next week. They shared at least half a dozen nationalities between them. Judging by the tense expressions they were wearing on their faces, the common denominator in the room was nervous anxiety.

Theo Bridges, the group's leader, swanned into the room accompanied by his lissom female assistant, Quattro. Angus had talked to the middle-aged, bearded therapist on a couple of occasions prior to the Encounter group. He was an Englishman whose lips carried a smug smile; the kind of smile that cast the impression he was privy to an inner secret about the human condition that only he knew about. An old hand on the therapy scene, he was a sensitive, benign fellow with a particularly wry sense of humour whose face was wizened beyond its years. When he spoke, his voice was confident and strong. Long, receding grey hair hung over the stooped shoulders of his tall, thin body, lending him the appearance of an academic wizard.

Quattro had a definite feline quality about her that extended further than the purely physical. Long tawny hair fell around her face. Her nose was slightly upturned below alert eyes. Ready to pounce, her movements were graceful, compact and precise like those of a large cat; more mountain lion than domesticated. Angus found himself imagining her working as a stewardess in the first class section of an intercontinental passenger jet. In a flash, her eyes locked on to his, signalling to him that she was a highly intuitive individual, capable of picking up on his thoughts if she chose to.

By the end of day one Angus knew where he stood in the eyes of his fellow group members. All but one of the women wanted to make love with him and all the men wanted to fight him. Before the session wound down for the day, everybody was given a homework assignment. Angus had to choose the woman in the group he felt least attracted to and take her home with him. He was tempted to cheat, but thought the better of it. He picked a South African woman who was a younger, dark-skinned version of Agnes Cameron, the widow who had nearly succeeded in melting his intestines when as a kid he ate her toxic brand of lumpy porridge.

The first real lesson in the Encounter group was learned that evening between the cool silk sheets of his bed. Never judge a jungle book by its cover, because you never know what's inside. They came together in the most wonderful of ways and, much to Angus's delight, he discovered that her vaginal muscles had the squeezing power of a mature boa-constrictor. She made savage, hot-blooded love, like an untamed creature out on the Serengeti Plain. She'd worked as a safari guide in a game reserve and Angus reckoned she'd learned a few tricks by observing the mating habits of wild animals, especially lions. When she reached a shattering climax she let out a deep-throated roar. It was so loud Angus thought his eardrums were going to burst from the pressure. After they'd caught their breath, she requested to have her bare buttocks spanked with a belt, the way her big game hunter Afrikaner father had punished her as a child. Angus tried to excuse himself by explaining how a leather strap had traumatized him when he was a schoolboy on Iona.

'Oh, I see,' she said, 'it's like that is it. I suppose you were one of those kids who hated doing their homework.'

'As a matter of fact I—'

'Listen A— ... Ang— ..., whatever your name is. This isn't just about having a good fuck. It's about facing our fears to be free of them.'

Angus expelled a theatrical sigh, stretched out an open hand and asked, 'Where's the belt?'

Lesson number two came the following morning. He had to put on a pair of leather boxing gloves to have an individual punch-up with each of the group's male participants. None of the men could stand the arrogant Scotsman who was 'full of shit'. The lesson was to never drop your guard, even if it looked like you were the champion. Angus was beginning to feel wobbly at the knees after winning two boxing matches and keeping his balance on the mattress-covered floor. His third adversary was a big Australian who weighed in at 300 pounds. His fuzzy hair made him appear like he had received the full electrical charge from a bolt of lightning. All of the group's participants were naked and Angus could see that the man from Oz was a tub of lard with little in the way of muscle development. Angus had honed his fighting skills on Glasgow's tough streets and after exchanging a few sparring punches he realized the Aussie was a cream puff who could not have fought his way out of a bag formed from wet toilet tissue. Letting his guard down to lend the Australian the illusion that he stood a chance of winning, Angus did not anticipate that the big galoot from the Antipodes would trip on the edge of a mattress and deliver a Glasgow kiss to his right eye. The Aussie won the match by way of a technical knockout. His opponent was out cold.

Angus came round realizing two things; he could not see out of his swollen right eye, and there was a commotion going on in a corner of the room. By mutual consensus, it was agreed that the man from down under was a bully because he'd head butted Angus in the face. He'd been overpowered, thrown to the floor and was now buried under a pile of foam-rubber mattresses. The other group members jumped on top of the bouncy mound and began a free-for-all groping session.

Beneath this heavy suffocating mass, the Australian's muffled voice could be heard pleading for his life. Angus felt sorry for the Aussie. He turned to Theo and Quattro, who were sitting to one side like a couple of long-haired garden gnomes enjoying a cup of Darjeeling tea on a high altitude Himalayan meadow.

'You've got to stop this,' demanded Angus.

Theo glanced up at him. 'What's the matter, Scotty, things getting too out of control for you?'

'Come on, man. Let him out of there, or he'll suffocate.' By now the Australian's cries had faded away.

'Listen Scotty, if this was an Encounter group, what do you think would be the next thing you had to encounter?' Theo nodded towards the pile of mattresses on the other side of the room.

'No fucking way,' shouted Angus. 'If you try to put me under there I'll fucking well murder someone.'

Theo shook his head and tutted. 'Didn't take us very long to discover your limitations now, did it, Scotty?'

Theo put two fingers to his mouth and whistled like a shepherd. The rest of the group members looked up from their frisky frolics on top of the mattresses. Nodding towards Angus, Theo said matter of factly, 'He's next.'

A panic grenade exploded in Angus's guts. He felt like he'd been booted in the stomach. Like a troop of aggressive baboons, the groupies pounced on him. He still had boxing gloves on and swung around defensively, managing to land a couple of hard wallops in the faces of two assailants. Someone punched him in the left eye and his eyeball squooshed in its socket. Angus was wrestled to the ground and the heavy slabs of foam rubber he'd tried to save the now unconscious Aussie from were thrown on top of him. Struggle was no longer possible. He was crushed against the cold concrete floor like a cockroach under the rubber sole of Godzilla's oversized boot. His lungs were collapsing as his breath was squeezed out of him. The last oxygen molecules burned away to leave his heart pounding frantically. His head was throbbing. Waves of red colour pulsed behind his eyes. There was a brilliant flash of white light as his mind imploded. He passed out.

'Welcome back, Scotty.' When Theo's words came to Angus, he thought he was being welcomed home to heaven by an archangel. The group's participants were kneeling around him in a circle, caressing his bruised body with sensitive hands. Angus could barely see out of his swollen eyes. He started to laugh and everyone in the room joined in.

126

Soon it was on to the next episode. A young Italian woman was reliving the trauma she went through as a child when her mother died of cancer. Angus felt so tuned in to her suffering he could smell strong antiseptic medicine and hear the liquid death rattle as mama's throat gasped out its final exhalation.

That evening Angus was taken home by a foxy French woman who'd chosen him as the man she was most attracted to, somewhat of a pleasant surprise for him because he wasn't exactly looking his best. Perhaps beat-up men with bilateral periorbital hematomas – black eyes – turned her on. She told him that her father was a rich diplomat, which explained how she could afford to rent a Bollywood star's villa that must have cost as much in one month as the average Indian family earned in a lifetime. When it came to sex Simone was a carnal junkie itching for a fix.

Sipping from a long-stemmed glass of blood-red wine, she ran a hand through her thick black hair, which was haloed by the last rays of sunset streaming into the bedroom. She took a few steps, opened the veranda windows and purred, 'Oh zut, I feel so terribly hot. Do you mind if I take off my bra? It feels like I'm wearing a pair of crepe Suzette on my boobs.' Her breasts were Sin-Doll jumbo XL prototypes, but even better because they weren't made from silicone. Simone used a curved Arabian dagger to cut Angus's long cotton shirt up the front. She took the stalk of his erect penis in her left hand. He breathed a sigh of relief when she threw the gleaming knife to the other side of the room, where it landed with a dull thud on a tiger-skin rug. 'Come', was all Simone said as she led him by the cock towards her empress-sized bed. They lay down and licked each other urgently like hungry cannibals savouring an appetizer. She turned away and reached under the bed. 'Voilà,' she laughed and lifted up a long pink suitcase. 'My toy box,' she giggled mischievously. Simone opened the case and handed Angus an onyx-handled, petrified armadillo snout.

Their two perfectly formed bodies slid and writhed together as waves of almost unbearable pleasure crashed over them when, with the aid of a string of marble-sized ball bearings, they performed the 108 tantric positions of The First Chakra Cult of Why Planet. She kept Angus up all night by strapping him into a Freon-cooled donkey harness. Its leather belts blistered his testicles, but the increase in his pumping powers defied belief. His damp body bumped into her in an accelerated rhythm of wet slaps, her jiggling breasts acting as buffers to cushion the impact. 'Ooh-la-la', cried Simone as she wrapped her slender legs around his waist, raked his buttocks with sharp nails and coaxed the build-up of energy that was demanding release to gush into her in one long, ecstatic pulse. Angus screamed when she popped a vial of amyl nitrate under his nose and the vapour exploded into his brain a second later. He thought he was going to die; yet he'd never felt more alive.

Wrecked by exhaustion, they lay entwined in a lovers' embrace, basking in libidinous rapture. A fresh breeze blowing in through the open windows caused steam to rise off the living yin-yang formed by their sweating bodies.

By day five, Bärbel, a German woman from Hamburg, had gotten it into her sick mind that Angus reminded her of her father, a businessman who ran a sausage factory in Schleswig-Holstein. Judging by Angus's appearance at the time, papa must have looked like a survivor from a high-speed crash on the autobahn.

'I hate you!' Bärbel yelled. 'I vant to kill you!' She dived across the room and brought Angus down with a professional rugby tackle. He was still recovering from his mechanically powered sex session with Simone, who was now playing scratch-your-eyes-out with the South African woman in the red corner. He struggled on the floor with the mad Hamburger like he was wrestling with an aggravated bull alligator. The blonde Aryan managed to free one of her hands and grabbed at his hair. It was too short to get a hold of. She settled for trying to rip his blistered testicles off. Angus screamed in agony. 'Aaghh! Get off me ya crazy fuckin' bitch!' He started to pummel the woman with his fists but she was strong, athletic and possessed by such a fury that she'd become immune to the punishing blows. Angus was desperate; becoming a eunuch at the tender age of twenty-seven was not on his agenda.

Viru, a sensitive looking Japanese man with a goatee, which curled forward at the end, came to Angus's rescue and pulled the grappling Teuton off him. Like many of his countrymen he was desperately trying to get in touch with his feelings. He'd spent five days battering away at a cushion chanting his personal mantra, 'I want to feel anglee.' The rest of the group decided that two men picking on one innocent woman was unfair. They set upon Angus and his rescuer with a vengeance. At the very least, this helped Viru come in contact with his feelings of being intimidated and beaten up. When at last a naked Quattro managed to claw her way into the combat zone, separating the attackers one by one, Angus found himself with three cracked ribs and, courtesy of an anonymous fist, minus two front teeth. His precious blistered balls remained painfully attached to his body, a physical fact that seemed far more important than what he saw as a few minor injuries. Quattro led a broken-nosed and tearful Viru over to a corner, helped him put on a giant nappy and made him lie down on the floor to keep him connected with his newly found emotions. Angus started to wonder if he'd signed up for a close encounter with a bunch of lunatics who'd escaped from the confines of a high security prison for the criminally insane.

During the early afternoon of the Encounter group's final day, another top therapist popped into the padded room for a visit. Her name was Patsy and her reputation as a brilliant counsellor was well known in certain circles around the world. Her appearance was that of a bag lady with a hangover. Middle-aged, her long straggly hair was dyed bright orange with a grey parting down the middle. Badly applied pink lipstick was smeared over her tight lips. A cheap plastic handbag had replaced her witch's broomstick. She clung to it with long fingers whose nails were decorated with cracked black varnish. One on one, she was pure psycho dynamite.

Patsy's powers of perception and intuition were honed sharper than a samurai's katana. She went round each of the groupies and cut straight through the superficial bullshit to the heart of each individual's problem. A wise man was once heard to say that God is not your uncle because he isn't nice. Neither was Patsy. If one wanted to get in touch with their inner child, she'd yank the brat out and spank its backside. Deemed necessary, she could turn on the sweetness and become a fairy godmother. In the case of the German woman, Bärbel, she requested all the men in the room to shower as much concentrated love and attention upon her as was humanly possible. Within half an hour the castrator had become a vulnerable fräulein, whose father had sexually abused her when she was in her early teens. An overdose of masculine, tender loving care was viewed by Patsy as the best cure to set Bärbel on a path that would one day lead to the healing of her wounds. Patsy had the knack of drawing the poison out of people. A New Age witch-doctor, she helped bring people in touch with a primitive, innocent and childlike part of themselves that had been buried underneath the psychogenic detritus that accumulates in the course of a human existence.

Angus was the last person in the group to receive Patsy's attention. 'Oh, dear,' she sighed, 'not another of those poor boys who grew up on the violent streets of Glasgow, and you were such a sensitive child.' Her sarcasm could have cut glass, but she managed to penetrate the marrow of Angus's psycho-bone. He wondered if Theo had been sharing his observations with her behind the scenes. Patsy's penetrating gaze stayed fixed on Angus's eyes. He was, overall, out on a shaky limb. He'd been through a lot during the last week. If having your ego flattened by a fifty-ton steamroller was therapy, he'd had the full treatment and now felt like he had been reincarnated as a human pancake.

Patsy worked her psychotherapeutic magic on Angus, revealing to him that he was wearing a tough skin of emotional armour. His psychological chain mail was perhaps necessary when he was a teenager. Now it was obsolete. Brought up into the light of awareness, his hyper-vigilant fight or flight programme evaporated. Having lost his protection, Angus felt insecure. Then, realizing he no longer needed it, he experienced a sensation of lightness, as if an oppressive weight he didn't know was there had been lifted off him. He looked at the naked men sitting cross-legged on the floor beside him and saw they no longer posed a threat. In fact, they appeared as quite the opposite; they were his soul brothers, supportive companions on his journey through life. Angus felt a strong sense of empathy for the big Aussie who had, like him, been crushed under the mattresses to suffer the same suffocating hell.

Looking deeply into Patsy's inscrutable eyes, her scruffy physical exterior dropped away, to be replaced by a vision of pure femininity, grace and intelligence. She had an aura that radiated in subtle shades of turquoise luminescence. He felt irresistibly drawn towards her.

Patsy had honey dripping from her tongue when she whispered, 'Do you feel attracted to me?'

Angus felt compelled to be honest. 'Yes, I do.'

'Would you like to make love with me?' The woman was more than twice his age, looked three times older and had a face like a blunt hatchet but in that moment it was the most tempting suggestion he'd ever heard.

He replied casually, 'I wouldn't mind.'

Smiling, she reached over and gave him a motherly pat on the cheek with a warm hand. 'Dearie me,' she breathed deeply and sighed. 'You're going to have to try a lot harder than that.'

Everyone in the room burst out laughing. She'd been using herself as bait to lure him into emotional openness. He'd been so mesmerized by her powerful presence he'd totally forgotten where he was. His cheeks reddened as he experienced an uncharacteristic bout of bashfulness. He looked around at his friends, returned their smiles and finally broke into laughter upon seeing the humorous aspect of the situation. When he turned to Patsy, she was gone, a fitting exit for a sorceress.

The Encounter group drew to a close with everybody embracing each other like it was the end of a loving family reunion. When Bärbel gave Angus a rib-cracking hug, her breath came hot in his ear, 'I vant to fuck you.' He squirmed and took a mental note to avoid her in future, in case she had a papa flashback. Theo gave a patronizing speech about how the group process had to be carried out into the world. Angus suggested that they'd better start building more hospitals to deal with the casualties.

All in all, Angus respected Theo, although one incident involving the group leader a few days earlier challenged this reverence. Angus had watched the therapist fuck the young Italian woman, who had looked very vulnerable during the one-minute quickie. In his eyes, the brief scene had a bestial quality to it, like an old bull mounting a young female calf after he'd cornered her in a muddy paddock.

Letting go of one's judgmental mind was seen as being par for the Encounter course. This practice certainly helped when confronted with the anomalies taking place within the padded therapy chamber. Angus's shocked eyes had been wide open when he'd watched Theo torpedo the young woman. Bizarre as it appeared, she'd put up no resistance to the situation, in fact, quite the contrary. She'd been passively receptive to having sex with a man who could have passed for her great grandfather. Angus perceived this to be the essence of the Encounter group experience. An artificial situation wherein it was possible to confront one's conditioning and go beyond the restrictive parameters set in place by convention and social taboos.

The sun was setting as Angus wandered home along a shadowy avenue lined by tall banyan trees. 'Didn't take us very long to discover your limitations now, did it, Scotty?' Angus stopped and shook his head when Theo Bridge's voice echoed in his mind. A friend rattled up on a rickety old bicycle, producing more squeaks than a large family

131

of excited mice, and asked Angus if he'd been in an accident. They exchanged a few words. The sad-eyed man had just split up with a girlfriend and was upset about it. As they spoke, Angus realized what a change had come over him during the last week. The process he'd undergone had released an unexpected emotional range and thus a new way of responding to people. Tears ran down his face as he gave his puzzled friend a long heartfelt hug. Without a word, Angus walked away, tears still streaming from his swollen eyes.

He saw that everyone was suffering in their own way, whether they were willing to admit it or not. This perception brought with it two sensations: a sense of humanity that had shifted him into a state of at-oneness with his fellow man, accompanied by a current of sorrow flowing through him, a not entirely unpleasant feeling as there was a depth to it that happiness lacked. Angus continued on his way and flashed on a Ritchie Havens song from the movie *Woodstock*. He started to sing it because the lyric captured so poignantly how it felt to be a motherless child a long way from home.

When he arrived back at his bamboo house, he threw off his clothes and soaked his battered body in a bathtub full of steaming hot water for an hour. Afterwards he stood under a cold shower. Drying himself, he caught his reflection in a full-length mirror and thought he bore a close resemblance to someone who had fallen into a gravel crusher. His body was covered in bruises. His testicles were so swollen they looked like a pair of maracas and he prayed to God that he hadn't contracted a dose of the gonocacacacas. He blinked and saw his eyes had two dark bluish-yellow circles around them. There was an empty space in his mouth where two front teeth should have been. Moving closer to the mirror, he stared at his face and noticed that a few blood vessels had burst in the whites of his eyes.

'Jesus,' he cried. 'I'm starting to look like Jimmy Bradley.'

9

SMOKE SIGNALS

Glasgow, Scotland. 1962.

Angus met Jimmy Bradley by accident. This was hardly surprising, because Jimmy's life at the time was composed of a string of disastrous mishaps.

Jimmy had been at the movies that afternoon. Being a big fan of westerns, he was feeling inspired having just watched the palefaces being massacred by the redskins on the banks of the Little Big Horn River in *Custer's Last Stand*. The 'Regal' was a local fleapit cinema on Glasgow's busy Georges Road. Jimmy stood up when they played 'God Save the Queen' at the end of the performance and walked out into the bright light of day. He looked up and saw a chimney on fire above the roof of a red sandstone tenement block, stained black in places by soot and a century of exhaust fumes. Seeing as how his current incarnation was that of a Sioux Indian brave, he encountered no difficulty in deciphering the smoke signals rising above the canyon's steep cliffs he imagined himself to be standing under.

'Heap many buffalo, puff, puff,' said the smoke clouds, 'roaming the plains of Kelvingrove Park, puff, puff. P.S. Good hunting.'

This came as good news to Jimmy because he had a squaw and several little papooses' hungry mouths to feed. All that he now required was a good spear and he'd be ready for the hunt.

Tied to a nearby lamp-post was Jimmy's white stallion 'Thunder', the invisible wonder horse. One of the temperamental beast's unshod hooves was pawing impatiently at the concrete pavement. Like his master, he could not wait to hit the trail. Unhitching the fabulous creature, Jimmy jumped on to its bare back and rode off at a gallop in the direction of his tepee pitched in West End Park Street. Startled paleface settlers made way for the young lad running by them as he rode like the devil crying, 'Hi! Hiyah! Hiyah!' Back at his camp he found a discarded broom handle and sharpened one end of it into a long tapering point. He used the Bowie knife he'd taken from Davy Crockett a week before and noticed there was dried blood on its razor sharp blade, a gruesome reminder of having scalped the frontiersman after watching *King of The Wild Frontier*.

'Heap good,' said the young brave, drawing blood from a fingertip with the spear. In a gravity-defying leap, he landed on Thunder's back and rode off to the Happy Hunting Grounds. On Woodlands Road he spotted a small group of buffaloes running along behind a number eight tram with a shower of blue and white sparks pouring down on it from overhead cables. Jimmy smelled the electricity in the air and reckoned the bison were heading back to the park to regroup with the main herd but he had other plans for them. His mouth watered at the thought of a big buffalo steak.

The Sioux hunter cornered the herd of long-haired, cloven-hoofed shaggy beasties outside the wrought iron gates of the Gibson Street entrance to Kelvingrove Park. Hissing and snorting, Thunder reared up on his hind quarters while his front legs thrashed at rising dust clouds. He whinnied anxiously in the direction of the herd's leader. A huge bull had separated himself from the rest of his family and was lowering his head preparing to charge.

'Whoa, Thunder,' said the fearless hunter in an effort to calm his highly-strung stallion. He raised the lance above his head, digging his heels into the horse's flanks to spur the animal on. Just as Jimmy was about to hurl his javelin, Thunder's front legs crumpled as they tripped on the edge of the kerb. The bareback rider went flying. When he sat up on the pavement, the only remnant of his Wild West fantasy was the sharpened end of the broom handle. It had broken off after it entered Jimmy's right nostril at an angle, made its way out through the left side of his nose and embedded itself firmly into the underside of his left eyebrow. A passing policeman came to his assistance.

'My God, son,' he said, 'what have you done to yourself?'

'A wiz hunting buffalo when my horse broke its leg in a gopher hole and I wiz thrown from his back. Could you lend me your six-shooter? I need it to put Thunder out of his misery.'

The constable took off his flat hat and scratched his close-cropped head. 'Last of the Mohicans, is it? Well, chief, by the looks of you, it's an ambulance you'll be needing.' He put his hat back on and resumed his official role. 'There's a police box down the road. You stay here lad, while I go and phone the emergency services. Don't move. You're looking a bit peely-wally.'

Jimmy watched the big bobby's back as he hurried off down the street, thinking that palefaces always spoke with forked tongues. It crossed his mind to make a run for it but he was feeling light-headed.

'Are you okay?'

Jimmy raised his head in the direction of the voice and saw a tall kid looking down at him. He recognized Angus from school. Some of the other kids called him 'The Choochter' because he'd come down to Glasgow from the Highlands and had heather behind his ears.

'Naw, a'm no' okay,' snapped Jimmy. 'I'm wounded and the Blue Coats are going to take me back to the Indian reservation at Fort Worth.'

Angus clicked straight away. 'Can I help you to escape?'

'You can that,' answered Jimmy. 'I need to get back to my tepee in West End Park Street.'

Angus offered his hand and pulled the injured boy to his feet. Looking more closely, he could see that the reason for all the blood was a piece of wood sticking through the poor guy's nose. At a slow run, the pair of them headed off up the road. If the bobby had been Davy Crockett, he could have tracked them down because drops of blood marked their trail.

Back at Jimmy's tenement apartment, Mrs Bradley took one look at her son and gave him a hard clout on the ear. Raising her voice she said, 'Ya scunner that you are. I'll never be able to scrub those bloodstains out of your clothes.' An injury of this kind was no big deal for his mother. Over the years she'd seen her eldest son do much worse damage to himself. Mrs Bradley had a lit fag stuck to her bottom lip, one eye shut tight against the smoke as she searched around in her purse and handed Jimmy some coins.

'Here,' she mumbled round her cigarette, 'this is bus fares for you and your pal. Off you go now and get yourself stitched up. My favourite programme is coming on the box in a few minutes.'

When they arrived at the Royal Infirmary, Angus was immediately impressed by the fact that Jimmy was on first name terms with practically all of the medical staff who worked in the Out-Patients Department. It took a skinny Indian doctor half an hour to remove what had once been the end of a broomstick from Jimmy's face. Another hour was required to stitch his nose and eyebrow into a semblance of normality.

During this time, Angus sat on a moulded plastic chair in the waiting room. Stark fluorescent light bounced off the blood-pressure-lowering, blue-gloss-painted walls. Saturday evening was the busiest time of the week in the casualty department. Orderlies in green nylon uniforms were pushing gurneys through the hospital's swing doors. Upon the rubber-wheeled trolleys lay the groaning injured, some of them so smashed up and covered in blood they looked like plane crash survivors. One could have imagined that there was a war going on and in a way would have been right, because Glasgow's streets were plagued by gang warfare. The root of the hostilities was grounded in a volatile social environment infected by religious sectarianism, alcohol abuse, poverty and the angry frustration that accompanies mass unemployment.

The building reeked of bleach, disinfectant and surgical spirit. Angus sat watching as every once in a while an old fag-puffing biddy, with holes in the knees of her stockings, would appear on the scene and mop up streaks of blood from the grey linoleum floor. She'd extinguish her cigarette in a large flowerpot containing hundreds of dog ends and an aspidistra that had died of asphyxia. A practised routine, she would then lodge the half-smoked stub behind her ear and, with a tired shuffle, disappear for a while. Angus wondered what his pals back on Iona would have thought about what he was witnessing.

It was six months since Angus had first arrived in Glasgow. He was beginning to get used to it. At first his small-island sensibilities took a hammering from the lively city's hustle and bustle. He'd been overwhelmed, as nothing on Iona could have prepared him for life on the streets of the city. Within a week of arriving he had two big bumps on his forehead from walking into cast iron lamp-posts. He found it difficult to keep his eyes focused on the direction he was walking, because his attention was constantly being drawn towards interesting things going on around him. Glasgow had its own smells. Burnt toast and the acrid reek of burning soot were the most dominant of these odours, although the distinctive warm hum of stale beer wafting out of open pub doors was a close runner-up.

Fitting into school had been the toughest part of his transition. He'd been forced to run the playground gauntlet twice and was badly beaten in the process. After school hours, he'd been in three fights. Subsequent to taking a kicking in his first square go, he toughened up and beat the crap out of his next two opponents. As a result, his schoolmates started to address him by his proper name instead of The Choochter, an appellation he loathed.

During his first month in Glasgow he'd missed Iona terribly, especially the peace and silence. Drunks shouting and singing as they staggered home on the street outside his bedroom window had kept waking him up at night. Steve's apartment had been near Govan Cross on the city's south side. Now they'd moved to a quieter area, he slept better and his memories of the island were beginning to lose their emotional content.

The more acquainted he became with the Glaswegians, or 'Weegies', as they liked to refer to themselves, the more he took pleasure in their company. They were always up for a laugh with a special brand of black humour that was particular to them. Glasgow's broad streets were a non-stop adventure playground, especially weekends when it seemed like every adult in the city was out to get drunk. The Weegies liked to have a wild time and, if the menfolk felt so inclined, they enjoyed a good punch-up.

On the home front, things were not going so well. Rose's relationship with Steve was driving a wedge between Angus and his mother. Rose was so caught up in her ardent love affair with the Glaswegian that she had little time for her son. They made noisy love every night and Rose had taken to locking her bedroom door after Angus interrupted one of their humping sessions. He'd rushed into the room thinking Steve was murdering his mother because of what sounded to him like her anguished cries for help. Angus knew that Steve only tolerated his presence because he was in love with his mother. Angus called Steve Uncle, refusing to call him Dad, in spite of the fact that his mother had tried to persuade him on countless occasions to address Steve as his father.

Daniel was dead and buried and nobody knew it better than Angus. Uncle Steve bore no resemblance to his real dad whatsoever and Angus tended to stay out of his way. Steve was a bricklayer, who acted like he was Harold Macmillan, the Prime Minister, and the less Angus saw of him the better it pleased him. His mother's lover had already threatened to thrash him with his leather Territorial Army belt when things had come to a head. Angus swore to himself he'd mix rat poison into the big ginger-haired brute's porridge if he ever hurt him or his mother, an idea he'd gleaned from watching television.

'Hey, pal, thanks for waitin' on me.' Jimmy had returned from the surgery with a bloodstained bandage on his nose, making him look like a macabre version of a circus clown. Angus could not help smiling. The injured lad smiled back, displaying two rows of jagged and broken teeth that he carried from a run-in with the tiles at the bottom of the pool in Maryhill swimming baths. Jimmy had dived off the high board with his hands behind his back and entered the water like a bullet. He'd bitten the bullet when his mouth smashed off the bottom of the shallow pool.

'What's your name, pal?'

'Angus.'

'Mine's Jimmy. Let's get outta here, a'm starvin'. If we use our busies we'll have enough to buy a big bag of chips.'

The two boys walked in silence as they dug into a huge helping of salted, deep-fried potato chips soaked in vinegar that they'd bought from a chipper on Byres Road. When they were finished, Jimmy wiped his greasy hands on the rolled-up ball of newspaper that had contained a kilo of French fries ten minutes earlier, and tossed it through the open window of a parked car. He sighed wistfully and said, 'I love chips.'

As they passed by some of the Glasgow University buildings they began to talk and exchange information about themselves. Jimmy was two years older than Angus and had two younger brothers and a baby sister. His father worked for Customs and Excise, in an office by the banks of the River Clyde. He was not exactly sure what his father's work entailed. All he knew was that his dad had a uniform and a hat, similar to a policeman's, which he sometimes wore when he had a job away from home.

'What's it like havin' brothers and a wee sister?'

'I hate them,' answered Jimmy in a matter of fact manner. 'They're always greetin', messin' up my room and fightin' with each other.' He spat on the pavement as if the thought of them left a bad taste in his mouth. 'What was it like in Iona?'

'It was great,' replied Angus, 'but I'm startin' to like Glasgow better. There's more things to do.'

'This is my street.' Jimmy pointed to a long road lined with parked cars glistening under tall streetlights. 'Where do you live?' he asked, turning to Angus.

'Woodside Crescent, a few doors down from the American Consulate.'

'Yer jokin',' exclaimed Jimmy. 'Are your family rollin' in it?'

'Naw,' replied Angus shaking his head, 'my maw got a job there as a caretaker in a big building and a basement flat goes with it. Me, her and her daft boyfriend moved there from Govan four months ago.'

'Aw I see. For a minute there I thought you were a toff or something,' responded Jimmy. 'Is yer maw not married? Where's your dad?'

'My dad died.'

'What happened to him?'

'He got a fever, fell asleep and didn't wake up again after he had an accident.'

'Well, that's somethin' I know about. I'm the King of Accident Castle. Look at this.' Jimmy rolled up one of the legs of his jeans to show off a deep scar running the length of his calf. 'And this.' He let his trouser leg drop and pulled up his jersey to display another healed wound running across his abdomen. 'I got this when I was ten,' he said proudly. 'I fell off the back of a lorry when I was gettin' a free hurl and got run over by a motorcyclist. He broke both his legs. Serves him right, he was drivin' too fast.'

'Hey, Jimmy, I've got to go home now or I'll get a row for stayin' out too late.'

'OK, pal, no problem, I'll see you later.'

Under the stark yellow glow cast by a sodium-vapour street lamp, the two lads stood still for a few moments and studied each other. They were the same height, with the same length of hair, long for the time, and if it wasn't for the fact that Angus had broader shoulders, one could easily have mistaken them for twin brothers. From that day on Jimmy and Angus became inseparable friends.

With a sigh, Hamish opened his eyes and left the boys back on Glasgow's streets. Of all Angus's childhood friends that had been described to him, Jimmy Bradley was his favourite, his name having become, for him, synonymous with accident-prone. 'A bit like me,' he thought, 'considering my current predicament.'

His mouth felt dry and his tongue furry. Having nothing to quench his thirst, he smoked a cigarette. Halfway down he examined its glowing tip, took another drag and then stubbed it out in the sand. He was eager to return to his twin brother's world.

10

THE HIGHLAND MAN'S UMBRELLA

Glasgow, Scotland. 1965.

It was the last week of the summer holidays. The Rolling Stones were topping the singles charts, but like Mick Jagger said, they couldn't get no satisfaction. For Jimmy it was the opposite because finally, after a month, the doctors in the General Hospital were ready to let him go home.

He'd really outdone himself that summer, managing to inflict two serious injuries on his head that could have killed him or left him brain-damaged. The first accident occurred in early June when Jimmy, his back teeth floating, rushed into his family's tenement flat. His mother had warned him time and again about the small step just inside the bathroom door, but he was in such a hurry to relieve himself he'd failed to navigate it. He tripped, smashed his forehead against the toilet bowl's curved ceramic surface and knocked himself out. He had to be carried down the stairs on a stretcher by two disgruntled ambulance men. They nearly ended up in a fight with a coalman who claimed he had right of way on the stairs because he was on his way up hulking a hundredweight bag of coal on his back.

The stretcher-bearers took one look at the brawny brute covered from head to tackety boots in glistening coal dust, told him he was being ridiculous and tried to edge past him. The staircase shuddered when the coalie dumped his sack of carbonised plant matter on the

141

middle of the landing, making it clear he was out to make a point. He pushed his filthy red bandana back on his head, folded his muscular arms across his chest and set his feet firmly apart.

'Listen, ya pair o' shites. Just because yer wearin' uniforms, don't think ye can boss me around. If ye want to settle this man to man, we can go doonstairs and step outside for a square go.'

The scrawny ambulance men immediately relented, pressing themselves and the stretcher against the close's tiled walls. This allowed the tough-talking coalman to go about his business. As he squeezed past, Jimmy's eyes blinked open. All he saw was the coalie's black face.

'Are we in Africa?'

'Are you tryin' to take the pish outta me, son? Cos if ye are, a'm no' fuckin' laughin'.'

Wishing to avoid another outbreak of hostilities, the ambulance men struggled to maintain their balance as they wound their way down the stairs and hurried out into the street to their waiting ambulance.

Apart from the thirty-two stitches running horizontally across the centre of Jimmy's forehead like a black zip, he had to wear a neck brace. His collision with the lavatory pot had also left him with two fractured cervical vertebrae. For Jimmy, the worst part of the accident was that he'd urinated in his pants when he was out cold. Besides that, it was just another notch on his well-worn crutches.

Angus went to visit his friend in the infirmary. They chatted for some time before Jimmy checked that they were not being observed so he could remove his bandages to show off his latest physical trophy.

'Wow! You look like young Frankenstein.'

It was true. Jimmy's stitches did give the impression that the top of his head had been sewn on. Obviously pleased with his friend's response, Jimmy said proudly, 'Fuckin' dead gallus, innit.'

A month after being released from hospital, Jimmy injured himself in an accident that would be remembered as one of his crowning achievements. Mrs Bradley asked her son to go down to the backyard to break up a pile of cement-covered builders' planks to make kindling. He began smashing away at the thick lengths of pinewood with a heavy-duty axe, meanwhile living out a fantasy about the choppy exploits of Paul Bunyan who was a legendary 'big man' Canadian lumberjack. As he swung his axe, he kept one eye focused on the job and the other on the lookout for grizzly bears. Clunk! The axe handle made a hollow sound when it hit a plank and jarred his hands. Grizzlies momentarily forgotten, he looked down and was surprised to see that the axe head had vanished. Jimmy was puzzled when he could not locate the three-pound wedge of cast iron. It should have been easy to spot as it was painted with bright orange gloss paint. His head felt oddly heavy on his neck and he'd broken out in a cold sweat. He ran a hand over his scarred brow. His palm came away covered in sticky fresh blood. Raising his other hand to the crown of his head he found what he'd been looking for. The iron axe head was embedded in his skull.

It was Angus who found Jimmy lying unconscious outside the front door of his home with a chunk of metal wedged in his cranium. There was an awful lot of blood. Not knowing what else to do, he rang the doorbell. Jaded though she was when faced with one of her eldest son's mishaps, Mrs Bradley fainted when she saw Jimmy lying on the doormat with his head in a pool of blood. Angus went into the Bradley's cluttered apartment and, for the first and only time in his life, dialled 999, just like he'd seen actors do in a television series about a friendly bobby called *Dixon of Dock Green*. He felt pretty chuffed with himself when he managed to explain the nature of the emergency to the woman with the sexy voice on the other end of the line.

Twenty minutes later, he was sitting in the back of an ambulance watching a medic put transparent plastic oxygen masks on the Bradleys' sickly white faces. A siren screamed on top of the vehicle as it sped up the road in the direction of the Royal Infirmary. Jimmy was hooked up to a life support system for a week. When he regained consciousness he complained about having a terrible headache, which didn't come as a surprise to anyone. Jimmy's powers of recuperation were almost as legendary as his misadventures. He was taken off the critical list and moved to a general ward. Three weeks after the accident had taken place, Angus's rubber soled boots squeaked on a linoleum covered floor as he once more made his way along the hospital's bleach and iodine scented corridors. As he approached Jimmy, sitting up in bed reading a book about deep sea diving, the image of a current TV personality popped into Angus's head.

'You look like the Invisible Man.'

Jimmy's bandaged head looked up from his book and spoke. 'Hiyah Angus. If I was invisible, I wouldn't be here.' He chuckled. 'The doctor said I can go home next week. That's good news to ma ears because I can't wait to get out of here.' Turning his head in the direction of an elderly yellow-faced man, mouth open and snoring in the bed next to him, he continued, 'That old fart keeps me awake all night with his haverin'. He must've been in the war. He's always

143

ravin' on in his sleep about the air raid shelter and Jerry sendin' over whizz-bangs, whatever the fuck that is. What about you, pal? How you doin' china?'

Angus sat down on the edge of the bed and helped himself to a big bottle of orange coloured Barr's Irn-Bru that was sitting beside a bowl of fruit on top of a small bedside cupboard on wheels. The carbonated drink made him burp.

'Scuse me,' he said, recapping the bottle. 'I'm doing alright. I've started goin' out with Linda MacDonald.'

'Get tae fuck! Ya jammy bastard that you are, how did you manage to get your mitts on Big Tits Linda?'

'She just came up to me one day after school, told me she fancied me and asked if I'd like to go steady with her.'

'Yer jokin'. Have you shagged her yet?'

'It's no' like that. I've had a feel of her diddies though.'

'Aw Angus, don't tell me. What was that like?'

'Like playin' with balloons filled with hot jelly.'

'Jesus. Ma chubber's turned into a stonner just thinkin' about it.'

'Yer no' the only one, I've been walkin' around with a glass cutter in my trouser tent for the past two weeks.'

'Do you think she'll let you shag her?'

'Well, if she doesn't it'll no' be from the lack o' me tryin'. But she says she'll no' go all the way until she's got a ring around her finger.'

'Aye right, pal. That's what they all say in the beginning,' said Jimmy the virgin.

'Naw, but I think she's serious like,' said Angus. 'She's a Catholic an' all that. Even goes to confession on a Friday afternoon.'

'Confession? What the fuck's confession?'

'It's to do with the Catholic Church.'

Jimmy looked worried. 'Linda's no' a Celtic supporter, is she?'

'Don't be stupid. Since when did girls know anything about fitba'?' Anyway, as I was saying, every Friday afternoon Linda goes in a box with a priest and tells him her sins.'

'What! Those Fenian priests are all randy old bastards. I'll bet he's away for a toss after that.'

The two teenagers burst out laughing.

'If you two can't keep it down a bit, your visitor will have to leave, Mister Bradley.'

The pair of them turned and looked up at a huge, square faced, overweight nurse, standing at the end of Jimmy's bed. Her chubby fists were wedged into her massive hips. She was dressed in a sky blue uniform that was two sizes too small, with a pair of black seamed nylons sheathing her tree truck legs. A starched white hat with an enamelled red cross in the centre of it adorned her cuboid head.

'Oh aye, right, sister,' said Jimmy. 'A'm sorry, we were just having a wee laugh like.'

'I could hear that,' she said haughtily, the dewlap under her chin waggling, 'but this is a hospital ward, not a public house. There are a lot of sick people around here, in case you haven't noticed.' She spun around on the heels of her silent white Scholls and marched away.

Jimmy whispered out the side of his bandaged face, 'Jesus, will you look at the arse on that. She looks like Billy fuckin' Bunter.'

They clasped their hands over their mouths to suppress ribald laughter.

'So, pal, a'm gettin' out of here on Monday.'

'Great,' said Angus. 'Let's go down the town Friday night.'

'A'm up for that. Hey, how's it gawn at home? That radje Steve givin' you any trouble?'

The smile vanished from Angus's face. 'It's goin' fuckin' awful. My ma hardly speaks to me anymore and it's all because of that ginger haired shitehead. When he tried to belt me the other day, I picked up my mother's frying pan and told him I'd batter him if he tried it.'

'For fuck's sake, pal, you're a pure mad dafty. You didn't mean it, did you?'

'I did that. I fuckin' well hate the wanker.'

'Keep your voice down an' take it easy with the language or you'll get yourself chucked out of here.'

'Sorry, Jimmy. Maybe we should stop talkin' about it then.'

'Aye, no problem pal. So see you on Friday night. Meet you outside the furniture shop at Charing Cross. Let's make it nine o'clock, right?'

'Okay dokey, Jimmy, see you there then.'

Jimmy watched his friend walk away along the aisle that ran between the patients' beds. He was tall for his age and must have had the longest hair in the school. Maybe that's why Big Tits Linda went for him. Long hair was starting to be really in. Jimmy felt sorry for the trouble Angus had with his parents. Threatening to attack his foster-father sounded like he better watch himself or they might put him in a home.

★

'Where the fuck have you been?' asked Angus. 'I've nearly been chibed twice in the last hour standin' here waitin' on you.'

Jimmy apologized by saying, 'A'm sorry, pal, I had a barney with my maw. She didn't want to let me go out of the house.'

'A'm no' surprised. Look at the state of you, with your bandaged head. You'll scare the shite out of people runnin' around like that.'

Jimmy swivelled at the hips, doing his version of the Twist, a popular dance craze imported from America. During the past year the two teenagers had taken to wearing identical outfits. Tonight they both had on black polo neck sweaters, sky blue drainpipe jeans and shiny black leather winkle-pickers. Angus had saved his pocket money for three months to be able to buy his pair of pointed shoes at the Barrowland Market. When he'd shown up at home wearing his most prized possessions, his mother hit the roof, saying that they would ruin his feet.

'C'mon, let's get going,' said Jimmy. 'It must be ten o'clock, the pubs are comin' out.'

Five minutes later, they were walking side-by-side along Sauchiehall Street, one of Glasgow's main thoroughfares. Last orders over, noisy drunks were spilling out of the crowded public houses on to the broad pavements. Filled with the pungent odours of beer and vomit, the air was fairly crackling with excitement. What the two friends were in search of was the possibility of witnessing some violent action. In those turbulent times, street brawls were as common as Pakistani bus conductors.

Someone shouted, 'Hey you, baw-heid. Who the hell do you think you are, the fuckin' Mummy or somethin'?'

Jimmy's head dressing had caught the attention of the very worst element of Glasgow's night-time pedestrian society. A Teddy boy had disengaged himself from a group of his drunken cronies, who were loitering on a street corner and passing around a bottle. The females in the small gathering had beehive hair-dos. They were cackling and cawing like a flock of boozed-up buzzards. Drunk to the point of being unable to walk in a straight line, the Tedzer zigzagged his way across the pavement towards the two young teenagers standing rooted to the concrete.

146

'Get ready to run for it,' mumbled Jimmy from within the confines of his bandaged head.

The Teddy boy was one of the few still in existence. An endangered dangerous species, he was a bad hangover from a sub-cultural style of the fifties. A lanky streak of malevolence, made even taller by his fat shoes' thick crepe soles, he had long black sideburns and a brilliantined hairstyle slicked up in a quiff. A livid scar ran in a jagged curve from his right temple to the corner of his mouth, making that side of his face unnaturally taut, completing a picture of a rock 'n' roller gone horribly wrong. Drawing closer to Jimmy and Angus, he undid the top buttons of his ultramarine coloured Edwardian jacket that sported a black velvet collar and then whipped out an open cut-throat razor from a convenient inside pocket. The razor boy brandished the wicked looking blade in front of the mesmerized teenagers' wide-open eyes. His foul, tainted breath filled the lad's nostrils with the repugnant odour of strong alcohol mixed with tobacco fumes and smokey bacon crisps.

The thug moved in close and personal, so near that Angus could see the blackheads on his pug nose. The Tedzer flashed a whiplash smile and asked a pertinent question. 'Can yer maw sew?' He was implying that if the pair of them stood there gawking for a moment longer he might be inclined to slash their cheeks open, leaving them with his personalised version of the dreaded six inch permanent smile. Something their mothers would have a terrible job sewing closed.

'Hey, Mister,' said Jimmy. 'Look at the flying saucer!'

The Teddy boy looked up to see what Jimmy was jabbing his finger at. Jimmy delivered a penalty kick to the Tedzer's groin like the Scottish Cup Final depended on its outcome. Crumpling to the pavement, the ruffian proceeded to spew his guts up. His similarly attired mates hurried over to see what had happened. Angus and Jimmy were running down the street like a couple of hungry greyhounds in pursuit of a tasty steak tied to a jet-propelled roller skate. Maybe the Teddy boy had only been fooling around, but Jimmy had learned that if someone pulls a sharp chib out, it's better to get the boot in first than suffer some flesh-slicing consequences. Having just broken the Olympic track record for the thousand-yard dash, the two runners slowed down, their throats rough from the abrasive intake of harsh breathing.

'Jesus, Jimmy, what a kick in the baws you gave that fuckin' bevvy merchant. You've probably ruined his chances of ever havin' any kids of his own.'

'Serves the radge right,' said Jimmy. 'My dad says that anybody who pulls a blade on a man is a coward, so I just taught that lanky choob a lesson.'

'You did that, pal,' agreed Angus, patting his mate's shoulder, 'but if his Teddy pals had caught us, they'd have cut us up into strips of streaky bacon. Ah mean to say, you're no' exactly blendin' in with the crowd with that mummified head of yours.'

Jimmy gave Angus a nudge in the ribs with an elbow. 'Well,' he laughed, 'it was you who said I looked like the invisible fuckin' man, so it shouldn't be too difficult to do a disappearin' act.'

Weaving their way through throngs of inebriated revellers, the teenagers headed down Renfield Street and found themselves in the heart of Glasgow, Argyll Street. It was there that they found exactly what they were looking for, big-trouble and lots of it, under the 'Highland Man's Umbrella'. This was the name given to a broad iron-girder railway bridge spanning a section of the street. Its massive trusses were pinned together by rivets as broad as a man's palm. The bridge had earned its name at the turn of the century when people came down from the Scottish Highlands and Islands in search of work in the city. They congregated underneath the railway bridge to exchange information and shelter free of charge from the rain.

Trains rumbled overhead on their way to and from the city's central station. Below, another kind of rumble was about to take place. On opposite sides of the street two rival gangs were shouting provocative insults at each other in a wind-up before battle commenced in earnest.

Approximately eighty men were preparing to go at it with no holds barred. This was to be no square go. Everybody was tooled up for this special occasion and ready to bury some steel. Weapons were a matter of personal choice, the more lethal the better. The overhead glow from incandescent street lamps reflected off the honed edges of a variety of nasty looking implements. Surgeons' hatchets, bayonets and sharpened bicycle chains were held aloft, poised ready to swing into action.

Angus and Jimmy settled into a convenient recessed shop doorway to stay out of harm's way and enjoy the brutal show about to erupt in front of their eager young eyes. One thing was for sure; Jimmy would not be the only one going home with a bandaged head after this spontaneous celebration of violence.

Squadrons of startled brooding pigeons flew from their nests on the overhead girders when loud cries of 'Fleet ya bas!' and 'Tongs ya bas!' cut through the charged atmosphere. The urban gladiators of the 'Maryhill Fleet' and the 'Calton Tongs' charged at each other. They met in the centre of the street and set to it with unbridled savagery.

The first noteworthy incident manifested itself when two grappling opponents crashed through the plate glass window of Watson's, the tailor. Well-dressed mannequins were knocked pell-mell by the helter-skelter movements of the two street warriors, fighting as if possessed by a maniacal fury. They clinched, underwent a metamorphosis and transformed into a chimerical two-headed octopus with flailing tentacles squirting blood instead of ink. After a furious slugging match, they separated and one of them collapsed on to shards of broken glass. His antagonist was not quite finished with him. Taking his time, savouring the pleasure of his triumph, the victor produced a flick knife to carve his initials into the unconscious man's face.

Somebody had been watching out for the fallen fighter because a half brick smashed into the side of blade man's head. He staggered, took two steps forward and fell face first into the street, where the brutal confrontation was ratcheting up a notch or two. Casualties were falling to the ground and groaning in the gutters; human garbage bleeding profusely from wounds inflicted by their enemies.

Angus and Jimmy could not believe their good fortune. Witnessing this barbarous melee of blood letting would fuel their schoolyard stories for weeks to come. The lads' jaws hung slack as they goggled on in astonishment, rapt by morbid fascination mixed with an overdose of adrenaline. The shrill sound of police whistles cut through the noise created by the pugnaciously battling combatants and the two transfixed spectators jumped to their feet. The 'Tarry Hats' had arrived on the periphery of the battleground. Uniformed men pushed their way through knots of bloodthirsty onlookers. In the background, frustrated drivers honked their horns in the build-up of traffic that had been brought to a standstill by the outbreak of gang warfare in the middle of the road. En masse, the bobbies waded into the heart of the battle zone, their weighted truncheons blurring with motion as they smashed down upon the belligerent brawlers' heads and shoulders.

Unity in the face of adversity was how the gang members responded to the onslaught of the boys in blue. Separating themselves from the main event, two rival scrappers set upon a lone policemen. The copper put up a good fight. Wielding his baton with precision and skill, he took out one of his assailants with a bone-crunching blow to the side of his head. Ducking below the bobby's swinging arm, the other aggressor popped up and slammed the crown of his head into the underside of the flatfoot's jaw. With a splintering crunch, the rozzer's teeth came together with such force that they severed off the end of his tongue. Blood streaming from his mouth, he howled in agony, fell to the pavement in shock and curled up in a foetal position. It was a good survival reaction because the hooligan decided to do some kicking practice with his steel toe capped right foot. The thug managed to get one good boot in before one of the fallen bobby's colleagues came to the rescue by playing unhappy camper. Using his truncheon, he hammered the villain's head as if it were a troublesome tent peg. Once the gang fighter was released from hospital after being treated for a fractured skull, he'd spend a few years behind bars contemplating the last time he'd had a kick-about in the free world.

In spite of quite a few policemen hitting the deck, it was predictable who was going to come out on top. Superior numbers plus brute force was to be the winning equation. Sirens wailed like demented banshees as fast approaching Black Marias rushed to the scene with reinforcements. The large police vans were screeching to a halt, leaving the smell of burnt rubber in the air to mingle with the metallic whiff of spilt blood and exhaust fumes. They formed an impenetrable roadblock cordoning off one end of the street. Angus and Jimmy decided to make a run for it – in the opposite direction. Flashing blue police warning lights were creating a stroboscopic effect under the bridge. The running boys' shadows flickered haphazardly off the graffiti-covered walls and concrete pavements in front of them. There was a resounding hollow dong when a distracted Jimmy ran straight into an iron lamppost. He toppled over and landed on top of an unconscious battle victim lying in the gutter with a belly full of stab wounds. The fighter's body cushioned Jimmy's fall but unfortunately this did not alter the fact that he'd broken his nose on the lamppost.

Angus ran back to his friend and pulled him to his feet. 'For fuck's sake, you look like you've got your head wrapped in a Japanese flag.'

Leaning unsteadily against his friend, Jimmy put a hand to the red splotch of blood spreading out from where his nose was hidden underneath the white bandages. He groaned and said, 'Maybe I could get myself into the worst accident section in the *Guinness Book of Records*.'

'Ya stupid numpty,' hissed Angus, looking around nervously. 'The only records we're going to get our names in are pollis wans. C'mon, we've got to get the fuck out of here.'

Halfway up Hope Street they skipped into a back alley and, gasping for air, sat down on some dustbins. Once their breathing settled, they heard passionate moans coming from a darkened garage entranceway. Drawn by curiosity they crept over to investigate. Peeping round the corner into the shadows, they saw an American sailor shagging a prostitute up against the wall. They were locked together like an excited four-legged animal. The sailor's white bell-bottom trousers and underpants were bunched around his ankles. Jimmy nipped back to where they'd been sitting and grabbed a couple of bin lids. Leaping out from behind the corner, he ran up to the back-lane lovers, crashed the aluminium lids together and screamed, 'Yanks go home!'

The seaman dislodged his torpedo, pulled up his pants and set off in hot pursuit of the party-poopers who'd gatecrashed in on his knee-trembling session. He needn't have bothered because his chances of catching the street rats were zero. If anything, the sailor's futile chase had given them the impetus to get up the road more speedily. Cutting over Sauchiehall Street, they ran up a steep hill, sat down on the steps of the Glasgow School Of Art on Renfrew Street and began an animated chinwag.

'Did you see the look on that Yank's face when I clashed my cymbals?'

'I did that,' replied Angus. 'It was as if a banger had just exploded in his arse.'

When it came to describing various scenes from the gang battle, the pair of them spoke in keyed-up, simultaneous outbursts, each trying to outdo the other's recounting of the events that had transpired beneath the Highland Man's Umbrella. They depicted the gang fighters in a heroic light and imbued their street names with awe.

'Did you see that radje, Bobo, chib Big Bannerman from the Tongs?' jabbered Angus. 'The big man went over like a pile of builder's bricks.'

'Och, that was nothing,' countered Jimmy. 'Did you no' clock it when that mad rocket berr, Doddsy, malkied that bobby on the konk with a mallet? What a fuckin' beezer!' Jimmy stood up and gave a physical demonstration of how a policeman looks when he's falling down after being hit on the head with a heavy wooden hammer. He collapsed, rolled down the stairs and across the pavement, and then banged his head against a parked car's bumper. The street seemed suddenly silent. Jimmy lay on his back without moving. He appeared to have stopped breathing. Fearing that Jimmy had done himself some serious damage, Angus jumped over the steps and landed at his side.

'Jimmy, Jimmy, for fuck's sake.' Angus knelt by his friend and gave his motionless body a worried shake. 'Jimmy, wake up. Are you all right?'

Jimmy screamed, 'Aaaargh!'

Angus leapt back and crashed over a pile of rubbish. 'Ya stupid twally,' he complained. 'What a fright you gave me.' Relieved, he pushed himself up from the ground. 'You really had me goin' for a minute there. I thought you were dead or something.'

Jimmy's shoulders shook with laughter. 'That'll be right. I kid you not, it'll take a lot more than a smack on the head to kill me.' He stood up, started walking along the pavement and called over his shoulder, 'Get a move on pal. Ma fuckin' nose is hurtin'. It must be way past midnight and I'm goin' to get it for stayin' out so late with this mummy disguise on ma head.'

'You're no' the only one,' added Angus, hurrying along behind him. 'If that shitehouse Steve's still up, it'll no' be to read me bedtime stories, you can be sure of that.'

At Charing Cross they stood around outside a Jaguar car showroom, their noses pressed up against the cool glass of its display window admiring the latest models.

'I'll bet that thing can do more than a ton,' said Jimmy nodding towards a brand new, bright red E-type, its wire wheels' polished rods gleaming.

'Aye, I'm sure it can but you don't even have the money to pay for one of its tyres.'

'No' right now, like, but one day I will and then I'll buy one.'

'In your dreams, you've got to be rich to buy an E-type.'

'No problem, pal, I'll just have to get rich. It's as simple as that. Hey, what a great night out though, eh? Wasn't it?'

'It sure was. It was absolutely brilliant.'

'So pal, see you Monday, right?' said Jimmy, raising a hand in farewell.

'Aye, Jimmy. See you later.'

Jimmy turned and headed off in the direction of home. As he hurried up the road, his bandages reflected the streetlights' luminosity, his head bobbing on his shoulders as if it were a fluorescent orange football.

★

When Angus had been sitting with Hamish, narrating this particular episode from his adolescent years, he'd paused for a few moments to add some personal reflections on those barbarous times.

'Nowadays,' he'd said, 'concerned parents fret over the impact that violent computer games are having on their childrens' impressionable minds because the graphics are virtually indistinguishable from the real thing. Jimmy and I were young teenagers back then, when we witnessed that brutal gang fight in Glasgow. That was no Play-Station virtual simulation, it was actual. For us two lads, it was great fun, an unforgettable experience. In spite of the fact that we saw a lot of gratuitous violence in our youth, we grew up to be happy, well-adjusted, human beings. If there is a moral to my story, it's that it is all right to let the children play because in the end they'll grow up to be who they're meant to be.'

Hamish protested. 'You are sick. You don't honestly mean to tell me that seeing people being seriously beaten up and stabbed in a gang fight was actually good for your development, do you?'

Angus's shoulders shook as he laughed and then he smiled ruefully, as if he were nostalgic for that bygone era when he and his best friend had watched two gangs of maniacs brutally injure each other. 'Well, not quite, as I was about to discover when I crept into my silent home in Woodside Crescent. I was feeling my way across the living room's pitch black interior towards my bedroom door when the lights suddenly flicked on.' Adopting a strong Glaswegian accent, Angus returned to his story.

'Where the bloody hell have you been?'

It was Steve. Never one to miss an opportunity to get on Angus's case, he'd waited up for him. He was dressed in a check-patterned dressing gown. His embittered eyes had a lot more life in them than the wooden television set's dead screen that he was standing beside.

Angus attempted to placate him. 'I was only out playing, Uncle Steve.'

'Don't you give me this out playing nonsense. Roaming the streets at all hours. Do you realize it is two o'clock in the morning? You were supposed to be home three hours ago. You're mother's been worried sick about you.'

'A'm sorry, Uncle Steve.'

'That's not good enough. I've a good mind to fetch my belt and tan yer bloody hide.'

Angus tried to remember where he'd last seen the blue packet with the skull and crossbones printed on the back of it that contained the rat poison. Steve took the strained expression on Angus's face to be a sign of remorse. He lightened his stance, under the illusion that his threat was having the desired effect. He was also well aware that hitting Rose's son would cause trouble with her and he didn't want that.

'You listen up now, lad. The papers are saying that Glasgow is the most violent city in Britain. Your mother and me don't want anything bad happening to you. You're going to be fourteen soon and you'll get that bike that's been promised to you for your birthday, but no more of this gallivanting around the streets in the middle of the night. Do you hear me?'

'Aye, Uncle Steve, I really am very sorry.' Angus was eating humble crumble because he wanted that bike more than anything else in the world.

'Right then, I'll believe you're sorry when I see it. Talk's cheap as far as I'm concerned. Goodnight, son,' said Steve sitting down in an armchair as he opened a crushed green and yellow packet of Golden Virginia rolling tobacco.

'Goodnight, Uncle Steve, I'm sorry.'

'Aye, aye,' said Steve impatiently. 'Away you go out of my sight.'

Angus lay back in his bed, folded his hands behind his head and watched a kinetic mural of lime-green angular forms dart across the ceiling. The effect was created by the reflected light thrown by passing cars' headlights. He listened to the cars swish by on the street outside. It had started to rain. Off in the distance he heard glass smashing and somebody shouting out. He thought about Steve. 'Maybe he's not so bad and I won't have to poison him after all. He could have grounded me from going out over the rest of the weekend and forbidden me to watch *Doctor Who* and *Danger Man* on TV, but he didn't.'

Raindrops were pattering on the window. The sound triggered a string of associations in Angus's memory. It had been raining one evening when Steve returned from work. The bricklayer had been caught in a sudden downpour and was soaked to the skin. He'd taken off his wet jersey and it was then that Angus saw for the first time the emblems of Steve's reservist regiment tattooed on his thick forearms. In spite of this, Angus did not perceive him as being a real soldier, unlike his uncles Arthur and Alfie back on Iona. The memory of them brought a feeling of warmth to Angus's chest. The sensation faded quickly and was replaced by a chill when Steve's face appeared in his mind. It had a square jaw, vertical anger lines creasing the centre of its forehead and wiry, sand-coloured hair. Jimmy had told him that you have to watch out for people with ginger hair because they're burning on a short fuse and can blow up in your face for no reason at all. Angus smiled to himself, remembering the fun they'd had sitting watching the street battle from the shop doorway. He burst out laughing when he recalled Jimmy clashing those dustbin lids together and the sailor chasing them along the alley. Gang slogans were the last thing he thought about before he fell asleep. There was something about the sound of 'Tongs ya bas' that he found exhilarating.

When he was almost twelve, Angus managed to pass a crucial school exam called the Eleven Plus. He'd studied for a year in preparation for this educational hurdle, not because of his academic aspirations – he didn't have any – but because of his sense of self-preservation. If he failed, he would have been sent to a junior secondary school on Georges Road. All the kids knew that your first day there meant getting lit cigarettes stubbed out on the skin of your back and having your head stuck down a dirty lavatory pot when it was being flushed.

Angus had now been attending Woodside senior secondary for two years. It was much better than Georges Road, but that still didn't mean he liked it. None of the teachers there matched Hitler for pure viciousness, although some of them came close. It was just that they were more skilful in hiding their nasty streaks. His Latin teacher, Mr Pringle, was a stuck-up homosexual who dressed as if he were on his way to Royal Ascot. Every morning Mr Pringle wore a fresh red carnation in the lapel of his dark blue worsted suit. He was squeaky clean and superhumanly mean.

On the last day of the autumn school term, Angus received a belting for what Mr Pringle described as insubordination. Out in the playground Angus's hands were still stinging as he looked around for Jimmy. After enquiring with some of his older friend's classmates he found out that his pal was dogging it. This came as no surprise because Jimmy hated school even more than Angus did, if that was possible. By Friday there was still no sign of Jimmy. Angus went in search of him. When he rang his front door bell, he noticed that the Bradleys' nameplate on the dark green door was missing and had left a blue rectangle where it once had been.

'The Bradleys have gone, son. The flat's empty,' said a cigaretty voice behind him.

Angus turned to face Mrs Knockerbee, the next door neighbour. She was dressed in a torn see-through negligee with a hair net on her head. There was an unlit dog-end in her mouth. The thick makeup on her face looked like pink icing on a cake.

Angus asked, 'What do you mean, gone?'

'Mister Bradley got a new posting with his work. They flitted during the week.' Mrs Knockerbee's soggy cigarette butt dropped to the floor. She bent forward to pick it up, giving Angus a peek at her ample, milky white cleavage. 'Wow,' he thought, 'look at the size of those things. They're nearly twice the size of Linda's.'

'Dover, that's right,' she continued, happy to have her stogie wedged back between her pink lip-glossed chops. 'That's where Missus Bradley said they were going, Dover, in the South of England. Would you like to come in for a cup of something warm, son? Ma man's on the late shift.' She gave Angus a cheerless smile and repositioned her sagging beach balls.

'Ehm … no thanks, Mrs Knockerbee, I have to get home for my supper.'

'Suit yerself, son.'

Back on the street Angus could not believe what had just happened. Not Mrs Knockerbee asking him into her flat, everybody on the block knew she was a slapper, but that his best pal had vanished out of his life just like that. He gave a passing tabby cat a boot in frustration. It yowled and clawed at the air as it flew over some railings.

11

NICOTEENS

In 1966 the Wild West era in the use of psychedelic drugs had begun. John Lennon met Yoko Ono. Bob Dylan crashed his Triumph motorcycle and was rumoured to have broken his neck. Comic genius Billy Connolly was rambling around the Scottish folk circuit and earning five pounds a gig by playing his banjo in a folk duo called The Humblebums. Left-handed guitarist Jimi Hendrix arrived in London to cut his first hit single, 'Hey Joe', and a powerful wave of new rock bands captured the hearts and minds of Britain's youth. Young people started to plan their lives with ideas they'd heard in pop songs. If they were Who fans they began talking about my generation and hoped to die before they got old.

Angus loved rock 'n' roll music even more than fondling Linda MacDonald's double D-cup breasts. Every night he would tune in his tranny and press it to his ear, in the hope of hearing some of his favourite bands' latest hits. Pirate radio stations, broadcasting from ships moored in the North Sea's international waters, played the music. He'd become a Rolling Stones fan. Mick Jagger lent a voice to the thoughts of teenage rebellion in his head, while the notes being produced by Keith Richard's rhythm and blues guitar-playing struck a chord with the hormonal explosion taking place inside Angus's adolescent body.

Apart from the occasional pesky pimple, he was showing signs of developing into a reasonably handsome young man. Long legs were pushing him up to level out at a couple of inches short of six feet. In

157

the face department, his high cheekbones and strong jaw created the illusion of being a few years older. Although his shoulder-length hair was curly, he cut it in a fringe in a vain effort to impersonate his fashion icon, Brian Jones, the flamboyantly dressed guitarist who had founded the Stones. Rose pestered Angus about his hair, telling him it was filthy and disgusting – completely false because a large percentage of what little money he had went on hair care products.

Fashion in general had become an increasingly important phenomenon in Angus's life. All of his favourite groups, The Yardbirds, The Small Faces, The Kinks, to name but a few, were all dedicated followers of fashion. He also wanted to join the Trendsetter Club and wear checked hipster trousers, wide-collared shirts and Cuban-heeled boots, all made readily available in boutiques if one had the money to pay for them. Angus received ten shillings a week pocket money from his parents. A half decent, paisley pattern kipper tie cost two pounds, which meant a month of saving to buy one, but then came the problem of buying a button-down shirt to go with it, costing three times as much.

The latest fashion gear was more expensive in Scotland than it was down south. Everything had to be transported up from London, the city that, during the swinging sixties, was the fashion capital of the world. Carnaby Street, on the edge of Soho, was the hub of the wheel from which the grooviest trends rolled out onto the streets of the U.K. to dress the fashion-crazed youth. Desire, the innovative sister of invention, prompted Angus to embark on a life of petty crime to obtain the money he felt he so desperately needed to become a fab dresser.

It began by taking an early morning job. He worked alongside one of his classmates, Alex Anderson. Alex had told Angus about the part-time job at Macrae's Dairy that had become available thanks to a drunken taxi driver, who'd reversed into a milk delivery boy as he rode by on his bike. An ardent Beatles fan, Alex styled himself on his pop idol, John Lennon, the man he considered to be the leader of the band. At times he went to ridiculous lengths to imitate Mr Lennon. Once a month, accompanied by Angus, he went to Big Nancy's, the ladies hairdresser, to have his thick black curly hair straightened. Angus would sit next to him to have his hair bleached in a vain attempt to make him appear more like his favourite Stone. Alex was constantly trying to impersonate the Liverpudlian accent that, when mixed with his Scottish brogue, came out sounding like an Irishman with a speech impediment who'd drunk one too many pints of Guinness. It was this way of talking that had earned Alex his nickname of Murphy. If Murphy wasn't singing a Beatles number, he was whistling one; during that period it was 'Paperback Writer'.

Murphy was always up to no good and had a tendency to look sly. He was often to be seen champing at the bit as if some unseen force was propelling him to behave in an impulsive manner. At school he'd earned himself a reputation for being a practical joker who enjoyed pulling dangerous pranks on unsuspecting victims. On April Fool's Day of that year he'd used a length of wire cable to tie the exhaust system of the headmaster's car to a lamppost, with catastrophic results. Due to his not wearing a seat belt, the principal's head went through the windscreen when his car jerked to a standstill, minus its exhaust pipe. One of Murphy's knots had gone round the car's drive shaft. Police detectives showed up the next day at school but left none the wiser. Murphy was not a great talker; just as well because he had a habit of rubbing people up the wrong way. If the wrong words were needed at the wrong time, he would be there to blurt them out.

Angus and Murphy liked each other from day one. It was the rebel in each other that brought them together and it would be this rebellious spirit that was to keep them together as close friends for most of their lives.

Macrae's Dairy was situated on Gibson Street, across the road from the park gates where Angus had first met Jimmy Bradley with a piece of wood sticking through his nose. Jimmy had finally gotten around to dropping his pal a line on a postcard showing the White Cliffs of Dover. All it said was, 'Sorry I did not write sooner. I fell off a harbour wall and broke both my wrists a month after I arrived here. Just got the plasters off today. See you later pal, Jimmy.' There was no address and therefore no way for Angus to write back to him.

Beginning at five a.m., every day except Sunday, Angus and Murphy cycled around the city's Kelvingrove area delivering their rattling cargo from large metal crates attached to the backs of their bikes. Winter months, when snow and ice were on the ground, were the most perilous. Going into a skid with three dozen glass bottles full of milk for company had to be avoided at all costs, unless one wanted to do a Jimmy Bradley impersonation. Hundreds of pints of milk had to be delivered before eight a.m. To the sound of milk bottles clinking together, the lads ran up and down tenement blocks' steep stairs collecting empties and dropping off their full replacements. Six mornings a week they raced to beat the clock. If they were lucky, they could double their money into the bargain when some housewives were feeling generous enough to leave a tip under an empty bottle. This was very much appreciated because their employer, Mr Macrae, was a stingy old miser who paid his milk boys a pittance for their hard graft.

A widower, Mr Macrae was so tight-fisted he would never have dreamt of splashing out on a pair of National Health spectacles, even though they cost next to nothing. Instead, he wore wire-rimmed glasses held together by Elastoplast, with enough grease on their cracked lenses to lubricate a rusty bicycle chain. He cut his own hair and rarely shaved because he thought razor blades were a waste of money. All year round he wore dirty woollen gloves, with the fingers cut off, to keep his hands warm whilst piling up his coppers in preparation for hoarding. The grubby penny-pincher was stone deaf and so preoccupied with counting his money that he would have been hard put to notice a passenger jet with its engines on fire making an emergency landing in the street outside his dairy's steamed up window.

Angus and Murphy began to pilfer the occasional packet of cigarettes from the well-stocked shelves behind the dairy's marble-topped counter. Later in the day, the filched fags would be sold in the schoolyard in the form of penny singles. By early spring, the thieving milk boys had graduated from pinching packets to stealing whole cartons. Although Old Man Macrae was no Einstein when it came to mathematics, he did know that one plus one doesn't add up to zero. He cottoned on to something being amiss when one day he spat on his bifocals, gave them a rub on his apron, put them back on his long, pointed nose and discovered his once abundant stock of cigarettes had completely vanished. Mister Macrae was surprisingly decent about how he chose to deal with the culprits.

It was a cold Saturday morning when Angus and Murphy returned from doing their rounds to find two mugs of steaming tea and a plate full of bacon sandwiches were waiting for them. While they were munching away on their greasy breakfast, Mr Macrae sat down beside them, lit up a fag, and blew two jets of smoke out of his hairy nostrils. From a grime-covered radio sitting in one of the dairy's dusty corners came the mournful sound of The Righteous Brothers singing 'You've Lost That Lovin' Feeling'.

'I've a wee bit of bad news for you lads.'

The milk boys stopped chewing and looked up like startled goats.

'What is it boss? Have we won the Golden Milk Bottle award?' asked Murphy.

'What ... what did you say?' asked Mr Macrae, adjusting his wonky hearing aid.

Murphy shouted. 'I said, are you going to give us a pay rise?'

'No, no, no lad,' replied the old miser, 'whatever gave you such an idea? Nothing of the sort, it's quite the contrary in fact. I'm sorry to have to tell the pair of you that I can't afford to keep you on any longer.'

Angus and Murphy took a guilty peek over at the bare shelves, where a solitary packet of Woodbines stood as a silent witness to the fact that the tobacco bandits had been getting very carried away with themselves of late. By employing what were by now the best-dressed milk boys in Scotland, the old skinflint's profits had disappeared into the cash registers of numerous boutiques.

Getting the sack was only a minor hiccup in the duo's burgeoning playground fag sales business. They were already planning their next move. Ascension of the financial ladder was waiting around the corner from Macrae's Dairy in the form of a newsagents shop.

A burglary was planned for a Friday night, just after the pubs came out, when the police would have their hands full with violent drunks and therefore be distracted from the illegal activities of three teenagers. Another youth's talents were required to help carry out the robbery. Raj Gupta was a seventeen-year-old Indian youth who'd left school and taken up employment at his father's garage as an apprentice car mechanic. Murphy knew Raj because his family lived downstairs from him. Mrs Anderson, Murphy's mother, was always complaining about the smell of curry that hung about in the close from Mrs Gupta's cooking. Raj was the first Indian that Angus had any real social contact with. At school, thirty percent of the pupils were Indian or Pakistani, children of the thousands of immigrants who'd come to Scotland after the partition of India in 1947. The foreigners usually kept to themselves, a social norm that was fine with the white kids because the Pakis and Indians had an unpleasant spicy smell about them. Besides, half of them could not speak English. This baffled Angus because it had been quite a task to pass the Eleven Plus examination in order to be accepted into a senior secondary school, yet here were these funny-smelling coloured kids sitting next to him in class who didn't even know how to write their own names.

It was difficult for him not to like Raj because he was one of the friendliest teenagers he'd ever met. The Indian made it his vocation to help everyone he ran into. Raj reminded Angus of a comic book character he'd read about in *The Hotspur*. The story had followed the exploits of a British officer in colonial India in the time of the British Raj. He had an Indian batman whose duties involved a lot more than carrying his superior's luggage. In every episode the servant saved his master's life by skilfully wielding his 'clickey bat' like a club to beat the crap out of the turbaned enemies.

Raj also had a cricket bat, although Angus never saw him use it on anybody's head. He was to learn later that Raj was a first class cricketer. The Indian nearly always had a monumental crescent-shaped grin on his face. His long black hair was parted down the middle. Chubby, he was as strong as a rhinoceros, and looked like a good man to have on your side if it came to a scrap. One physical characteristic that distinguished Raj from his fellow countrymen, and just about everyone else for that matter, was his eyes. They were a luminescent green blue that gave off the impression they would glow in the dark. When Angus first met Raj, he could not help but be fascinated by his eyes. Every chance he got he looked into them. Raj eventually talked to Angus about it. He spoke with a strong Glaswegian accent. 'I see you find my eyes interestin'. My father says that our family has for generations always had at least one person who carries this colour of eyes. Accordin' to him, it stems from the period when Alexander the Great and his armies invaded India. I like my eyes and, more importantly, so do the comely besoms.' Raj Gupta was the only person Angus ever met who called attractive females 'comely besoms'.

The Indian Scotsman had joined them on the robbery because he knew how to break into cars without smashing their windows, hot-wire their ignitions and drive them away. Angus reckoned he just came along for the ride. Judging by his appearance, Raj didn't really need the money. He was as well-dressed as his fellow burglars.

As it turned out, he was the perfect man for the job. At 10:15 p.m. he pulled up outside the newsagents in a brand new Ford Zodiac, a powerful car with a boot as big as a wardrobe. Breaking into the premises was a simple task that went as smooth as a packet of Silk Cut. A dozen cardboard boxes packed with cartons of cigarettes were loaded into the car without anyone on the street paying the slightest bit

162

of attention. The booty was then transported and stashed in a derelict building's basement.

On Monday morning, the real work began when Angus and Murphy started touting their packets of stolen fags in the schoolyard. The other kids were eager to buy, since the cigarettes were being offered at a quarter of the price they were being sold for in the shops. For the first time the nico-dealers were faced with the problem of oversupply.

The teachers at school were starting to become aware that a pall of blue-grey smoke was hanging over the playground during break times and piles of dog-ends were forming mole hills in the lavatories. Also, they could not fail to notice an outbreak of smokers' coughs in their classrooms. Angus and Murphy took time out from their boring studies to establish a cigarette dealing network in half a dozen other schools on the west side of Glasgow. If the trio were not out breaking into tobacconist shops on the weekend, they were going round the pubs on Friday and Saturday nights supplying hundreds of inebriated customers with their cut-price fags. Raj was a fan of the American pop group The Byrds, and their hit song, penned by Bob Dylan, became their theme tune. After a busy night's work, they'd walk home along empty streets singing 'Mr Tambourine Man', their boot heels wandering and their back pockets jingle jangling with spare change.

Angus, now flush with money, was looking very trendy indeed. This was having the desired effect upon Linda, who was slowly but inexorably getting around to going all the way with her expensively dressed boyfriend who'd also bought her a small diamond ring. On a couple of occasions they'd discussed using condoms, even though Linda saw this as a terrible sin. With fluttering eyelashes as long as a cow's, her sad eyes looked across a Wimpy Bar's red Formica tabletop into Angus's as she made the sign of the cross and said, 'I'm scared, Angus. I don't want to go to Hell when I die but, if you can get a packet of those things, I'm willing to risk it because I love you. Do you love me?'

'Ehm … well, ehm … aye, Linda, I do.' He bit into a hot-dog that tasted like it had been vulcanized and added, 'I'll see what I can do about getting the rubbers.'

'Say you love me, Angus.'

He looked at her incredible bazoombers, took another bite on his hot-dog and mumbled, 'I love you, Linda.'

'Holy Mary, Mother of God', she gasped, her eyes brimming with guilty tears.

After that, Linda took to going to confession twice a week to unburden herself. Her priest had taken to making strange grunting sounds on the other side of the confession box as she spoke. She was beginning to wonder if her confessor was going deaf because he kept asking her to repeat some of her sins half a dozen times. At the end of each session the cassocked priest was no longer telling her to do Hail Marys, but urging her to return as soon as possible in order to protect her from what he described as the Devil's temptation. Linda was not quite sure what to make of the leery-eyed priest, but consoled herself with one of her mother's favourite sayings, 'The Lord works in mysterious ways'. Meanwhile, Angus was trying to build up the courage to brass neck it and walk into a chemist shop to ask for a packet of Durex and a tube of spermicide.

On the home front, it was downhill all the way. Angus could barely relate to his mother, and as for Steve, not at all. The couple's honeymoon period was over, but Rose was still besotted with her man. In their free time they were often to be found either squabbling over nothing, or looking at maps of Australia and making plans to emigrate down under. Back then the Australian government was paying people to come and populate the country; not surprising as far as Angus was concerned. To him it sounded like a desert inhabited by fuzzy-haired spear-chuckers, kangaroos and big brown venomous snakes. His uncle Steve made a point of letting Angus know he was not included in their plans by saying, 'It's high time you learned how to fend for yourself.' Steve thought he was being smart when he described the vacuous space that existed between them and Angus as the 'degeneration gap'.

Angus's parents were, of course, suspicious about the source of their son's newfound wealth. It was something impossible for them to ignore, he had clothes in his wardrobe that would have taken Steve a year's overtime to be able to afford. Angus fed them a string of thin lies to disguise the fact that his money came from the wages of sin. For the most part, they accepted his fabrications at face value for convenience sake, not wanting to be distracted from indulging themselves in their very own brew of emotional roller-coaster realities. In short, his parents' apartment had become an insecure perch for him to roost on for a few hours before taking off to where he really felt at home – Glasgow's lively streets.

Murphy had a brain wave; a visit to Mr Macrae to offer him loads of cigarettes at a price he could not refuse. The old miser recognized a good thing when it came strolling into his dairy. From then on, he bought as many cartons as the lads could supply. A family relative with a shop in Greenock had promised to buy as much as the dairyman could come up with.

Business was booming, the Beatles were living in a yellow submarine and Angus had a stash of bank notes hidden under a floorboard in his bedroom amounting to £5,000. This is what Steve earned in three years working as a bricklayer. The fag barons were by this time doing a tobacconist shop every weekend, going as far afield as Edinburgh to seek out new targets. Thanks to Mr Macrae's new role as a tobacco wholesaler, the trio was set to make a packet.

Riding a wave of excitement, Angus surfed into a pharmacy on a Wednesday afternoon after school. 'A packet of spunkbags and a tube of spunk ointment, please,' he said to the young woman with a spotty face serving behind the counter. He'd become embarrassed when the shop assistant said she didn't understand what he wanted. He'd explained and turned scarlet when she'd asked, 'What size?' She'd been referring to what size tube of spermicidal cream he wanted, but he'd thought she meant what size rubber Johnnies he needed. He'd never imagined that he'd be asked such a thing.

'Ehm … eh, normal, please, I think.'

'I'm sorry, sir, we only have small, medium or extra large.'

Angus thought he'd show off a bit. 'Extra large, please,' he said, as cool as a big cucumber. He was surprised when he walked out of the shop with a small packet of condoms and a tube of spermicide as big as a giant salami.

When he arrived home, he locked himself in the bathroom, visualized Linda's breasts and tried on a condom. At first he found the rubber sheath slightly uncomfortable, but once he started masturbating he found that its slippery lubricant had an erotic feeling to it. He became extra hard at the thought of trying one of these things out with Linda, something that was already planned for Saturday, when her parents would be away for the weekend. Just imagining what it was going to be like filled the little sack on the end of the prophylactic.

There was a loud knock on the bathroom door.

'Angus, what are you doing in there?'

'Nothing, Ma,' he gasped. 'I'm just getting ready for the weekend.'

Rose sounded irritated. 'It's Wednesday evening. What are you talking about?'

★

On Friday night the shop-crackers drove on to the main Glasgow-Edinburgh motorway in a stolen Ford Transit van. They were headed for a well-stocked tobacconist's shop in Regent Road, which was situated off one end of Edinburgh's busy Princes Street near to Calton Hill. Raj and Murphy had cased the place a week previously and could not believe what a lucky find it was. One Yale lock to pop, to become a full vanload of ciggies the richer. The vehicle had a radio and Raj tuned it to Radio Luxembourg just in time to catch The Byrds' hit single, 'Eight Miles High'. The song was at least twenty years ahead of its time and described perfectly how the three young bandits felt that evening as they flew along the highway on their way to their next robbery.

As they drove east along Princes Street, Angus pointed towards an illuminated Athenian acropolis on the summit of a large prominence. He asked, 'What's that supposed to be?'

Murphy looked up to where Angus was pointing and answered. 'That's Calton Hill and the monument you see was built as a memorial to those who lost their lives in the Napoleonic Wars.'

'Oh deary me,' snorted Angus, 'I didn't know you were such an educated Archie. How come you know all that?'

'From a history book, stupid, maybe you should learn to read.' Murphy nudged Angus in the side and received a punch in return.

'Pack it in you two,' urged Raj. 'Can't you see I'm trying to concentrate on my driving?' Angus and Murphy snickered.

Raj parked outside the tobacconist shop. The three young men stepped out on to the pavement. A gaggle of mini-skirted teenaged Dolly birds checked them out and giggled. The lads looked more like fashion models than burglars. Dressed in tight-waisted, three-piece 'made to measure' suits with flared trousers and handmade Chelsea boots; they were living mannequins for the latest trends.

When the coast was clear, Murphy began to work on the shop's door with a crowbar. He soon managed to jemmy open the flimsy lock. A loud alarm system went off, startling the robbers and attracting the attention of two bobbies who were cruising the neighbourhood in a squad car. The lads raced for the van. The patrolmen pulled up in the street outside the shop, looked up at the clanging alarm bell and decided it was time to earn their salaries. As the cops were about to get out of their 3.5 litre Rover patrol car, Raj began a spontaneous demonstration of how not to make a quiet and speedy getaway. He rammed into two parked cars and knocked over a lamppost. A crowd of passers-by gathered to cheer on what looked like someone practising for a demolition derby. When Raj finally managed to manoeuvre the large van into position for a clear run at the street, he floored the accelerator and with a loud screech the van shot away, leaving two black lines burnt into the grey asphalt. Zooming through a red light, on the wrong side of the road at a busy traffic intersection, Raj left the stunned cops behind to savour the modern day flavours of burnt rubber and exhaust fumes. The bad taste in their mouths spurred the police into giving chase to the vehicle that was driving into oncoming traffic with no lights on. Following the burglars, on the correct side of the road, the police driver sped through the same red light. It was a big mistake.

Coming in from the right was a ten-ton lorry loaded with potatoes. Patrick Mackracken, the man behind the wheel, had just driven over from Dunoon. He was running late due to having been held up by a Campaign for Nuclear Disarmament rally being held on the banks of the Holy Loch. They'd been protesting against the American atomic submarine base located there, chanting that the Yanks should go home and take their Polaris nuclear missiles with them. When the long-haired demonstrators, who looked like a bunch of over-educated bearded beatniks to Patrick, staged a sit-in on the A 815 he'd had to wait three hours until police reinforcements showed up to arrest the dirty drop-outs. Despite the delay, Patrick was in a good mood; he had a fat pay packet in his back pocket, the lights were with him and he was singing along to Tom Jones on the radio, who was crooning on about the green, green grass of home. In half an hour he'd be home in Leith with his wife Mary. Her lips weren't the colour of cherries, more like bruised tomatoes, but when it came to suction power they worked a treat. After a few lines of whizz on a Friday night, Mary liked to put on her red rubber Mondo Bondage outfit and get down and dirty on top of a plastic sheet spread over the kitchen floor, with a bottle of cooking oil in one hand and a stainless steel triple-ripple butt plug in the other.

Patrick the trucker groaned as he recalled how it felt to have the anal device pulled out of his rectum when he shot his load. He pushed the pedal to the metal. The needle was passing the speedometer's 50 mph mark as he approached a road junction with the green lights burning bright for him. He saw the white police car crossing his path. The roll-up he was smoking fell out of his mouth when he shouted, 'Jesus fuckin' Christ!' and slammed on the brakes. It did not help. The lorry's tyres were screeching and producing clouds of smoke when it crashed into the squad car's front wing. Tom Jones's voice warbled away in the background and Patrick looked on helplessly as his truck sandwiched the cops between itself and a bus full of American tourists taking in the sights and sounds of Bonnie Scotland's capital city by night. So far, so good, it seemed, for the three burglars.

Fortunately for the police officers, they'd been wearing their seat belts, a safety measure that had saved their lives. Apart from one fractured wrist, mild concussion and hundreds of tiny face cuts – making them look like they'd been severely blighted by acne – the two cops were in good physical condition, more than could be said for their patrol car. The Rover was a complete write-off. Their first concern after the accident was what their superintendent was going to say when he found out they'd been involved in a serious road crash after driving through a red light.

The only things left functioning in their crumpled vehicle were a flashing blue light on the roof and the police radio. One of the cops called in a description of the Transit van to police headquarters, requesting an all points bulletin be implemented immediately.

Meanwhile, Raj had sweat dripping off the end of his nose as he set about providing months of work for Edinburgh's auto mechanics and panel beaters by crashing into dozens of parked vehicles, as well as causing various traffic accidents. The city's shocked motorists were making frantic efforts to get out of the way of the battered van that was coming towards them on the wrong side of the road.

'For fuck's sake man!' shouted Murphy, catching a glimpse of Edinburgh Castle's illuminated ramparts behind Raj's head. 'You're going to get us fuckin' well killed.'

'Don't panic, ma friend,' responded Raj. 'Everything's under my control.'

Angus and Murphy exchanged anxious glances as Raj took off a taxi's side mirror and clipped a motorcyclist. The fragmented sounds of shouts, squealing tyres and blaring car horns were sucked into the van through an open side window. Raj drove on to the correct side of the street. By the time the van entered Corstorphine Road, heading west, so had three police cars behind them. They tore past the exit for the city's Zoological Gardens with Angus and Murphy holding on for their lives as Raj demonstrated his non-existent skills in high speed driving. He did however show a lot of potential as a stunt driver. As the speedo passed eighty miles per hour, Raj remembered the gearbox had a fourth gear. The silence was deafening when the van's straining engine stopped screaming after he stepped down on the clutch pedal and shifted up.

Raj wore spectacles for night driving, although they didn't seem to help him see much. He was bouncing off other vehicles as if he were steering a king-size dodgem. His glasses were steamed up from the damp heat of excitement the three young men's bodies were generating. He removed both of his hands from the wheel to give his misty lenses a quick wipe. The stolen van he was supposed to be in control of swerved, sideswiping an oncoming maroon-painted Corporation bus. A few of the double-decker's side panels were torn off in a cloud of sparks accompanied by the sound of an oil drum being crushed under tremendous pressure. Horrified bus passengers looked out the windows, in time to catch a fleeting glimpse of a long-haired Indian youth sitting in the driver's seat of a speeding van using both his hands to clean a pair of specs as he shot by in the opposite direction.

Raj had driven through his eighth red light that evening by the time he returned his attention to the road. He took a firm grip of the steering wheel, blinked rapidly, smiled to himself and said, 'Ah, that's much better,' just before completely losing control of the van. Murphy had switched on the radio and 'The Last Time' by the Stones was trying to blow the loudspeaker out of its mounting when, careening off the back of a parked car at high speed, the van hit the kerb and sent a jarring shock wave through its occupants' skeletons. For a few seconds the Ford Transit was airborne as it flew over the pavement. The three flying van boys joined together as one when they spontaneously roared out a single, unrelenting primal scream. Angus perceived the world to be passing by in slow motion. As he screamed, he glanced out the passenger side window and noticed an elderly man standing on the pavement with his mouth hanging open. He was wearing a dark military jacket with a row of medals pinned over the left breast pocket and holding a leash with a little black dog on the end of it. This was Mr Barry Macrivens, an old age pensioner who was taking his wife Maggie's toy poodle, Foo-foo, out for a walk. When the vehicle ripped past him, Mr Macrivens caught a glimpse of a slant-eyed, open-mouthed face, belonging to a young lad with long hair. 'It's a screaming Jap,' thought Macrivens. Later he gave his eyewitness account to a cub reporter who was following up the story for a local newspaper.

'I was taking Foo-foo out for a piddle when I heard a terribly loud bang, like a cannon being fired. When I looked up, there was a big black van flying through the air. Above the whine of its engine I could hear a horrible scream. It put the fear of God into me because it reminded me of the Japanese troops screaming out 'Banzai' when they attacked our positions in Burma. I was taken prisoner and the Nips tortured me for months. Do you know the little blighters stuck bamboo slivers under my finger and toenails? It's still very painful for me to do anything that requires applying any sort of pressure with my fingertips, like making a phone call. That's why I was relieved to see the police arrive on the scene so promptly. I didn't want to dial 999 and hurt my fingers. Name, rank and number, tha—'

'Excuse me, I didn't quite get that,' said the bored tabloid fodder collector who was writing all this down in shorthand.

'Name, rank and number, that's all the slanty-eyed bastards got out of me.'

'Oh aye, right,' said the reporter, barely able to suppress a yawn. 'It's been fascinating talking to you. Thanks for being so helpful.'

'No problem at all son, I'm always happy to be of service to Queen and country.'

'Right then, thanks once again, Mister Mac—.'

'Here, hold on a minute, son. I haven't told you about how I won these medals.' The old soldier patted his gongs. 'I was awarded this one for—'

'Goodbye, Mister Macrivens.'

Angus was still screaming when he looked away from the old man and saw a brightly lit shopfront. The sound the airborne vehicle made as it smashed through the broad plate glass window and crash-landed on top of a dozen front loading washing machines was horrendous. It was like the entire collection of the BBC's sound effects department being played simultaneously, at high volume, backwards. Many of the refrigerator-white housewives' dream machines crumpled under the impact as the Transit bounced off them and smashed through a partitioning wall, finally coming to a standstill in the shop's main showroom. Looking into each other's shocked eyes, the three youths burst out laughing. Miraculously, Murphy was the only one hurt. He'd banged his nose on the dashboard. Giving his bloody beak a wiggle, he sighed with relief and said, 'Thank fuck it isn't broken.'

Unfortunately for Murphy, this was not to be the case for much longer. Squads of furious policemen were piling in through the devastated shop front. They made their way to the wrecked van. With an effort they managed to prise open its badly dented doors and haul out the three well-dressed youths. Fists flying, Murphy punched a bobby in the mouth. A truncheon swung into Murphy's face. It broke his nose. After receiving the beating of their lives, the three robbers were handcuffed and unceremoniously tossed into the back of a waiting Black Maria.

Battered and bleeding, Angus soon found himself sitting on the cold concrete floor of a white tiled holding cell in Edinburgh's Central Police Headquarters. He felt like a hit and run victim.

'Help me, God. Please help me, King Kong's coming oot o' the chanty pot an' ma cell's full o' vampire bats. Heeelp! I swear I'll never touch another drop again.' The voice of dementia came from the cell next door, where a wino was going though the delirium tremens, after having dined on a boot polish sandwich washed down with a bottle of turpentine.

'Get tae fuck, ya silly auld jakey. It's no' ma fault if you've got the DTs,' shouted Murphy's harsh voice from a cell further along the corridor.

Angus chuckled when he heard his friend voice his complaint. It hurt to laugh. One of his ribs was broken. He rubbed his bruised face, like he was washing without water. Sucking on the back of his teeth he tasted blood and felt movement. Something was pressing against his backside. He put his hand into his back pocket and retrieved the one thing the cops had overlooked when they'd searched him, a packet of condoms. For lack of anything else to do, he opened the small carton, exposing its contents. Examining the glycerine packets, he applied pressure with his fingertips, stained black from fingerprinting ink, and felt the lubricated rubber prophylactics squish around inside.

'Shit,' he cursed through his loose teeth. Just when Linda was ready to go all the way, he'd managed to get himself banged up in jail. Fidgeting nervously with the closed packets, the reality began to sink in that he would not be in need of the kind of protection they provided for quite some time to come.

'Help meeee!' screamed the wino, lending a voice to Angus's troubled thoughts.

12

ANGUS IN BLUNDERLAND

The teenage tobacco bandits were shunted around various cells for a month. The immaculately dressed man in charge of their investigation, Detective Inspector Brown of Edinburgh CID, who had the face of a toad suffering from indigestion to match his personality, ceased his remorseless questioning when he reckoned he had a clear enough case to take it to court. The few old friends who remained loyal to the inspector swore that he'd been a charming fellow when he first joined the force, determined to do some good in the world. Twenty years down the identity parade had changed all that and now he thought everyone who wasn't wearing a uniform was a criminal. As far as Angus and his mates were concerned, he was right. They were charged with breaking and entering into eighteen shops, stealing fifteen vehicles, damaging private property and endangering the lives of the public. Two years the senior of his accomplices, Raj was singled out as being the ringleader, plus it was ascertained that it was he who had stolen the cars and vans.

The trial was held on a rainy Monday afternoon. It only lasted for an hour, because all three culprits pleaded guilty to the charges brought against them. They had little choice in the matter. Highly unprofessional, the trio had left fingerprints on all of their handiwork.

Dressed in black and wearing a lopsided wig on top of receding grey hair, a brooding ruddy-faced judge presided over the court proceedings. Peering through a pince-nez jammed onto his red bulbous nose, the judge's sharp gaze rested on the accused standing before him with heads bowed. He listened with growing agitation as the prosecutor read out a list of charges as long as the arm of the law. Glancing down at the teenagers' unopened social reports on his desk, he pushed them aside like an unwanted meal. He'd already decided these young hoods were going to be majorly rogered. Over the weekend his wife had run away with a younger man and these delinquents were going to pay for it. As he listened, Angus felt like the catalogue of enumerated charges went on forever. When the long-winded prosecutor finally closed his case, he requested that the maximum possible punishment be handed down to what he described as dangerous menaces to society. His Nibs' complexion turned the colour of beetroot as he glowered at the three reprobates, barely able to suppress his rage. Clearing his throat, he took a sip from a glass of water that was almost pure vodka and asked if any of the accused had anything to say for themselves. Murphy could not resist the temptation to blurt out something stupid.

'Aye, your Honour, could you please be so kind as to send us to a women's prison?'

One could have heard a snowflake drop in the cold silence that followed Murphy's request. Angus shivered and shrunk inside his clothes, thinking that Murphy had probably earned them an extra six months inside. The effects of the alcohol on the judge's bad liver began to manifest when he started banging down his gavel as if it were closing time on Wall Street's trading floor. Before sentencing, he described them acrimoniously as being young representatives of a malignant social cancer bordering on pure anarchy. Therefore, he was left with no other choice than to deliver a punishment that would teach them that in Scotland, at least, law and order still ruled the land.

'Mr Raj Gupta, I hereby sentence you to six years in prison.'

Raj gasped and slumped forward in his seat as if he were an inflatable mannequin who'd suddenly lost half his air. Perhaps the judge was seeking inspiration when he glanced over at the courtroom clock; seeing it was 4:30 p.m. he sentenced Angus and Murphy respectively to four years and six months in a young offenders' custodial institution.

No matter how the penal authorities deemed fit to describe the place that Angus and Murphy were sent to, Broomhill Borstal was a prison. Instead of high walls, a heavy-duty chain-link fence, capped by coiled barbed wire, surrounded the conglomeration of grey buildings that comprised the custodial institution. It was to become a permanent home for what, to them, would seem a very long time. When he arrived there, Angus made a phone call to his parents, from whom he had heard nothing since being arrested. It was Steve who answered.

'Hello, this is Steven Boyd speaking.'

'Hi, Uncle Steve, it's me, Ang—' The line went dead. In the course of settling into the idea that he'd lost his freedom, he also had to get used to the fact that his parents apparently didn't want anything to do with him.

Angus had been locked up with a pack of aggressive lunatics for three months when, one grey afternoon, a warder with mocking eyes and a complexion like a bucket of rusty bolts approached him in the exercise yard. 'Macleod, come with me. It's visiting time at the zoo.'

Angus felt extremely nervous when he was escorted to the communal visiting area for the first time since he'd been incarcerated. He threw a wobbler, not when he saw his mother and Steve looking over the smoke filled room towards him, but when the figure sitting next to them raised his head. It was Angus's paternal grandfather, Robert Macleod.

Angus sat down on a plastic chair to join the family reunion. Nobody said a word at first. He glanced around the table. His mother looked crestfallen, Steve disinterested and his grandfather appeared grimmer than the reaper.

Rose played the guilt card first. 'How could you have done this to me and Steve?' Tears welled in her eyes as she blew her swollen pink nose into a well-used hanky.

'Done what, Ma?'

'For God's sake, your name's been in the papers. I've had the police and reporters round at the house asking me all sorts of questions. I feel so ashamed.' She began to sob.

Feelings of remorse overwhelmed Angus. He'd never considered the consequences and social repercussions of being caught and convicted. He'd been too busy planning the next robbery or thinking how he was going to spend the money. Linda's breasts bounced into his mind, but he canned that thought for later when he was alone in a shower stall.

Steve used the opportunity to put in his tuppence worth. 'Now look what you've gone and done to your mother. You're a disgrace.'

'I didn't do anythin'. I'm just listenin' to her goin' on at me.'

'If you're so bloody innocent, what are you doing locked up in a borstal?' asked Steve, his voice rising in anger. 'Take a look around you. It's where you are that's breakin' your poor mother's heart.'

Angus checked out what was going on in the room. About thirty people were grouped around white plastic tables, all talking at once. The buzz of their intense conversations rose into the stuffy atmosphere, which smelled of strong coffee and cigarettes. A couple of blue-shirted guards stood in a corner with their arms crossed. They were having a chat, their watchful eyes roving over the occupants of the green-painted room. His attention returned to the table when his grandfather spoke.

'I always said you were going to be trouble.' Angus looked at his granddad. He'd only met him a couple of times before, back on Iona when he was a kid. His face gaunt and deeply lined, he looked much older now as he bent forward in his seat and leaned heavily on his brass handled walking stick, although his faded blue eyes still contained a spark of vigour. His thick tweed cap was tilted at a rakish angle upon his close-shaved head. Turning to Rose, Rab said, 'Come on, woman, tell him.'

She blew her nose again, took a deep breath and said, 'Me and Steve are emigrating to Australia.'

'What? You're leavin' Scotland?'

'We'll have to do that if we move to Australia, won't we?' chipped in Steve, never the one to pass up a chance to demonstrate his alacrity in the realm of dunderheaded sarcastic wit.

'Not that, woman,' clucked Rab impatiently, 'the other thing we've talked about.'

Dabbing at her flushed cheeks with her handkerchief, Rose had a pained expression on her face when she said, 'Angus, I have to tell you somethin' that will come as a shock to you, but I have to tell you anyway.' She paused for a moment and then blurted out, 'I'm not your real mother.'

Angus's eyes narrowed into slits as he took a double take on Rose. 'What do you mean, Ma?'

'You're adopted, son. Your real ma died on the day you were born.'

'What the fuck?'

'Mind your language, boy,' warned Grandfather Macleod.

Angus was thunderstruck. A dam opened, inundating him with a rushing torrent of thoughts. One of them separated from the others, turned into a question and floated to the choppy surface of his mind.

'But Da was my real dad, wasn't he?'

'No son, he was your real father's brother,' replied Rose. 'Your dad was lost at sea. He went down in a trawler within a few days of your mother dying, as far as anybody knows.'

'Lost at sea, my mother dyin', you've got to be fuckin' joking. Come on Ma, tell me you're makin' this up.'

Rab banged his fists on the table. The screws looked over, but went back to discussing the life and times of Hibs Football Club when they saw it was only some old geezer losing his cool.

'I'll no' tell you again, laddie. Mind your tongue in front of your Aunt Rose. I can swear to you everything she's telling you is God's honest truth.'

'Your grandfather's right,' added Steve. 'How dare you speak like that in front of Rose?' Steve curled an arm around his wife's shoulders as if to say she needed protection from this young maniac. Angus felt heat churning in his stomach. His dislike for Steve was turning into burning hatred. Focusing on Rose, he tried to keep the lid on his inner pressure cooker that was full of pent-up rage and just about ready to explode.

'Why didn't you tell me this before?' he asked.

'I ... I ... thought, I mean your grandfather thought it would be better if—' Rose's voice was blotted out by the shrill ringing of a loud electric bell.

Visiting time was over. Plastic chairs rumbled and squealed as their occupants pushed them back from the tables. Hugs, kisses and warm handshakes were being given and received by the other young prisoners. There were to be no such tactile displays of affection for Angus. Thoughts clattered in his head like steel chisels in a rolling oil drum. He remained seated and looked up in desperation towards the woman he'd always believed to be his mother. Feeling weak at the knees, he willed himself to rise unsteadily to his feet. He pleaded with Rose one last time.

'Please, Ma, I'm beggin' you. Tell me what you've said isn't true.'

The look of sorrow flew from her red-rimmed eyes and the vacuum it left was quickly filled by cold anger. Her raw-edged nostrils flared. 'No son of mine would have ended up in a prison,' she said, steel in her voice.

Steve backed her up. Jabbing a finger at Angus, he said, 'Rose is right. You're nothing but scum, a complete waste of time.'

The pressure cooker inside Angus reached its limits of containment and blew its top. He lost control and a furious force possessed him in an instant. Screaming, he leapt over the table, grabbed Steve by the neck with both his hands and fell to the floor on top of him. Steve Boyd was no pushover. His body reacted violently to being strangled. He fought back with all his might, punching Angus on the side of the head with hands made hard and calloused from years of manual labour on building sites. His young attacker managed to deliver a nut-cracking knee to his groin before being restrained by the guards. Angus was dragged from the room struggling, spitting, and shouting.

'Fuck you. Fuck the lot of ya,' he cursed the world that had deprived him of his freedom.

Angus spat out the last words his visitors were to hear from him before a third warder appeared on the scene and smacked him on top of the head with a billy club. The blow knocked him unconscious. After that tragic afternoon, Angus never heard from any of his three visitors again for the rest of his life.

As a punishment, the borstal's governor had Angus locked up in a cramped cell for two months to discover the rigours of solitary confinement. This presented the angry young man with plenty of time to cool down.

For two days Angus lay on a cot that was bolted to the bare concrete walls of his isolation cell. A pack of wolverine thoughts howled in the tangled undergrowth of his mind. He had no idea how much time had passed because nowhere could daylight enter the cupboard-sized room. Illumination was supplied by a low wattage transparent light bulb recessed into the ceiling behind thick wire mesh. It burned twenty-four/seven. Angus lay on his back, staring up at its glowing element, going over and over the details of what Rose had said to him, trying to fit the jagged-edged pieces of information into the already fragmented picture that formed the jigsaw puzzle of his life.

Now that he thought about it, he realized he bore almost no physical resemblance to Rose. As for Daniel, there could be no doubt that they had shared a number of physical characteristics. This tied in with him being his real father's brother. Angus had the Macleods' broad forehead and big-boned skeleton. His light blue eyes were biological carbon copies of his grandfather's.

Despite feeling more and more estranged from his foster mother, deep in his heart Angus had never stopped loving her. Now that she'd completely shunned him, an old, well-worn expression that Daniel had liked to use came to mind and, although it was becoming increasingly difficult to recall his face, he could still remember his voice saying, 'You don't miss the water until the well runs dry.' It rang shockingly true as he suffered the unexpected loss of Rose's love for him. It was something he would have to learn to live with. His biggest struggle lay in coming to terms with Daniel not having been his real father. Angus's cherished memories of his da were for the most part realistic, albeit somewhat idealised. He knew that no matter what, Daniel, had he been alive, would never have rejected him the way Rose had.

He began to ask questions that had no chance of being answered. What had his real parents been like? What had they looked like? How had their voices sounded? It was such thoughts that robbed him of the solace of sleep during those first days in solitary. After forty-eight hours, exhaustion finally took him to a place where he no longer existed and the burden of individual worries dissolved into the darkness.

He awoke the next day when a uniformed guard entered his cell carrying a plastic tray with a plastic bowl of potato soup on it.

'How you doing, son?' enquired the apparently friendly screw. Angus was trying to remember where he was as he sat up on the edge of the cot rubbing sleep out of his eyes with balled fists.

'I'm okay,' he answered, but the guard didn't hear it because the heavy door had already closed behind him. A key turned in its lock with a reverberating clatter of metal as oiled tumblers slotted into place.

Angus was still contemplating the bowl of soup five minutes later when he heard the spy-hole in the door slide open. Looking up, he caught a glimpse of an eyeball and then the small hatch slid closed with a dull clunk. He realized they were checking to be sure he didn't try to top himself with a bowl of soup. Angus never once entertained thoughts of attempting suicide during his time in solitary, although there were a few hours when he'd thought he was going insane. He soon settled in to the reality of life in an oversized concrete coffin.

The idea of exercising to keep fit had never before occurred to Angus. He was always in A-One physical condition with not a gram of fat on his body. For lack of anything else to do, he started to perform a few push-ups and sit-ups to pass the time. He found out later that there was a law that said every prisoner was allowed one hour of fresh air each day. That page of the rulebook must have been torn out and thrown away in that particular institution because he did not leave his cell for two months. There was a small sink recessed into a corner with a button set in the wall that supplied a trickle of water if he kept his thumb pressed hard against it. In the other corner was a squat-down toilet that made gurgling sounds and every once in a while delivered some gas into the room that smelled like rotten eggs. Screwed to the wall was a warped rectangle of shatterproof polished plastic. The dim overhead light bulb gave off enough illumination to see a distorted shadowy reflection in this suicide-proof mirror. Even if a prisoner felt like attempting to take his own life, it would have been well nigh impossible unless he wanted to bash his head open on the graffiti-covered walls.

After a fortnight, he was up to three hundred sit-ups, push-ups and crunches a day. Two weeks later he'd graduated to a thousand of each. If the warders peeped through the spy-hole and saw he was not lying on his cot, they didn't enter the cell, delivering his meals instead through a hatch at the bottom of the door. He started to make a point of standing up when he heard the screws coming with his food so that they did not open the metal door. He found their presence disturbing. In his book, anyone who wanted to earn money by locking other people up was below contempt.

One day, a month into his time in solitary, he'd just finished a strenuous set of push-ups that involved launching himself off the floor and clapping his hands in mid-air, when his lunch was pushed through the hatch. Apart from feeding his hunger, the meals helped to gauge what time of the day it was. Not that it made much difference, but in isolation little things can become very important to a prisoner, so as not to become too alienated from the world that he will one day have to return to.

Whoever it was that had delivered the meal had obviously taken pity on him because, rolled up beside his bowl of soup, two slices of doughy white bread and cup of strong tea, was a copy of *Playboy*. Unrolling the glossy mag, he became instantly erect as he came face to face with Miss December. So starved was he for sensory input that the busty pin-up girl looked three-dimensional to his fascinated eyes. He could have sworn he heard the sexy paper lady whispering to him.

Twenty-four exhausting hours later, Angus threw in the sperm-stained towel. When he finished lunch, he returned the magazine when a warder knocked for him to pass the tray out through the hatch.

No longer satisfied with his basic callisthenic exercises, he began to develop more complex movements to work on different muscle groups. One evening while sitting on the edge of his cot, tensing his biceps and delighting at how firm they were, his cell door swung open. Framed in the doorway was the Governor flanked by two uniformed guards.

'Well, prisoner 2025, have you learned your lesson?' asked the autocrat, the scent of his cheap aftershave wafting into the cell. Angus stood up and took a deep breath. He almost spat in the man's piggy-eyed face and told him where to shove his lessons, but didn't for one simple reason: he was looking forward to seeing Murphy.

'Right then, lad, out you come,' said one of the screws, stepping to one side and motioning for Angus to leave his cramped environment. The fizzing fluorescent tubes in the windowless corridor dazzled Angus and the sour smell of sweaty armpits, dirty socks, and disinfectant assaulted his nose. He turned and looked back into the dark cave that had been his home for the last two months. He smiled. In a way, he'd really quite enjoyed his spell of solitary. He took a mental note to do something in order to be sent back there if he needed a break from the tedium of life in the big tank.

'Get that smile off your face, 2025. We haven't got all day to stand around waiting for you while you enjoy the scenery,' said the Governor. Angus felt like punching his fist through the prison boss's smug face, but he'd finally started to take control of his emotions and felt a subtle sense of power in discovering that he was no longer so easy to manipulate.

As he approached his old cell, Angus felt like a man coming home to his family after a long absence. The grey-painted metal door was ajar. When he peeped inside, sure enough, there was Murphy the bookworm lying on his cot reading *One Flew Over the Cuckoo's Nest.* Angus pulled open the door and his cellmate lowered his hardback.

'Good book, Mister Macmurphy?'

'Yeeeah! Welcome home, Angus.'

'It does feel a bit like that. How you doin', Murph?'

'I'm doin' all right,' replied Murphy. His voice rose a notch. 'Jesus, what have they been feeding you in solitary? Nuclear fuel rods? You look like Charles Atlas.'

Angus smiled at the thought of being compared to the godfather of modern-day bodybuilding. He sat down on the narrow bed opposite his cellmate. 'So what's new, pal?'

'What's new? You're as white as the Pope's dick and you've got huge muscles, that's what's new. How did you manage that?'

'Och, all I did was a few push-ups.'

'A few fuckin' push-ups my arse. You look amazing. Come on, tell me. How did you do it?'

'Discipline.'

'Will you teach me?'

'Of course I will,' replied Angus in between chuckles. He reached over and gave his mate a friendly jab in the side. Murphy winced from the unexpected physical contact.

'What's up with you? You're no' gettin' soft are you?'

'Naw, nothin' like that,' replied Murphy pulling up his regulation lime green tee shirt with a bright orange band round the collar. 'Look at this.'

Angus was shocked to see that his friend's rib cage was covered in dark blue bruises.

'How the fuck did that happen?'

'I got jumped in the shower room last week by Jamie Kilroy and some of his goon squad. I refused to pay him his fuckin' protection money. I didn't stand a chance.'

Jamie was a tough street kid who came from Glasgow's notorious Gorbals slum area. He was inside for nearly stabbing a man to death and ran the prison like a feudalistic barony. The guards let him do as he pleased because his father, Jack Kilroy, was a well-known gangster who controlled Glasgow's Southside.

'What's the time?' asked Angus.

'Seven thirty.'

Lock-up was at eight p.m.

'I'll be back in a minute.'

'Angus, wait. Don't—'

He was gone before Murphy had a chance to blink. Angus returned ten minutes later. There were bloodstains on the front of his tee shirt.

'Fuckin' hell,' exclaimed Murphy. 'What happened to you?'

'Nothing,' replied Angus as he sat down on the cell's only chair, nursing a pair of chipped knuckles. 'But somethin' happened to Jamie fuckin' Kilroy's face. He'll be payin' us protection money from next Friday on.'

'For fuck's sake, Angus, you've just been let out of solitary and you're in a fight within half an hour.'

'It wasn't a fight. Kilroy's all talk, I had the fucker beggin' for mercy in one minute flat and I stuck the head on that fat prick he calls a bodyguard as well.'

'What's come over you? You're like Desperate fuckin' Dan in a bad mood.'

'All that's changed is that I'm no' takin' shit from anybody anymore.'

The two friends sat in silence, staring at the white walls as if they were windows to the outside world. Out in the corridor a guard was closing and locking the cell doors. Then theirs was slammed shut and a key turned in its lock. The prison sounds brought the two friends back to their situation.

'Angus?'

'What?'

'It's good to have you back, man. I fuckin' well missed you, you know that?'

'I missed you too, Murphy. It feels good to be together again, doesn't it, pal?'

'It sure does, Angus.'

They stood up and embraced each other. It was a manly, warm-hearted hug, which brought tears to Angus's eyes.

Angus and Murphy were never bothered again by any of their fellow inmates. It hadn't taken long for them to assess the lay of the alien world they'd been banished to and it soon became so familiar that it felt to Angus like he'd been there for years rather than months. Inside the confines of the fenced-in prison compound, it was survival of the fittest and soon the other prisoners knew that he was the best fighter in the place. Nobody else had ever dared to take on Jamie Kilroy. The following Friday, Jamie sent one of his lackeys round with his protection money. And so began a routine, involving weekly payments, that was to continue until Jamie was released a year later. He was granted six months off for good behaviour by the parole board.

The two friends watched the months pass slowly by as if adrift on an ocean of time in a boat going nowhere.

Raj Gupta was locked up in 'D' hall in the Bar L (Barlinnie Prison), on the outskirts of Glasgow. Raj kept Angus and Murphy up to date by writing letters. Going by his weekly ten-page diatribes on the 'Riddre Hilton', as he referred to the house of detention, it was the most agonizingly boring place on the planet. A hellhole of misery, the deprivations the inmates lived with were designed not only to dispossess a man of his liberty but also his dignity and self-respect. He was locked up with a recidivist called Johnny McBride. Illiterate and an alcoholic when he was out on the street, the reoffender had spent twenty years of his life behind bars for committing petty crimes, the most serious of which was stealing money from gas meters. According to Raj they'd become good friends. This was just as well, seeing as how they had to spend twenty-three hours of each day petered up, with only each other for company, in a small cell with a circle worn into the floorboards from a century of pacing and a plastic chamber pot in a corner that had to be slopped out every morning. Fresh air breaks took place in a tennis court-sized, walled yard along with hundreds of other prisoners. Raj had the right colour of skin to attract xenophobic hostility and the right size to limit racist aggression to the occasional gob of spit on his back. It was boredom that was the real enemy, hence his long, monotonous letters.

Angus and Murphy had read detailed accounts about Raj and his cellmate's chess marathons. Some of their matches went on for days on end without sleep. This was made possible by snorting lines of the amphetamine sulphate powder that Johnny kept secreted in a piece of rolled up plastic wedged behind his top lip. If Raj wasn't playing chess or writing to his friends he kept himself busy by helping Johnny cover his body in prison tattoos. These designs were created with a pin and the ink from different coloured ballpoint pens. Raj spent six months filling in a chest tattoo of a big red rooster. This image was so bizarre it gave Raj nightmares, which always ended with him being chased by a belligerent red cockerel. He persevered with the tattooing because it required concentration and thus was a good way to kill time.

It was through the jail mail connection that Angus received word that Linda MacDonald was getting engaged to Mark Simpson, one of Raj's old weekend cricket-playing friends. Angus fell into a depression for a couple of days after he read this, even though Linda had never bothered to send him so much as a postcard in the past twenty months. He'd often fantasized about how it was going to be when they were together again. He added an extra two hundred push-ups to his exercise programme and stopped himself crossing the border into a state of bitter melancholy.

Part of the prison system's policy was to provide training initiatives for the inmates. It was thought that by teaching the young prisoners some basic skills, they would have a better chance of gaining employment upon their release. To entice the young men into these courses, there was an added incentive of a small cash reward. It was the £2 a week hook that caught Angus and Murphy. They studied and applied themselves to learning the spark-filled trade of a welder. Their newfound wealth was invested in Murphy's skills as a red-hot poker player. When it came to seven-card stud, he was unbeatable. Every once in a while fights broke out around these card games but nobody said a harsh word to Murphy because standing right behind him, watching his back, was 'Mad Boy' Angus, and nobody wanted trouble with him. The guards viewed violence as par for the course and rarely intervened unless somebody used a blade.

The warders spent most of their working hours behind the safety glass of their office windows. Angus despised the screws, most of whom had a vocabulary of twenty words or less. To him they were the real prisoners in the institution.

Raj had received the longest prison sentence of the three, yet it was he who was released first on parole, because his father guaranteed to give him his old job back in the garage. Two years and six months after the judge's gavel banged down, Raj Gupta was once more a free man who, twice a month over the next year, had to go and talk to an extremely bored-looking probation officer. Murphy followed six weeks later. He was freed on the day an American space-cowboy performed a giant leap for mankind on the surface of the moon. Angus had to wait out another two months, not because he was a tough, young unrepentant criminal who had absolutely no respect for authority, but because he'd made the mistake of displaying what is seen to be the most dangerous quality a criminal can have – intelligence. Reports had been written about Angus Macleod's skills as an organizer. Angus had, on several occasions, marshalled the inmates to form meeting groups in order to demand improved living conditions. As a result the young offenders were, much to the governor's scorn, eating more nutritious food, reading contemporary books and enjoying more sports activities.

Finally the day of his release arrived. Angus picked up a brown paper bag and tipped its contents out on to the supervisor's desk. A packet of condoms, a picture of Linda Macdonald's smiling face, a Yale key, some small change and the clothes on his back were his only worldly possessions. Linda's photo was torn in half before being deposited in a waste paper basket. The key, condoms and coins went into his pockets. A guard led him outside and opened the main gate.

'See you when you get back, son.'

Angus stopped and looked at the screw for a moment. It was a sunny morning. The strong sunlight outlined the blue-uniformed man in sharp contrast to the grey buildings in the background. Badly out of shape, the guard's face was the colour of old newspapers and home to about as much emotion as an empty goldfish bowl. He was breathless from pushing the reinforced aluminium gate aside. Angus suddenly felt a mixture of contempt and sympathy for the man who stood watching him with eyes as lifeless as pebbles.

'I don't think so, pal,' said Angus taking a step towards him, 'but you, you'll be here for the rest of your life until you retire, if you don't drop dead from a heart attack first.' He spat to one side, and then fired off his parting shot. 'In fact, I'm havin' a right fuckin' job believing you were ever alive.'

Angus turned and left the guard to his duties. There was a reassuring metal clunk when the gate swung closed. He took a deep breath; the air smelled of freedom, fresh with the hint of a gardener's fire upon it. He stretched his arms, causing the seams on the back of his suit jacket to split apart. Looking down at his trouser legs, they were three inches too short. The whole suit was a few sizes too small for him but in that moment he did not give a damn because it was August 1969. He was seventeen, a free man, and it felt great to be alive.

Walking along the pavement in the direction of the bus stop, Angus started singing the Rolling Stones' 'Satisfaction' at the top of his voice. When it came to the 'Hey, hey, hey' part, he pumped his arms in the air. There were a few people standing around waiting to catch the bus into Edinburgh. They gawked at the sight of a muscular youth, apparently drunk, singing out loud and dressed in clothes that obviously didn't fit him. Oblivious to the stares directed at him, he was still singing when he stepped off the train at Glasgow's Queen Street station.

Angus had learned his lesson well within the rigid boundaries of prison life. He'd made a huge blunder entering into the world of crime, totally unprepared for the repercussions that came with being caught.

186

In future, if he was going to break the law, he would do everything he could to avoid capture.

There was a lot of lost time to be made up for. He'd done enough floor-mopping and shower stall masturbation to last him for a lifetime. Angus was two years late for the 'Summer of Love' and number one on his list of priorities was to lose his virginity as quickly as possible.

13

LOVE AND PEACE

It was difficult at first to believe what he was hearing. Hamish knew his brother would have described it as synchronicity, because he believed that this kind of simultaneous occurrence could in no way be coincidental. This did not prevent Hamish from perceiving the sound as uncanny. Perhaps an unconscious sensory receiver had picked up on the song that Angus had told him he sang on the morning he'd been released from prison over thirty years ago. Whatever the case might be, there was no mistaking the distinct chord sequence of 'Satisfaction' by the Rolling Stones, coming from somewhere in the distance.

The music was growing louder. Sir Mick Jagger's voice could be heard delivering the lyrics to the classic sixties anthem of discontent. Bending forward, Hamish turned his head to the right. He could make out the shadowy form of a boat hugging the coast and heading in his direction. Slapping the waves, its pointed prow threw up water that shone with white phosphorescence. He could distinguish the throaty growl of a powerful outboard motor penetrating through the music.

When the craft was a hundred metres from him, Hamish raised his fingers to his mouth to produce a loud piercing whistle. The helmsman must have had ears like a dog, because when the boat was almost directly in front of Hamish, he cut the engine and switched off the music. Now that the vessel had drawn level with him, only a stone's throw away, Hamish recognized it as a longtail. These narrow boats, common in Southeast Asia, are so named for the exceptionally long propeller shaft that extends back from the large outboard motor mounted on a pivot in their stern. This makes the longtail the perfect craft for manoeuvring in sometimes-shallow waters because by leaning on the motor, the propeller can be lifted out of the water with ease when obstacles beneath the surface are encountered.

Silhouetted against the moonlit sea, the boat was now close enough for Hamish to see three people aboard: the helmsman, a seated figure in the middle and, in the prow, a man wearing a baseball cap.

A powerful searchlight came on, its beam directed towards the beach. When it spotted Hamish, the light stopped moving. Staring into the glare, he began waving his arms in the air, so carried away by his enthusiasm that he almost stood up. He remembered where he was and thus prevented himself from being blown into flying, burning bits. The people in the boat were calling to him.

Hamish hollered back. 'Over here, I'm over here! Help me! Heeeelp!'

He shaded his eyes with his hands to see the fishermen more clearly. Blood throbbed in his neck, driven by an excited heart pounding out a techno beat on his eardrums. A few deep breaths succeeded in slowing down his pulse enough to let the Cambodians' voices filter through. They were shouting, 'Farang, fak off, fak off America!' and laughing.

Their words thudded into Hamish's chest like ice-cold darts. With a wet growl, the boat's outboard motor started up again. Music came back on, played at an even louder volume than before. God must have been out for a smoke, leaving the Devil to run things, because the being in charge of the world in that moment had a wicked sense of humour. Mick Jagger's plaintive voice floated over the water singing 'You can't always get what you want.' Hamish knew the song's lyrical hook of getting what you need in life, from hearing it on a classic rock radio station that he often tuned into back home in Scotland. Considering where he was, the rock ballad sounded perversely ironic to his oversensitive mind

The longtail surged off, continuing on its course along the coast. Hamish watched the craft's progress until a passing cloud crossed in front of the moon to reduce the light, making it impossible to differentiate the longtail's form from that of the glimmering sea. The rumble of the engine faded and merged with the sounds of small waves slapping onto the shore. Still, he could hear snippets of music floating back to him. It was choral music. He remembered that the song ended with the voices of the London Bach Choir.

Hamish felt like a man lost on a mountain road during the night, when suddenly a car drives by with its headlights on. For a moment, the gloom is thrown back and he can see where he is. Hope flares in his heart, but when the car disappears around a bend, he is left facing a darkness that has become even denser than it was before.

Hamish's hopes of being rescued had spiralled out of control; only to be dashed on the rocks of the Cambodians' shouted insults. To them, he must have appeared like a crazy foreigner on the beach. How were they supposed to know he was in a life-threatening situation? All very logical, but Hamish still hung his head in despair. 'What ya neeeed, awwww yeah', Jagger's voice haunted him, buzzing around in his head like a lyrical wasp. His mind returned once more to its usual programme of forming associations. A rolling stone gathers no moss, rolled into Bob Dylan's 'Like a Rolling Stone'. With shocking clarity he realized what the master bard had been driving at when he'd asked how it felt to be left on one's own, a stranger with no idea of how to find his way home, like a …. Hamish had to get away from his mind or he would go mad listening to it.

Having managed to forget about the landmine for some time, the dreadful object was now making its presence felt with increased intensity. His backside was almost without sensation, although not quite numb enough to get rid of the pressure of the detonator button pressing into his flesh. His soul reached out to reconnect with his twin brother's. Music had never been a great source of inspiration in his own life, whereas for Angus, it had been for some years the fulcrum of his existence.

Glasgow, Scotland, the summer of '69.

'Honky Tonk Woman' by The Rolling Stones had been topping the pop charts for five weeks. Those weeks had, for Angus, been an angst-ridden, strangely disconcerting period of time during which he'd struggled to rise above feeling like an extraterrestrial misfit who had just stepped out of a black hole and wandered into the bright light of the so-called normal world.

After he had been released from the young offenders' institution and the novelty of being free again wore off, it came as an unpleasant surprise to find himself living through an intense period of social alienation. His dreams of freedom had quickly evaporated in the intense heat of the friction produced by rubbing up against life's hard realities. At times he felt more uncomfortable on the outside than he had on the in, to the point of missing the orderly routine of prison life.

In middle age, viewing the past through the prismatic reflection of hindsight, Angus would acknowledge the value of the time he'd spent in prison as having been beneficial for him in terms of learning personal discipline. As many who have lost their physical freedom will declare, there is no place quite like a prison cell for studying philosophy. Angus was no exception to this perk, in that falling foul of the law and being forced to relinquish control over his external circumstances, he had in turn learnt three fundamental truths: that the world is a mirror of one's inner state; that life is what one makes of it; and that this aphorism is a lot more profound than it sounds. At first it was not easy for Angus to shoulder the burden of responsibility for what happened to him and how he chose to view it. This psychological weight built up his inner strength and it soon became apparent to him that blaming others and his surroundings for how he felt only served to weaken him. Looking back, he would recognize that time in his life for what it was – a trigger-point from where the old Angus disappeared and the new Angus started to materialize.

When Angus had adjusted to the beginning of this new chapter in his life, one of the first things he did was to go round to his parents' old basement apartment and ring the doorbell.

Dressed in a pink plastic housecoat, a plump middle-aged woman answered the door. She had a lime green mudpack on her face, a thin slice of cucumber over one eye and, clutched in her left hand, a red ball of wool with two plastic knitting needles pushed through it. Angus had to bite his lower lip in order to prevent himself from bursting out laughing. He looked down to her feet and noticed she was wearing a pair of fluffy pink slippers with glass eyes stitched on to them. They looked like radio-active rats.

'What can I do for you, son?'

'Good morning, Missus,' he glanced at the brass nameplate screwed onto the doorframe, 'Missus Puddock. I used to live here with my parents. My name's Angus.'

The housewife cocked her head and spoke like a human parrot. 'Angus ... Angus ... Angus, that will be Angus Macleod. Am I right?'

'Aye Missus, you are that. So as I—'

'Are you in the army or something?' she asked, looking at his dark blue nineteenth century cavalryman's jacket adorned with gold braid and fastened with shiny brass buttons.

'Naw, I'm not. So as—'

'Would you like to come in for a cup of tea, son?'

'Thanks, I'd love a cup of tea.'

Over a fresh cup of tea with too much milk in it and a plate of chocolate biscuits, Angus explained to the housewife that he'd left some important papers in her apartment. He asked if she'd be so kind as to let him look for them.

'I'm not so sure about this son,' she said. 'I haven't noticed any papers in the house that don't belong to me.'

'I'm no' surprised, because I hid them.'

'Hid them,' she repeated pursing her lips, scepticism entering her mind. 'Why did you hide them?'

'Because they were important.'

'Oh, I see. Well, son, I don't know about this. It all sounds a wee bit strange to me.'

'I can understand that, so I'll give you fifty quid to help you overcome the strangeness of the situation.'

'Fifty pounds?' Mrs Puddock's eyes sprung open at the thought of such an amount of money. The slice of cucumber fell out of her right eye and splashed into her teacup. Angus gazed up at the picture of Jesus that was hanging on a wall. The good shepherd stared back with soulful eyes. He looked like he'd just had a heart transplant.

'Help ma boab, if you put it like that son, please be my guest. Away you go and look for your important papers. I'll get back to my knitting. My casa is your casa, as they say in Mallorca.'

'Cheers. I was hoping you'd say that,' said Angus, wondering what a casa was. He stood up and walked through to what had once been his bedroom. It felt odd to be back in there after so much time had elapsed. He shrugged the sensation off as he lifted a carpet and, using a penknife, prised up a loose floorboard in a corner. The money was as he'd left it. Removing a black plastic bag from his jacket pocket, he placed the wads of bank notes in it, keeping the eyes on the back of his head peeled in case Mrs Puddock became curious. He pushed the plank back into place and then stuffed a handful of blue fivers into his inside pocket.

When he returned to the living room, Mrs Puddock was seated by a sewing machine, blowing smoke out the side of her mouth. She appeared almost hypnotized. Head slumped; she was staring blankly at the curling threads of smoke rising up from the tip of her cigarette. Through a filter of dirty smudged glass, a yellow shaft of Glasgow sunshine shone down into the basement room, highlighting clouds of grey smoke swirling around her. She snapped out of her trance when she heard Angus approach and, raising her head, looked up at him. She smiled, sending cracks through the dried gunk on her face.

'Would you like another cup of tea, son?'

'No, but thanks anyway.'

She looked at the bulky plastic bag. 'So you found your important papers?'

'Aye, I did that. Here ye go.' Angus counted out ten crisp five pound notes and handed them over.

'That's an awful lot of money to be giving me for a carrier bag full of papers.'

'No problem, I just had a wee win on the pools, so a'm well flush the now.'

'Don't tell me, you didn't, did you? My man did the pools for donkey's and he never won a penny.'

'Well, he'll just have to keep trying. You can't win if you don't play.'

'That's very true son, but I said he did. You see, ma man died of cancer nine months ago. God rest his soul.' She looked up to the picture of Christ with his bleeding heart exposed, raised a hand to her left breast and stood up. 'Listen son, if you need to come looking for any more papers just pop round. I'm always happy to oblige, so I am.'

'That's very nice of you, Missus Puddock. If I remember anything else, I'll come by. Sorry to hear about your husband. See you later then.'

Angus offered his hand. She gripped it and then wouldn't let go of it. She was staring into his eyes with a deep meaningful look that he found difficult to fathom. Suddenly, understanding dawned on him.

'Are you still missing your husband?'

The housewife's eyes glistened. She gave a wan smile to show she wasn't offended by her young visitor's direct question. 'Yes son, you could say that. I think about my Sandy every minute of every day. I don't know if I'll ever be able to come to terms with the loss.'

She sniffed and then let go of Angus's hand. 'Cheerio then, Mister Macleod, it's been very nice to meet you.'

Angus had a lump in his throat as he walked up the stone steps that led to the pavement outside. 'Fuck it!' He turned around, went back to the door and, reaching into his plastic bag, pulled out about a thousand pounds and stuffed it through Mrs Puddock's letter box. He hurried back up to the street and, after walking a couple of blocks, deposited a Yale key into a gutter drain's murky depths. He was glad that the key was no longer of use to him, thanks to Mrs Puddock's cooperation and lack of guile.

Walking down the road with a carrier bag full of cash at his side, his exuberance bubbled over. He began to sing an old American dance song that had been covered by the Beatles and the Stones, 'Money (That's What I Want).' That's what he'd wanted also and now he had it, plus he'd done his good deed for the day.

The winds of change had blown into Glasgow and deposited flower power's seeds between the cracks of the city's dirty, litter-strewn pavements. Those seeds soon germinated and began popping up all over the place like magic mushrooms.

When Angus had first observed a group of hippies dressed in clown-bright kaftans wandering down the road with beatific smiles on their stoned faces, he'd written them off as 'a bunch of fucking fairies'. He began to lighten up when he lost his virginity at the top of a pair of delectable quivering thighs belonging to Jenny, an advocate of love and peace.

Angus met Jenny one evening in the State Bar, a public house he frequented, just off Sauchiehall Street. He was standing at the bar nursing a pint of Guinness, feeling sorry for himself because his mates were out with their girlfriends and he was alone. He was thinking about Linda and how it might have been if she'd waited on him. His mood was reflected in the background music. The Animals were playing 'I'm Crying'. Eric Burdon's blues soaked voice delivered evocative lyrics so vivid, the band should have been awarded an Oscar for best screenplay.

'A double gin and tonic with lots of ice, please.'

A silky female voice beside him had ordered the drink. He smelled its owner before he looked at her. She was wearing enough patchouli oil to stock the perfume section in a head shop catering to the growing hippie population's desire for strongly scented fragrances.

Finding a lover does not always depend on personal efforts. In Angus's case, it simply happened. When their eyes first locked in to each other's, a synchronicity occurred that would shape their destinies for some time to come.

Angus stared down into a pair of honey-coloured eyes filled with wildfire. There was so much ardent spirit contained within those flaming orbs that had their full force been unleashed, the State Bar would have gone up in smoke and been burnt down to its foundations in a blazing inferno. The woman blinked, avoiding such an eventuality.

She was of medium height, in her mid-twenties, with unbound, reckless, long wavy hair hanging in golden tendrils down to the mid-point of her back. There was something of his foster mother Rose in her overall appearance and therefore he did not see her as being beautiful, however he did feel strongly attracted to her. Her face was perfectly made up and glowing with health. A smile played upon her full lips that he found difficult to comprehend: amused, curious, hungry or perhaps seductive. Whatever was behind them, they certainly looked alluring. Her cheeks were slightly concave, with a small mole at the corner of her right eye accentuating her unblemished olive skin. He found out later that her mother was Italian. His first impression was that she was perhaps Eurasian because of her slanted eyes. In fact, this had nothing to do with her parentage, and everything to do with being permanently stoned out of her mind on hashish. The layers of her loose, emerald green, crushed-velvet dress, embroidered waistcoat and Afghan coat made it difficult to gauge what kind of figure lay beneath them. Angus was sure that if a miracle happened and he was allowed to find out, he would most definitely not be disappointed.

Jenny had noticed Angus before. Tall with shoulders three feet wide, he'd caught her roving eye a week earlier when he'd removed his jacket at the bar to display sculpted biceps under a tight tee shirt. It was his military jacket that had really grabbed her attention. It was the ultimate men's fashion statement of the time and must have cost what would have amounted to a fortune for Jenny, due to her meagre earnings. She remembered that he'd been in the company of two other guys. One of them was also muscular, with a crooked nose and thin moustache. He'd seemed like a bit of a joker because he had his two mates in stitches with whatever it was he'd been saying to them. The other guy had struck her as being very unusual; a big, longhaired Indian with chubby cheeks and eyes that shone like light-reflecting studs set into the road. She'd found it curious to see two white men obviously good friends with an Indian; a social phenomenon frowned upon in most circles in those racist times.

As she stood looking up into the stranger's eyes she sensed a deep sadness that drew her to him. She noticed a small scar on his chin that lent a hint of machismo to an otherwise gentle face. His hair was thick and curly, reminding her of get-it-on, banging-his-gong, child-of-the-revolution himself, Marc Bolan of T.Rex fame, for her the sexiest rock star around.

It was the jacket that did it though. Any guy wearing something as far-out as that deserved her attention. She knew straight away that she was going to take this young hunk home with her and make love with him.

To her delight, it was he who broke the quickly melting ice by sparking up a conversation with her about music. This then led into a discussion about ex-Stones guitarist Brian Jones. He'd been discovered three months earlier, floating dead in his swimming pool, purportedly after an evening of heavy drinking.

'He was bumped off,' said Jenny, fidgeting with a silver snake ring, wound around one of her long fingers.

'But the papers said it was an accident. Who would've wanted to murder him?'

'A lot of people.'

'Like who?'

'People who are against the revolution.'

'Revolution,' repeated Angus, justifiably bewildered. 'What revolution?'

'Man, where have you been for the past couple of years?'

He told her.

'Wow, man, that's really heavy,' she said, sympathy for the devil in her eyes.

Over in a corner of the bar, a television flickered with the sound turned down. On it was a black guy with fuzzy hair playing an electric guitar with his teeth. The guitarist lowered his instrument and continued playing in a more conventional style. When the camera zoomed in, Angus had a closer look at him.

'Jesus,' he exclaimed. 'Who is that?'

Jenny tossed her thick mane to one side, making her long rhinestone earrings flash. She glanced up at the TV set. 'You really have been away for a long time, haven't you? That's Jimi Hendrix, the hottest guitarist in the world.'

'So that's the 'Wildman of Rock' in action. I've heard 'Purple Haze' on the radio a few times but I haven't really had a chance to get into anything else by him. What does his music sound like to you?'

'The gods making love with a lot of bluesy feedback mixed in,' replied Jenny knocking back her drink in one big gulp and taking hold of his hand. 'Come on, man, let's go.'

'Where to?' In that moment he would have gone anywhere with her.

'Back to my place.'

'What for?' asked Angus barely able to suppress a grin that was threatening to break his jaw. He couldn't believe his luck. Jenny turned and drew his head to hers, planting the hottest kiss on his lips that he'd ever tasted. He stepped away from her in fear of being burned.

'A lot of things,' said Jenny, hoping that he'd drop his immature ploy of asking stupid questions.

In the background, Marvin Gaye's deeply emotional voice brought a whole lot of soul into the bar via the house system as he sang 'I Heard It Through The Grapevine'. Gaye's incomparable vocal scorched Angus's ears. From that moment on he would forever associate that wonderful song with Jenny because he was just about to lose his mind.

Jennifer Fraser was twenty-four years old and worked part-time in a children's nursery. She'd been wearing the multi-coloured mantle of hippiedom for two years and lived in a groovy little pad in the Cowcaddens area. When she switched on the lights of her small apartment, Angus took a look around.

'What happened to the furniture?' he asked.

'Chairs are for plastic people,' answered Jenny, hanging her coat up beside a Mexican poncho and a pair of castanets.

The living room was bare except for a dark red Afghan carpet, a few black and white op-art cushions, a yellow bean bag and, taped to a purple-painted wall, a solitary psychedelic poster advertising a gig at the Fillmore West auditorium in San Francisco with Led Zepplin topping the bill. Angus wondered if he was in for a whole lotta love. He didn't have to wonder about it for more than a few seconds because when he turned round he saw that Jenny was stepping out of her green velvet dress.

'What are you doing?'

'What do you think I'm doing? Do you always ask daft questions, or are you just having an off day? Come on, man, what are you waiting on? The bedroom's through here.' She wandered through the doorway, naked except for her high-heeled, red leather boots. They clicked out a beat on the wooden floor. A Nancy Sinatra song came to mind as he studied her swaying form before it disappeared into the room's shadows.

When Angus pulled his zipper down, his engorged cock popped out like a mini version of Casper, the very friendly ghost, because it was straining against the tightly stretched white cotton of his underpants. He escaped from his clothes quicker than Harry Houdini in a hurry.

The orgy of riotous fantasies he'd entertained in the past about losing his virginity, rose into the air and merged with the fragrant jasmine incense smoke fuming out of a brass Aladdin's lamp lying to one side of Jenny's waterbed. She sensed immediately that he was not an experienced lover. By the light of a flickering Buddha candle, whose head had melted into Nirvana, she parted her legs, pulled him down on top of her and let him enter her with the minimum of fuss. His big body shuddered. Unfamiliar with hot vaginal walls, Angus was unable to contain his excitement. He came as soon as Jenny started grinding her hips against him. She pushed him off her in frustration.

'What the fuck's up with you, man? That's no way to treat a woman. The way you're behaving you'd think you were a virgin or something.'

'Well, I was until a moment ago,' said a scarlet-faced Angus.

Jenny's tone became more playful. 'Wow man, far out. I've never made love with a virgin before. You could have said something.'

'Said something,' repeated Angus. 'You mean like, good evening darling, my name is Angus Macleod and I'm a virgin?'

Her lips drew back in a wide smile to reveal two lines of even teeth. She ran her fingers through his thick hair and began to kiss him passionately. Their tongues flicked and danced until raw sexuality suffused every cell in his body. He penetrated her for the second time and began to glide in and out with slow, deep, squishing strokes, lubricated by his earlier premature delivery of over 100 million overeager spermatozoa whose procreative potential was thwarted by the pill.

An hour later, Angus lay back in bed feeling very contented with himself. Jenny went into the tiny kitchen and returned with a cup of herbal tea. It was cold in the room and she was still naked. He stared, fascinated by the puckering pink nipples of her lemon-shaped breasts. Leaning over, she pressed them against his mouth. He sucked on them and it dawned on him that he'd really missed out on something when he was a baby.

Taking a sip of tea, Angus screwed up his face and asked, 'What's this? It tastes like hot water with perfume in it.'

'That's Mister Wong's Red Ginseng Tea. It's very yang and therefore good for potency.'

He drank his medicine down and after another wild bout of fucking he commented, 'I think Mister Wong should change his name to Mister Dong. That stuff really works. For a minute there my knob was so hot I thought it had caught fire.'

'I just love making love,' said Jenny, exhaling a long sigh. She had introduced Angus to the term, which sounded to him like a chocolate cake recipe. He thought 'shagging your brains out' captured the essence of what they'd been doing together much more accurately.

Jenny lit up a joint of hashish and took a few long drags on it before handing it to her new-found lover. The free love part of his initiation into flower power had flowed smoothly enough and then some, but the peace part, when he inhaled it, brought on a coughing fit.

Although Angus had sold hundreds of thousands of cigarettes, he'd never before smoked tobacco, something Jenny had used to mix with the hashish. He was totally unprepared for the stupefying effects of his first nicotine rush. A cold sweat, accompanied by dizziness, turned his face the whitest shade of pale Jenny had ever seen. She knew what the problem was. Picking up a small soapstone box, she began rummaging around in her stash. Using a single cigarette paper, she skinned up a pure grass joint using marijuana that had come all the way from darkest Africa. Minutes later, the Durban Poison lit up his brain in a neural fireworks display. There was a mindless smile on his face when he asked Jenny to turn up the music that was playing in the background. He'd never heard the likes of it before. He started sniggering when he was carried off on a Number Nine cloud bound for Funniesville.

A couple of tracks into the album he said, 'That music sounds incredible. Who is that?'

'Captain Beefheart and his Magic Band.'

'Did you say Beefheart?' asked Angus, a fit of the giggles coming on strong.

'Yeah,' she said, chuckling under her breath. 'The album's called,

Safe as Milk.'

It sounded absurd, but the music was brilliant. He felt like he was listening to the work of a musical genius. The Captain's legendary five octave vocal range hollered out bizarre lyrics to the intricate musical spell cast by the Magic Band as they played their unique style of electrified drop-out boogie. When side one was over, Angus wanted to continue along Beefheart's zigzagging yellow brick road and hear side two immediately.

'Later,' said Jenny, pushing him back on to the pillows. She straddled his hips and Angus saw for the first time that she'd had a red rose tattooed on the inside of her left thigh with the words 'Dangerous Mystique' written below in Celtic lettering. The sight of it made his young blood run wild. He was about to discover that the marijuana plant opens the doors to many different levels of experience when the THC crystal-coated petals of her flowers are inhaled.

Hours later, a slash of brilliance shone between the curtains as the sun rose over the chimney pots of Glasgow's mottled grey-slated rooftops outside Jenny's bedroom window. 'Mmmmh,' Jenny let out a satisfied moan. She'd curled up and fallen asleep on top of Angus. He ran his hands over her warm buttocks. They felt as boneless as a velvet jellyfish. Her body was still a mystery to him. He toyed with the idea of slipping into her as she slept. A throb of lust pulsed through him at the thought of it. She'd done a good job of converting him to her credo of love and peace. He lay still and listened to the joyful sound of early morning birds singing single notes as if practising for the celebration of a brand new day. Sleep took him with the suddenness of a light bulb being switched off.

Jenny lived for sex, drugs, and rock 'n' roll. Angus was happy to supply her with the first part and she had plenty of the other two good-time ingredients close at hand. Monday morning she phoned in sick for work. For the rest of the week they spent most of their time in bed, making love, getting stoned, and listening to her great collection of rock music. The only time they left their cosy nest was to buy supplies from the Pakistani corner shop. Angus was at first puzzled by his new-found voracious appetite for sweets. He found it hard to believe that he'd developed the capacity to devour a bag of marshmallows, half a dozen bars of chocolate, a tub of ice cream washed down with Coca-

Cola, and still be left desiring a Kit-Kat. Jenny explained that his sugar craving came as a result of smoking lots of hash and grass, creating a side effect that lowered the glucose level in his blood.

Angus popped the top off a tube of Smarties, smoked another joint, lay back against a surrealistic pillow, listened to Jefferson Airplane and dreamt about a hookah-smoking caterpillar giving him the call. He didn't get a chance to listen to Jimi Hendrix because Jenny had loaned all the axe man's vinyl long-players to a friend. Angus decided he'd buy the guitarist's albums for himself next time he passed a record shop.

After an astral week together, Jenny decided it was time to catch up on some sleep in preparation for returning to work on Monday morning. This was cool with Angus because, after having stretched free love to its red-raw breaking point, he was feeling more than a little shagged out and curious about what Murphy and Raj had been getting up to in his absence. There was no talk of falling in love with each other, only a loose arrangement made to meet up again next weekend at the State Bar. Jenny saw herself as a free spirit who valued freedom above love, something Angus could more or less relate to now that he was once again beginning to enjoy liberty himself.

Van 'The Man' Morrison was singing 'The Way That Young Lovers Do' in the background when Angus shared a long goodbye kiss with Jenny over the threshold of her hippy dream pad, before heading downtown in search of his mates. It was Saturday evening. He did not bother to go home, knowing full well he stood a far better chance of catching up with the lads in the State Bar at that time of the weekend.

14

LOCK, STOCK AND DIETHYLAMIDE

All across Glasgow the message was hot and smoking. During the time that Angus had been becoming acquainted with Jenny and *cannabis sativa*, his two mates had also been getting familiar with Mary Jane. Over a pint that turned into a few, the three friends brought each other up to date on what had been happening since they'd last seen each other. Raj had not lasted very long working in his father's garage. Mr Gupta Senior had the habit of nagging his eldest son about how he'd brought disgrace upon the family name by breaking the law and ending up in jail. Raj loved his dad but his constant hectoring became too much for him. One morning he threw in the spanner and walked out of the garage. Work-shy Murphy, like Angus, had somewhere down the line decided that nine and five were two numbers he'd never form a close relationship with. Before leaving the bar, Murphy had a brief chat with a local dope dealer and, after a quick transaction in the men's toilet, returned with a half ounce of top quality zero-zero Moroccan hashish wrapped in aluminium foil.

The three ex-cons had rented a top-floor, unfurnished, three-bedroom apartment on Great Western Road, in the vicinity of Glasgow's Botanical Gardens. The landlord did not ask too many questions when they offered to pay a year's rent in advance, telling him the half-truth that they were university students studying economics.

When they arrived home that evening, the young dopers blew a few joints, got smashed and talked a lot of intoxicated nonsense, which sounded incredibly interesting or ridiculously funny. Levelling out, the topic of conversation rolled around to how they were going to improve their financial situation. What with paying their rent, furnishing the flat, buying a fifth-hand Mini Cooper, a stereo system and all the other things necessary to create a comfortable home, the kitty box was almost empty.

Murphy, always full of ideas, some of them good ones, brought his mates up to date on how he proposed to deal with the material question. Walking through to his bedroom, he returned a moment later with an oil-stained curtain bound with pieces of string. He placed it on the coffee table's glass top and sat down in a worn leather armchair.

'What's that?' enquired Angus.

'Oh, it's just a little something that Lanky Lenny gave me in return for helping him out of a sticky situation,' replied a non-chalant Murphy.

'Lanky Lenny!' Raj's eyes widened in astonishment. 'I didn't know that you knew him. He's supposed to be a dangerous nutter. In fact, somebody told me a couple of days ago that he's been locked up in a padded cell in the loony bin.'

'That may well be but Lenny is all right in my books,' said Murphy, hinting that he and Lanky had a positive story running with each other.

'Can I open it?' asked Angus.

'Of course, my horse,' answered Murphy, smiling benevolently.

Angus was surprised by the weight of the mysterious package as he pulled it over to his side of the table and started untying the knotted string. Sensing that whatever was wrapped in the cloth should not be seen by the nosey-parker neighbour with a penchant for binoculars who lived across the street, Raj rose to his feet and pulled the thick blue velveteen curtains closed over the room's large bay window.

'What the fuck?' exclaimed Angus.

Raj walked across the white flokati carpet and peered over Angus's shoulder to see that he was examining a well-oiled sawn-off shotgun. Sighting down the gun's blue-grey stubby twin barrels, Angus aimed towards the corner of the room where the television was showing *The Birds*, a black and white Alfred Hitchcock movie. He gently squeezed on one of the gun's triggers. Click. There was a thunderous boom as the shotgun discharged a cartridge full of tiny ball bearings in the direction of the TV set, blowing it instantly into smithereens. Angus was knocked out of his chair by the weapon's recoil. All three of the young men had a ringing in their ears that might have been the call of the wild because when the smoke cleared they went apeshit.

Murphy: 'Ya fuckin' idjit.'

Angus: 'I didn't know the thing was loaded.'

Raj: 'For Christ's sake, look at the hole you've blown in the wall. How the fuck are we going to explain that to the landlord?'

Angus: 'Ya stupid bastard. Why didn't you tell me the fuckin' thing was loaded?'

Murphy: 'Because you never asked, ya fuckin' dunderheaded twat. What the hell did you pull the trigger for?'

Raj: 'The pair of you are off yer fuckin' heads. Angus, you … you … you're a fucking madman. Look what you've done to the telly. You could have killed somebody. Murphy, you're pure mental. For fuck's sake, man, what are you doing bringing a loaded gun into the house?'

Angus: 'Yeah, man, Raj is right. Murphy, this is your fault.'

Murphy: 'My fuckin' fault? It was—'

The argument was interrupted by another kind of ringing in their ears – the doorbell.

'Fuckin' shite, what now? It's probably the fuzz.'

'Come on, Murphy, calm down. It's probably just a couple of Jehovah's Witnesses,' said Raj. His hands were shaking like he was suffering from Parkinson's disease. He turned to Angus and ordered, 'Go see who it is. It can't be the filth. Even in Glasgow they don't move that fast.'

'Me? Why should I bloody well answer the door?'

'Cos it was you who fired the—'

The doorbell rang again; this time twice. It was after midnight so it wasn't the postman.

'Stop fannying around. Go and answer the fuckin' door, Angus,' hissed Murphy.

Angus surrendered, left the room, walked across the hall and, taking a deep breath, pulled open the front door. A pleasant surprise awaited him; standing before him was Miss Wood, the nubile neighbour from downstairs who worked as a gym teacher at the girls' academy around the corner.

'I'm awful sorry to bother you,' she said, a worried look on her innocent face, one eye blinking from beneath a neatly trimmed auburn coloured peek-a-boo hairstyle, 'but I heard a loud bang and shouting, so I came up to see if everything was all right.'

'Oh … I … I see. Thanks, Miss Wood that was … ehm, very thoughtful of you. Am sorry about the noise, it's just that the TV imploded when we were watching a horror film. It gave us a bit o' a fright, like.'

'Gee whiz, that sounds terrible. Crikey, no wonder you're looking so pasty. Would you like me to come in and make you a cup of tea?'

Angus was thinking that Miss Wood was in the right place at the wrong time because she was just a little bit too scantily dressed to be appearing on his doorstep at this hour of the night purely to check out the state of his health. The low cut neckline of her semi-transparent blouse was exposing one shoulder. A black bra strap contrasted sharply with her pale skin. His thoughts were dampened by the acrid whiff of gunpowder smoke floating out from behind the open door on to the landing. He had to get rid of her, even though he would have liked to ask her in for a sausage roll, an electric eel sandwich or something else equally appropriate.

'That's awful nice of you, Miss Wood, maybe some other time. I'm fine. You don't need to worry yourself. I better go in now and clean up the mess.'

'I can help if you like,' said the young woman, taking a step forward.

'No,' protested Angus, raising his hands. 'I mean, no thanks, Miss Wood. My flat-mates are already tidying up.'

'Are you sure, now?'

'Aye, I am, Miss Wood.'

'You can call me Charlotte.'

'Oh … aye right, that's a nice name.'

'Thank you. I like your name too. Angus, isn't it?'

'Yeah, that's right. Well then Charlotte, thanks again. Good-night now.'

'Goodnight Angus. See you later.'

Closing the door behind him, he leaned back against it for support. His knees were trembling.

Murphy peeped out from behind the living room door. 'What the fuck was all that about?'

'That's a good fucking question, man. It was Miss Wood from downstairs. I couldn't get rid of her. I think she fancies me.'

'For fuck's sake, fancies you? Why the hell did you not ask her in?'

'Aye right, that's a brilliant idea, Murphy. Come on in, Miss Wood. Don't mind the mess like, because it just so happens that I've accidentally blown away ma fuckin' telly with a sawn-off shotgun that I found lying around in my livin' room.'

'What's so funny?' asked Raj wondering if it was safe enough to venture out into the hall.

'Miss Wood,' replied Murphy.

'Aw, that's who it was? She's a wee stoater, that one. I wouldn't mind giving her ma piece o' wood.'

'Ya dirty Indian,' retorted Angus. 'Keep your cricket bat in your trousers an' away and make us something to eat. I'm famished.'

Raj had, by this time, taken on the role of 'Mum', treating the lads to recipes he'd learned from his mother: pakoras, bhaji and the best chicken curries this side of the Shish Mahal Indian Restaurant on Gibson Street.

After cleaning up the mess, a late-night feast was served up. Spicy poppadoms and hot chapattis covered in strawberry jam were washed down with big mugs of Ty-Phoo tea sweetened with honey.

'We'll have to get a plasterer in to fix that bloody mess,' said Raj nodding towards the damaged wall.

'We'll have to buy a new telly as well,' added Angus.

'We're going to need a wee bit of extra cash,' said Murphy, a conniving tone in his voice, 'and I'm the one who knows how to go about getting it.'

'How?' asked Angus and Raj in unison.

Murphy went on to explain how, a week before, an acquaintance of his, no names mentioned, had asked him if he was interested in holding up the Byres Road branch of Scotland's National Bank. He'd declined the offer, and the next day wandered into the bank to check it out for himself. What he saw confirmed what he'd already been told, the place had zippy in the way of security, making it a miracle that nobody had gotten around to knocking it over before.

'I'm telling you,' said Murphy, 'the place is a dawdle.' Putting on his best Al Capone accent, he condensed the whole idea down into a double-barrelled question. 'Right then, are you guys into a bit of daylight bank robbery or aren't yazz?'

Silence hung between Angus and Raj as they looked blankly into each other's bloodshot eyes. The searchlights were on but the sky was empty, so they didn't find any answers in that vacuous space. In the end, what crystallized their thoughts was the depressing idea of ending up stony broke. Once they'd shook a shaky hand on it, all that remained to be done was to plot a course of action.

★

They hit the bank the following Friday afternoon, just before it closed for the day. Angus and Murphy strode in, wearing over their heads the black seamed ladies' nylon stockings that Raj had embarrassed himself by purchasing that very morning in Marks and Spencer's lingerie department. By democratic vote, Angus had been nominated to carry the shotgun, since he'd already demonstrated his skills as a gunman on their TV set. One devastating blast into the polystyrene tiles of the bank's lowered ceiling almost brought the roof crashing down on their heads, but served their purposes well, bringing the bank's terrified employees completely under the bandits' control. The incompetent bank manager should have been fired in the same instant as the shotgun. He would have been better employed sweeping the streets than running an establishment with over £40,000 in cash lying in an open vault. Angus had time to study the man while Murphy was helping himself to the money. His dress code was as sloppy as the security of the business he was supposed to be managing; a crumpled dark-grey flannel suit with a mismatched striped shirt and coffee-stained pink tie only added to his general air of unsuitability for the job. Angus decided to scare the shit out of him.

'What the fuck are you lookin' at? Get your fucking face on the floor or I'll blow your fuckin' head off!' shouted Angus, waving the shotgun in front of the man's frightened eyes. The bank manager hit the deck like he'd been run over by a lead-filled oil drum.

Murphy was ready to go, having cleaned out the walk-in safe and shoved all the bank notes into a sports bag. Backing out of the place, Angus took a final glance around the bank's interior, not quite believing what he was in the process of doing. He yelled at the half dozen or so people standing with their hands in the air, looks of abject terror upon their horrified faces.

'Anybody comes out after us – they're dead.' It was hardly necessary to say it, but he'd seen gangsters do this in the movies so he thought he'd try it out just to add a bit of realism to the situation, which was beginning to feel totally unreal to him.

Four minutes after entering the bank, the two masked robbers walked casually out into the street, still wearing the stockings over their heads. Murphy carried the bulky black canvas bag with the loot in it on his shoulder. Angus wielded the big gun in his gloved hands. It couldn't have been more obvious what they'd been up to, even if they'd put a full-page announcement of their intentions in the early morning papers. Shocked pedestrians stopped and stared as the masked men strolled over and slid into the back seat of a gleaming, dark-green Jaguar parked in the street outside the bank. Raj had picked the vehicle up from the nearby university car park where some absent-minded professor had been kind enough to leave the keys in the ignition.

The Jag's eight-cylinder engine purred as it shot up the road like the sleek jungle cat it had been named after. Raj spun the wheel. The car screeched into a narrow street at break-neck speed.

'For fuck's sake, Raj, take it easy,' shouted Angus from the back seat. 'I don't fancy going through another shop window, courtesy of your stunt driving skills.'

'Don't be worried man,' said Raj over his shoulder. 'Everything's under my control.'

Sitting side by side, bouncing around in the rear seats, Raj's two passengers exchanged anxious glances and hoped they weren't in for a catastrophic *déjà vu*. The two stick-up merchants tore the nylons off their heads and chucked them out the window.

'Raj, get that thing off your head,' ordered Murphy. 'You look like a bogeyman,'

The interior of the car smelled brand new. Hardly surprising; its owner had just picked it up that morning from a Jaguar showroom. Angus examined the backs of his hands. Like his two accomplices, he was wearing tight-fitting black leather gloves that matched the Jag's upholstery perfectly. They made him feel like a real professional, like Napoleon Solo in *The Man from Uncle*, or some other sharply dressed spy. He remembered Neil Ferguson, his childhood friend from Iona who wanted to be a bank robber when he grew up, and thought to himself, 'If only Neil could see me now.'

Three hundred miles to the south of where Angus sat in the back of the speeding Jaguar, Neil was in the process of torturing a successful gem dealer in order to extract out of his tightly sealed and bleeding lips, the combination to the safe in the wall of his luxurious home. If nothing else, the man was stubborn.

'Okay, Boris,' said Neil, turning to his partner, a seven-foot troglodyte in a Savile Row suit. 'Let's go to work on his missus.'

Both men turned to face a shapely, long-legged, middle-aged brunette, tied up, gagged, and wriggling on the double bed of the couple's master bedroom in a gated community on the outskirts of Birmingham.

'40, 28, 36,' gasped out the panic-stricken gem dealer through his broken teeth.

'Thank you very much, Mister Goldstein,' said Neil, before smacking the distraught man on the top of the head with a lead cosh.

Mr Goldstein was still unconscious on the floor, with his wife desperately trying to untie herself on the bed, by the time Neil unlocked the door of his London penthouse apartment on the South Bank of the River Thames. After Boris and he had stashed over half a million pounds worth of cut stones, Neil kicked back and lit up a cigar. Picking up the phone he dialled a number.

'Hullo, Gloria, it's Neil here. Get your lovely ass over here and bring that wee pal of yours – Rita, or Mona, or whatever the fuck her name is, with you. I'm gonna shag the pair of you stupid.'

He hung up the receiver, took a drag on his long corona and blew a perfect smoke ring in the direction of the French windows framing the excellent view of the Houses of Parliament on the Thames's opposite bank. Neil contemplated the buildings glowing in the gentle amber tones of the late afternoon sunlight and sighed with pleasure.

'If only Angus could see me now.'

'What's that, Boss?' grunted Boris.

'Nothing. Do me a favour and fetch a bottle of that Krug for me.'

'Anything you say, Boss. Which one is it?'

'The champagne with the pink label that's chilling in the fridge.'

Raj parked the stolen Jaguar in an empty car park behind a cinema at Anniesland Cross. He'd managed to drive it there without putting a scratch or a dent in its polished coachwork, a miraculous feat considering the speed and reckless manner in which it had been driven. A quick change of clothes, three tickets on the bus and they were back in their apartment just over an hour after having robbed the bank.

'Come on, Raj, get the kettle on,' said Murphy, tipping the black canvas bag's contents out on to the coffee table. Lying in the centre of a big pile of bank notes was the sawn-off shotgun.

'Careful,' warned Angus, 'one of the barrels is still cocked and loaded.'

'Listen to who's talking,' remarked Murphy, looking over to a freshly plastered wall. 'Dead-eye fuckin' Dick himself.'

As the two friends sat counting the money, outside on the road police cars could be heard speeding by with their sirens howling, in hot pursuit of the elusive bank robbers.

'So that's £14,325 each,' said Murphy patting three neat piles of bank notes. 'Not bad for an afternoon's work, even if I do say so myself.'

'It's fucking brilliant if you ask me,' said Raj, setting a plastic tray, loaded with mugs of tea and fresh chapattis, down on the middle of the table.

A hard day's work over, the merry bank robbers were ready for a spot of rest and recreation. Money now stashed under the gas cooker in the kitchen, a stiff joint was being passed around when Murphy produced a small cellophane bag containing a handful of orange pills.

'What's that?' asked Raj.

'This is acid, man.'

'Aw,' groaned Angus.

'What's the matter with you?' enquired Murphy, when he saw a disappointed look on Angus's face.

'I was hoping you were going to say that it was some of that LSD stuff. Jenny told me about it and it sounds fantastic.'

'You know, man, maybe you should look up the meaning of ignoramus in the dictionary.'

'Why?'

'Because that's what you are, ya fuckin' idjit. Acid *is* LSD – short for lysergic acid diethylamide.'

'Awwww, now I get it.' Angus slapped his forehead.

'So you're into it?'

'Dead right I am,' answered Angus, settling into a worn leather chesterfield.

'Raj?' Murphy raised his dimpled chin.

'Yeah, why not? What exactly does it do to you?'

'I'm not sure,' replied Murphy. 'The guy that I bought it from said it's really good stuff.'

'Come on then,' said Angus. 'There's only one way to find out, right?'

'How many pills should we take?' asked Raj, picking up on his friends' enthusiasm.

'Just one to begin with, I think,' replied Murphy, who, apart from knowing the chemical compound's name, really had not the faintest idea what he was holding in his hand.

'Only one?' asked Angus. 'Those pills are really small. Surely one won't have any effect on us.'

'Naw, Murph's right. We should only take one. I just remembered reading in the papers last week about some guy in East Kilbride who took LSD, imagined he was a bird and jumped out the window thinking he could fly. Turns out he couldn't, which must have come as a bit of a shock to him because he was on the sixth floor of a block of flats.'

Angus and Murphy assumed a sceptical air, looked at their Indian friend and began to laugh.

'Maybe you've been listenin' to too much of The Byrds' music,' said Murphy through his laughter, 'if you believe that fuckin' nonsense.'

'I think we should just start with one, to be on the safe side,' said a more cautious Angus.

The three friends swallowed their first LSD trip and washed it down with Ty-Phoo tea. Typhoon tea would have been a more appropriate name for the beverage in this case, because they were about to be seriously blown away.

15

DON'T BE LATE

The extremely powerful doses of Lysergic Acid Diethylamide that the three adventurous pals had just ingested had undergone a long and circuitous trans-continental journey before reaching their stomachs.

The ergotamine tartrate alkaloid to make this particular batch of LSD had been manufactured five years earlier in the laboratories of a well known Swiss pharmaceutical company situated on the outskirts of Basel. Eighteen months later, forty kilograms of the substance was sent by airmail to a fictitious address in Phoenix, Arizona, set up explicitly for receivership of this package. After that it was stored in a sterile deep freeze for over a year until a clandestine lab could be set up in Reno, Nevada. During this time there were about thirty people in the United States who knew how to cook high quality LSD. Most of them worked out of the San Francisco Bay Area. Their skills were much sought after. Another year passed before an underground chemist called 'The Wizard' began to work on the ergotamine. It took him nine months to create just over ten kilos of odourless, sparkling crystalline powder. It was ninety-nine percent pure LSD. The Wizard was paid five million dollars for doing an excellent job by Buck Baggins. Buck was a well connected Californian surfer from Mill Valley who had masterminded the whole operation, which was financed by 'The Sons of Thoth', a subversive Los Angeles based drug dealing syndicate formed by a group of Ivy League dropouts. Buck was very pleased with what was contained within the aluminium suitcase that he loaded into the back of his Mercedes station wagon before hightailing it back to the West

Coast - enough LSD to turn on fifty million people.

One kilo of the crystalline compound was transported to New York City. When it arrived in the Big Apple, the powder was divided up into hundred-gram deals and so on down the line. An enterprising English dealer called Acid Mike flew over to New York from London and bought twenty grams of the crystal acid. After getting a tidy haircut, a new pair of Levis and a woollen sports jacket, he flew into Heathrow Airport with the small cargo concealed in his leather boots' hollowed-out heels. In those days, Her Majesty's Customs and Excise officers were laboring under the misconception that the drug smugglers of the time had long hair and wore kaftans. Nobody paid Acid Mike the slightest bit of attention as he breezed through the customs hall with a knot in his stomach and a fortune in his boot heels.

Once safely back in his apartment in Notting Hill Gate, things were going great. Acid Mike's pill compress was working perfectly, cranking out little orange pills at the rate of thirty a minute. He'd done his arithmetic and calculated that if each pill contained 200 micrograms it meant he would be able to make 100,000 pills. Selling them wholesale at £2 a trip, he was doing very all right for having brought back to England something that would easily have fitted into an empty cigarette packet and cost him, altogether, £18,000.

A dose of LSD that weighs in at one five-thousandth of a gram is enough to make a person want to kiss the sky for eight hours. Mike decided to make up a batch of 1000 extra-powerful tabs, containing 500 micrograms of acid, to share with his seasoned buddies once he'd taken care of business. A month later he'd deposited his money in a Swiss bank account and returned to London ready to try out one of his mindbenders. He flew solo. Blasting through the ozone layer, he was flying so high he blew his nose in a Kleenex to check he didn't have a nosebleed from the altitude.

A couple of hours into the trip, Mike felt like his tongue had been transformed into a mile high sand dune in the Sahara Desert with a herd of mangy camels wandering about on it looking for a drink of water. To relieve his thirst he poured himself a glass of Coca-Cola. Suddenly he heard fireworks going off. He went to his living room window and looked outside. Portobello Road was deserted on a blustery grey afternoon, a few leaves dancing in their death throes on the pavement before they turned to dust. Still the sound of firecrackers exploding continued. After a couple of unsettling light years he realized that the loud crackling noises he'd been hearing were being produced by the carbonated gas bubbles in his glass of Coke.

The phone clamoured, sounding to Mike like King Kong dinging his dong against Big Ben inside his head. The noise was so unexpected he jumped out of his skin and circled the room twice before picking up the receiver. On the other end of the line was a young woman trying to sell him cheap car insurance. Crossed wires in Mike's brain circuitry led him to believe he was receiving an ultrasonic message from a fifth dimensional entity on Venus. Due to his altered state, he could understand Venusian perfectly. He listened attentively and transcribed everything on to several pages of a notepad. When the alien hung up, Mike was reading back what he'd written down when he remembered that he was an extraterrestrial agent who had taken on a human form in order to carry out a secret mission on Planet Earth. This was all part of a conspiracy that had been planned eons ago to lift the consciousness of mankind onto a higher plane, something that would not happen until many coastal cities were submerged under water from rising sea levels. Mike looked out of the window again. It was raining. The process of transformation had begun at last. To celebrate its arrival Mike decided to skin up a tasty doobie of hand-rubbed Parvati hash.

A few tokes into his smoke, he placed the still burning joint in an ashtray. He searched along a long line of record sleeves until he found what he was looking for. When he removed the vinyl LP from its cover he handled it with reverence and marvelled at the rainbow curves of reflected light upon its shiny black surface. For Mike, The Grateful Dead's *Anthem Of The Sun* was the Holy Grail of psychedelic music. After placing the disk on the turntable he lay down on the floor, placed a cushion under his head, closed his eyes and slipped into a dream.

He floated down the River Styx in an old canoe and passed by a big green alligator, wagging his tail as he sunned himself on a sandbank. The beast's saurian purple eyes blinked and it smiled at Mike as if it knew him. It slithered down the bankside and with a soft splash disappeared into the dark waters.

The canoe meandered for a while, entered some rapids, shot over a thundering waterfall, and next thing Mike knew he was standing naked on an endless flat plain made from non-reflective black glass. In the distance, under the light of a dark star, he could see a glowing white mound. He walked towards it and found that it was a pile of protoplasmic clay. Bending down, he grabbed a handful. It was warm, pliable and crackled with static electricity. An inspirational idea came to him; he would sculpt a figure from the material. First he made feet –

not just any feet but the most delicate feet he could imagine, the feet of a veritable goddess. 'Yes, a goddess,' he thought, 'that is why I've come here, to bring the most beautiful creature imaginable into existence.'

Well proportioned calves to support lovely long legs, the curving hips of a belly dancer, a rare orchid for a vagina, a belly button window, breasts like ripe pomegranates, buttocks like a coco de mer, arms that could circle the world, the svelte hands of a pianist and a slender neck to support the most gracious of heads; slowly but surely they began to form. Mike stood back to appraise his work and noticed celestial beings were gathering above to gaze down in wonder at his fabulous creation. Mike paid little heed to the beating of their wings or the hushed murmur of their heavenly voices. He was too busy visualizing a luscious pair of lips – lips that looked good enough to eat. Picking up another dollop of electro clay he began to shape them.

Mike laboured long and diligently. How long it was not so easy to gauge, for the rigid hands of time held no sway in the flexible space he now inhabited, a space that imbued him with an ever-deepening sense of love. The eyes of his goddess alone took ages to shape. Earthly needs like hunger and thirst did not exist for him. All that mattered was the completion of his manifestation of love in action.

Her hair was like the angel falls and, when it was ready, he formed feathers to make a crown to place upon her magnificent head. One last time he moved back to admire his work from a distance. 'Yes,' he gasped, tripping over his feet due to his excitement, 'she's perfect.' Not only that, she was sexually attractive.

He drew close again, breathed in her intoxicating musky scent, brushed his fingers across her nipples until they were pebble hard and whispered a name in her nautilus shell-shaped, spiralling ears. 'Aphrodite.' His wildest fantasy remained silent. He bowed down like an acolyte at the feet of a deity.

She spoke to him. 'What would you have me do for you, my beloved Michael?' Her honeyed voice came to him as an arpeggio of lust.

He looked up at his dream megababe, her moist vagina's labial petals directly in front of his nose. Fire rose up in his loins. He felt as horny as a heathen attending a slurp orgy in a five star brothel packed with sex-starved nymphomaniacs. He wanted to split her with his tongue. She placed her hands on his head and gently pushed him away saying, 'Not now my love, first you must rest.' The goddess made him lie down and knelt beside him. Mike didn't want to relax because his cock was so stiff it felt like it was about to explode. Her warm hands gripped his phallus, and taking its swollen purple head into her mouth the goddess of his dreams sucked on it with the power of an industrial vacuum cleaner. Mike cried out in ecstasy as he gushed a geyser of white-hot magma that splattered across his stomach and chest. Energies spent, mercurial molecular sperms danced, died and faded into oblivion on the inside of his eyelids as he entered a state of deep relaxation. In the background he could hear people's voices out on the street, chattering in his mind like nagging thoughts made audible.

The following morning, Acid Mike woke up with a start and a painful erection when the telephone rang. He sat up and banged his forehead on the underside of the kitchen table. His head and hard-on were throbbing as he stumbled into the adjacent room to answer the jangling phone. It was an important call from a friend who needed his help and required Mike to write some information down. Casting around for his notepad, he found it on the floor and wondered absently who had drawn all the neat hieroglyphics on several of its pages. Telephone conversation over, he hung up, glanced down at his wilting penis and realized he was shivering from cold. He looked around, in search of his clothes. 'What the fuck!' Scratching his balls, he walked over to his expensive hi-fi. 'Where the bloody hell did this come from?' He was looking at the turntable. It was turning and upon it was a crude, foot-high female figure made from wet mashed-up newspapers; its head was a mouldy doughnut with burnt matches sticking out of it.

Acid Mike had used LSD on many occasions, but decided to go easy on the special orange pills. In future maybe only take a half pill at a time. Three days later he was down at 'The Gold', a public house on Portobello Road, enjoying a pint of bitter and a ham sandwich. As he sat gazing at the black and white framed photographs hanging on the pub's walls, anybody checking out Mike's tie-dyed outfit with matching headband and spaced-out expression on his unshaven face could have guessed he was a doper and not a Member of Parliament.

'Hey, how you doin', ma man?' said a coarse Scottish voice behind him. Mike turned and looked up into the eyes of an exceptionally tall, thin man dressed in a black leather motorcycle outfit who, missing some back teeth, had sunken cheeks that emphasized the shape of his skull.

'Please allow me to introduce myself. My name's Lenny.' Lanky Lenny offered a calloused hand. Not knowing what else to do, Mike shook hands. There was such strength in Lenny's grip Mike felt like he'd jammed his hand in a car door.

'Would you like another swally?' asked Lenny.

'I beg your pardon?'

'A bevvy, man. Would you like another pint?'

Mike looked at his empty glass. Not wanting to upset what he took to be a tough moron, he nodded in the affirmative. Being an ex-public schoolboy, Mike had a touch of the snob about him, especially when it came to working class Scots like Lenny, who, judging by his uncouth accent, hailed from the Glaswegian hinterlands. Four pints later, Mike was beginning to change his mind. Lenny was a comedian who seemed to take a lot of enjoyment out of poking fun at his very own lanky self. The Scotsman told him joke after ridiculously funny joke.

'Did you hear the one about the old age pensioners having a shag against an electric fence?'

'Hold on a minute, Leonard, would you like to come back to my pad and smoke a few joints?'

'Does His Holiness The Pope wear a funny fuckin' hat, Mike? C'mon man, let's go, a'm dyin' for a smoke.'

Acid Mike and Lanky Lenny ended up hanging out with each other for a week. They were an unlikely pair, but the ex-public-schoolboy-meets-the-hard-nut-street-brawler got on like an oil refinery on fire. Lenny eventually told Mike that he was looking for some good acid and was willing to pay £4 a trip for it. Mike was one of those strange species of people who have lots of money stashed away but live like paupers. He couldn't resist selling his special acid trips at such a good price. Before Lenny returned to Glasgow, Mike gave him his private phone number. Lenny did not realize what a privilege this was, because only a handful of Mike's closest associates were deemed trustworthy enough to be given such a token of his respect.

On the train back to Glasgow, Lanky Lenny was already bored by the time it rolled out of Kings Cross Station. He decided to try one of the acid trips – it took him a lot further than the ticket he'd paid for. He was very relieved when he returned from a journey to the outer reaches of the Upper Megadon Galaxy where aliens calling themselves Goorantians had held him captive. They looked like giant toasted, kidney-shaped marshmallows with cyclopean gamma-ray eyes. The Goorantians had forced Lenny into slave labour where, for a thousand years, he'd toiled by a conveyor belt sorting through coloured jelly babies. He'd survived by chewing on the rejects. When he arrived in Glasgow his jaws were aching

Four days later, Murphy, who did not have a clue how much LSD cost, was his first customer. Lenny owed Murphy a big one because he'd saved him from being stabbed in a street fight three months before, but this did not stop him from taking Murphy for a ride and doubling his money when he sold Murphy fifty pills. Two nights before, Lenny's girlfriend, Sheila, had flipped out on his acid and thought she was a mermaid. When she hallucinated a pod of dolphins sporting in the Clyde she had jumped off a bridge into the river, swallowed a lot of filthy water, and had to be taken to hospital to have her stomach pumped. Lenny, with faint twinges of guilt, was starting to think twice about his new role as an acid dealer, so when Murphy asked him where the LSD had come from, Lenny told him and gave him Mike's phone number. Not thinking much of it at the time, Murphy soon forgot about the slip of paper he had deposited in the inside pocket of his signal red corduroy jacket. By the time Murphy left Lenny's dirty downtown flat, he had also become the owner of a sawn-off shotgun and a small cardboard box full of orange cartridges.

Lenny's next customer was a woman, Diana Walsh. She was a real tough oatcake from Drumchapel who sported a rainbow-coloured Mohican hairstyle, long before Malcolm Mclaren assembled The Sex Pistols and punk stormed into town. As sharp as a tomahawk, Diana felt that Lanky Lenny was trying to scalp her when he tried to sell her his acid at the ridiculously high price of seven pounds a trip. They smoked a joint together. When Lenny went to the bathroom, Diana took ten hits of the super-acid from the bag on the kitchen table and dropped them into the rip-off merchant's half-finished bottle of Guinness. Diana made sure that Lenny finished the rest of his drink and then left him to get on with it.

An hour passed and freaked-out Lenny found himself viewing the world through an electron microscope. Not only that, he thought his skin was on fire. He tore off his clothes and ran out into the street. A fire engine had to be called in to rescue a crazy, stark naked man from the top of a high lamp-post in Argyll Street. After a hair-raising struggle, helmeted firemen managed to bring Lenny down from his perch. Bringing him down from his monster acid trip was to take a lot longer. When he became violent, Lenny was belted into a straight jacket and locked in a padded cell in a mental hospital.

Two years plus a lot of electro-shock therapy later, Lenny was back on the streets, literally. He was employed by Glasgow Corporation as a garbage collector. His best friend at work was

Peter Petford. Pete was always going on to him about how he used to be a bank manager on Byres Road until two guys with a sawn-off shotgun robbed the place. He'd been given the sack and as a result suffered a nervous breakdown. Lenny didn't believe him, but they remained good friends and workmates for many years to come.

A kamikaze mosquito dived into Hamish's left cheek. He slapped his face automatically. His eyes sprang open and he stared blankly at the moonlit sea.

'Oh-oh, no mind,' he chuckled and lit a cigarette. Another insect buzzed around his head. He blew smoke at it, hoping to deter any more of its friends showing up for a blood feast. Raising his left arm, he looked at his wrist and remembered he'd thrown his watch in the sea. Three more puffs on his cigarette and he was ready to return to his brother's story.

★

Side one of Chicago's classic debut album drew to a close. One of the songs on the record was called 'Does Anybody Really Know What Time It Is?' Angus looked at his watch. Half an hour had passed since he'd ingested his first acid trip. There was an unusual metallic taste in his mouth. Apart from feeling strangely strange, but oddly normal, he thought that perhaps Murphy was the victim of a swizzle and that the pill he'd swallowed was a dud. He leaned forward in his armchair and spoke to his two friends sitting across from him.

'Do you guys feel anything?' 'Strange,' he thought, 'I've never noticed an echo in the room before.'

'I feel a bit weird.' Raj sounded nervous. Angus was very surprised indeed when he saw the words come out of his friend's mouth encapsulated in rainbow-coloured bubbles. The five transparent spheres floated into the centre of the living room and burst with wet popping sounds.

'Wow, man, look at the white rabbit.' Murphy was pointing to a pile of old newspapers stacked up in a dimly lit corner of the room.

Thinking to himself, 'Rabbit, what bloody rabbit?' Angus peered into the shadows. Sure enough, sitting up on its hind legs in the corner was a large albino bunny rabbit with floppy ears, buck teeth and sparkling fluorescent pink eyes. The mysterious snow-white creature smiled at him. A soap bubble emerged from its mouth. There was a three-dimensional orange-coloured word suspended in it. Angus leaned over to read what it said. It said – boof! The bubble burst before he could make it out. Zzzzt! There was a burst of light in the corner, like a flashbulb going off. The bunny vanished.

'For fuck's sake,' hissed Angus, pressing his back into the padded armchair's contours. His breathing laboured, unaccustomed feelings of insecurity rose from the pit of his stomach to overwhelm him. Worried thoughts circulating in his mind made a break for it through the sutures of his skull, spread their wings and took flight for destinations unknown.

Another half hour passed and, much to his amazement, he found himself strapped into a space capsule on the front of Apollo 25, its guidance system controls set for the heart of the sun. Judging by the way that Raj and Murphy were gripping the arms of their chairs, they too were blasting off. Murphy broke the silence when he began blabbering gobbledygook from Planet Gonzo spoken backwards. Fortunately, Angus and Raj had intergalactic language translators hard-wired into the frontal lobes of their brains. They switched on automatically and deciphered Murphy's unintelligible mumbo-jumbo. He was in the midst of giving his personal rendition of what had taken place in the bank, a million years ago that very afternoon, when Angus had blown a hole in the ceiling. Floating down like snowflakes, small particles of polystyrene had filled the air, creating the illusion that it was snowing. Murphy described it as having been a blizzard in the bank. The acid was now coming on strong. So was Murphy's description, resulting in the funniest thing they'd heard in their entire lives. They began guffawing until in no time at all, the three of them were on the floor, helpless with laughter. They soon forgot what had started them off in the first place, which only served to make the situation more hilarious. It was fun at first until Angus's ribs began to ache from the unusual physical exertion.

Angus rose to his feet and tried to pull himself together to counter his feelings of being blown apart. He headed for the record player with the idea of putting some music on, an absurdly funny thing to be doing. The first record cover that came to hand was one he'd bought the day before. It was Jimi Hendrix's first album, *Are You Experienced?*. Angus studied the picture on the sleeve. Jimi looked groovy in a black cape stretched out like bat wings, with his two musical sidemen, Mitch Mitchell and Noel Redding, staring off the cover like a pair of arrogant schoolboys. Giggling to himself, he pulled the black vinyl disc out of its protective sleeve. Squinting through the hole in the middle of the record, he performed the incredibly delicate and complex task of placing it on the turntable. Angus had to focus all his available attention units on the player's arm so he could successfully place its needle in the groove at the beginning of side one.

Beautiful noise exploded out of the loudspeakers. The feedback from Hendrix's guitar sounded like a jet fighter had just screamed into the room. Angus's body started moving to the music on its own volition. A rock and roll shaman, Hendrix's wild spirit filled the room and took possession of the three acid trippers' minds. From not so mellow yellow to bloody red, the furniture was going through colour changes in time to the pitch and scale of the music. Raj was bouncing around on the sofa doing the dance of Shiva, while Murphy was jerking around, electrocuted after having been plugged into the national grid. Angus went over to the amplifier and cranked up the volume. The dancers went cosmo-ballistic, moving to the musical universe's equivalent of the Big Bang in full living colour. The album's moods were multi-flavoured, from flat-out no-holds barred rock 'n' roll to brooding, moody electrified acid blues. The music took the three friends on a magic carpet ride through a non-stop psychedelic extravaganza of weird and wonderful sounds.

When Jimi played the blues number 'Red House', Angus pictured him walking along a dusty track with his guitar slung over his shoulder, on his way to sell his soul to the Devil down at the crossroads, something he may well have done to learn to play like that. Hendrix played the trippers' souls on the neck of his guitar in his musical opus created for those who wished to be freed from the limitations of the squared-off world. A voice of his generation, Jimi, the celestial musician, sang his message of love and freedom. He told of a previous lifetime in days gone by when he'd visited the new mother earth before vampiric businessmen sucked her dry and in so doing brought on a high temperature planetary fever.

Jimi asked strange questions: Would it burn him if he touched the sun? Will I live tomorrow? Was it the end of time?

Angus wondered if this had something to do with Hendrix being a voodoo chile who'd been born during a night when the moon shone fiery red. Before Jimi's spirit left the room, he said he was not destined to be in this world for very long, but that was cool because he'd see everyone in the next world and don't be late. 'Don't be late?' Angus asked himself, 'What on earth is that supposed to mean?'

Two Jimi Hendrix Experience albums later, the three friends collapsed on the floor, grooving to the buzzing aftermath reverberating in their heads.

Angus lay on his back, his supercharged brain undergoing an atomic flash deluxe as he watched fractal patterns spread out over the ceiling and walls. He could not imagine himself feeling any higher, when the cosmic elevator shot upwards and left his stomach in the basement. With a hiss of compressed air, the automatic doors of perception flew open and he stepped out into the astral zone.

To his utter astonishment, he was back in the bank, just before he fired the shotgun. His eyes locked into those of a young bank teller. She was about the same age and looked back at him through a pair of oval gold-rimmed glasses, her thin black hair tied back in a ponytail. Next thing he knew, he was in her quivering body looking at himself firing the gun into the ceiling. Terror shot through his soul. Whoosh, he zapped back into his own blood-filled bag of bones where his adrenalized heart was thumping like a big bass drum.

Looking over at another bank employee, much older than himself and dressed in a neat, navy-blue polyester trouser suit, Angus could see that the lady had once been beautiful. Parted down the middle, her grey hair was gathered into a tight bun at the back of her head. Although the passing years had done their mischief and left deep wrinkles on her face, she was a woman who hadn't tried to recapture her youth with the overuse of makeup. From beneath slack lids, her bright, timeless orbs stared back at him with a mixture of proud dignity and disgust. Angus felt a rushing sensation. A dazzling blue light flashed and he found himself perceiving the scene from inside her head. Once again he saw himself pull the gun's trigger. Unlike her young colleague, this lady experienced no fear, only revulsion. Her thoughts centred on the kind of world her grandchildren had been born into, where maniacs like this long-haired miscreant standing before her could live with themselves having committed such violent, greedy, and repulsive acts.

What Angus experienced was a heavy-duty dose of instant Karma. He'd never heard of such a thing, but that did not matter because it had heard of him and it was not finished with him yet. There was a sound like a cotton sheet being ripped in half. The floor of the astral bank opened up. Down he went, sucked into a vortex. Angus spun and knew where he was bound. He could already feel the heat from the flames of Hell rising to meet him. Having little in the way of a religious education, he flashed on something he'd read in the Bible when he was a kid trying to find out what death was. 'As a man sows, so shall he reap,' echoed over the Sea of Galilee. He realized that he had not been reading a Farmer's Manual. A vile stench filled his nostrils.

'Angus.' He heard the Devil calling his name. 'Angus.' Hell was getting closer by the second. It was becoming hotter. The sulphurous smell was making him gag.

'Angus.' He opened his eyes and sat up. It wasn't Satan calling his name, it was Raj. He'd just returned from a journey that had begun when, dressed in his astral body, he'd climbed Jacob's ladder to reach the stairway to heaven and then, staggering up to the pearly gates, Raj ran into a bureaucratic hassle.

'What do you mean I can't come in?' asked Raj.

'You cannot enter because you're sixty years too early,' replied a Hindu Brahman, a white thread strung across the grey hair on his chest.

'Is it because I robbed a bank?'

'That's not the problem, young spirit. Everybody makes mistakes, the biggest mistake being to keep repeating the same ones. Keep that up long enough and you'll end up in purgatory.' The gatekeeper chuckled and consulted a sheaf of papers attached to a clipboard. 'We have regulations here in Seventh Heaven and one of them says, no disembodied entity is allowed in until the preordained moment has arrived.'

'B-but what can I do about it?' asked a bewildered Raj, sitting down on a bench made from hydrogen with a large 'No Smoking' sign beside it.

'You'll have to reincarnate immediately.'

'Reincarnation!' gasped Raj. 'You mean all that spiritual stuff is true?'

The Brahman's translucent eyes would have looked up to heaven but he was already there. Agitated, he lit up a Ganesh beedi and asked,

'How did you get here? This is highly irregular.'

'I ... I took some LSD, left my body, floated up through the ceiling, passed through some clouds and ... and—'

'Ah, now I understand,' said the Brahman, blowing smoke at the glowing tip of his cheap cigarette. 'Now that I think about it we have had a few souls turning up here prematurely, due to those psychedelic drugs that are so popular just now.'

'I ... I had no idea that this could happen t-to me' stammered Raj.

'Listen up, Raj Gupta,' said the Brahman, tossing his foul smelling beedi away to land at the feet of a patron saint dozing on a nearby cloud. 'I'm a very busy man and I've wasted enough time today already. You will have to return to third dimensional reality immediately.'

'How?' asked Raj, momentarily distracted by a squadron of giggling cherubim flying by overhead.

The divine official studied his clipboard. 'Well, there are two possibilities. The first is for you to reincarnate as a Bengal Tiger.'

'Oh no, man, I can't handle that,' moaned Raj. 'Tigers are big meat eaters and I'm trying to become a vegetarian. What's the other possibility?'

'To be reincarnated as the totem bird of blue funk.'

'A musician?'

'No, a chicken.'

'A chicken?'

'Yes, you can be reborn as a chicken. It's a good way to earn karmic merit. The thing is, you'll have to leave without delay or risk spending eternity in the void,'

'Okay, okay,' said Raj, wondering what he was getting himself into. 'I want to be a chicken.'

'So be it,' said the gatekeeper. 'I'll see you in sixty years.' The Brahman raised a hand in farewell and Raj found himself spinning through space. He entered a tunnel composed of rainbow light and next thing he knew, he was a chicken. A cock crowed from somewhere in the distance.

'Cluck, cluck, cluck.' Raj was amazed to discover he was fluent in the local tongue. He looked around and realized he was in a fenced-off yard. There were half a dozen hens scratching and pecking at the earth in search of grubs.

'Cluckety, cluck, clucky.' He called to his new companions.

'Cluck, cluck, cluckety,' they replied.

Raj felt hungry. He began looking around for something to eat. He came across some yellow grains of corn and began to peck on them. They were delicious.

It was a bright sunny morning and a fresh breeze stirred the grass surrounding him. 'Wow man', he mused, 'who'd have imagined that being a chicken could be so far out?'

'Cluck cluck cloo, cluck cluck cloo.' He voiced his enthusiasm to his feathered friends.

'Clookety clook, coo coo' said a big old hen, her brown plumage tinged with grey. Roughly translated this meant, 'Your days are numbered, dear. Nothing lasts forever.'

Raj was chewing on a tasty worm when a horrible sound ripped through the air. 'Cock a scedaddle dooo!'

Startled, Raj looked up to see a huge red rooster strutting in to the compound. 'Jesus,' he thought, 'look at the size of this guy. I hope to hell he's not feeling horny.' Raj let go of his intestinal juices in a steaming white and olive-green jet.

The cockerel preened himself, did a few indignant laps round the yard and then, using talons as sharp as razors, he grabbed a pullet by the neck. ''Ere you,' crowed the rooster, ''ow many eggs 'ave you laid today?'

'Squawk! I … I'm sorry boss. I've only laid two eggs today, but I'm going to lay some more, I … I promise.'

'Kaka-dada,' screamed the cockerel. 'Too late.' And with that he tore the pullet's head off and tossed it over the fence, leaving its body to run around like a, well, like a headless chicken.

'Fucking hell,' clucked Raj in alarm, realizing Mr Rooster was a psycho.

'Cluuuck, cluuuck,' cried another terrified chicken, feathers flying everywhere as she struggled in the farmyard villain's clutches.

'And you?' screeched the cockerel. 'How many eggs 'ave you laid today, you fat little bitch?'

'One, cluck, one.'

'Kaka kaka, doodoo,' screamed the cock, ripping open the plump boiler's throat and throwing her to the ground. Blood gushed from a mortal wound in her neck and pooled round her twitching body.

Raj was in a panic, flapping around in search of an exit.

''Ere you.' Mr Rooster caught hold of Raj's tail feathers and jerked him closer. 'Your new 'ere, how many eggs 'ave you got for me?'

The cock's claws closed round Raj's throat. Gasping for air, he cried out, 'None, Mister Rooster, none, but I'm trying man, I'm trying.' He was straining with all his might to lay an egg. It was painful, he felt faint but, miracle of miracles, he could feel something coming out of his body. He was on the point of laying an egg in a supreme effort to save his life. He called out, 'Angus, help me.'

'What is it?' asked Angus, sniffing the air. He could still smell Hell.

'I've messed my pants.'

Angus looked at Raj's face in astonishment, it appeared to be undergoing a process of accelerated decomposition, and asked, 'You've done what?'

'I've shit myself. I need to go to the toilet.'

'Jesus, Raj, what a stink.'

'I'm sorry man, I thought I was a chicken. A … a big red rooster was strangling me. He … he scared the shit out of me.'

'Yeah, I can smell that. What a bloody pong.' Angus burst out laughing.

'Hey man, this isn't fuckin' well funny,' complained Raj, close to tears.

'Sure, Raj, anything you say, man.'

Raj started to cry like a child with sobs and hiccups. Snot was running from his nose.

Angus said, 'Let's go.'

He stood up and led the smelly, wide-eyed toddler to the potty room. They edged past Murphy lying on his back. A fluttering was visible beneath his closed eyelids. A beatific smile graced his sealed lips. His arms were folded cruciform over his chest, flattened palms on top of his shoulders. He'd become a Pharaoh resting in a sarcophagus on the deck of a solar boat crewed by Captain William Blake at the helm. Frederick Nietzsche and Socrates were on the oars. Lady Kundalini was the navigator and Aleister Crowley was up in the crow's nest, keeping a lookout in case he sighted the Beast 666.

While Raj cleaned himself up, Angus went through to the kitchen. After putting on the kettle, he sat in a chair and watched his bare feet melt into the concentric patterns on the linoleum floor.

'What's that noise?' asked Raj, returning from the bathroom, his breathing audible. He was gnawing anxiously at his lower lip after hearing startled clucks coming out of the toilet pot and catching a glimpse of the murderous red rooster's face when he'd looked into a wall mirror.

'What noise?'

'Like a train in a tunnel.'

Angus looked around. 'It's the kettle heating water. Relax, there's nothing to worry about,' he said, unsure if that were true.

Over a cup of tea and a joint, the two trippers tried to relate what they had been going through, and still were judging by the direction their conversation was taking.

'You know,' said Raj, 'we've done a dreadful thing. We have to bring the money back to the bank.'

Suddenly overwhelmed by guilt, Angus agreed wholeheartedly. They started making elaborate plans about how to go about returning the cash.

'We could write a wee note saying that we're really sorry.'

'Hey, that's a really good idea,' complimented Raj. 'How about we buy a big bunch of roses? We'll use our own money of course.'

'Of course,' echoed Angus, his own voice sounding strange to him. 'That's a brilliant idea, man.'

'Let's do it now,' suggested Raj positively bubbling over with enthusiasm.

'Do what now?' The voice startled Angus and Raj. They looked up to see Murphy hovering in the kitchen doorway like a fugitive Highland warrior with a suspicious look on his weather-beaten face. Angus explained.

'Nice flowers, a wee fucking note?' exclaimed Murphy, his eyebrows doing the boogaloo half way up his forehead. 'Are the pair of you off your fuckin' trolleys? Please, guys, tell me you're joking.'

Hearing his friend speak like that Angus snapped out of it. Looking at wild-eyed Murphy framed in the doorway, a wave of brotherly love swept over him. 'Jesus', he thought, 'give back the money? I must have seriously lost the plot.' He stalled for a moment to let tension build up, and then, when he could see it was making Murphy uncomfortable, he lied. 'Of course I was joking.' Murphy laughed in relief and Angus joined him. Raj, now cognizant enough to realize he'd just experienced a complete lapse of reason, clicked in a few seconds later and began guffawing louder than both his friends combined.

Back in the living room, a chunk of hash went into making a joint the size of a millionaire's cigar. It took a lifetime to smoke and when it was finished Murphy nervously stubbed the cardboard roach out in an ashtray. 'What's that light coming from behind the curtains?' he asked, wringing his hands. Three dilated pairs of pupils stared at the undulating velvet curtains. Murphy was right, there was a bright light emanating from behind the edges of the thick drapes, as if a powerful searchlight were being directed up at the window from the street below.

'Maybe it's the cops.' Raj, too, was scurrying down 'Paranoia Avenue'.

Angus stood up and went over to investigate. After peeping round the edge of the curtains, he turned towards his friends. His face twisted into a mask of worry. 'Shit,' he hissed.

Raj and Murphy jumped to their feet, their worst suspicions confirmed.

'What the hell is it?' asked Murphy in trepidation.

Angus pulled the curtains apart and laughed as light speared into the room. 'It's the sun coming for you, ya fuckin' clowns, it's Saturday morning.'

A couple of underworld hobgoblins caught in the rays of the rising sun, Raj and Murphy fell back into their armchairs. In the timeless realm of their LSD experience, time had flashed by on Mercurial winged feet.

The two psychonauts stood up and went over to join Angus at the window, where he stood watching life wind up in preparation for another day in the clockwork city. Bug-eyed vehicles whooshed past early morning pedestrian androids, walking purposefully along grey pavements beneath tall trees whose shiny metallic leaves shimmered with a scintillating light. The three young men stood transfixed, fascinated by the scene, as if they were visitors from another solar system, observing life on Earth for the first time. The concerns of the planet's inhabitants were as foreign to them as microchip technology is to Bushmen living in the Kalahari Desert.

It was while sitting back on the sofa bathed in sunlight, sipping on an excellent cup of hot chai that Raj had brewed up, that Angus initiated the next move by saying, 'Hey, listen. This acid is amazing stuff. Does anybody fancy taking another one?'

Nobody actually said a direct yes but three minutes later when Murphy produced his little bag of LSD, there was no doubt in anyone's mind what was going down. 'Trips, anyone?' he asked with a California sunshine smile on his face.

Second dose of acid buzzing through their synaptic channels, Raj put his favourite album of the week on the record deck. Cream, a power trio who'd split up in '68, had been the first of what came to be known as supergroups. A blistering rendition of blues legend, Robert Johnson's 'Crossroads' roared out of the speakers. Cream's guitarist, Eric Clapton, was without doubt one of the era's most gifted and electrifying musicians. During that period, graffiti artists had taken to the streets and sprayed 'Clapton is God' on the city walls. Angus was never to subscribe to the idea. If there was a God of Rock, at the feet of whose guitar-wielding image the devotee could lay his blown mind to attain sonic salvation, he had decided it was Jimi Hendrix. While listening to Hendrix's music under the influence of LSD, Angus soon realized that Jimi, more than anyone else, knew how to jack a guitar lead into the heart of a fabulous untamed beast and unleash a sound that was to become the defining spirit of a musical epoch.

As the morning passed, so did the music. Jethro Tull, The Mothers of Invention, Ten Years After, The Moody Blues and half a dozen other great bands spoiled the trippers for choice on their psychedelic rock 'n' roll journey. By mid-day, ground control communicated that it was time for the Major Toms to leave their capsule and embark on their first space walk. It was Raj who brought up the subject of the shotgun and its box of orange-coloured cartridges. 'We should get rid of that stuff,' he said. 'I don't think I want to do another bank job and I really don't like the idea of having a gun in the house.'

Angus nodded his head. 'I'm with you all the way on that one.'

'What a couple of party poopers you two turned out to be. No pun intended, Raj,' said Murphy, mischief playing on his face. 'But to be honest, I have to admit I went through a few things last night that made me realize I don't want to do another stick-ups either. So let's dump the fuckin' thing.'

Angus was nominated to carry the weapon in a knapsack. When they walked along the street and passed a newsagent shop with a billboard outside proclaiming 'Armed Robbers Get Away With £40,000 Haul', he almost x-bombed in his underpants.

After an eternal trek, the three space travellers entered Kelvingrove Park through a gateway opposite Glasgow's Public Art Gallery. Walking over a broad Victorian-era cast iron bridge, they stopped and gazed down at the River Kelvin's dark green murky waters flowing by below them, its banks edged with soap scum. Flatulent as a glutton's alimentary canal, it was known locally as the 'Smelly Kelly'. They looked around to check that they were not being observed, then everyone nodded when the coast was clear. Angus opened his backpack. The sawn-off shotgun and its oil-stained box of ammunition tumbled into the river. Surrounded by bursting gas bubbles, a small rainbow-coloured slick floated on the water's surface until it faded and disappeared. The trio's brief career as armed bank robbers was over. It was a welcome relief on the one hand to be rid of the gun, and a comfort on the other to have wads of cash stashed underneath the gas cooker at home. To celebrate the occasion, Murphy decided they should go and score some hash. 'Andy Burns lives over the back of the Kelvin Hall,' said he. 'Let's go pay him a visit and see if he's got any good dope for sale.'

The acid trippers continued on their way through the park. They looked up when startled pigeons flew from their perches on verdigris-encrusted statues of famous Victorian personages. Streaked in bird shit, the sculptures' stern faces looked unhappy to Angus, as if the stability they'd strived so hard for while alive had left them frustrated. Cast in bronze, they stood reaping their rewards in the only way that it's granted – being given a place among the forgotten relics of their time.

As Angus, Murphy and Raj approached the gates, they passed an old park keeper who was sitting on a wooden bench. He was a short, thickset man in a shabby dark-green uniform with a peaked hat on his head that would have better suited a North Korean general. His tired face appeared to Angus like it had been made from mouldy cottage cheese. The old man stood up and looked the young men up and down.

'What the fuck are you staring at?' asked Murphy.

'That's just what I'm asking myself,' replied the warden. 'These days I can't tell the difference between the boys and the girls.'

Murphy spat on the ground in front of the man's feet. 'Yeah, like fuck you can't, ya cheeky old cunt.'

The warden's eyes blazed. He rose to the challenge and took a few hurried steps towards Murphy. For a moment, Angus thought the old boy was going to take a swing at his friend. So did Murphy but he didn't look worried about it. He was smiling.

'Come on then,' goaded Murphy 'fuckin' well try it.'

The park keeper wasn't altogether stupid. He could see that Murphy was built like a well-trained middleweight boxer. It was therefore that his attack was limited to a verbal one. His voice rang with indignation when he spluttered into Murphy's amused face. 'No … no respect, that's the problem with young people today. Bring back national service and the birch rod, that's what Harold Wilson and his bloody Labour government should do. I'll have you know I fought in the war so the likes of you could walk about in freedom.'

'Aye right granddad, if that's the case why don't you bugger off an' polish your fuckin' medals?'

The warden was visibly shaking as he stammered, 'Y-y-you're scum, th-th-that's what you are, scum!'

'C'mon, man,' said Raj, taking hold of Murphy's arm and pulling him away from the confrontation. 'What are you playing at? Winding up the parkie like that, you'll give the old fart a heart attack.'

'Aye, that's right,' shouted the old man to their backs as they walked off along the pavement, 'run away like the big Jessies that you are. Get a bloody haircut!'

Andy Burns was an easygoing, slim man with a sallow face who always wore thick black sunglasses. If they weren't covering his permanently bloodshot eyes they were jammed into his thatch of fair hair like a plastic crown of thorns. He lived on the top floor of a grime-stained tenement whose filthy stairwell stank of territorial tomcats' scat mixed with the smell of shit emerging from a waterless communal lavatory out on the landing. He was at home in his flea-infested flat after having returned from London the evening before with three weights (pounds) of Kashmiri twists. The mouldy lumps of potent hashish were a tasty smoke. Nobody disagreed when Murphy decided to splash out and buy four ounces. After sharing a few joints with his customers and getting everyone heavily stoned, Andy asked a question that, unknown to him, would change the course of his three clients' lives forever. 'Have you guys ever thought about going into business as dealers?' Up until that point they hadn't.

An hour later, sitting on top of Hill Sixty, a high vantage point on the edge of the park, the three space cadets began discussing how to go about starting up in the hash trade.

'Maybe my Uncle Suleiman has connections down in London,' said Raj, rubbing his shins. He pulled his trouser legs up. 'Aw for fuck's sake, I'm covered in flea bites.'

'What do you mean, connections?' asked Murphy, glad he'd tucked his jeans into his cowboy boots before entering Andy's grotty apartment.

'Uncle Sulei is shunned by the rest of my family because he's a bit of a gangster,' answered Raj. 'He lives in London's East End, in Hackney. One time I overheard my mother and father saying something about him being involved in the narcotics business.'

'He sounds like our man. Can you get in touch with him?' enquired Angus.

'I think his number's in the phone book in my parent's house. My dad would become suspicious if I ask for it, so I'll just have to write it down when they're glued to the telly watching some shite like *Opportunity Knocks* or *This is Your Fuckin' Life.*'

'When?' asked Angus impatiently, sensing they might be on to something good.

Raj considered briefly and then shrugged, saying, 'Tomorrow?'

'Sounds good,' said Murphy smiling deviously. He, too, felt like a bright new future might be shaping up, so bright in fact that he thought it would be a good idea to invest in three pairs of shades just like Andy's, for himself and his two partners.

Looking out over the city to Glasgow's south side, the tall cranes in Clydebank's shipyards were clearly visible on the horizon, standing like long-legged mechanical war machines from an invading alien civilization. The sun was beginning to set. It was the kind of sunset that Hollywood's cowboy heroes ride off into. Below them the park was a veritable oasis in the heart of the industrial city. Due to the combined effects of the intoxicating hashish and the LSD that was still hooking up unlikely combinations of brain cells, the scene was reminiscent of a pointillist painting in the style of Georges Seurat, whereby the viewer is tricked into believing that dotted patterns are people and things. A hum was rising off the busy city, sounding to their banged out senses like an Om although, at that point in their lives, they still had not heard of the Hindu mystic syllable that is considered to be the most sacred of mantras.

Sauntering home, the trio struck up their customized version of an old Glaswegian pub song, 'I belong to Glasgow. Good old Glasgow town. A couple of trips on a Friday night and Glasgow belongs to me.'

After a good night's rest, Raj went round to his parents' house in search of his uncle's phone number.

Later that evening:

'Hullo, Uncle Sulei, it's me, Raj.'

The voice on the other end of the line rattled and buzzed in Raj's ear like an angry bee trapped in a tin can.

'I'm fine,' said Raj.

'Buzz, buzz zarens?'

'No, I don't live with them anymore.'

'Crackle. Buzz, blurpee?'

'Because me and a couple of ma pals would like to come and have a wee talk to you about a business we're thinking about startin' up.'

'Crackle, dood zzt, bzown.'

'That's right. Hold on a minute.'

Standing inside a vandalized, windowless red telephone box, Raj started to write on a piece of paper with a ballpoint pen.

Knock! Knock! Knock! Impatient to use the phone, a drunken woman with runny eye make-up was rapping on the wooden doorframe with a broken stiletto-heeled shoe.

'Fuck off!'

'Bzztor roopay?'

'Naw, naw, Uncle Sulei, I'm sorry. There's a drunken wifie outside annoyin' me.'

'Zzzt, zzzt, eddy?'

'Yeah, I'm listening.'

'Burble.'

'Is that with an A?'

'Bzzion.'

'Right, okay, square.'

'Bzzt, arzoo oomin?'

'We'll be down on the weekend.'

'Gorgoo. Zoit zoosee.'

'I'm looking forward to seeing you too Uncle Sulei.'

'Gorguy.'

'See you, then.'

Click.

16

THE RETREAT

'The Retreat', Unawantuna Bay, Sri Lanka, November 2004

It was Lara, Angus's lover, partner and friend, who'd designed and overseen the construction of 'The Retreat'. Her Irish father had been a successful architect before he died in 1979. As a child she'd often sat by his side on weekends, when he'd put in extra time at his Dublin office. Although she'd never studied architecture, some of her father's skills as a draughtsman had rubbed off on her while she'd watched him working at the drawing board.

The Retreat had been Angus's dream, but it was Lara more than he who had brought it into reality. In January 2001, they'd bought a large, dilapidated Dutch colonial house set in five hectares of overgrown land on top of a cliff that was the face of a disused granite quarry.

Work had commenced on the day that the title deeds had been signed. With the help supplied by a small army of skilled tradesmen and a gang of hardworking Tamil labourers, the house was restored to its former splendour of a century before. Various annexes were constructed. A huge infinity edge swimming pool was built and gardens lain out and planted. After two years of non-stop work, performed to the sound of cement mixers churning out concrete, wheelbarrows squeaking under heavy loads, mechanical diggers tearing up the ground and power tools whining, the project was finally completed. The small community was entirely self-sufficient. Lines of solar panels provided electricity. Ethanol made from fermented sugar cane juice provided fuel for motorized transport. Angled roofs directed rainwater into underground deposits. Hydroponic fruit and vegetable gardens provided organic food. Nothing was thrown away and all waste matter was recycled. A small farmstead, set in a nearby jungle clearing, was home to chickens, goats and cows. Lara referred to it as 'Animal Farm', minus the pigs. If only one adjective were to be used to describe how The Retreat looked, 'impressive' would be the most appropriate. Angus saw the community as an eco-friendly model for the future.

The 'Rain God' was having an elemental sparring match with the 'Lord of the Wind'. 'Look at my tears of joy,' he cried, bombarding the rooftops of the meditation centre with an unrelenting hail of golf ball sized raindrops.

'That's nothing comparrrred to my powerrrr!' roared the wind, bending a row of tall Washington palms into a line of giant archer's bows.

D.J. Donner was mixing in a booming rumble-in-the-jungle ambient soundtrack. Blitzen Special EFX Company Unlimited provided vibrant forked lightning, streaking across a billion-litre vapour screen.

Inside The Retreat, Hamish sat facing his brother at the opposite end of a long dining table, his stomach filled to bursting point after feasting on a breakfast fit for the King of Gourmetland. Eating over, the twins began to colour in blank spaces from the past.

'And this old crone, what did you say her name was?' asked Hamish.

'Nancy Stewart,' answered Angus.

'And she was demented, you say?'

'Put it like this, when I handed her a couple of fifties, she blew her nose in them, crumpled the money into a ball and swallowed it.'

Hamish cracked a smile. 'Yet it was this madwoman who was instrumental in bringing us together. What did she say to you?'

'We smelt Nancy before we saw her. Lara and I had been on Iona for a couple of hours. I was surprised about how much of Baile Mor as I remembered it was still there, although everything appeared smaller. After paying an emotional visit to my stepfather Daniel's and our mother, Margaret's, graves in the old cemetery, I took Lara to see the cottage where I grew up. The house had been renovated. It had a conservatory attached to the back, which served as a small tea room. It was there that we had lunch. I tell you, it felt strange to be sitting on that spot after all those years.' Angus shook his head, remembering. 'We'd just started eating a skimpy looking salad with too many tomatoes and oodles of mayonnaise in it when Lara turns to me and asks, 'What's that awful smell?' I look up and there's Nancy, smelling like a badly run sewage treatment plant.'

'"Come back to smash the abbey's windows again, have you?" she says. "You were always a cheeky wee bizzum, Angus Macleod."'

'"Nancy, Nancy Stewart," I say. "I don't believe it." Then she snaps at me, "Well you better believe it laddie, because that's who you're bloody well gawking at."'

'What did she look like?'

'That was the unbelievable thing. She looked exactly how I remembered her, except her mouth was a dental write-off because she only had one broken tooth left that was sticking out the middle of her top gum like the Old Man of Hoy. She wasn't a pretty sight. She had a big, dirty white sock with holes in it on her head for a hat. The colour of fallen leaves, her face was a mass of wrinkles. Nancy didn't have hands, she had claws, and they were filthy. But it was her eyes, I'll never forget her eyes, they were amazing.'

'You mean they were beautiful?'

'Yes. Clear and sparkling, like a baby's, even though she must have been well into her nineties.'

'What else did she say to you?'

'Well, the lady who ran the restaurant wanted Nancy to leave immediately. There were a few tourists in the place and the guff rising off the old girl was causing a mass exodus. The manageress was a stiff faced battleaxe. I told her Mrs Stewart was an old friend of mine and I was willing to reimburse her for any losses incurred due to Nancy's malodorous presence. I passed her a few quid and she left us to get on with it.'

'Amazing the effect money can have upon people,' added Hamish.

'Yes. Sometimes sad, but that's the way of the world that we live in. Anyway, Nancy sits down at our table, picks up the hot coffee pot and proceeds to drain it by sucking on its spout. Lara can't believe her eyes. She doesn't know whether to laugh or cry. Next thing we know the old bat's digging in to the butter with a soupspoon. She polishes that off in ten seconds flat.' Hamish slapped his sides at the thought of it and Angus continued. 'Throat well and truly greased, Nancy starts blabbering away like a ventriloquist's dummy on speed. Neither of us could understand a word she was saying. I put my hand on her shoulder to try and calm her down. "Get your bloody hands off o' me, you cheeky wee monkey that you are," she says, brushing my hand away from her dirty torn coat. And then, as clear as a bell she says, "In search of your twin brother, are you?" When I heard that, the pieces fell into place.'

'What pieces?'

'Let me tell you. It started the day before, when we were in Oban and a couple of strange things happened. We had an hour to wait before the ferry to Skye left, and we went into that pub opposite to the big hotel near the harbour. You know that one with the tartan wallpaper. What's it called? The ... the—'

'The Crofter?'

'Yes, that's it. So Lara and I are in The Crofter, enjoying a pint and listening to the Eurythmics' greatest hits coming out of the sound system. Annie Lennox is singing 'Sweet Dreams', I still love that song, as long as I don't hear it too often, and this squinty-eyed drunk with a scar running across his nose, staggers up to us and blurts out, "Oh aye, what have we here? I'll bet thon stuck-up wife of yours doesn't know aboot her." He's nodding towards Lara. "I've a mind to pop oot and make a wee phone call and drop you right in it."

'I look at Lara and she shrugs. The boozer has by now moved in close enough for me to smell his hundred-percent-proof halitosis.

'"Who tha fuck do you think your talkin' tae, pal?" says me, putting on my best Weegie accent.

'He looks a bit shocked and takes a step back. "My name's Cruickshank. Do you no' mind who I am?"

'I adopt the Glasgow hard man role and answer, "Yeah pal, I mind very much who you are, so you better fuck off right now before I decide to do somethin' about it."'

Hamish's shoulders shook with laughter. 'That will have been Andy Cruickshank. I gave him the sack a few years back for stealing copper wire off one of my building sites.'

Angus went on. 'To cut a long story short, Lara and I had noticed a few of the locals casting curious sidelong glances in our direction, and a couple of strangers had said hello to us on the street. At first we'd put this down to us being suntanned strangers in the land of the palefaces but—'

Hamish cut in. 'They thought you were me and when Nancy Stewart asks if you're in search of your twin brother, the penny drops.'

'Precisely.'

'Then what?' asked Hamish, toying with his plastic lighter.

'We start making enquiries on Iona. The only person I was able to get a hold of that I could remember from my childhood days was wee Morag's snobby mother, Eleanor Simpson. She's an old woman now, who needs a Zimmer frame to get around, but her memory's still working fine.'

'And it was her who told you where I was?'

'Not exactly, but she knew you ran a building company somewhere in Oban and, well you know the rest.'

'I'll never forget the day you and Lara strolled into my office.'

'You're not the only one.'

'I can imagine. But even though my foster-parents told me I had a twin brother on my eighteenth birthday, it still came as a shock to meet you face to face. Still, I recognized you as soon as I saw you.'

'All things considered, that's hardly surprising,' quipped Angus.

'You know, there are a couple of questions I've been meaning to ask you about The Retreat.'

'I'm listening.'

'Well for a start, where on earth do all the people living here come from? There must be at least forty of them.'

'Good guess, forty-two to be precise. In answer to your question, I'll put it like this. The internet is a great tool in terms of networking. It's helped me stay in contact with my large extended family and people who like to get away from it all, which is one of the needs we cater to. Apart from that I like to share what's been created here with people who appreciate it.'

'But don't you get tired of having so many people around you all the time?'

Angus shook his head. 'On the contrary, I love it. Since the sixties, I've always had a soft spot for communal living. As long as I can withdraw from it when need be. There's plenty of room here. People are like plants, in the sense that they need plenty of space and fresh air if they want to grow and stay healthy. Anyway, what was the other thing you wanted to ask?'

Hamish looked around. 'How are you able to afford all this?'

'Imports and exports,' replied Angus.

'What kind of imports and exports?'

'I managed to get myself a seat on the board of directors in the M.H.C.'

'M.H.C.,' repeated Hamish. 'I've never heard of them. Are they an international company?'

'Yes. You could say that, very international, in fact.'

'What does the M.H.C. stand for?'

'Moroccan Hashish Company.'

'Drugs!' exclaimed Hamish. 'Jean and I were wondering where all the money came from. You're a drug dealer?'

'Was,' said Angus leaning over to one side to retrieve a fallen napkin from the teak wood floor's fine-grained surface.

'What kind of drugs?' Hamish asked, nervously tapping his fingers on a packet of Marlboro Lights.

'Good ones, the kind repressive, democratically elected governments have made illegal, denying their citizens what should be their inalienable right to explore their own minds – that is, if they feel so inclined. Parallel to this, people who live in less economically advanced, non-democratic nations still have the freedom to delve into their consciousness with mind-expanding substances. I'm talking about hash, marijuana and psychedelics, like mescaline and LSD'

'That's quite a mouthful,' said Hamish, lighting his fourth cigarette that morning. 'But LSD, my God,' he gasped, expelling the word God in a cloud of smoke, 'that's a Class A drug. How could you have sold that to people? That stuff drives teenagers mad.'

'So do narrow-minded uptight parents.'

'That's an absurd assertion.'

'Maybe it is, but that rapid-delivery nicotine tube you're puffing on, tobacco, "the red man's curse", is the most addictive substance on earth. Indians introduced it to the white man and since then it's killed tens of millions of people. It may well be the cause of your death one day. So, before you accuse me, take a look at yourself and no, I don't want one of the filthy things in case you're thinking of offering me one.'

Hamish had been considering asking his brother exactly that. By now he was accustomed to his brother's mind-reading ability, although when he'd asked Angus about it he'd replied that he had more interesting things to read than people's minds.

Angus continued. 'Since we began breakfast, many people have taken their last breath as a result of being addicted to tobacco. By this time tomorrow, more people will have died from cigarette smoking than in the entire history of the psychedelic counterculture, so please don't get too carried away with your accusations.'

Hamish stubbed out his half-smoked Marlboro by twisting and breaking it in an ashtray, realizing as he did that it smelled disgusting.

'Sounds to me like you're applying salve to a guilty conscience. Even if only one person ended up in a mental hospital or jumping out of a high window as a result of taking drugs that had passed through your hands, it's still a terrible thing to live with.'

'To a certain extent I agree with you and, even though I experience no feelings of remorse about what I've done in the past, I won't try to excuse myself. My views on these matters have changed over the years and in my own way I've tried to make amends for any human casualties that I may have been partly responsible for.'

'Really? How?'

'Well, for a start, I've funded two free clinics for the poor. They've already saved hundreds of people's lives by supplying medical attention and medicines that they would otherwise have been unable to obtain.'

'I didn't know you'd done such a thing.'

'Neither do the doctors and nurses who are employed by the clinics.'

'Does Lara know about all this?'

Angus had to laugh at this reference to his spouse.

'What's so amusing?'

'Lara helped me to sell over a hundred tons of hashish.'

'A hundred tons of hashish?'

'Yes, that's what I said, but I'm exaggerating, it was probably closer to eighty, which isn't really so much over a period of years when you take into consideration that's what's consumed in London alone in less than a month.'

'Good grief, you mean to tell me Lara is a drug dealer too?'

'Was.'

'Why do you say was?'

'Because it's over fifteen years since either of us pulled off a deal.'

'How could the pair of you have stooped to such a low level? Was it the lure of easy money?'

Angus looked up towards the ceiling fan's slowly rotating blades, searching for inspiration to lift up their conversation before it descended into an argument. In spite of his heart's desire to keep the peace, he spoke his mind.

'It's easy to criticize. If they become skilled at it, some people even manage to make a living from it. But in this case, I'm sorry to have to inform you that I don't think you know what you're talking about.'

'What exactly do you mean by that?' Not for the first time Hamish felt that his brother was adopting a patronizing attitude towards him.

'I don't mean to sound in any way superior to you,' said Angus.

'Well, that's how you did sound whether you meant it or not,' snapped Hamish, who was annoyed at his brother's ability to read him so easily.

'I see I've ruffled your feathers.' Angus extended his arms sideways with palms facing outwards in a physical expression meant to convey openness. 'You know, I could go into a long rap about some of the people who really do make easy money: corrupt politicians, corporate vultures and so on. But I won't because I don't wish to appear like I'm trying to justify my past actions. It was just one of those things that snowballed over the years. I never thought, right then, I'm going to become a big drug dealer. I just grew into it over a long period of time and hey, I'll be honest, I did it for the money.'

'Well I didn't think you'd have done such a thing to be awarded a CBE by Her Majesty The Queen, and I am aware of the corruption that exists in the world. The broadsheets announce it on an almost daily basis. But the newspapers also report on the huge profits made by black market drug barons.'

'Drug barons,' repeated Angus contemptuously. 'Where did you pick that up from? The *News of the World*? You really want to get on my case about this, don't you?'

Hamish remained silent, trying with all his might to suppress a guilty smile.

'Come on, let that smile out.'

'For goodness sake, how do you do that?'

Angus chuckled. 'There's nothing supernatural going on. It's just a case of being open and receptive. Relax, it's no big deal.'

The tension that had been building up in the room dissolved. Hamish laughed in relief and Angus joined him. Mental barriers dropped and they experienced the special bond that existed between them as twin brothers.

'You know,' said Hamish, 'sometimes I feel attacked by you and I want to—'

'Fight back? I'm aware of that and for my part I ask your forgiveness. You see, I often feel that I'm not getting through to you. It's as if you've written me off as being a talkative eccentric loony who's permanently out to lunch at the Pie in the Sky Cafe.'

'You're right. I do think you talk too much. Anyone listening to you would think that you were in love with the sound of your own voice. Not only that, half the time I haven't the faintest idea what you're waffling on about. And yes—'

'Hold on a minute, Hamish. Let me remind you. It was you who asked me to tell my life story.'

'I haven't forgotten that. Anyway, as I was saying, I do find you weird at times. I know you think I'm unaware,' Hamish used his fingers to make inverted commas above his head, 'but I'm conscious enough to realize that I'm a proud father who did a damned good job of raising my three daughters. Something, I might add, you know very little about.'

'Being proud is nothing to take pride in,' commented Angus. 'You sound like somebody who counted up the gold stars on your report card when you were a schoolkid. Forty years on, you're still running on the same programme.'

'Don't be so bloody well smart, Angus. It's your turn to listen to me for a change. One of my biggest problems with you is that your life is so full of contradictions I don't know what to make of it. Like me, you're a stubborn old dog. I suppose that's part of the Macleod's genetic inheritance. After I found out I'd been adopted, I made some enquires and it turns out that our father was, by all accounts, very headstrong. When—'

'Well I'm glad to hear that you admit to us sharing at least one thing in common. Being obstinate is—' Angus's mobile phone started to play 'Auld Lang Syne'. He picked it up, flipped it open, listened and said, 'That was thoughtful of you Jeeps, bring it in.' He closed the phone, put it back on the table and a moment later there was a sharp knock on the thick wooden door.

Angus twisted around in his seat. 'Come in,' he called, his voice echoing off the wood-panelled walls, bare except for a large, oblong, multi-coloured Australian Aboriginal dreamtime dot painting.

The door swung inwards and a short, chubby man entered the room. He was bearing a copper tray with a stainless steel coffee pot balanced upon it. His bare feet slapped on the floorboards. He wore a

243

baggy khaki jungle trekker's outfit with a bright orange scarf wrapped around his head to form a slipshod turban. His long grey beard had coloured beads threaded into it. Large gold rings hung in both of his pierced ears. He might have been mistaken for an eighteenth century pirate had it not been for his pair of yellow-tinted, aviator style Ray-Bans and the absence of a neurotic green parrot squawking on his shoulder. There was a note of affectionate amusement in Angus's voice when he welcomed him. 'Good morning, Jeeps, how are you doing?'

'Morning, Commander,' said Jeeps as he bowed from the waist after placing the tray on the reddish-brown mahogany tabletop.

'I'd like to introduce you to my brother. Hamish, this is an old friend of mine, Jeeps.'

'Pleased to meet you.' Hamish stood up, extending his right hand.

Jeeps appeared suddenly nervous as he took Hamish's hand between both of his. 'Fit like? The pleasure's all mine. Jings,' he gasped, studying Hamish's face. 'Ye look just like the boss here.'

Hamish knew by the Doric dialect that he was a Scotsman from the Northeast Coast. He made an educated guess. 'You're an Aberdonian.'

Jeeps shot him a suspicious look. 'Aye, that's right. How did you ken that?'

'Your accent.'

'Oh aye, right,' said Jeeps, his surprised face as open and innocent as a child's. He burst into song and started to waltz around the room with an imaginary partner. 'The Northern Lights of Old Aberdeen mean home sweet home to me, tra-la-la-la-la-de.'

Hamish glanced at his brother and saw he was grinning from ear lobe to ear lobe.

The ballroom dancer paused by a wall-to-wall window. The rain was beating out a staccato rhythm as it hit the glass and ran down in a continuously flowing opaque sheet, making it difficult to see what lay beyond.

'Christ,' Jeeps called out, startling Hamish, 'will you look at that weather. Mother Nature's fairly chuckin' it down today. Good for the wildfowl, though, eh? Quack! Quack! Quack!'

The barrel-chested fellow put his fists under his armpits, started flapping his arms and began to circle around the table calling out like a distraught duck. Hamish couldn't believe his ears or eyes. He looked once more to his brother, in search of a sane reflection. He didn't find one.

'Quack! Quack! Quack!' Jeep's squawking was becoming more frantic, accompanied by him pumping his arms up and down like pistons. He stopped by a corner, squatted down and gave one last, very loud, agonizing 'Quaaaack!' Without further ado, he stood up and walked over to Hamish with something in his hand. Opening it, he offered Hamish a large blue duck egg. Incredulous, Hamish took the egg and stared at it as if it were a rare zoological exhibit from a natural history museum.

Jeeps shouted. 'Extra, extra, read all about it. Scotsman lays an egg in Sri Lanka.' He fell silent and crossed his eyes.

'What are you up to today?' asked Angus.

'Trying to get rid of me, commander?'

'No, no, relax. I'm curious, that's all.'

'Oh inquisitive, it's like that is it? Well now, let's see ... I just thought I'd bring you a pot of fresh coffee. Err ... no ... that's not quite right. You see I simply brought you coffee because I felt like it. It just happened. I didn't think about it. Now I'm going to head back to my cave to smoke a chillum and have a wee play on my guitar. That said, I have to add, that's only the mind talking because as everyone whose got a bit of sense knows, there's an awful lot can happen between the here and the there. Nobody knows what's going to happen next. There, how does that sound?'

'Fine, Jeeps, fine,' replied Angus.

'Well it sounded like a load o' bollocks to me. In fact there are only three words that don't sound like nonsense to me.'

Intrigued Hamish asked, 'And what are those three words, Mister Jeeps?'

'Who am I? Mister Macleod. Who am I?'

'Well, I don't know about you but I'm in no doubt as to who I am. I'm Hamish Macleod.'

'That's a name.'

Hamish hadn't a clue what Jeeps was talking about, and reached for his cigarettes. A look of alarm took hold of the little Scotsman's face.

'Oh no, Mister Macleod, you have to stop smoking those horrible things right now, or very soon they'll bring you into terrible danger.'

Uncomfortable, Hamish glanced at Angus who in turn looked up into Jeep's worried eyes.

'That's enough out of you, Jeeps. I'll be seeing you later.'

'Aye right you are, Commander, God willing that is. Insh'Allah, you know.' Jeeps raised his hands prayer-like. 'Good day to you, Mister Macleod, it's been nice meeting you.' He turned to face Angus and said, 'I knew you were trying to get rid of me.' He bent closer to him and whispered in his ear. 'Listen, man, I'm not fooling around. I dreamt about him last night. He's got to stop smoking. You have to get him to pack it in, or he's had his fuckin' chips.'

Jeeps bowed, turned and walked out of the room. Before closing the door, he looked back over to Hamish and flashed a peace sign with two fingers. The door closed silently behind him.

Hamish was visibly relieved to see the back of Jeeps. 'Good heavens, who on earth was that?'

Angus reached for the coffee pot. 'That was the "wee man".'

'I could see that, but who is he? He was behaving like he's out of his mind on drugs.'

'That's because he probably is. Jeeps believes you have to be out of your mind to know God.'

'What? I thought there was no drug use allowed in The Retreat.'

'True, but that's mostly for the guests. The drug policy is flexible. Besides, Jeeps is a very special case.'

Hamish lit a cigarette, inhaled and then blew a jet of agitated smoke up into the air, which was his idea of a concession towards his non-smoking brother. 'I've never met such a nervous person in my life. What's so special about him?'

'He's ... he's ... well, he's a crazy Buddha,' replied Angus.

'You've got to be joking.'

'No, straight up, the wee man's a living example of crazy enlightenment.'

'Well, I can understand the crazy part. He's obviously certifiable.' Hamish studied the blue egg for a moment. 'I find it extremely hard to believe there's anything illuminated about your Mister Jeeps whatsoever.'

'As an old friend of mine used to say, belief and doubt are two aspects of the same coin,' countered Angus.

'Did I hear him say he lives in a cave?'

'That's right, over in the jungle.'

'Where do you know him from?'

'Oh, way back, we used to hang out and take LSD together in the sixties.'

'And now you mean to tell me he's some kind of wise man?'

'Yes. And not only that, Jeeps is the funniest person I know. He makes me laugh and, as any good doctor will tell you, laughter is good for your immune system.'

'Why does he call you Commander?'

'What is this, twenty questions?'

'I'm curious, that's all.'

'That's understandable, but I'd like to return to what we were discussing before Jeeps popped in to entertain us.'

'Hold on a minute, Angus. Aren't you the same person that said to me a couple of days ago that you can't step in the same part of the river twice?'

'You got me,' conceded Angus. 'I was quoting a sixth century Greek philosopher called Heraclitus. What he said still holds true but, as I see it, there's no harm done in trying to step in the same part of the river twice, unless you don't like getting your feet wet.'

'I see that, like your no-drug policy, your philosophy is also flexible.'

'Touché. Now where were we?'

'We were talking about you and Lara having been drug dealers in the past; successful ones, from what I can gather.'

'Yes, it was a lucrative business to be involved in. We made a few bob.'

Hamish turned at the waist and looked over at the imposing window. The rain had slackened and a patch of blue sky could be seen appearing from behind rainbow-tinged charcoal-grey clouds. Over to his right he could make out the edge of the black tiled Olympic size swimming pool, which he'd taken great pleasure in diving into every day since first arriving at The Retreat a month before.

'Judging by the looks of this place, you're making a colossal understatement.'

'Well, all right then. We made a lot of money.'

Hamish was enjoying himself. His brother was not being as forthcoming as he normally tended to be. He wondered about the source of Angus's evasiveness.

'Weren't you worried about being caught?'

'Of course I was. Unfortunately, as is so often the case, worrying didn't help. I still ended up in jail.'

'You've already told me about the time you were locked up for stealing all those evil nicotine-filled cigarettes.'

'My, you're sharp today,' said Angus. 'Thing is, that was only my first time inside.'

Hamish feigned surprise. 'Don't tell me it's my brother, the recidivist. Is it?'

'Not quite,' said Angus, smiling slightly.

There was a bright flash followed by a loud peal of thunder. The window reverberated, the air conditioning unit fell silent and in the same instant the fan above their heads stopped turning.

'So what was it like being a drug dealer?'

Angus quickly ran a complicated story through his mind and whittled it down to a short statement. 'At first it was fun, like a Felliniesque big dipper ride. Later it turned into an exciting gentleman's sport. In the end it was business as usual while trying to keep one step ahead of the Heinekens.'

'And for the benefit of the English-speaking listener in your one-man audience would you mind explaining who or what are the Heinekens?'

'Spanish custom's patrol boats are painted the same colour as the Dutch brewer's beer cans.'

'Oh, I see. Now I get it. Speeding across the Strait of Gibraltar under the cloak of darkness, I presume. Anyway, I have to say, I'm a bit surprised by your reticence,' said Hamish unaware that he was, in fact, being reeled in for a storytelling marathon.

Angus expelled a force five sigh between his lips and made a whistling sound. 'I don't mind telling you everything, but you have to understand this is a long and winding story.'

It was pouring again. Hamish looked out at the torrential rain, which was falling in grey sheets and said, 'It doesn't look like we will be going anywhere this morning.'

Angus stood up and walked over to the expansive window. Normally from this elevated position it was possible to have a panoramic view that took in the coastal town of Galle to the north and a line of golden sandy bays stretching away into the distance along Sri Lanka's southwest coast. Mist had moved in to shroud the garden and reduce visibility to twenty metres.

Facing his brother, Angus said, 'It will require some time to recount that part of my life. You see, I wasn't only a dealer, I also played the smuggler's role.'

'Well, shiver me timbers, if it isn't old Captain Angus, the buccaneer. I can hear the Jolly Roger flapping on the halyard and you ordering people to walk the plank.'

Angus smiled, returned to his seat and poured himself a large mug full of coffee. Hamish found its tangy aroma impossible to resist and asked for a refill. He looked over towards Angus, now sitting with his hands steepled, staring into space, as he was apt to do before launching off into one of his narratives. They sat in companionable silence for some time, Angus absorbed in his thoughts, while Hamish listened to the rain as it pounded out an abstract rhythm on the roof tiles.

'Listen,' said Angus suddenly, 'what you have to understand is that the word "drug" is generic. It includes a whole gamut of substances from aspirin to Zyban. I never—'

'Hold on,' interrupted Hamish. 'What, might I ask, is Zyban?'

'It's a drug that's used to relieve nicotine withdrawal symptoms. Maybe you should try it because smoking, I've been told, is not good for you, for reasons other than you might imagine.'

'Oh, I see, go on.' Hamish added another cigarette butt to the half dozen or so already lying bent out of shape in the glass ashtray.

'As I was saying, apart from cigarettes,' Angus winked at his brother, 'I never sold a drug that I wasn't into myself. Take cocaine, for example. It's an easy substance to abuse and at present enjoys a reputation of being a status gourmet drug for those who can afford to pay a hundred dollars a gram for something that's been stepped on so many times they'll be lucky if it keeps them high for half and hour. If my memory serves me well, I think it was the American actor, Robin Williams, who said, "Cocaine is God's way of telling you you're making too much money." It's a thin line that separates a recreational coke user from a habitual one. I've seen a few friends get seriously messed up when infected by white line fever. Others I know enjoy it and if the company is right and the Peruvian flake's as pure as freshly driven snow, I might be tempted to have a wee toot myself.'

'I take it that this is another example of your flexible attitude, is it?'

'Yes, I suppose you could say that. As for the business side of things, I never sold a gram.' Angus paused, clearing some obstacle in his throat. 'There was a period in my life when I might have gotten into it. Now I like to imagine that I knew better. Coke dealers often rattle on about the "heavy karma" that goes with dealing Charlie, but still they keep selling it. In a world where money appears to be king, I can't say that I blame them because after cutting pure cocaine with baby laxative or cheap procaine powder, the profits can be astronomical. The general attitude in those circles is, "if I don't sell it somebody else will." As for heroin, I detest the stuff and the people who deal it. Coke might be borderline but smack's a flat line for sure. When it comes to mind-expanding chemicals like LSD and—'

'Angus.'

'What?'

'Would you please do me a favour and go back to the time in your life when your career as a drug dealer began?'

'I actually prefer "dope dealer". That's a title I'm more comfortable with.'

'Whatever, will you just do as I request?'

'Are you sure you're up for this? I wasn't exaggerating when I said it's a long story.'

'So was *Once Upon A Time In America* and I enjoyed that'.

'Great movie, nobody could have played Noodles like De Niro.'

'What about Al Pacino?'

'Nah, he'll always be Scarface for me.'

'God, that was such a violent film. Don't tell me you liked it,'

'No I didn't like it. I loved it. That's one of my all-time favourite movies. Do you remember that scene when Tony Montana's getting tore into that big pile of yay-yo? He was like the beast unleashed, absolutely brilliant. And that shootout at the end when—'

'For crying out loud, will you just get on with your story?'

'All right, muthafucka, don't say I didn't warn ya,' said Angus Montana. 'First ya get the money, then ya get tha power and then ya get tha wom—'

'Angus!'

Once upon a time in Cambodia, Hamish was sitting on a landmine, smiling as he recalled how later that day, in The Retreat's small Dolby-Surround cinema, he'd watched *Scarface* with Jean, Lara, Angus and a few of his friends. He'd had to admit that he enjoyed it, although he couldn't bear to watch the scene where one of Tony Montana's Cuban cohorts was killed by a chainsaw. It came to mind how he'd laughed with everyone else when Al Pacino got up on a Miami discotheque's dance floor to strut his stuff with a gorgeous, coked-up Michelle Pfeiffer.

Angus had met more than most when it came to gangsters and drug-dealing sharks. None of them were in the same league as Tony Montana when it came to pure viciousness and depravity, but some of them were equally as twisted. Raj's Uncle Sulei was no exception.

17

THE DEALERS MACDOPE

London. 18 September 1970.

'What's with the golden gun, Uncle Sulei?' enquired Raj, nodding towards the chrome-plated semi-automatic pistol lying on the low round table in his uncle's office. The only illumination in the musty-smelling room came from a shaded standard lamp with a yellow light bulb in it, reflecting gold off the handgun. The thick curtains in the middle-aged Pakistani's basement office were permanently drawn. Periodically under police surveillance, the CID were well aware that Mr Suleiman Khan was involved in nefarious activities but experienced difficulties when it came to pinning his name to any them.

Picking up the weapon and clicking on its safety, Suleiman answered his nephew. 'My dear boy, this is nothing more than a hearing aid. Many of my business associates need to pay close heed to what I say. This little beauty helps them listen more attentively.' With an unsettling metallic clunk, Suleiman placed the gun back on the table in front of Raj.

Angus felt an icy chill blow down the back of his neck and he wondered if Raj's uncle was being ironic. He asked, 'Mister Khan, what are all those pictures on the wall?'

'Please, Angus, call me Uncle Sulei. Raj has told me you're a close friend of his and therefore you're part of the family now. Those pictures that you're referring to are photographs of my beloved Mecca. I've been on the Hajj three times in my humble life.'

'What's the Hajj?'

'Why, my boy, it's the great pilgrimage to the holy city of Mecca in Saudi Arabia that all Muslims must undertake at least once in their lives – that is, if they can afford to do so.'

Angus perceived Uncle Sulei to be a man who was so bad that he was good. He'd liked Raj's uncle from the moment he had set eyes on him. Suleiman was dressed in a spotless long white cotton shirt and matching trousers, an embroidered prayer cap perched on the back of his head. He had black oily hair, a neatly trimmed beard, a mouthful of gold teeth and wore thick Buddy Holly glasses. Because of the power of the lenses, his eyes darted about at the bottom of two deep pools and appeared smaller than they actually were. The appellation Uncle suited his benevolent personality; a clever ruse intended to disarm people. Underneath his friendly veneer, Suleiman was as deadly as a basketful of anvil-headed, virulent vipers. One had to be alert to catch it, and Angus was, because every once in a while he saw an expression of controlled violence flashing across the criminal's otherwise genial face. There was no doubt in his mind that respect was a key word in Suleiman's vocabulary. He knew that if the Pakistani sensed anyone being in the least way irreverent towards him, he would spare no time or weight in coming down hard on his or her impertinent head.

Sitting in a dimly lit corner of the large, comfortably furnished room was Mustapha, Suleiman's dogsbody. Uncle Sulei sometimes called him Mustaphafag, teasing the man-gorilla escaped from a cage in Regents Park Zoo for being a chain smoker who in all probability fell asleep at night with a lit fag stuck between the thick lips of his craggy face. Suleiman's restless tiger-shark eyes peered out from behind his spectacles as he gave a broad smile to the three young men sitting before him, flashing enough gold to pay the dowry of a Pakistani princess. 'Well my boys, how can I be of service to you?' he asked, striking a match and leaning forward to give flame to a pair of thick candles that, a moment before, Mustapha had placed on the centre of the table.

Raj did the talking while Suleiman listened, his gold-ringed fingers drumming impatiently on his knees to some rhythm in his head.

'And how much are you boys wishing to invest in your business venture?'

Raj handed his uncle a plastic bag containing the money. Suleiman counted the bills with the speed of a skilled bank teller. He made a quick calculation on the coloured wooden beads of an abacus that, like the steel grip of his automatic, was always close at hand. He summoned his gofer. 'Mustapha.' Suleiman peeled off £300 from a bundle of twenties, set them aside and, standing up, gave the rest to the swarthy man whose shaved bullet head glistened in the fuzzy light. When addressing his aide, Suleiman spoke in his mother tongue. With a look of dog-like devotion, Mustapha said nothing, only nodded now and then to let his master know that he understood an important point. After receiving a pat on the back, the hulk growled and strode out of the room.

Uncle Sulei returned to his seat and his guests. 'Tea?' Before anyone had a chance to respond he called out, 'Fatima!'

A moment later his youngest wife entered the room, her slippered feet padding over thick woven rugs with patterns like fantastic animals' hides. Dressed from head to toe in black cotton, Fatima was demure when she approached her husband. She was wearing a veil, and the slit of pale skin that revealed so little of her face accentuated the thick kohl makeup surrounding her sparkling eyes. The distinct fragrance of attar of roses emanated from her mysterious form, bringing with it a note of female tenderness.

'You wretched woman, where have you been? Can't you see I have guests? Bring tea and sweets at once,' ordered Suleiman, clapping his hands in an effort to speed the process up.

Fatima bowed and, accompanied by the swishing of her skirts, disappeared through a doorway. Her elegance would have been better suited to the environment of a Bedouin tent belonging to a desert prince.

Uncle Sulei made a show of studying his thick gold Rolex. 'You will have to excuse me, boys. It's time for my afternoon prayers.'

Left alone, the three prospective dope dealers sat back in large stuffed armchairs arranged around the circular hammered–brass table and looked at each other expectantly.

'What do you think?' asked Raj.

'I think he's too much, man,' answered Angus. 'He's like a character out of a book'

'I like him too, but I'm not taken in by his "Uncle" trip.' Murphy paused, and then went on. 'He's like a hyena; one wrong move and he'd bite your arm off sooner than look at you.'

'Murphy, take those sunglasses off,' ordered Raj.

'What for?'

'Because I get the feeling Uncle Sulei does not like to speak to a man if he can't see his eyes.'

Murphy removed his circular, dark blue, John Lennon sunglasses and deposited them in the breast pocket of his red corduroy jacket that had an enamelled black and white peace badge pinned to a lapel. With a rustle of fabric, Fatima returned carrying a brass tray laden with delicate pastries and glasses of steaming spicy tea. She didn't say anything. For a brief moment Angus caught her eye. An exotic butterfly's wings, the serrated curves of her long eyelashes fluttered. With a graceful movement she averted his gaze and swished once more out of sight, discreet like a shadow from the tomb.

Angus sighed and inhaled the lingering scent of her perfume, which hung on the room's still air like strands of silk. He said, 'I wouldn't mind finding out what's under her robes.'

'For fuck's sake, Angus,' hissed Raj. 'Cool it, man. If Uncle Sulei heard you say that he'd cut your nuts off and barbecue them for breakfast.'

'He's right,' added Murphy. 'These Muslim geezers are dead serious when it comes to their women. Careful what you say in here, I wouldn't be surprised if this place was bugged.'

'Everything all right, boys?' Uncle Sulei appeared out of nowhere and sat down.

Angus raised a glass of tea to his lips. 'Cheers, Uncle Sulei, everything's just grand.'

Half an hour later, Mustapha returned and handed his boss a canvas bag with a tennis racket sticking out of it. Suleiman tugged on the sports bag's zipper and removed seven red cellophane-wrapped slabs of black hashish stamped with golden crescents. He made a neat pile of the hash and patted it affectionately.

'There you are, boys, seven good kilos.' Suleiman turned to Mustapha, who had an unlit fag dangling gangster-style from one side of his mouth, and said, 'Give me one of your cigarettes.' Suleiman used the tobacco to make long tapering joint. He lit it with a solid gold Cartier lighter, took a few puffs and handed it to his nephew after blowing a large smoke ring into the room. 'Taste and try before you buy. Always remember to sample the goods, Raj, my boy.' The master gave his apprentices a nod of encouragement. Once the spliff had gone around, he asked, 'Well, boys, what do you think?'

The gear was a mediocre smoke. It was commercial border hashish, made in the no-man's-land of the Pakistan-Afghan frontier region. Containing a sprinkling of opium, the high obtained was more of a heavy stoned that mellowed the smoker out in preparation for a night of dreamless sleep. Its price was its selling point. The three novice dealers would encounter no difficulty in selling it quickly and doubling their investment in under a week.

'I think its fine, Uncle Sulei,' said Murphy, his eyes hooded from the drug's narcotic effects. 'Will we be able to come back for more?'

'Whenever you boys have the money to invest, I'll always be at your service. Now, then, before you go, would you like to share a drink with me?'

Without waiting for an answer, he clapped his hands. On cue, Fatima wafted into the room carrying on her tray four glittering, cut-crystal whisky glasses. Mustapha fetched an unopened bottle of Johnnie Walker Black Label from a liquor cabinet set into a corner. The movements of their well-rehearsed roles were fluid and unobtrusive.

The fledgling dealers would soon discover that polishing off a bottle of Scottish whisky or two concluded all business transactions with Uncle Sulei. The Pakistani's idea of 'one for the road' was a pickled liver. Suleiman loved drinking whisky almost as much as playing with his tribe of children who lived upstairs in his end of terrace Victorian house.

Outside, the temperature had dropped. Rush-hour traffic was building up on the streets.

'Fuck me, I'm half pissed,' said Angus as he and his two friends crossed the square in front of Uncle Sulei's home.

'Me too.' Raj's boot soles scuffed the pavement in testimony to the fact that he was not altogether in control of his legs. Murphy turned round to look back at the run-down exterior of the building they'd just exited.

'What a sly old fox,' he said, 'who'd ever guess what was going on behind those shabby walls? I feel like I've just spent a week in Karachi. Oh!' Murphy retrieved a slip of paper from his jacket's inside pocket and, pulling open the glass-panelled door of a phone box, spoke over his shoulder. 'Just remembered, I need to make a quick call.'

'Hurry up, then.' Raj was squinting at his watch under a streetlight's neon green glare. The city hummed in the background. From the direction of a nearby roadworks, the sound of a pneumatic drill ruptured the air like a heavy-bore machine gun firing on automatic. Keening in the distance, a lone police car's siren ululated. It was starting to rain and Raj knew their train left at six o'clock. 'We've got half an hour to make it back to King's Cross Station.'

Murphy didn't catch that because the hinges on the telephone kiosk's door screeched like an overdone sound effect in a Hammer Studio's B-movie horror film. He fumbled for some coins in his pocket and took in a deep breath of cold air, trying to clear Uncle Sulei's whisky miasma from his brain. 'Phew!' The filthy call box stank of incontinent tramps. He dialled a number, still not sure what to say to Acid Mike if he picked up the phone on the other end of the line. 'Tring-tring, tring-tring.' Analogue sounds rang in his ear – digital was still an unrealized dream.

'Mike here, please leave a message after the beep and I'll get back to you. Stay cool.' Peep.

'Hi, Mike, my name's Murphy. I'm a friend of Lenny. He said that you might be able to … err … emmmh, help me out with a few small things. Here's my number. So give me a ring when you've got the time, like. Thanks … ehm … stay cool, man.'

Murphy had forgotten about the message he'd left on Acid Mike's Ansaphone by the time a taxi deposited him and his two mates outside Kings Cross Station. As he slipped his wallet back into his jeans back pocket he glanced up and said, 'Keep the change.'

'Thanks, Guv,' said the taxi driver.

Groggy, Murphy turned away from the cabby's jaded countenance, thinking that whisky and hash was a bad combo.

Loud announcements about arrivals, departures and delays echoed off the station's cavernous glass roof as the three friends wound their way through knots of commuters and boarded the Glasgow Express. Raj had bought an evening newspaper and when the train rumbled through a tunnel he looked up from it. He said, 'Shit, man, I just read some really bad news.' Murphy and Angus looked over to where he was sitting. 'Jimi Hendrix died this morning.'

'How?' asked Angus.

Raj consulted the newspaper. 'It says he died this morning at the Samarkand Hotel, Bayswater, London, and there's going to be an inquest.'

Their compartment shuddered when a train shot by, moving in the opposite direction.

'What a fucking drag, man,' said Murphy. 'Mister Purple Haze won't be kissing the sky anymore.'

'Not in this world at least,' added Angus.

The Stones kept on rolling and Mick Jagger was singing something on the radio about seeing a red door and wanting to paint it black. Angus was thinking what a great drummer Charlie Watts was and Andy Burns was taking a corner cut of brown border hash away from his finely tuned nostrils.

'At that price,' said Andy, 'I can shift ten of these a week.' He looked over at his three business acquaintances and took a double take. 'Hey guys, what's going on? You're all wearing the same style of sunglasses as I am.'

'Yeah, man, sign of the times,' said Murphy. 'Move over Andy and let the Dealers MacDope sell the candy. Here's a present.' He handed Andy a plastic bottle.

Andy took it and asked, 'What's this, man?'

It was Raj who answered, 'That's DD fuckin' T, and if you don't use it to get rid of the fleas in this shit-hole you're living in you won't be seeing us again.'

The dealer coughed up a lungful of blue smoke and thus began what is known as 'a good working relationship'.

The next morning, Angus and Raj were back on the train to London, on their way to see Uncle Sulei again. It turned out to be a carbon copy of their previous visit two days before, except they left his house with fifteen kilos and slightly more drunk, having shared a bottle of Chivas Regal between the three of them. Two months later, the Dealers MacDope levelled out at twenty kilos a week. Their customers were asking for better quality gear and the lads invested in a white three-litre Ford Granada for their business trips down to London and back.

It was a cold January evening in Glasgow and the three dealers had their feet up. Donovan was on the stereo singing 'Sunshine Superman'. Out in the hall the phone rang. Murphy went to answer it, happy to get away from the vibrato voice of Scotland's answer to Bob Dylan.

'Hello. Speaking. Who? Oh yeah, Mike. Sorry, man. Yeah, that's me. I'll be down in London next week. Hold on a minute somebody's taken the pen.'

Murphy hurried into the kitchen. He rummaged in the odds and ends drawer. He returned to the phone with the best he could come up with, the stub of a pencil.

'OK Mike, I'm listening.' He scribbled on the wallpaper. 'Right then, I'm looking forward to meeting you. Thanks for the call.'

Murphy returned to the living room, took a seat and started to roll himself a dovetail joint. Donovan's next song, proclaiming how mellow and yellow he was, came to an end.

'Sounds like the cunt's got jaundice,' complained Murphy. 'Come on guys, take that shite off and put on some decent music.'

'What's wrong with Donovan?' asked Raj.

'There's no oomph in his music, that's what's wrong. I ask you, mellow yellow?' Getting up from his seat Murphy walked over to the turntable and intentionally pulled the stylus over the long player's shiny black surface. Riiiip!

Angus glanced up in annoyance. 'Take it easy, Murph.'

Murphy put on Santana's first album. The conga and drum intro to 'Soul Sacrifice' pattered out of the speakers. When the bass kicked in he twisted the volume control clockwise.

Murphy said, 'Now that's what I call high energy music.'

Nobody disagreed.

'Who was that on the phone?' asked Raj. He had to shout because of the loud music.

'A guy called Acid Mike.'

'Interesting name, who is he?' enquired Angus.

'A guy down in London who sells acid.'

'Even more interesting,' said Angus. 'Where do you know him from?' He was thinking it would be great to get their hands on some more LSD. They'd almost managed to gobble up the entire contents of Murphy's little plastic bag.

Murphy did not want to mention Lanky Lenny's name, so he fabricated his answer. 'I met him one Saturday afternoon, down Portobello Road at a free Hawkwind concert under a flyover and we swapped phone numbers.'

Angus could read Murphy's face like an 'A to Z' and could tell that his friend was not being straight with him. He let it pass knowing that Murphy enjoyed having a few secrets on the go. 'What's he like?' he asked.

'You'll find out when you meet him.' Murphy answered casually, realizing Angus had probably picked up on his fib as being casual was something he was not very good at.

Meanwhile, Acid Mike was sitting in his apartment down in London, nursing a mug of hot Yogi Tea and feeling pissed-off about Leonard passing his number on to a complete stranger. He'd just returned from California with a hundred grams of crystal LSD stashed in the soles of his cowboy boots. He'd spent a month in Venice Beach waiting to score. The day had started badly when he'd gotten a tug while strolling through the customs hall in Heathrow Airport that morning. Dressed in a uniform which would have looked more in place on a bowling green, a female customs officer had searched his suitcase, which was crammed full of underground rock albums. She'd been more intent on asking him a string of dumb questions and studying his suntanned face for telltale twitches or revealing eye movements. Her own face was home to nervous eyes, a pasted-on smile and caked with enough makeup to render a wall. Not registering anything to raise the needle on her suspicion meter, she'd closed Mike's bag and mouthed something polite that sounded empty.

Mike squirmed when he recalled her hollow voice and how he'd broken two of his golden rules for dealing with the customs. First, he'd looked her directly in the eye, big mistake, and then he'd said, 'That's all right, Officer. I know you're only doing your duty.' Upon hearing this, her double chin had merged with her throat and she'd looked twice at him, meaning she would remember him. 'Shit,' he cursed before drinking the rest of his cinnamon flavoured tea.

'Bloody hell.' His thoughts returned to his brief telephone conversation with Murphy. When he'd first heard the Scottish voice on the Ansaphone, he'd decided not to call back but, during the afternoon, he'd changed his mind when he found out his main buyer had been busted.

The police had caught mouth-wateringly gorgeous, strawberry blonde Wendy B. White with her knickers down, her well hung Nigerian boyfriend handcuffed to a four-poster bed, a rolled-up fifty pound note stuck up her nose and a pile of illegal substances on her kitchen table big enough to start up her own pharmaceutical company. This had happened in the early hours of a Sunday morning, when the Thames Valley drug squad decided to nip round to Cheyne Walk in order to pay Miss White a visit. The police officers used a battering ram to knock on her Chelsea apartment's solid oak front door, smashing it clean off its hinges. Wendy's stepfather, a prominent Conservative Party MP, wouldn't be able to help her much with that kind of evidence stacked against her. Mike reckoned it would be three to four years before he saw her again. He was confident that she wouldn't grass him up because he had insurance.

Before flying over to the States, Mike had been up to his usual game of pretending to be hard-pressed for cash. His logic being, why use his own hard earned money, tucked safely away in Zurich, when he could use other peoples'. He'd persuaded his biggest customer, Wendy, to invest in his latest lysergic smuggling venture. She'd fronted him the cash for the whole deal when he'd promised to double her money quickly. Mike was a parsimonious skinflint but he was also a man of his word and therefore he'd fulfill his promise. The only thing that had changed was that Wendy would have to wait a little longer than expected to count her profits. Mike knew that the thought of returning to the free world, where a briefcase full of crisp bank notes sat waiting to be collected by her, would make Wendy's time in prison that much easier to do. 'Real money,' mused Mike, 'doesn't always need to talk – sometimes it only has to whisper.'

If the Dealers MacDope could make the right connections, the cash would start to roll in even faster, on solid gold wheels. Murphy met up with Acid Mike in a pub in Ladbroke Grove which smelled of spilled beer, damp plaster and mildewed carpets. The place had an atmosphere of muggy despondency dripping off the wallpapered walls, which created the kind of ambience that the British love to get drunk in. It seemed to Murphy like he could not get away from Donovan; his 'Season of the Witch' was picking up the musical stitch from a glowing jukebox in a corner of the sleazy smoke-filled dive. He'd been worrying about how he would recognize Mike. He needn't have bothered because when he approached the bar the acid dealer was looking over his shoulder at him and Murphy realized that apart from himself Mike was the only white cat in the place. Due to his tie-dye outfit, Acid Mike was sticking out like a multi-coloured snowman on a pile of coal dust.

'Hi, Mike. I'm Murphy.'

The acid dealer spun his barstool round and shook the newcomer's hand, relieved at what he saw before him. Mike was thinking, 'Unless the drug squad have become very innovative of late, there is no way on earth that this freak in a red corduroy suit with bell bottom trousers, waist length hair, circular sunglasses on a cold dark night and Frank Zappa style facial hair, could possibly be an undercover cop.' He nodded towards a vacant stool and said, 'Please, take a seat. Would you care for a drink?'

'Yeah sure man, I'll have a pint of whatever it is you're drinking.'

'Two pints of Black Velvet,' ordered Mike. A busty Jamaican barmaid with a head full of fake dreadlocks poured the drinks, half a pint of Guinness with the same again of cider. This was not a combination Murphy usually drank. He didn't like the taste, it could give you a bad hangover and, last but not least, it was a student's drink. The piano intro to The Lovin' Spoonful's 'Summer In The City' began ringing out of the record machine, sounding highly inappropriate seeing as how it wasn't hotter than a match-head but a chilling minus five outside. Murphy was halfway through a drink that he wasn't enjoying when, much to his relief, Mike suggested they go back to his place for a smoke. Some of the stares that were being directed their way by the local clientele weren't exactly saying Ladbroke Grove's black community wants to funk it up now my white soul brothers.

Murphy took a look around the spartan interior of Mike's bachelor pad. It was entirely devoid of clutter. Two framed Grateful Dead posters, hanging on the living room's orange painted walls, hinted at Mike's profession. Murphy found himself inexplicably drawn to a papier mâché sculpture sitting on the bricked-up fireplace's granite mantelpiece. There was something powerfully feminine about it. Upon closer inspection he found that its head was made from a very mouldy doughnut. A pair of electrostatic loudspeakers wired to a state of the art Leak hi-fi system made it loud and clear that the man liked to listen to his sounds in style. Mike placed a vinyl disk on a turntable that must have cost a platinum arm and a gold plated leg.

'Its nature's way,' sang a wistful voice.

Murphy recognized the music immediately. 'Hey, man, are you into Spirit?'

Pouring green tea into two handmade Japanese teacups on top of a teak opium table with short curved legs, Mike nodded. 'The Dead, The Allman Brothers and Spirit are my favourite bands.'

Due to the powerful mind-altering substances that a lot of people were enjoying during those mind-blowing times, music had become a real communication highway. Many psychedelic drug-takers experienced a strong sense of togetherness with each other, wherein the kind of music a person was into revealed a lot about who they were. LSD-fuelled listening sessions, out there in the twilight sonic-zone, made it possible to imagine a close relationship with the musicians who played the soundtrack that accompanied trips on the cosmic escalator. Spirit's sound was an acquired taste in the world of psychedelic music. Unfortunately, the boys in the band never received the recognition they deserved, mainly due to a massive career blunder. They'd turned down an offer to play at the Woodstock Music Festival and instead went on a radio promo tour. The slot they rejected in the biggest rock and roll jamboree ever was the act preceding Jimi Hendrix's legendary performance.

From music, Mike and Murphy moved on to a discussion about the self-styled guru of the LSD experience, Timothy Leary. The ex-Harvard professor's chant of 'Turn on, tune in and drop out' was fanning the flames on the bonfire of radical chic, whose highly reactive molecules were pulsating through the underground scene. By the time they were a few loaded joints into their stoned conversations, both of them decided simultaneously that the other was a cluster of excited electrons whose nuclei were spinning in a positive synchronous orbit.

During the summer of '71, the Dealers MacDope were, in a big way, helping to supply the West of Scotland with hash, marijuana, LSD and anything else that could keep stoners floating high above the sunny side of the street. Acid Mike had been instrumental in the advancement of their careers by selling them his special product in bulk. He'd started using violet dye in his pill mix, creating a brand of LSD called 'Purple Haze', named after the late Jimi Hendrix's ode to getting blasted. Like the song had in its time, Mike's acid became a very popular hit within the underground psychedelic community. Mike had also introduced them to a friend of his called Ozzy. His speciality was exotic smokeables at affordable prices. Sputnik from Morocco, Manali from Northern India, Thai sticks from Southeast Asia; if it provided the connoisseur with a tasty high, Ozzy had it on his well stocked shelves. The money the Scots were making by this time no longer fitted into a Danish biscuit tin. Even the large metal cash box that had been its replacement was soon to become obsolete.

A change of address was on the cards for a number of reasons. First and foremost, the Glasgow drug squad had begun to make discrete enquires about them on the street. There's no dope smoke without a lit joint and the Dealers MacDope still had not learned how to play generals and let foot soldiers do the frontline work. Neighbours were starting to pay attention to the fact that the long-haired hippies were driving fancy cars that belonged to a more affluent part of town. At the time, Angus was driving a third-hand E-type Jag, but the only attention it drew was mechanical. It was chrome yellow, a real lemon and constantly in Mr Gupta's garage for ridiculously expensive repairs. Angus was beginning to curse the day he'd bought it. The car was a great looker, but the engine kept overheating and therefore he'd never driven it above 60 mph.

Another thing that was boiling over was Angus's affair with Charlotte Wood, the downstairs neighbour. She'd gotten it into her mixed-up New Age mind that Angus was her soul mate. He was beginning to wish he'd never jumped into the sack with her after he'd gone downstairs one evening to borrow a cupful of sugar and taken three days to return with it. Meanwhile Raj had bought a whole boxful of Tate and Lyle sugar lumps for a liquid acid project he was working on. When Angus returned home with his cupful of sweetness and grey suitcases under his eyes he found Murphy complaining because his bedroom was directly above Miss Wood's.

'Welcome home, Casa-fuckin'-nova. I've not been able to sleep a wink, thanks to the racket you've been making downstairs with Woody the Woodpecker, the bedroom fuckin' banshee. What the hell were you doing to her? It sounded like an alley cat being boiled alive.'

'Sorry, Murph,' apologized Angus. 'Charlotte likes to let it all hang out, man.'

'All howl out, more like,' sniffed Murphy.

Relations turned hostile a week later when Charlotte revealed a bitter side to her normally saccharine sweet personality. Angus came home with Jenny one night and ran into Miss Wood on the stairs.

'Who's this?' Charlotte was glaring cyanide-filled hypodermics in Jenny's direction.

It came to a head two days later, when a perfume-scented note arrived in the letterbox. The jilted lover was threatening to blow the whistle on their drug dealing activities. Angus had never said anything to Charlotte about how he made a living. He didn't need to because the hordes of hippies tramping up and down the stairs at all hours made it obvious what was going on. It was inconvenient, but as far as Angus was concerned his attention lay elsewhere; he had fallen deeply in lust with Jenny.

'Angus, my man,' said Murphy, 'me and Raj have decided to draw lots for it.'

'Lots for what?'

'We need to move out of here,' replied Murphy. 'Somebody has to go to a rental agency, so that means one of us has to get a short back and fuckin' sides, man.'

'No way, man,' protested Angus. 'I'm not cuttin' my hair.'

'Murphy's right,' added Raj, 'none of this would've happened if you hadn't started shaggin' that screaming bitch downstairs.'

Angus drew the short straw. His two friends snickered.

'Did you two fuckers stitch me up?'

Murphy and Raj were grinning like a couple of drunken orangutans attending a cocktail party at the zoo, but there was nothing Angus could do about it.

The following morning, while waiting for a barber to go to work on him, Angus tore out an ad from the Glasgow Herald's Classifieds section. 'Next,' said the grinning hairdresser, looking over at Angus. He rose to his feet and sat down in the barber's chair. He closed his eyes because he couldn't bear to look in the mirror. It felt like bits of him were being lopped off as his shoulder length curls tumbled to the floor. Snipping session over, he was left with the chilling sensation of how it felt to be an army recruit home on leave.

Back on the street, his now exposed ears felt like ice lollies. He decided to track down the address he'd found in the newspaper. After driving for about an hour, he steered his car between two rusty iron gates flanked by black granite pillars, the perch for a pair of eroded stone lions' heads whose frozen snarls sported blunt fangs. The too-tight jacket of his new, cheap, off-the-peg business suit strained at the shoulders as he parked his freshly waxed sports car on the loose gravel driveway, fronting a country house twenty-five miles from Glasgow's city centre. After a quick gander around the place, Angus was suitably impressed. So was the toffee-nosed landlord wearing a deerstalker, when he was offered a £1,000 deposit and a year's rent in advance.

The countrified gent asked little in the way of questions after Angus spun him a line about being a rock concert promoter who longed for the peace and quiet of such a rural setting. Deal done, Angus drove back into town and managed to make it to Gupta's garage before the radiator of his Jag blew its top. He sold the car a week later, for half of what he'd paid for it, and swore he'd never buy another Jaguar no matter how good it looked.

18

THE BIG ONE

Murphy, Raj, Angus and Jenny, a permanent item by now, moved into Killearn Lodge in July '71. Their new residence was a Neo-Gothic red sandstone hunting lodge built at the turn of the century. The only things they didn't like about the house were the fifty or so dusty antlered stags' heads mounted on plaques (soon to be sprayed with day-glo paint) that were hanging on the mould-stained walls above the great open fireplace in the spacious living room, the chintz-covered antique furnishings that were riddled with woodworm, the sepia-coloured photographs of serious looking gentlemen with drooping moustaches posing beside a variety of very dead animals and a grandfather clock, which minus hands rang out a sporadic time line that was unique to itself.

On two floors, the Lodge had six bedrooms with pointed arch windows looking out onto a sprawling garden, so overgrown that a herd of giraffes could have hidden in it. The nearest neighbour was a deaf old farmer who used a hollowed-out ram's horn as a hearing aid. One of the household's first purchases was a blow-your-shirt-off sound system that could have powered a medium sized rock venue. Sound levels restricted by an urban lifestyle had always stymied the MacDope's efforts in holding a noisy party. This had been, up until then, a source of much frustration for them because they all considered loud stereophonic music to be the twentieth century's greatest technological invention.

A long way from the city's ubiquitous hubbub, their new environment was a far cry from what the young Glaswegians were accustomed to. Angus felt reconnected to his country roots and sat for hours in the garden with Jenny by his side. She would laugh and shed the occasional tear while listening to her lover narrate various episodes from his childhood on Iona. If they were facing west they could see a long stretch of high moorland called the Campsie Fells.

Within an hour's walking distance was an isolated 1600-foot hill called Earl's Seat. From its summit, panoramic views could be had that included the far distant shipyards of Clydebank and their towering cranes. Overhead, clouds swept by, flirting with the countryside as their shadowy presence constantly changed the colours and moods of the surrounding landscape. The steep fern-clad hillsides provided endless opportunities for rambling hikes and picnics by small gurgling streams worn into the black earth. The amber-coloured water tasted of decomposing bracken, rumoured to be the secret of Scotland's famous malt whiskies.

During the night it was rare to hear the motorized sounds of modern-day transport. It was as if the roads were rolled up at sunset and stored in hangars overnight. Out in the garden, tall fir trees creaked and moaned in the breeze, complaining that the weight of their broad boughs was too heavy for their tired old trunks to support. The big-city hippies soon adapted to their new environment and wondered why it had taken them so long to discover the wonders of living close to nature. All things considered, the scene was set and it was high time to let the good times roll.

It was a warm, sunny summer morning a year later when, in the kitchen, over a pot of jasmine tea and a plate of fresh pancakes soaked in maple syrup, the MacDope's were in the midst of their weekly business discussion.

'Come on you guys, we should count it,' urged Murphy.

'Aw, man, you're becoming too materialistic in your old age,' complained Angus, drawing on a crackly joint of Jamaican. 'Next thing you know, you'll be caught up in the system.'

'Fuck the system and fuck you too, Angus,' said Raj. 'Murphy is right. It's a bit daft not knowing how much money we've made.'

'It won't become any less if we don't count it, will it?' Angus blew a thick cloud of sweet smelling marijuana smoke in Raj's direction and grunted, 'Oink, oink, capitalist pig.'

'You fuckin' smart ass, stop hogging that joint, man.' Murphy stretched over to take hold of the burning spliff, and coughed after drawing on it. 'Rasta man v-v-vibration,' he spluttered, his head disappearing in a cloud of smoke.

The reefer did its work and served as a motivator. Half an hour later, the three stoners were sitting on a burst mattress up in the loft counting out neat piles of bank notes. They were into telephone numbers by mid-day, with plenty to go. Murphy used a £50 note to light the next jay.

'Hey,' cried Angus, 'that's a waste of money, man.'

'Who gives a shit? Anyway, it was you that was calling me a fuckin' bread-head this morning and now listen to you.' Murphy nearly set fire to the mattress trying to stub out the burning paper. 'We've got more dough than we know what to do with.'

'Take it easy, man,' said Raj, who was rolling a joint, his hands busy sorting out the stalks and seeds in a plastic bag full of Jamaican herb, 'if this place catches fire we won't have any.'

By late afternoon the final tally came in at nine grand short of half a million pounds. The sound of 'Ziggy Stardust and The Spiders From Mars' rose up from the living room. Completely zonked, the MacDopes lay back against piles of money bricks and listened to David Bowie singing about making love with his ego. They were too buzzed to climb down the ladder to the landing beneath them. A shaft of golden sunlight shone through an open skylight, illuminating clouds of swirling dust motes. Angus studied them and thought, 'Spinning planets! I wonder if there are people living on them who are looking up into the sky and asking each other if it might be possible that other intelligent species could be—' His contemplations were interrupted when Raj clicked his thumb and forefinger.

Raj spoke excitedly. 'Man, I've just had a megaton idea. We should throw a big party to celebrate our success.'

Murphy rolled his eyes and made it clear that his friend's words weren't exactly making a seismic impact on his jaded mind by saying, 'Life around here is like living in a non-stop fuckin' party.'

'Naw, Murph, I know what Raj means,' said Angus. 'We should organize a garden party with a stage, a psychedelic light show, rock bands and lots of drugs. And then invite all the freaks we feel connected with.'

Murphy did not require much in the way of convincing. One word from him was all it took to set the mirrorball rolling – 'When?'

The August full moon was chosen as the date. 'The Big One'

was the name of the event. From there it branched out into what the party was going to consist of. Over the next three weeks, in between deals, everyone did their bit to make The Big One a happening that would be remembered by the cream of the crop of Scotland's hippy population as one of the best parties ever. A red-and-white-striped marquee was erected on the Lodge's grounds with a wooden stage built inside. When Murphy was over in Edinburgh selling twenty thousand hits of microdot acid to a festival organizer, he booked a band called 'Damaged Goods' to play at the party. Murphy was by this time very excited by the project, so when the rock group's manager suggested hiring a support band called 'The Brain Dead' he handed him five hundred pounds and said, 'Bring 'em along, man.'

During this time there were a dozen or so permanently stoned 'heads', as hippies were now calling themselves, living in the Lodge. The honeymoon stage a long way from over, Angus and Jenny were involved in a lovers' rhapsody. Raj and Murphy were stuck with a couple of air-headed hippy chicks who had somehow managed to superglue themselves on to them. Helium-headed was a more accurate description of the girls' bubble-brained condition. Lighter than air, they were floating so high they were being blown around by solar winds in the heliosphere. Part-time models, the kind who remove their clothes instead of wearing them to make a living, Alice and Nina made up for their lack of brain cells in the curvaceous looks department. Their pantyless, mini-skirted, eclectic fashion sense bordered on the erotically bizarre. They looked good in anything, especially silk bed sheets. Both of them sported dyed black, fuzzed-out Afro hair-dos. From a distance they could have been mistaken for sisters, but their faces, on closer inspection, broke the illusion. Alice had high cheekbones, her features hard and angular, while Nina's face was more rounded, bordering on being cherubim. They had blue eyes, but this was difficult to see because their pupils were permanently dilated to the point that they completely occupied their irises, making it impossible to distinguish their colour. The girls were so well formed that, had black plastic rubbish bags been placed over their crazy heads after their voluptuous naked bodies had been tarred and feathered, they would still have looked like a pair of exotic birds.

Alice and Nina were great cooks, prone to spicing up their delicious creations with LSD or magic mushrooms. At the beginning of the summer, their proclivity for spiking the food with psychotropic drugs sparked the only heated row ever to take place in the Lodge during the Macdope's tenancy. One evening, they'd served up scrumptious plum duff dosed with PCP. Phencyclidine Hydrochloride, a veterinary anesthetic known as 'Angel Dust' on the street, is a dangerous, highly unpredictable, mind-bending hallucinogen. Everyone who ate the doctored pudding went completely loco for twenty-four hours. Raj, who had been suffering from the munchies at the time, devoured twice as much of the sticky sweet as anyone else. As a result it required four of his friends to physically restrain him in order to prevent him phoning for an ambulance, because he believed phosphorescent centipedes were burrowing into his brain. After that the female chefs limited their celestial seasonings to hash and marijuana – for a couple of weeks. For the most part, everyone in the house enjoyed having Alice and Nina around, although not because of the girls' conversational skills. Their vocabularies were pretty much limited to 'oh wow', 'far out', 'cosmic', 'groovy', 'right on', 'outta sight' and the ubiquitous 'man'. In spite of this linguistic shortcoming the girls were always good for a bubbly laugh.

Dave Eldritch, 'Shortwave' to his friends, was the gardener with the mean green thumb, who had cut down the wilderness surrounding the Lodge and created a beautiful garden after six months of labour-intensive work. His magic ways with the botanical dimension were not limited to the garden. In a small paddock, round the back of the house, he had a marijuana plantation that by the summer's end would produce a crop of sweet smelling sinsemilla buds. Their fragrance was so strong it could be detected half a mile away on a hot day. This posed no problem because back then most hippies, let alone the country bumpkins or local pedal-pushing policeman, didn't know what a marijuana plant looked like. On that level it could honestly be said that Dave was a head of his times.

He'd earned his nickname of Shortwave by being the recipient of a lot of electro-shock therapy over the years. His family history was plagued by chronic schizophrenia, both of his parents having committed suicide when he was a child. A beautiful soul with messed-up circuitry hard-wired into his defective brain, Dave was not so schizoid, more manic minus the depressive. Connected to a powerful battery of nervous energy, he could go for days without sleep. Hyperactive, Dave was always busy with some task, be it tending his grass plants, trimming a hedge, or listening to a snail sharing his woes from a cauliflower leaf. He was always totally into what he was doing.

Medium height, his supple body was nearly fleshless in its

muscularity. His gentle eyes gleamed with a dreamy light. Long, straight, light brown hair cut in a fringe gave his guileless face an effeminate look. Nobody had a clue how old Dave was. Angus reckoned Shortwave was in his mid-thirties because of the crows' feet etched into the flesh at the corners of his eyes. Dave was unconcerned about material possessions. As long as he had enough to eat and a warm place to sleep, his physical needs were fulfilled. A borderline case, he was a tightrope walker who balanced on the thin line that separates a sage from a madman. He was host to an uncontaminated form of pure intelligence, the kind which is not recognized by insensate intellectuals. Academics whose clever minds are caught in a mental web, their ears plugged by mouldy old thoughts, will never hear, let alone understand, the parlance of true wisdom – that simple and uncomplicated language spoken by the tribe of the wide open-hearted. To the average citizen, Shortwave would have appeared as a smiling imbecile who spoke with a lisp, but in reality he was an earthbound abstract angel who would not have harmed an amoeba and broke into a panic if he accidentally cut a worm in half with the edge of his spade.

Everyone in the Lodge loved Dave. He was the extended family's mascot. He could become a bit intense to be around when he tripped on LSD, his usual Sunday afternoon activity. It was the wee man, Jeeps, who'd brought Dave to the Lodge when the pair of them returned from India after spending a year in Neem Karoli Baba's ashram. The holy man was brought into the spiritual limelight in 1971, when Richard Alpert, using his spiritual name Ram Dass, had a groundbreaking book published called *Be Here Now*. An ex-Harvard professor who'd left his teaching post to take up the role of spiritual seeker, Alpert had first been thrown in the spotlight by becoming known as Timothy Leary's right-hand acid-dropping man. His life, as well as that of his guru, is well documented and it is thanks, in part, to these two wonderful men's lives that a lot of the so-called Woodstock Generation's spiritual aspirations got fired up by the idea that living in the present is the best place to be.

One thing that was never mentioned in any books was that Jeeps and Shortwave Dave were asked to leave the guru's ashram in Northern India because they'd been allegedly running around naked in the nearby jungle and as a result upset the local villagers. Jeeps denied that he was guilty of the bare bottom crime but, to put things in perspective, it might be possible that he did not recall accurately what was going on at the time since the two of them were popping acid drops like they were

Smarties. As Gerry Garcia of The Grateful Dead so aptly put it, 'If you can remember the sixties, you weren't really there.' In Jeep's case this saying was very appropriate because he was a person who often forgot what he was trying to remember.

The rest of the Lodge's residents were fairly typical of the times. They had either just blown in or were involved in the process of being blown out – of their minds. Wee Jeeps was the in-house guru. He loved to play acoustic guitar and encourage his friends to sing along in spiritual bhajans. It was mainly due to Jeeps that all things Eastern were becoming increasingly popular in the Lodge. From chanting 'Om' to lighting incense sticks in front of a brass statue of Ganesh, the Hindu elephant headed deity. Due to his upbringing, Raj was already familiar with the Vedic pantheon. His father was a practising Hindu and his mother had dropped her inherited Islamic faith when they married. Therefore, burning joss sticks in front of bizarre-looking idols was not new to Raj and the same went for devotional singing. Raj was not overly impressed by idolatry. In essence he was a peace-loving soul who reckoned that God did not reside in a temple, church, mosque, synagogue or statue but in the hearts of people around the world no matter what their religious beliefs were.

During this particular period in Angus's life, Jeeps, Shortwave, Raj and one other person were the only individuals he was close to who were genuinely interested in developing a spiritual side to their lives. Murphy saw the world as one big cosmic joke. When confronted by what he conveniently labeled as 'Spiritual Bullshit', Angus had often heard Murphy proclaim, 'I don't need anyone to tell me what the meaning of life is because I already know. Life is for living. If there is a God, he must be off his fucking rocker. Who else but a nutter would create midges and Celtic Football Club?' Angus, for his part, was positioned somewhere in between the way his closest friends perceived the life process. He had, in fact, had a couple of flashes when high on acid where he saw himself sitting at the feet of a bearded wise man. When he told Murphy about this, he'd laughed and said, 'You've been spending too much time with Raj and wee Jeeps.'

Just before The Big One, the other main hippy characters hanging out at the house were Mad Montrose Max, Panorama Anna, and the one other spiritually inclined person that Angus had formed a close relationship with, Sandra the Head-expander. Sandra was a middle-aged mother who, due to a life-changing LSD experience, had dropped out of her family life and job in Glasgow University where she'd taught psychology. It was 1969 when Sandra decided she'd had enough of everything except music, dance and serenity. She shaved her head, put on an orange robe and paid an international news magazine to print her message to the world. The announcement was printed in big black letters and used up a whole page of advertising space and cost her most of her life savings.

Her message was:

TRUE COMMUNICATION HAPPENS BETWEEN PEOPLE IN SILENCE. WHEN THE MEANINGLESSNESS OF WORDS IS FULLY UNDERSTOOD AND PERCEIVED TO BE NOTHING MORE THAN HOT AIR THEN ONE WILL KNOW THAT THEY ARE TRULY ALIVE AND BLESSED WITH THE CAPACITY TO COMMUNICATE WITH ANYONE. PEACE AND LOVE. SANDRA.

Those were the last words Sandra ever said and even though she'd chosen them carefully, everybody concerned thought she'd gone insane. Worried that she might do some serious harm to herself they, quite naturally, wanted to have her committed to a locked institution, where psychiatrists could fill her up with barbiturates so that she could watch cartoons on TV with a group of screaming people obsessed with examining their own faeces. The only person who was totally unconcerned about anything whatsoever was Sandra the Head-expander who, after a long plane flight, took a vow of silence and entered a Buddhist nunnery in South Korea where she communicated by employing a variety of innovative hand signals. After a year in the convent she tired of the sisterhood's incessant chattering and returned to Scotland where, by way of a serendipitous meeting, she bumped into Raj in Glasgow's Botanical Gardens when they were both coming down from an acid trip. Raj was immediately struck by the thick aura of quietude that surrounded Sandra and asked her back to the Lodge where she soon became part of the family. Sandra and Shortwave Dave became close friends and, during the evenings, were often to be found in the garden sitting by a campfire. It was there that they'd hold hands, stare into the bright circle of flames and laugh about absolutely nothing.

On the Thursday evening before the party, Alice and Nina tied their fuzzy hair into pigtails and like a couple of Heidi-high-hoes baked, blended and mixed five hundred brown pellets of mescaline, the condensed essence of peyote, into everything edible in the kitchen. Angus discovered that the coffee tin had not been immune to their cosmic chicanery.

By midnight, everyone was flat on their backs in the garden staring up at the spirit of Mescalito dancing in the sky. Mescalito looked like a thousand foot high scarecrow with solar eclipses for eyes and had a voice that bellowed louder than a foghorn. Nobody could understand a word he was saying because he spoke in Spanish, but that didn't matter because even though it was a day early, The Big One had begun.

The following evening, Shortwave Dave lit a bonfire at the bottom of the garden to guide the UFOs in. Underground friends and oddballs started landing at all hours. Everyone was excited about the big bash on Saturday night.

Acid Mike drove up from London accompanied by three stunning Chelsea girls and two suntanned Californian freaks who looked like Cheech and Chong.

The God Squad arrived in the form of half a dozen orange-clad Hare Krsnas on bicycles. Alice welcomed them to Wonderland and poured them glasses of fresh orange juice spiked with LSD. An hour later the Hare Krsnas stopped singing devotional songs, put down their drums and finger cymbals and spent the rest of the night sitting silently in a circle under a fir tree. They held hands and with eyes wide shut watched God descend into their midst disguised as a blue-skinned Hindu deity. His devotees bowed at the feet of the thief who had stolen their hearts and listened to him reveal the essence of devotional theology. Lord Krsna's voice was as sweet as honey when he said, 'I am the source of all spiritual and material worlds. Everything emanates from me. The wise who perfectly know this engage in my devotional service and worship me with all their hearts. The thoughts of you, my pure devotees, dwell in me. Because your lives are fully devoted to my service, you will derive great satisfaction and bliss from always enlightening one another and conversing about me.'

Tears of ecstasy streamed from the Hare Krsnas' eyes like torrents of rain when their lord played a haunting melody on his wooden flute. The instrument's notes echoed across the heavens. In a blinding flash Lord Krsna revealed his true form. His devotees were suffused with an all encompassing light of awareness, which contained within it a pervasive peace that was the source of all and everything.

Meanwhile, a black Rolls Royce was pulling up in front of the

Lodge. Dressed in a flowing white robe, Uncle Sulei emerged from the limousine, accompanied by his three veiled wives, a tribe of screaming children and his driver, Mustapha. The chauffeur was wearing a grey uniform, leather gloves and a shiny black peaked hat. He hung around in the shadows until Nina brought him into the light fantastic by feeding him a pancake covered in her special psilocybin mushroom spread. Noticing his faithful servant out on the dance floor, spinning Dervish-style with the addition of Elvis Presley hip thrusts, Uncle Sulei called out to Raj, 'My dear boy, what have you done to Mustaphafag? He looks like an oversized camel jockey with scorpions in his jock strap.'

By the time The Damaged Goods took to the stage, at ten o'clock on Saturday night, three hundred people were swaying in front of them, getting off on the buzz from the band's Marshall amps. The Goods sounded like Iggy Pop and the Stooges, and performed well until half an hour into their set. That's when the mega-doses of lysergic acid that Alice had popped into the band members' beer glasses began to make their presence felt. Halfway through a song whose lyrical content was centred on not needing a doctor, the vocalist, a fat Irishman with long greasy black hair who went by the name of Mickey Bates, screamed during the guitar solo, tore off all his clothes, leapt from the stage and ran into the woods pursued by a hideous apparition. Mickey Bates disappeared completely from the rock 'n' roll scene after that. He was not heard of again until a decade later when one of his friends saw his photograph on a New Age magazine's cover. It was the haunted eyes he recognized, although the thin man with a shaved head staring off the periodical's glossy cover bore little resemblance to the crazy rocker of bygone years. Mickey was now called Master Bates and he'd opened a tantra school called 'The Lingam' near a town called Peccioli in Tuscany.

The band played on although, minus their front man, it was jarringly obvious to everyone's ears that the heart had gone out of their music. The Brain Dead were the transcendental surprise of the night. Big on percussion, they laid down a beat that brought the writhing mass of trippers in touch with their tribal roots. Playing extended jams that blended smoothly right through their four-hour set, The Brain Dead were trailblazers for what would one day be called Trance Dance. The sun popped up over the misty horizon like a big red bald head and the party raved on. By Sunday afternoon the event began to wind down. Spaced-out revellers sat around in the garden, resembling brightly clad, shell-shocked refugees. Everybody had the munchies and wondered why every time they ate something, served up by the two gorgeous chicks dressed up like nurses, they'd end up leaving the planet for another few hours. Not content with pushing the psychedelic envelope, Alice and Nina decided to blow holes in it by using hypodermic syringes to inject a solution of liquid LSD into fruit, which was then strategically placed around the house in bowls.

Sunday evening, Murphy remembered that he'd purchased a vanload of fireworks. Enlisting Mike and Raj's help, they went round to the back of the house, careful not to trample on Dave's marijuana plants, and lighting the blue touch paper, stood well clear. Big rockets shot into the air and exploded. They lit up the sky like the aurora borealis going ballistic. Blessed with warm weather, everyone was out in the garden enjoying the fresh air before it filled with gunpowder smoke and the smell of singed brain cells

The only person who was not taking pleasure in the pyrotechnics was Shortwave. He thought Armageddon had begun. Sandra the Head-expander came across Dave running around a mulberry bush, too hysterical to be taken seriously. By employing an amalgam of hurried hand signals and facial expressions twisted into big happy smiles, she did her best to alleviate his fears about what effect the fireworks' bangs and flashes would be having on his four-legged and winged garden friends. It wasn't easy at first, but after ten minutes, Sandra's skill as a silent communicator won out over the noisy tribe of paranoid thoughts that were troubling Dave and he started oohing and aahing along with everyone else.

At the stroke of midnight, the wee man summoned everyone into the marquee for a sing-along. It kicked-off with a noisy rendition of the Plastic Ono Band's, 'Give Peace A Chance'. Maybe it was the drugs, perhaps it was the time of the season, or it could have been the Hare Krsnas singing their hearts out and thumping out the rhythm of life on their drums, whatever it was, Jeep's magic worked that night, lifting everyone into a wonderfully transcendent feeling of communion in heartfelt song.

On Monday morning it started to rain and the guests began to disperse. Acid Mike drank a big mug of strong coffee before taking his leave to begin the journey back to London with his friends. He managed to make it to the bottom of the road, where he skidded and crashed his rented van into a telephone pole. He could hardly speak by the time he and his shaken passengers made it back to the Lodge. His coffee had contained enough mescaline to keep Don Juan and a tribe of shamans in orbit over Acapulco for a week. Mike and his companions ended up staying on until the following weekend. After a few stimulating walks in the hills, Mike was talking about buying himself a pair of wellies and moving up to Scotland for good.

'I wouldn't do that,' advised Murphy, 'until you've seen what the winter's like.'

All in all, The Big One was a big one, and a fantastic success. Still flying high, the MacDopes were already planning another party for the September full moon. Alas, this was not meant to be. Someone had been spying on them for quite some time and had something else in mind.

19

SNOWMEN IN NEGATIVE

After midnight on the third of September 1972, Angus and Jenny went to bed, made love and fell asleep in each other's arms. The past few days had been hectic. The MacDopes had bought half a ton of 'soaps', cheap commercial Moroccan hashish, that wouldn't get a fly high, being just a step above smoking dried banana peel. The average punter liked to score the stuff, which was shaped like bars of soap, because it seemed like they were getting a lot for their money. Now that it was out on the street, all the MacDopes had to do was wait for the cash to come in.

At three a.m. the lights in young lovers' bedroom were switched on. Angus opened his eyes and found himself looking up into a gun barrel. It looked like a long tunnel, but unlike the tunnel that one normally hears about, with light at the end of it, this one was filled with impenetrable darkness. Half awake, his first take on the situation was that the lads had decided to play a bizarre prank on him. The realization that it was no joke came quickly and painfully when he was pistol-whipped on the cheek. Adrenaline kicked his heartbeat into overdrive. Wide awake, he glanced up from the business end of the gun into rat-like beady eyes belonging to a masked man who smelled of Brut aftershave and strong alcohol. Jenny woke up and squealed with fright as she stared into an equally malevolent pair of eyes, belonging to another masked marauder. The two lovers were forced naked out of their warm bed. Their hands were tied behind their backs with nylon cord that bit into the flesh of their wrists. Duct tape was unceremoniously stuck over their mouths before they were frog-marched downstairs to the living room, where they were united with their bound and gagged housemates. Angus had never seen a trussed-up turkey, but he imagined this was how a flock of them would look if they somehow managed to make it into the house.

As far as he could determine, there were six intruders in the Lodge. Their masks had been made from black woollen ski hats pulled over their faces, with holes cut out for the eyes and mouth. Apart from hiding their assailants' identities, the masks added an air of terror to the situation. It's one thing being tied up and gagged. It's another having it done by men who look like snowmen in negative. The raiders formed what is known in the underworld as a wrecking crew. These rip-off merchants had somehow found out about the MacDope's illegal and highly profitable business activities and kept a predatory eye on them for weeks. Like a pack of crafty wolves, they'd lain in wait, preparing to pounce on their unsuspecting prey in the middle of the night. Now all that remained for the crew to do was find what they were after – the money. Angus looked into his gagged companions' bulging eyes. Everybody looked shit-scared, a sensation that his frantically beating heart could relate to on a level that was powerfully existential.

Stepping forward, the thug who had struck Angus in the face with his revolver took command of the situation. His skin-tight black leather outfit accentuated the musculature of his massive frame. One could be left in no doubt that this bull-necked Goliath's main preoccupations in life were, apart from robbing people, dining on breakfasts composed entirely of anabolic steroids before entering a weightlifter's gym to spend countless hours pumping iron. He gave out orders with a guttural Glaswegian accent, so thick and dark it could have been used as a substitute for asphalt.

'Right, lads, no rest for the wicked, tear this fuckin' place apart. These hippy cunts have been rakin' it in big time. The dosh is around here somewhere and I want every penny of it, so get fuckin' crackin'.'

Turning to face a Sumo wrestler dressed in denim, the leader of the pack's voice was full of gall when he gave a direct order. 'Joey, if any of these shites moves a fuckin' muscle, you've got my permission to give them a wee tap on the napper with that bat of yours. Get the fuckin' picture?'

Angus felt the message was intended as much for him and his friends as it was for Joey who, using neck muscles twice as broad as his head, nodded once and remained silent. He stood grinning like a chimp and used the varnished baseball bat to slap out a regular beat on the palm of his left hand as if he were a human metronome. The slope-head's primitive eyes looked out of their fleshy circles, daring anyone to budge so he could put in a spot of batting practice. It wasn't going to happen because his captives were so frightened they would not have attempted to take a badly needed deep breath, let alone move.

Shortwave Dave was having a particularly hard time of it because he was suffering from a bad cold. Pale yellow snot was bubbling out of his nose. Aided by gravity, the slimy goo was making its way over the silver-grey duct tape covering his mouth and dripping off the end of his pointed chin. For a while Angus was distracted from his own plight, worrying that Shortwave might throw a fit and go catatonic.

The hippy family sat around on upholstered furniture, shivering with fear in an obscene parody of a group of bondage freaks posing for an art class. From all around came the sounds of chaos on a vendetta to wreck the harmony of their home. The soundtrack from a violent movie, broken glass tinkled and was crushed under foot, fabric ripped and wood splintered, all accompanied by a thumping backbeat provided by thick-soled boots as the crew went about their destructive duties.

Angus's worried thoughts stampeded around like wild horses in the echoing ravines of his mind. How had the villains gotten on to them in the first place? The permutations were infinite. His thoughts began to gallop out through the top of his skull. He reined them in. This was neither the time nor the place to lose his self-control. The crew's leader was a Weegie for sure, but what difference did that make? His gang of hoods had invaded their home and they would not leave till they found the cash. This was the only fact that Angus could be sure of in those terrifying moments. He had no idea where these vermin had come from, but even if he did what good would it have done him? Phoning the police was not an option once the wreckers had gone.

'Good evening, Officer, we've just been robbed by a gang of thugs who've made off with our drug-dealing profits from the past couple of years. There will be a handsome reward in it for you and the fine men of the Strathclyde Constabulary if these villains are apprehended, taken into custody and our money returned.'

Dream on. Angus knew that he was a criminal, but he was way out of his depth when it came to this school of bottom-feeders who were swimming around him. Feeling impotent, he sat in the midst of his stunned friends and waited for events to unfold.

The big boss man strode back into the room with his revolver stuck into the waistband of his trousers. Angus tried to will the gun to go off and blow the bastard's balls away. When it came to telekinesis, he was no Uri Geller and could not have bent a teaspoon at a distance even had it been rubberized.

The leader spoke to bat man and pointed to Jenny. 'Joey, bring Blondie over here.'

The missing link pulled Jenny to her feet. Visibly trembling, she looked vulnerable and ashen-faced.

'Which one of you hippy cunts is Angus?'

Hearing his name spat out by this hard man, Angus nearly let go of the entire contents of his bowels in one smelly second flat. Tightening his basement sphincter, he nodded his head vigorously.

'Stand up, ya fuckin' piece of shit that you are.'

Angus complied.

'Right, then, ya hairy fairy, I'm going to give you one chance, so listen up. When I take that tape off your mouth, you're going to tell me where the readies are stashed. Got me?'

Angus nodded. The ogre did a bit of nodding too, in Jenny's direction. 'If I don't like what I hear, me and the boys will take Goldilocks here upstairs for a gang bang.' It was clear that he was a man who believed being cruel gave him power over life. Roughly fondling Jenny's left breast with a leather-gloved hand, he added, 'Nice pair of paps. I might be tempted to give her one anyway the fuckin' wind blows.' He glanced over to his lackeys. 'What do you say, lads? Fancy a wee bit of hippy nooky?' All of the wreckers had filtered back into the room. A pack of feral tabby cats surrounding a mighty tiger, they were smoking nervously and stamping their dog-ends out on the living room carpet. When their boss addressed them with his lewd suggestion, they snickered and mumbled the kind of remarks that passed as wit in their maggoty minds. Smiling, the beast walked over to Angus and ripped the duct tape off his lips.

'The ... the money is in the loft. The ... the ... there's a hatch above the upstairs landing, at the top of the stairs.'

Now that he'd said it, Angus felt relieved and wondered why the thug hadn't taken this course of action right from the start Before he had time to take an in-breath the tape was slapped back over his mouth. As he turned away, the boss's right fist shot out and struck Angus on the chest, knocking him backwards. Angus fell to the floor and was glad that he had long hair, thick enough to absorb the impact against the back of

280

his head. Stunned, he sat up in time to see Jenny flump back on to a sofa, making its cushions gasp.

Rubber soles crunched on shattered glass as the crew marched upstairs. The cold, sharp smell of fear hung in the living room. Angus watched Joey patting his baseball bat, marking out the seconds with the efficiency of a grandfather clock. With a cold, soggy lump in his guts, he thought about what the wreckers were about to find, just under half a million pounds in hard-earned cash. It had been fun when they'd been stoned and counted it. Now it was tragic.

When the leather-clad gang leader returned for the second and last time, his mood had changed. Obviously chuffed with his nasty self, the edge had gone out of his voice.

'Well now, although you tosspots didn't know it, you've been workin' for me all along. Congratulations, love-children, you've done me proud.'

Nodding to the rest of his crew, he signalled that it was time for them to make an exit. Now only the human clock remained standing to the right of his master.

'Gimme that bat of yours, Joey, and get the fuck outta here.'

The brute did as he was told and left the room, his knuckles trailing along the floor behind him. Swinging the baseball bat in his right hand, the boss seemed to be enjoying his captive audience's petrified attention.

'Don't forget that I know where you cunts are. I might pop in again for a visit sometime.'

All things considered, Angus thought this was a pretty lame parting shot and he wished the muscle-bound creep would crawl off back to whatever stinking sewer he'd been spawned in.

'Angus, stand up.'

Angus's heart missed a beat and with a struggle he managed to do as he was told. The gangster walked slowly over and looked him squarely in the face. Angus instinctively knew something terrible was about to happen.

'Angus, my lad, close your eyes.' The soft voice the villain used did little to hide the malice that motivated it.

Angus kept staring into the black pits of his captor's eyes.

There was an almost hysterical edge to the thug's voice when he shouted, 'Close yer fuckin' eyes.'

Angus obeyed.

'This is a wee present from Jamie Kilroy.'

In a split second, all the connections were made. The name answered all the questions. Jamie Kilroy was the king rat in the young offenders' institution whom Angus had thrashed for setting his goons on Murphy. He and Angus both realized that this was Jack Kilroy, Jamie's father, the notorious gang boss from Glasgow's Southside. Jack Kilroy did not know it then, but he'd just made the biggest mistake in his very violent career.

Angus's eyes blinked open. They didn't stay that way for very long, just long enough to see Kilroy swing the baseball bat towards the left side of his head. He heard a whooshing sound, and then bang. Murphy jumped out of his seat and received a hard punch in the guts for his trouble. Jack Kilroy quickly left the room.

Angus felt his body falling to the floor and, for a few moments, his consciousness floated out of his earth suit and hovered by the ceiling, where he witnessed what was going on in the room below. He watched Murphy double over and then trip over his prone body. Angus could see dark red blood seeping from his own head onto the cream-coloured woven carpet. Like a camera shutter in slow motion, blackness closed in from all directions and for a timeless duration he slipped into non-existence.

Car doors slamming and the revving of a powerful engine broke the deathly hush. Whatever kind of vehicle it was mashed over the gravel driveway, its fat exhaust pipe emitting a loud repetitive growl. After a long and penetrating hi-octane howl, sound faded until silence crept back into the house.

Murphy groaned and rolled off Angus's unconscious body. Raj and Jeeps struggled to their feet. They made it through to the kitchen and, using a serrated bread knife, cut each other free. Hurrying back to the living room, the two friends unfettered the rest of the family. Murphy rose unsteadily to his feet. Angus lay splayed out on the floor, thick blood still dripping from his temple. Jenny and Murphy dropped to their knees beside him. She pushed her hair to one side and lowering herself, listened for a heartbeat.

'Jesus!' she cried, 'I thought the bastard had killed him!'

Murphy's face turned scarlet as silent tears ran glistening over his drawn cheeks. Raj knelt beside Jenny. 'What shall we do?' he asked.

'Do?' repeated Jenny. 'We've got to take him to a hospital immediately. That's what we have to do.'

'Wh-wh-what's with Shortwave?' stammered Alice.

Everyone turned to look at Dave. He was lying on a sofa. The whites of his eyes were showing, his body jerking spasmodically. Jeep's rotund naked body rushed over to him. He peeled the duct tape off Dave's mouth and looked up at the others, shock registering on his face. 'Christ! He's having an epileptic fit or something. His tongue's gone down his throat. Quick, somebody get a spoon.'

Angus regained consciousness six days later. He was lying on a bed in a private room in Killearn Hospital, which was situated a few miles away from the Lodge. His head was swathed in bandages. There was a sharp pain shooting up the left side of his skull and a drip feed's needle inserted in his arm, held in place by a square of white sticky tape with a spot of dried blood at its centre. Not knowing who he was, where he was, or how he'd managed to get there, he gazed blankly into the radiant eyes of a golden-haired angel staring back at him, her concerned expression morphing into one of relief.

'Thank God you've woken up. I was beginning to think you were going to spend the rest of your life in a coma.' Her features reconfigured into a most beautiful smile.

Angus blinked. 'Who are you?'

'Don't tell me you've lost your bloody memory? It's me, Jenny.'

Cogs began to turn in his concussed brain.

'Jen, what the fuck happened?'

Jenny explained. The pieces of information began to click into place. When she informed him that Shortwave Dave had almost died from choking on his tongue, Angus tried to sit up. He groaned, put his left hand to the side of his head and lay back on a starched white pillow.

'The doctors say they want to keep you in here for a couple weeks under observation.'

'Two fucking weeks!'

'Look, man, you're lucky to be alive, so don't start complaining. I had to tell the doctors you slipped in the shower and banged your head on the taps. Try to remember that.' Jenny stood up, removed her embroidered Afghan goatskin coat and laid it over a small grey TV by his bedside that up until a day before had been monitoring his vital signs. She searched in her fringed, brown leather shoulder bag and produced a compact mirror.

'Look at the state of you.'

He looked at his reflection. His eyes and left hand side of his face were shadowed by yellow bruising. Blood red, his left eye had no white in it. Angus sniggered and discovered it hurt his head.

'What's so bloody well funny, Angus Macleod?'

'When I saw my bandaged head, it reminded me of an old pal of mine.' He heaved a sigh and asked, 'Where's Murphy and Raj?'

'I haven't the faintest. They were here a couple of days ago. The pair of them stood around in silence gawking at you for five minutes, said they had some important business to attend to and then walked away whispering to each other. That was it.'

While Jenny sat at her lover's bedside, his two partners were sitting in a rented white van on the south side of Glasgow in the Queen's Park area. Across the road was a pub called the Talisman. It had taken a few rounds of drinks and some discreet enquiries to discover that this was Jack Kilroy's watering hole. Half an hour earlier, they'd watched the gangster park a dark blue Aston Martin on the opposite side of the street. Going by its number plate, the sports car was five years old. Mister Kilroy was still wearing the same tight leather outfit he'd had on a week before when he'd ripped them off for half a million pounds. Jack had walked into the bar, accompanied by a bald-headed monkey-man who, judging by his clumsy gait, was the masked galoot who'd been so fond of nursing the baseball bat that had brained Angus.

Now that they had located the gangster, Murphy and Raj had no clear plan about what they were going to do. This kept them occupied by discussing endless possibilities while waiting for Kilroy to exit the bar.

'We've got to follow the bastard back to whatever rat hole he lives in, kidnap him and torture him to find out where our money is.'

'Aye right, Raj, brilliant idea.' Murphy put his feet up on the plastic dashboard. 'Excuse me, Mister Kilroy, would you like to come along with us? We won't take too much of your time, just enough to tie you up and put a couple of electric cables to those big hairy balls of yours.'

'Then let's get some guns.'

'From where?'

'What about your mate, Lanky Lenny?'

'He's locked up on the funny farm, remember?'

'Oh, yeah, that's right. Do you not know anybody else who sells heavy equipment? I could phone up Uncle Sulei and ask him to send up Mustapha and some growlers for backup. Whadaya think, Murph?'

'I think you're starting to sound like Al fuckin' Capone. Away and score us some sausage rolls, a'm fuckin' starving'

'Me too. Keep your eye on the Talisman. I'll be back in a minute.'

'Aye, right you are boss, I'll do that.'

Murphy twirled the dial on the radio. 'Schools out for … ' he didn't like Alice Cooper and wondered to himself why the disc jockeys played such crap music during the week. He wished it were Saturday afternoon when Radio One's 'Top Gear' show was broadcast and John Peel came on spinning the underground sounds. The passenger door opened. Raj clasped a white paper bag made transparent by grease. A mouth-watering aroma filled the van's cab.

They were half way through their second sausage roll when Jack Kilroy walked out of the public house, accompanied by bat man and two Stone Age creeps wearing black leather bomber jackets and blue jeans. With a roar, the sports car laid some rubber on the street and shot off in the direction of downtown Glasgow. Murphy swapped places with Raj because his Indian friend was the more skilled driver – hard to believe, but true. They managed to get four cars behind the sleek blue Aston by the third set of traffic lights. When the lights changed to green, Mr Kilroy floored it. The coupé seemed to devour the street and spit it out from its roaring twin exhaust pipes. Speed limits were something the gangster obviously held little respect for. Within a minute the Aston Martin was a noisy dot disappearing down Pollokshaws Road.

'Our Jack obviously doesn't believe in cutting a low profile', commented Murphy.

'Now what?' asked Raj.

'Back to the Talisman.'

Raj performed a tyre-screeching U-turn. A couple of blocks past the Denistown Palais dance hall, Murphy shouted, 'Stop!'

Raj stamped down hard on the brake pedal. 'What the fuck is it now?'

'We just passed an interesting shop. Park the van.'

Murphy stepped out onto the pavement, noticing absently that there was a lot of chewing gum stuck to it. He walked back along the street. When he pushed open the shop's glass door, a buzzer rang out. Ten minutes later he returned to the van carrying a neat oblong package wrapped in brown Kraft paper.

As they drove up the road, Raj glanced over at the parcel sitting in his partner's lap. 'What's that?'

Murphy lit up a joint and answered, 'A wee present for Mister Jack Kilroy.'

'What the fuck is that supposed to mean?' asked Raj, leaning over to take a closer look at the mysterious parcel.

'Look out,' shouted Murphy, dropping the joint.

Raj swerved to avoid crashing into the back of an orange and lime green-painted Glasgow Corporation double-decker bus that had come to a sudden halt to pick up some passengers. Angry motorists tooted their horns.

'Come on, tell—'

'Raj, shut the fuck up, stop asking me questions and keep your eyes on the road.'

'Don't worry, everything's under my control.'

'Aye, like fuck it is. Here, want a hit on this?'

Raj took the joint. A rush of air plucked at his shirt as he blew a cloud of smoke out the open window and then the spliff was sucked out of his hand. Murphy looked out the back window, shook his head and said nothing.

The van was parked on the same spot it had been half an hour before. On the radio, the Monkees were singing, 'I'm a Believer'.

'For fuck's sake, can you not find anything better to listen to than that bubblegum music?' complained Murphy.

Raj fiddled around with the black plastic tuning knob. He tuned into Them playing Mississippi blues singer Big Joe Williams's 'Baby Please Don't Go'. The band's vocalist, Van Morrison, spat out the song's lyrics loud and clear.

'That's better.' Murphy pulled out three rolling papers from his pack of Rizlas. 'Who's playing the guitar on that track?'

Raj shrugged. 'I'm not sure, but I think it might be Jimmy Page.'

When the Four Tops came on singing 'It's the Same Old Song', Murphy cursed, 'It fuckin' well is an' all,' He switched off the radio and said, 'It's not true.'

'What isn't,' asked Raj.

'That there's a pub on every street corner in Glasgow.'

'I never said there was.'

'Yeah I know you didn't, but everyone else does.'

'Man, this thing stinks,' said Raj, pulling a green tree deodorizer off the rearview mirror. He pitched it out the open window.

They sat in stoned silence, watching drops of condensation race each other down the inside of the windscreen until eight in the evening.

'Aha,' said Murphy. 'James Bond's back.'

The Aston Martin was once more parked outside the Talisman. It was gleaming under the streetlights like a streamlined predator on wheels. Two hours later, Jack Kilroy exited the pub, staggered over to his car and drove off, very slowly this time. Jack must have had a right skinful because it took him five minutes to realize he was driving down the road without any lights on. Raj kept a few cars behind. About ten minutes later, the Aston's right indicator flashed orange as it pulled into a side street off Paisley Road West, not far from the Clyde's South Bank.

The street lights were haloed by misty drizzle. Parked cars lined both sides of the narrow street and glistened with raindrops. The Aston's powerful engine grumbled in complaint at being driven at a stop-go-stop, looking-for-a-parking-place crawl.

Murphy spotted an empty space. He pointed and said, 'Pull in there.'

It was a tight fit. As Raj manoeuvred the van into position, he heard the sound of paper being torn. He glanced over at his partner. Murphy was holding a large stainless steel meat cleaver in his gloved hands. The van crunched into a Morris Minor's back lights.

'Fuckin' Hell, Raj, watch what you're doing.'

'What the fuck are you doin' with that?'

'I'm cleaning my nails.'

'You've got gloves on.'

'Park the fuckin' van, will you.'

By the time Raj switched off the lights, Jack Kilroy could be seen a block away, walking along the pavement with his hands dug into his packets. He was on the same side of the street as they were, headed in their direction.

'Murphy, I—'

'Shut it, Raj.' There was something in Murphy's voice that Raj did not want to tangle with. He sucked in his cheeks and gulped down the words he had on the tip of his tongue.

Jack Kilroy drew closer. When the leather-clad gangster was a few feet away from the front of the van, Murphy opened his door. He stepped out onto the pavement. In the distance, a ship's bleak foghorn blew twice.

'Good evening, Mister Kilroy.'

'Huh, what the … how the fuck did—'

Swish, the butcher's chopper swung down hard and cleaved into the crown of Jack Kilroy's closely cropped, grey-haired skull. There was a sound like a ripe melon bursting open. Murphy delivered the blow with such force that it split the gang boss's head neatly down the centre of his face. The two halves began to separate, displaying what looked like seaweed inside. Accompanied by a disgusting gurgle, blood spurted out of the gangster's open throat. There were now five pounds of Sheffield Steel embedded in Mr Kilroy's breastbone. Murphy let go of the blade's wooden handle and Jack's rotten soul floated away into the darkness. Headlights swept into the terraced street in the same moment that Murphy grabbed Kilroy's jacket lapels. He lowered the convulsing body to the pavement. He glanced into the van. Raj ducked under the steering wheel. Murphy knelt by the corpse. There was a bad smell rising from it. A police patrol car cruised slowly by. A CB radio's static crackle rose above the throb of the vehicle's engine. Murphy caught a glimpse of its two occupants. Hatless, their faces were illuminated by the dashboard's glow. He could hear them laughing. The driver flicked a half-smoked cigarette out the open window. It spiraled through the air and landed at Murphy's feet. He picked it up and took a long drag on it. Inhaling deeply, he nearly coughed his guts up. It was a Gauloises. When the squad car turned left at the bottom of the street, Murphy spluttered and stood up. Placing a booted foot on the cadaver's chest, he used it as leverage to work the curved oblong blade loose from the dead man's sternum. Bloodied cleaver in hand, he opened the van's passenger side door.

'J-Jesus, man, you've got blood on your face. What have you d-done?'

'Shut yer fuckin' mouth, Raj. Just drive. If you fuck up, I'll kill you too.'

'Wh-what about the money? We—'

'Fuck the money. I told you to shut the fuck up and I meant it,' said Murphy, grabbing Raj's arm and jerking him round to look in his eyes. 'Get a fucking move on and drive no faster than thirty.'

When they drove over the Kingston Bridge, Murphy lowered his window and chucked the bloody butcher's knife over the railings into the River Clyde. Twenty minutes later, Glasgow's brightly lit streets receded and gave way to bungalow suburbia then shadowy country roads. Like an odour, thick silence hung in the van's cab until they drove between the Lodge's big iron gates. When the van crunched to a halt on the driveway, Murphy turned to Raj. There was a wild light in his eyes.

'Not a fuckin' word of this to anyone.'

Raj remained silent and stared at the steering wheel.

'Do you fucking well hear me?'

'Aye, Murphy, I hear you.'

Hamish shuddered, opened his eyes and caught a fleeting glimpse of a large fruit bat flying in front of the moon. He remembered how Angus's voice cracked with emotion when he recounted how it happened that his friend Murphy became a killer. Six months passed before Angus found out about Jack Kilroy's murder, when Raj broke down and confessed to him, by which time a lot of water had flowed under the bridge, although not enough to wash away the emotional impact of Murphy's horrific act.

'But how could he have done such a terrible thing?' asked Hamish.

'To this day, I've never been able to figure that out,' answered Angus. 'He was always impulsive, sometimes to the point of being dangerous, but I still can't bring myself to say he was deranged.'

'The guilt must have driven Murphy mad.'

'You only say that because I've not told you enough about him. Murphy had a conscience but it wasn't a guilty one. I eventually talked to him about it and he responded by saying that I should feel grateful for what he described as "taking care of" Jack Kilroy.'

'What about the money?'

Angus shrugged. 'That's another story.'

'I'm listening.'

Hamish looked away from the moon, closed his eyes and could have sworn he smelled marijuana and melting candle wax.

20

ROLLING THUNDER

It would be an easy thing to imagine Angus and his two partners being completely devastated by the loss of so much money. They weren't. Most people who lose a lot of money have a few obsolete tape loops running in their minds about what they had planned to do with it one day. They didn't. The MacDopes had been so busy making it that very little time had been spent dreaming about a cash-filled future. Life did not exactly return to what passed for normal in those crazy times, but it most certainly was not the end of the world, unless your name was Mr Jack Kilroy.

The hash-dealing scene in Great Britain is unique in Europe in that, for the most part, it runs entirely on a credit system. Big dealers 'lay on' their product to smaller dealers. Selling wholesale for cash rarely happens. On most levels the trade operates without a schedule because nobody delivers or pays on time. Bulk movers wish the dream of hash for cash would come true so they could be done with the interminable waiting that often accompanies supplying. For once, this nerve-wracking aspect of the business worked to the MacDope's advantage. When the wrecking crew hit them, they still had over two hundred thousand pounds worth of drugs out on the street. Slowly, over the next three months, the money came home to roost.

Angus had a small birthday party in December 1972. By this time his head injury had healed, although he was to suffer from the occasional migraine for the rest of his life from the vicious blow he had received at the hands of a man he still did not know was dead. He was preparing to blow out twenty-one candles on a round birthday cake coated in dark chocolate. Smiling into the eyes of the seven people seated around the kitchen table, he spoke to Alice and Nina.

'I hope you two didn't drop a few trips of acid into your baking mix this afternoon. I don't really feel up to blowing the doors of perception off their hinges right now.'

'Och no, Angus,' said Nina, who had a cone-shaped party hat on top of her head that sparkled in the candlelight. 'Maybe a wee bit of grass, that's all.'

'Oh wow,' exclaimed Alice, her face shadowed by the oversized blue cardboard bowler hat that she was wearing. Her eyes were held wide open in their customary expression of perpetual surprise. 'Did you put in weed as well?' She gulped. 'So did I.'

Angus blew out the candles. He cut the cake and began to distribute it among his friends.

'Here we go again,' said Raj, biting into a slice of green-coloured sweetness.

Murphy chomped into an extra large wedge and mumbled, 'Mmmh, delicious.'

'Can I have a bit?' Shortwave Dave's voice was that of a child requesting something special. He was never the same after the night of the wrecking crew. He'd become withdrawn, spending even more time than previously with the rabbits, squirrels and birds that inhabited the garden.

'Of course you can, David,' said Jenny from behind a Venetian carnival mask that made her look like a white crow. She handed a plate to Sandra, who was dressed in a bright orange sari. Sandra placed a slice of cake on the plate, silently passed it to Dave and ruffled his hair. He smiled and looked down, uncomfortable with outward shows of affection when more than one person was present.

Later in the evening, everybody was lying around in a high vacuum, thanks to Alice and Nina's grated marijuana baking ingredient. Jeeps put Santana's *Abraxus* album on the turntable and 'Black Magic Woman' belted out of the speakers. Angus, Murphy and Raj staggered through to the kitchen.

Raj brewed up a pot of Columbian coffee. 'Fuck me, I'm toasted. My legs feel like they're made out of rubber,' he complained, leaning against the cooker. 'I can hardly stand up straight.'

'I'm the same,' said Murphy, glancing up from a Fabulous Furry Freak Brothers comic he was engrossed in. 'One of these days those witches are going to OD somebody messin' around with their tricks.'

'You're right, Murph,' added Angus. 'I'd rather smoke dope than eat it. I feel like somebody's put a heavy spell on me and I'm moving around in an extra six G's.'

The coffee looked like bitumen, and tasted worse. A few cups laced with tablespoonfuls of sugar later, the conversation picked up.

'So what do you think about my idea on wheels?' asked Angus.

'The bus, you mean?' enquired Raj, screwing his face up Carlos Santana style and playing an air guitar solo to the music screaming out of the living room.

'Yeah, Carlos, you got it, the bus. Welcome back to Planet Earth.'

'Fat Freddy's cat is so fucking funny, man,' said Murphy turning a page of the comic book. He giggled and looked up. 'Overland to India, I'm into that, man.'

'Me too, as long as I get to drive.'

'Oh, yeah, Raj,' groaned Murphy. 'Don't worry, everything's under my control.'

Raj let out a great belly-shaking laugh. It echoed through the house and could be heard out in the garden where the winds of change were gathering strength and preparing to blow.

A week later, the MacDopes drew a step closer to what they were searching for when Angus read a small advertisement in the Commercial Vehicles section of a classified magazine. He and Jenny, with Raj and Alice squeezed into the back seat, drove down to Harwich on the southeast coast of England to investigate. Murphy stayed at home with Nina to work on retrieving the money still out on the street.

The six-wheeled, single-decker, left-hand drive Mercedes bus had white oval German Zoll plates and was a mechanical paraplegic that should have been drinking oil through a straw in an old omnibus home. Broken shock absorbers made her list to one side like a holed battleship. She still drove, but only just. Clouds of black diesel smoke belched out of its cracked exhaust pipe. Once the bus was rolling, it was almost impossible to change gears up or down. Metal ground together causing the vehicle to judder like it was riding along a street lined with fat sleeping policemen.

Angus looked at the odometer and said, '972,021 kilometres, where's this old girl been? To the moon?'

'No rust on the bodywork or the chassis,' called Raj from underneath the back axle.

'I like her,' said Jenny, patting a cracked headlight.

'I think she looks far out,' chimed Alice, checking her lips in a broken side mirror.

'How much do you want for her?' asked Angus.

'Four grand and you can drive her away right now,' replied the broken-down vehicle salesman, who had enough grease in his hair to lubricate the cables of an Alpine ski lift. The pasty-faced man looked like Sméagol dressed in a shabby pinstriped suit. His anorexic, pimple-splattered face spoke miles for his predisposition for enjoying a daily well balanced lunch of three gin and tonics with a packet of salt and vinegar flavoured crisps thrown in, to increase his fibre intake.

'Four fucking grand!' exclaimed Angus, his face hardening.

'Three,' chirped the weasel, glancing at his filthy fingernails.

'It's a deal,' said Angus, offering his hand to the smiling salesman whose stained teeth had so many holes in them they could have played a sonata composed for an organ grinder if the wind picked up. When Angus felt the trader's clammy palm against his own he made a mental note to scrub his hands with hot water and carbolic soap as soon as an opportunity presented itself, in order to ward off the possibility of being infected with bubonic plague.

'What about the number plates?' asked Raj.

'I can sort that out for you in twenty-four hours,' replied the salesman, 'for an extra two hundred quid.' He gulped, making his protruding walnut-sized Adam's apple yo-yo between the taut cords of his scrawny neck. He caught Raj and Angus exchanging a wary look. 'Take it or leave it, mate. It's all part of the service.'

'Okay, get it together, man. Here,' said Angus, producing a wad of twenties from inside his fringed buckskin jacket.

The weasel's face lit up at an unscripted success in a life that contained few of them. He grabbed the money and said, 'Thanks mate, see you here same time tomorrow.' A vulgar bubbling sound gurgled in his throat. He was laughing.

Angus and his friends spent the evening in Clacton-On-Sea, a coastal holiday resort that, like the bus, had once upon a time seen much better days. It was the kind of place where even the seagulls looked desperately bored. The weather was bleak. A cruel wind was howling in off the slate-grey North Sea. After dining on big plates of fish and chips in an empty restaurant that had the ambience of an abattoir, the weary travellers checked into a half-star hotel with creaky floorboards, red flock wallpaper peeling off the walls and bath water that was brown.

Raj was singing 'Route 66' with Alice humming along in accompaniment by his side when, just outside of Gretna Green on the A74, the bus rolled by the 'Welcome to Scotland' sign. When he felt the engine lose power and heard a sound like large knitting needles tapping frantically on glass behind him, he immediately knew what had happened. 'Shit,' he spat out the window, 'the big end's gone.'

He pulled over on to the hard shoulder and waited for Angus and Jenny to show up in their Triumph Stag. The turquoise-coloured sports car drew up and Raj explained what the problem was. The rest of the day was spent ordering up a flatbed truck to transport the dead-duck single-decker to Glasgow. Three days later she was lowered down a ramp on to a piece of waste ground beside Mr Gupta's garage. Work began the next morning.

Shortwave Dave was broken-hearted when he found out the Lodge was about to become history. He'd dug his soul into the garden and could not imagine himself leaving it behind. He knew every tree, bush and blade of grass on the lawn, and his best friends were the little creatures living there.

'Come on, Dave, it's time to go,' said Jenny, shepherding him away from the trunk of a tall cedar tree that he'd been hugging all morning.

'I know I shouldn't have, but I've allowed myself to become attached to this place. Now I'm paying the price and it hurts.' Tears welled up in his reddening eyes.

'We've rented a big flat in Glasgow. There's a room waiting there for you. When the bus is ready, you can come to India with us.'

'Thanks, Jenny; I know you guys are my family but I just can't handle the thought of living in a city right now. If we really are leaving the Lodge I might head up to the Black Isle on the northeast coast with Sandra. She has some friends there who are running a commune with a big vegetable garden and lots of animals to talk to.'

'Are you sure, Dave?'

For once he did not start to wriggle when Jenny gave him a heartfelt hug.

'J-J-Jenny?'

'What is it, Dave?'

'I … I really love you, Angus and all the rest of them. You know that, don't you?'

'Och, Dave,' she said, a runaway two-ton teardrop streaking across her left cheek.

The following morning, Dave and Sandra caught the train up to Inverness. They stood at a carriage window; he waving a red hanky with the enthusiasm of a six year old, while beside him she smiled the smile of a person who has learned to witness life as a drama. The whole family had come down to Queen Street station to bid Shortwave Dave and Sandra the Head-expander a fond farewell. When the train lurched and started to move away, Angus was the only one on the platform who was smiling. Raj nudged him in the side and said, 'Don't tell me you're happy to see Shortwave and that wonderful woman go?'

'Not at all, Raj, I'm missing them already.'

'So why are you lookin' so pleased with yourself?'

'I opened Dave's wee tartan suitcase with the peace sign painted on it before we left the house.' He began to laugh.

'What's so funny about that?'

'He had a little brown teddy bear in there with a third eye sown on its forehead. The only other things in his case were a toothbrush, an Alan Watts book called *The Wisdom of Insecurity* and a worn copy of the Bible.'

'Yeah, Dave's told me a few times that if everybody obeyed the Ten Commandments the world would be a lot more peaceful place to live in. Maybe he's right. Anyway, what the fuck were you doing rakin' about in his bag?'

'Trying to find enough space to leave him a little good luck money.'

'How much?'

'Eight grand, I sold his crop to Andy Burns.'

'Nice one,' said Raj, giving Angus such a hard slap on the back that a misaligned vertebra, which had been bothering him for days, clicked back into place.

In mid-February, three heavy wooden crates arrived from Stuttgart, West Germany. They were unloaded on to the snow-covered ground outside Mr Gupta's garage. Bound with blue steel bands, the long, bulky boxes contained a brand new eight-cylinder diesel engine, gearbox, brake system, replacement windows and every imaginable spare part the bus would ever be in need of once she was roadworthy. The contents of those three crates had cost more than five times what had been paid for the bus. With money to launder, nobody cared.

The Mercedes bus was shaping up nicely, bearing little resemblance to how she'd looked a month before. The interior had been completely gutted and now had three separate sleeping compartments with double mattresses installed, a shower, and a toilet. Mounted on the roof at the back of the bus was one of Mr Gupta Senior's brilliant innovations, an upstairs observation bubble made from transparent Perspex that could sit three comfortably.

'I don't understand why you're spending so much time welding in an extra brass-lined water tank,' said Mr Gupta, crouching down to take a look under the bus. His puzzled Indian features looked strangely incongruous framed by the urban setting of Glasgow. His bushy moustache was turning grey at the edges. Angus saw him as an Indian gentleman who would have looked more in place performing his ablutions on the banks of the Ganges than standing in one of Glasgow's numerous back lanes with an oily monkey-wrench in his grease-covered hands. The source of the mechanic's bewilderment was a hatched tank, which was being fitted into the bus's chassis. Angus and Murphy had been working on it for a week. Mister Gupta would have had a fit if he'd realized that what the lads were constructing was a secret stash big enough to hold five hundred kilos of hashish.

One piece of equipment that had been brought into town from the Lodge was the five thousand watt sound system. Along with a voltage converter, it was installed with suspension-rocking results. Air-conditioning, mirrored tinted glass windows and hydraulic seats; no expense was spared in the creation of the rock and roll juggernaut that said yes to every excess. Spare tyres, snow chains, a large khaki-coloured army tent, primus stoves, copper cooking pots and a box full of mirrors were stored in the below-deck luggage compartments. Nina had a brainstorm one night after ingesting a couple of hash cookies.

'What's with the mirrors, Nina?' enquired Murphy.

'I've had an absolutely magic idea, Murph. We can use them for trading when we meet pygmy tribes in the jungle. I'm thinking of nipping round to Woolworths to buy frying pans and strings of plastic beads. The wee women would really go for those. What do you think? Is there enough room on the bus for a couple more boxes of tradeables?'

Murphy looked into his girlfriend's eyes. They were spinning like flying saucers. Her eyelids blinked like an owl's. Her frizzy black Afro definitely lent her appearance a jungle queen flavour. Although he did not foresee them running into Pygmy tribes on their overland trip, she was so pleased with herself he didn't want to break her illusion.

'I think it's a great idea, Nina. Maybe you should buy a few boxes of lighters, as well.'

Nina gave him a look of adoration that could only have been mustered by an infatuated young woman or somebody who was completely stupid. 'Wow, Murph,' she gushed, 'that's a hot idea. That's why you're so groovy, man. You always think positive. Come closer, wild thing, I think I love ya.' He received a slobbery kiss for his good vibrations.

'Start her up, son,' ordered Mr Gupta a week later, when the engine had been installed to his satisfaction. The motor came to life as soon as Raj turned the ignition key. Twin jets of light grey smoke shot out of the new exhaust system. After he'd floored the accelerator a few times, not a trace of smoke could be seen escaping from the two thick stainless steel tubes at the rear of the bus underneath the three hundred horsepower turbo-charged engine. Angus and Murphy went over and shook Mr Gupta's hand.

'Thanks, Mister Gupta, you've done a great job,' beamed Angus.

'Right-on, Mister Gupta, I don't know what we'd have done without you and your mechanic's help,' added Murphy.

'Come on now, boys. The pleasure was all mine. It will do Raj the world of good to visit the Motherland. The missus and I are very happy about that. Anyway, I'll have made up your bill by the end of the month. You better start saying your prayers to Goddess Laxmi because it's not going to be cheap, I'll tell you that right now.'

Raj's Punjabi father was very Scottish when it came to money matters. He expected to be paid well for his hard work, family or not.

'What a sound, eh lads?' he said, referring to the rumble of the bus's powerful engine. 'It reminds me of the sound the thunder made when the monsoon rains rolled in.'

Angus and Murphy looked at each other. They knew they were both thinking the same thing. Mister Gupta had unwittingly helped them find a name for their home on wheels.

It took a talented spray artist a week to give the bus her new skin of paint. When he'd finished, he pulled off the masking tape and everyone gathered around and cheered. 'Rolling Thunder' looked magnificent. On a navy blue background, galaxies swirled beside stars that were going super-nova on the side panels. In the foreground, pink-tinged, bubbling grey clouds shot out yellow lightning bolts. Under the windscreen, a winged Jolly Roger was painted over the ventilation grill. The skull was wearing a crown.

'Man, that looks a bit heavy,' said Raj, nodding at the skull and crossbones. 'Whose bright idea was that?' he asked, looking over to Murphy, who was sitting on an oil drum.

Murphy pretended to be deaf and gazed up at the sky. The devilish smile on his face said much more than words ever could.

A few bottles of Champagne were cracked open and, much to Mr Gupta's disdain, a couple of joints were passed around. Raj's father would have been a lot more taken aback if he'd known that most of the bus's sewage tank had been removed to make way for a secret compartment. The welding skills the lads had learned in borstal had finally come in handy. Unless somebody knew how to gain access to it, the stash was virtually undetectable.

Rolling Thunder and her crew were now ready to hit the road and, like Jack, they would not be coming back.

Hamish lit one of his six remaining cigarettes. He exhaled smoke through his nose. Never before had a Marlboro Light tasted or felt so good. 'What an addict I am', he mused. 'Angus was right when he said to me that smoking might well be the cause of my death one day. If it weren't for my nicotine craving I'd be cuddled up next to Jean instead of sitting on top of a bloody landmine.' He stubbed out his half-smoked cigarette.

'Fucking shit!' he cursed, wondering how on earth what he was going through could ever be turned into a blessing. He asked himself, 'Could it be that this is my destiny? What was it that Angus said to me? You only have two choices in life, and those are whether or not to accept that everything that happens to you is preordained.' Hamish could remember clearly how his brother's deep voice had sounded when he'd made that statement. He contemplated its meaning. 'All right, Angus, I accept that fate propelled me to sit on a mine, now what?'

Somewhere in the distance a cockerel crowed, mistaking the bright lunar disc for the sun. Hamish looked up and saw that the moon was encircled by a silver grey halo refracting a tinge of rainbow light. He was struck by its immediate beauty and stared at it for some time. The air was cooling. Out over the sea, beyond the horizon, there was a flash that could only have been caused by lightning. A few moments later he heard a distant rumble. It was the sound of rolling thunder. Free of thought, he closed his eyes and found himself tottering on the brink of a great abyss. He jumped.

ACKNOWLEDGEMENTS

I am immensely grateful to my beloved wife, Prita, for all and everything, and her outstanding performance in the demanding role of devil's advocate. My gratitude goes out to Helen "Editorina" Gosch, for overseeing my efforts with remarkable care and enthusiasm. I am thankful to Anita Maria Avey, for lending her proofreading skills. Don Miguel Cabezas deserves many thanks for his technical expertise and jokes.

I would also like to extend my thanks to the following people: My sister, Helen, for always being there for me. Johnathon Clifford, for his publishing advice. Petra Von Lehsten, for designing The Landmine Chronicles logo. My dear old Scottish friends Alon, Lex, Neil, Mac and Moira, for those wonderful years we spent together exploring The Highlands. Joshua Pantel Rice for reminding me about the stories I told him during his childhood. Liese for giving me the female cobra. Ce Meij and Ian Lima for creative feedback. David Buschman, Kamal, Martin, Shivani, Tonebone, Chicago, Premal, Declan, Utah and Walter for listening. Anna Wood for her young reader's perspective. Bhishu Mohammed and all the staff at the Unawantuna Bay Hotel in Sri Lanka for their hospitality. Timotheus and Natasha for bringing their beautiful son, Kianu, into the world, who helped me to once more see life through the eyes of a child. All of my friends, from all over the planet, for being who they are. The musicians of the world, for providing me with the soundtrack that's always playing somewhere in the background. And last but not least I'd like to thank Melrose Books for publishing my book.

I'd like to thank the purchaser of this book on behalf of the Cambodian landmine victims who will receive a substantial percentage of the author's profits generated by the sale of this book. There are still over six million unexploded landmines buried in Cambodia.

Luke Mitchell, October 2007.

The Cambodian Children's Painting Project (CCPP)
is a Cambodian non-governmental organization (NGO).
CCPP is a non-profit, grassroots project created by British artist,
Roger Dixon, to help underprivileged Khmer children. Donating
money to a NGO can, in certain countries, be tax deductible.
If interested in helping these beautiful and intelligent children to learn
how to paint and make a living for themselves,
log in to: www.artcambodia.org